Creative Truths in Provincial Policing

PAULA LICHTAROWICZ

WINDMILL BOOKS

1 3 5 7 9 10 8 6 4 2

Windmill Books
20 Vauxhall Bridge Road
London SW1V 2SA

Windmill Books is part of the Penguin Random House group of
companies whose addresses can be found at
global.penguinrandomhouse.com.

Penguin
Random House
UK

Copyright © Paula Lichtarowicz 2015

First published by Hutchinson in 2015
First published in paperback by Windmill Books in 2015

www.windmill-books.co.uk

A CIP catalogue record for this book is available from the British Library.

ISBN 9780099592273

Typeset in Bembo MT by Palimpsest Book Production Limited,
Falkirk, Stirlingshire
Printed and bound by Clays Ltd, St Ives plc

To the bee and the bear

A Very Important Policing Mission

Looking back on the day when everything began to go so horribly wrong, most people came to agree that the sun was to blame. For the murder that occurred at one o'clock during the Dalat Wedding of the Year took place not only in the prize rhododendrons in the Valley of Love, but also entirely in the dark. Yes, people agreed, it was a most pernicious sun.

Seven floors up in the very pent of a peppermint-painted townhouse, early in the morning of the big day, Chief Duong's wife hears hail strike the television aerial on the concrete roof and she howls.

'This was not forecast!' she cries, opening up the hot tap of the reinforced bath with a toe. 'This hammer and nail throwing and snowing was not said to be so. But so it goes. So it goes once more.'

She no longer expects much, the police chief's wife. Little beyond the comfort of sesame shrimp crackers, TV medical dramas and these hot baths in which she might close her eyes if she chooses – as indeed she does on this already disappointing day – to lose herself in a familiar fantasy.

She will take her husband's razor from the soap dish and pluck out the blade. This she will slide lengthways into her left wrist. She will press down through the buttery fat and open a green thread of vein. Next she will do the right. With her big toe she will pull the plug. Her blood will begin to slurry down the sides of the bath and congeal on the floor like cooling chocolate. Soon enough she will shrink. The balloon of flesh about her will shrivel smaller than a walnut, harder than grit. And she will go slinking down the drain with a gurgle of dirty water to ride the underground rivers of sewage, ever diminishing, until, in some unhurried moment in future days or weeks, a single, irreducible atom of her being will go shooting out of a coastal waste pipe to bob and dance forever on the swells of the South China Sea.

There will be a time soon to come when Mrs Duong will wish she had slipped away while she still had the chance. But, lying in the bath, she opens her eyes. The police chief's wife – whom he, along with everyone else left alive in her life, knows as Po – clears her throat.

'Husband!' Her voice, a ten-decibel baritone undaunted by the disappointments of time, blasts a cockroach into retreating behind the bathroom mirror. 'Your presence is required, husband. It is hair-wash time on the seventh floor.'

The bathwater trembles in the answering silence.

Most likely he is betting on the cow racing!

On his daughter's wedding day!

To that unfortunate creature!

Mrs Duong grinds her teeth and gets her breath back.

Silence still.

She reaches to the crown of her head and tugs. A thin grey chignon uncoils. Not one split tip remains of the black drape that once glistened in sunlight like molasses and danced on the wind like the feathers of a cormorant;

that bewitched a bush-browed soldier boy in bloody Highland mud. Hair that was once strong as first-spun silk and plaitable twenty different ways by fingers that were soft and pencil thin.

Mrs Duong looks to the rain-drenched window where the day is still struggling to break. She eyes the razor in the soap dish. The bathtub groans as she shifts to the side. 'Viens, mon petit soldat de singe,' she whispers. 'Viens, mon mari.' She reaches past the soap dish to thump her fist on a switch wired to the bathroom wall.

Seven floors down in the corrugated tin lean-to behind the peppermint house, a bulb buzzes unobserved above a filing cabinet. A to-do list flaps unticked on a nail. Pages of an abandoned wedding speech curl by a phone in the dirt.

Astride his Honda Hero 125, Mrs Duong's husband is heading out of town. It is still early and the roads are quiet. Chins in to keep the rain out, Chief Duong is humming the victory refrain from the Hanoi operetta *Oh Most Glorious Liberator of the Viet People*. For a man cannot but be cheerful on the open road with the scent of the pines about him. And in any case today is a great day – the greatest of days, is it not? He has come far since his own paltry wedding in a dusty shed, has he not? As runty as a cripple-backed piglet, his mother had said of him at the time, and likely less juicy. A sudden smile comes to his lips; a smile, it was often said, that made it seem as if all the lights over Vietnam had just been switched on. And now, Mummy, look where your piglet is heading now.

Chief Duong swerves the moped past a hummingbird,

broken-necked on the tarmac, and turns onto a potholed road that twists down into the cold and forested part of town.

Eighteen-year-old Lila Duong lies on her bed, motionless as an effigy on a marble tomb. A closer inspection behind the mosquito drapes is required to spot signs of life. Here may be seen a trembling of silk-clad thigh, and a flickering of lips that count out *one thousand and forty-eight, one thousand and forty-nine, one thousand and fifty*. For despite her seeming stillness, Lila is engaged in a crucial pre-nuptial activity. Clamping her legs together, she is building her strength against the hands that will soon be reaching to tear them apart.

'Make no mistake, ma chérie, marriage is a battle-ground,' Mrs Duong had growled maternally on hearing the sad news of the betrothal just three weeks before. 'Men fight with the boneheadedness of the buffalo and the lust of the boar – even the unfortunate ones. We women must deploy our cunning to resist. Resist, or die in the trying.'

A conjugal defence strategy was initiated without delay. 'Tighten those frogmeat legs of yours!' Mrs Duong barked, directing Lila into a brace position on the bed. 'Kick with the toes. Thrust with the knees. Punch on these two plums here. Crush them, pulp them, chew them, spit. Again. Kick. Thrust. Harder. Better.'

'We shall soon have you strong as a wildcat,' Mrs Duong purred, hacking at her daughter's hamstrings with a backhand slice. 'And for those times when your strength fails before the insistence of his tusks, I shall teach you a woman's greatest art – sneakiness,' she concluded with a sorrowful volley of whacks. 'This shall be my gift to you.'

So Lila was instructed in feminine wiles: simulated headaches, toothaches, bad breath; the cultivation of lice in the bush, scabies, fake rabies, a phobia of babies. Into her daughter's trousseau Mrs Duong placed essential props: sleeping powder, poison ivy and a stash of thirty-six betel-stained sanitary towels that could be wetted and applied to suggest menstruation at a moment's notice. 'These should see you through the first three years,' she sighed. 'Pass this gift to your own daughter, if you are unfortunate enough to breed yourself.'

Lila submitted. She didn't repeat to her mother the words she had used with her father when he revealed Commissar Nao's agreement to the full terms and conditions of the match: 'It is of no matter to me.' Words that were spoken calmly and from the heart, and had unnerved the police chief slightly. 'He can be as well-armed as he likes, Daddy,' she went on to say, fluttering her fingers over the contours of his face, 'I am just relieved that my affliction will no longer be a burden to you.'

'Oh my most precious silkworm, this affliction of yours has never once been a burden to me.' Beneath their bushy brows, her father's eyes began to leak. Tears plopped and burst on his rubber sandal straps. 'Consider this a Very Important Policing Mission you can help your family with. He is Hanoi-bound, it is said. The highest level of the Interior. Most influential. They have beautiful lakes in Hanoi, Lila, and beautiful homes for Interior wives. Did I also mention he's a talented bonsai artist? Gold medal position at the Spring Flower Festival seven years running. Must be a man of some poetry, mustn't he?'

Lila, whose dry eyes looked out far beyond her father, answered as she always did – pragmatically. 'In the circumstances, it is an admirable solution for all concerned. Well done, Daddy.'

'My most wise and beautiful silkworm,' the little chief blubbed, 'I knew you would see it like this.'

'Just as long as I can start my reflexology course a week on Monday,' said Lila, who as well as being beautiful and pragmatic was also sensitively fingered. 'I signed up for it six months ago and I don't want to miss out.'

So, on this wedding morning, as Lila lies listening to a mosquito struggle in the net, waiting for her mother's descent, she reflects that she doesn't mind too much, in the circumstances. Though being of a practical bent, she continues to jam together her thighs and test her reserves of strength.

Seconds later Lila's bed begins to quake. Four floors up, Mrs Duong is on the move. A square of towel flailing about the folds of her back, she thunders from the bathroom to the window in the bedroom. Here the towel drops, a pelican jaw is unhinged and a glass pane cracks beneath the blast of a maternal yowl. The sky has turned greyer than the concrete on the unpepperminted back wall. At eight in the morning the sun remains no more than a circular stain in the east.

Mrs Duong reaches for the telephone. 'Mr Duma!'

A pause. A shake of pelican jaw, of unwashed hair strings. 'Wrong, Mr Duma, all wrong, I tell you. I demand a redrawn up-to-the-minute accurate astrological chart at once. Vite, Mr Duma, vite! Doom is dangling in the heavens above. There is simply no time to lose.'

A Warm Welcome to Paradise

Dismounting his moped, Chief Duong pays no heed to the whipcrack of electricity in the black sky above. Ahead of him is the white house, rearing from the surrounding vegetation like a lone tooth in a jaw of decay. Paradise Plantation it is named. It is whispered to be the grandest of the old French residences west of Saigon.

There are many other rumours about the place and its owner, of which Duong, as the town's police chief, is not unaware. 'I must inform you it is categorically untrue, not to mention most slanderous, to say Mr Mei operates outside the law.' Such is the warning he has had to dole out to wild-eyed husbands and fathers appearing at the police station clutching pink sheets of paper and demanding with a shout or a tremble an immediate civic response. 'Please remember, here we deal with hard facts not fancy rumours, yes? Besides,' he would usually soften at this point, 'the corporation HQ is situated two kilo-metres beyond our civic jurisdiction, so what can we do? Besides all this, you have in your hands self-signed docu-mentation, yes? Most probably it is legally binding.'

At these times Chief Duong would smile – never unkindly – and sometimes offer a peppermint from his tin on the desk. 'If you are loved, most likely you will be reunited at the contractual end date. The eagle may take

to the distant plains but it will always return to the nest.'
The chief, who had long possessed an affection for proverbs, tried to send the men away with an assortment of
maxims. Any other result he considered impossible.

Yet on this great morning here Chief Duong stands
himself, patting down his eyebrows and waiting for the
electrified gate to yield to the peeps of the Hero's horn.
He removes his helmet to inspect the board by the gate.

WELCOME TO PARADISE
FULL DISARMAMENT REQUIRED
NO PHOTOGRAPHY

The print is adorned with four laughing pink skulls.

The chief takes a peppermint from his pocket tin and
reminds himself he is not a man who could ever be cowed
by gaudy paintwork. He tightens his sandal straps. He
begins to wonder whether a third peep on the horn might
be considered impolite when the left gate clicks and grinds
open sufficient to allow pedestrian access. Clearing his
head of townsfolk tittle-tattle, Duong steps inside a curtain
of thick bamboo. A host of giddy dragonflies pursues him
into the gloom.

'So Commissar Nao finds himself a wife at last!'

On the marbled verandah of the great white house,
astride a glass-eyed buffalo stiffened into an eternal gallop,
a tiny figure is draining a coconut through a silver straw.
'A warm welcome to Paradise, Chief. We have been expecting
you. Please approach so I may offer congratulations on a
most providential match – one that has been, shall we
say, *fingered* by fate?'

Duong is hit by a blast of laughter, not dissimilar in

sound to the screaming hyenas he once watched on a documentary about the African Serengeti. The tiny man – much scrawnier than the town gossips implied – is naked but for a silk leopard-print loincloth currently being rasped back and forth against the buffalo's rump. 'Ascend the marble, Chief! Full steam ahead!'

Duong hurries up the steps. He does not glance back at the overgrown drive and the cross hairs he could have sworn were trained on his every step. And he knows better than to look up at the immensity of the building's façade, so he does not spot the painted eyes that crowd at the iron grille of a window high above. Nor for that matter does he notice the wisps of black eyelashes that are cart-wheeling slowly down from this grille and beginning to settle on his shoulders. Would that he did. But Chief Duong is here as a man of business. Visiting a man of business. On business. He flaps dragonflies from his face and bows before the buffalo, keeping his eyes averted from the loincloth reputed to conceal the stub of a tailbone that a succession of Bangkok surgeons has failed to remove.

'Permit me to say, it is the highest of honours to be invited to the home of a renowned captain of industry.'

'And permit me to reply, Police Chief, there is no shame in what you are about to do. Little, in any case, that will stick permanently.'

Duong has a go at joining in with the scream of laughter. 'A good joke, Mr Mei, a very good one indeed.'

'Uncle, please, Police Chief.' Up close Mei's smile is twenty-four-carat plated, his eyes the green of stagnant ponds. 'Shanghai gangsters, Hanoi ministers, even a Yankee once came visiting. In matters of enterprise Uncle Mei knows no prejudice.'

'It is most comradely of you, sir.'

'Uncle Mei is the little man's friend.'

'Certainly, sir—'

'*Uncle,* please, Chief. Uncle Mei is the needy man's family. He tries to give what a father cannot.'

'Well, if there's ever anything I can do for you – Uncle – officialdom being what it is. I am myself a man of not inconsiderable connections and not insignificant provincial position and—'

'Bring out the papers!'

But Duong has no papers. Shrimp from last night's supper lurch in his gut. There was something papery on his to-do list today – was this it? 'A thousand apologies, Mr Mei—'

'*Uncle.*'

'Uncle.'

But no, it seems the order was not addressed to him. The great ebony door of the great house is swinging open. A blank-eyed dark-skinned boy appears, naked but for a camouflage-print loincloth and two belts of bullets lashed across his chest. He carries an upturned turtle shell containing a bottle of Mekong, a glass tumbler, a vacuum-packed green block and a sheaf of pink sheets of paper. The boy pours out an inch of whisky and presents it to Duong.

Mei raises his coconut. 'So, Chief, first we salute our newborn friendship.'

'To friendship.' The Mekong crashes into Duong's belly. His glass is refilled.

'Now to fortune.'

'To fortune.'

'To your beautiful daughter's future.'

Duong beams at the liquid sloshing in his glass.

'And, naturally, your own.'

'Naturally,' he stifles a hiccup, 'my own.'

'And now, Chief, to our business.'

The boy refills Duong's empty glass, bows and presents the chief with the plastic-wrapped green block. It is about the length of two cigarette packets and looks as light as a rice-paper roll. Duong is not a greedy man. He knows he has never been that. Nevertheless, his fingertips tingle with the urge to stroke the block that is granting him and all the family such a happy future!

'Touch it, Chief, if you wish. It will not bite you! There you go! You will find your five hundred as requested, in twenty-dollar bills, Chief. Your Uncle assures you that all is present and correct. One hundred per cent guaranteed.'

Mei clicks his fingers. The block is snatched away from Duong and dropped inside a blue plastic bag. A small beetle – a cockroach or some such thing – is scrabbling about inside.

'You will permit me a final toast. To your well-connected son-in-law. To you being, shall we say, Chief, well armed for the future.' Mei screams with laughter and scratches his rump. 'Very well *armed* indeed.'

So the rumours about the commissar race this way too? But that must not be minded now. Duong drains his glass, beaming at screaming Uncle Mei, beaming at the blank-faced boy, beaming at the shadow of the cockroach racing along the block in the bag. And for a moment, just a moment, as whisky drowns the shrimp in his gut, dreams rise like perfumed dancers in the police chief's mind and whirl their charms before him. Hanoi. A crime-fighting desk job in the Interior. Retirement with full honours back to the Highlands. Perhaps that will be the time to agree to a commemorative statue in the town centre. Underneath the Petit Eiffel or on the roundabout outside the station. Chiselled from local limestone and certainly nothing grander than life-sized. For he is not a greedy man. No one could ever call him that. Duong beams at the cockroach. What possibilities there are!

'You will find the terms and conditions of the loan clearly stated. Immediate courier delivery to destination is thrown in free of charge. Uncle Mei takes the risks so you don't have to.' Mei points to the whisky glass that is somehow back in Duong's hand and sloshing with honeyed liquid. 'Please, we are now as good as family, you will oblige.'

Duong beams and obliges.

'Uncle Mei will now mention one additional clause to you.' He pauses to rasp his rump along the buffalo hide. 'After all,' he sniggers, 'who knows to what heights your new son-in-law will give you a helping *hand*!'

'Who knows,' the chief beams, blinking back Hanoi desk jobs in Interior ministries.

'An entirely insignificant clause, Chief. More of an agreement between old friends. Chums. Closer than family, old chums like us.'

'Anything you like, Uncle,' Duong beams, blinking back life-sized statues on Dalat roundabouts, 'anything at all.'

'I knew you would see it like that, Police Chief. It's your daughter.'

'Excuse me?'

'Your daughter.'

'I'm sorry? My—'

'Your daughter, Chief. My price. Your gamble. Our bit of fun together.'

The glass trembles in Duong's hand. 'I'm afraid I don't quite understand.'

'What's there to understand, Chief? It is of no great consequence, I assure you. Consider it but passing amusement between bored businessmen. It's fun to share things when you are chums.'

'My *Lila*?'

'That is her name?'

'You want my *Lila*?' Duong's eyes start to sparkle.

'It is a very simple game, Chief. If you renege on the clearly stated terms and conditions, you will facilitate your daughter's divorce from the Commissar and deliver her here within twenty-four hours.'

Duong's knees begin to shake. 'I'm sorry, sir, but I'm a little confused, yes.'

'Please speak up, Chief.'

'I mean, it wasn't mentioned previously. I mean, with the greatest respect, we have our financial repayment arrangement, yes? All agreed, yes. All A-OK. However – *Lila*?' Duong tries to say, but all that whisky seems to have scorched his lips. The softest easiest word in the world is snagging in his throat. 'Please, sir, for what purpose do you want my daughter?'

Uncle Mei slaps his thigh and enjoys a long scream of laughter. 'Oh my dear Police Chief, what a good one! You too listen to the town gossips! You think this old buffalo likes to eat young grass! No no no! I do not want her *myself*! Whatever do you take me for?'

Duong's mouth opens and closes. Tears leap from his eyes.

'I am a man of business, that's all there is to it.'

'And this is business, my *Lila*?' Tears tumble onto Duong's cheeks, onto his tummy, onto the eyelashes fallen about his sandals.

'Come, Police Chief, no need to water the plants so heartily. I have gardeners for that. And you have a wedding to get to, I believe. Blow your nose, Chief. There is no place for emotion in business.'

A silken handkerchief appears in Duong's hand.

'Blow it again, while I articulate your position. You are an honourable man who came to his Uncle for financial assistance. Nod for me. Excellent. We are both honourable men, are we not? And we both understand – as honourable men – that an honourable man will never renege on a business agreement. Therefore an honourable man, such as yourself, Chief, will quickly deduce that this additional clause, such as it is, in an otherwise excellent financial package, by the way, is entirely hypothetical and will remain entirely hypothetical. Consequently, it is both dishonourable and highly tedious of you to get overexcited with the details of where and when and which daughter and so forth. All irrelevant in your honourable case, and entirely hypothetical.' Mei's gaze slithers to the green block in the blue plastic bag. 'Although it is of course up to you, Chief. Entirely.'

Duong blows his nose. With as much dignity as he can muster he turns his attention from the blue bag to the pink sheets of paper that the boy is holding in front of him, a pen in his hand. He sees the terms of the loan, as have been agreed on the telephone: ten years at six per cent. Difficult at present, but not unmanageable with a little belt tightening. And surely the years after today's marriage will be belt-loosening ones. That is what a man must hope. After all, what is life – he has asked of many a remorseful miscreant – what is life without hope?

And curiously now, for a man moved mostly by practicalities, the little police chief's gaze is pulled upwards; up beyond the stuffed buffalo, up white stuccoed walls; up to a high-grilled window. And for just a moment, the planet on which he stands seems to cease its spinning. And in this moment, for all future reference, and despite all the evidence emerging from astrological charts being redrawn elsewhere in town, there is a chance that a day of doom is not assured, but merely possible. Indeed, it only takes one man's decision to prevent it.

But here at Paradise Plantation low clouds are veiling the view of painted eyes at a high window, and down on the verandah silk is rasping impatiently on hide.

'I'm sure there are other lenders available, Chief. If you wish to devote some time to looking. Da Nang perhaps, or of course the ports of Saigon.'

Fingers are clicking. A blue plastic bag is swinging away.

'Wait! No! Mr Mei, wait, please wait!'

'Police Chief, you begin to offend me. You will do me the honour – Uncle.'

'Uncle, forgive me, all respect to you, but you do know my daughter is—'

'I hear she is – what is the polite term – afflicted?'

'Indeed, yes. A vehicular accident.'

Mei plucks a thread from his loincloth, nodding. His sudden grin is golden. 'But most exquisite in spite of this, is she not, Chief? This is what I hear.'

Chief Duong sniffs, cursing the whisky cramping his unhappy gut and the tears still dripping from his eyes. Eyes that are drawn back to the green block in the blue bag. It is only a little belt tightening that is required. Does not everyone have some sort of belt to tighten in life?

Mei clicks his fingers. 'Take it away, boy.' Mei swings

his leg to dismount the buffalo. 'Please consider the beverages on the house, Chief. Non-rechargeable.'

'Wait!' Duong lurches at the boy. 'Stop him, Mr Mei, uncle sir, please wait!' He smiles. It is less than stellar but it will have to do. 'Mr Mei – *Uncle* – so sorry, a minor misunderstanding. My daughter, of course, a simple game. Between friends. Businessmen. As you say, honourable. Hypothetical, you say. Ha! So tell me please, Uncle, tell me where do I sign?'

It is swiftly done, the business, on three pink sheets and carbon copies.

It is done with a chirped-up whistle and a focus on belts and statues on roundabouts and the like.

It is only once he is outside the plantation gates that the chief's whistling wavers and the tremor in his legs becomes a wobble. Here on the grassy verge he vomits whisky and shrimp in a tangerine fountain that narrowly misses his sandals.

Slipping through the gate behind the chief, a dark-skinned blank-eyed boy jumps onto a bicycle. Swinging from his wrist is a blue plastic bag with a green block and possibly a small cockroach inside. He consults an address Duong has written on a slip of paper and sets off pedalling up the hill towards the governmental district of town.

The little policeman finds he has no strength in his lungs for operatics on the return journey. A second appointment on his day's to-do list remains overdue and unremembered. Which is a shame because his appointment is with the Venerable Chaura, and although there are many monks in the world it would be safe for a forgetful police chief to cross, this Chaura is not one of them. Beneath soft lemon robes lurks the heart of a charlatan; a man with gambling hands and feet that are happiest on the run.

A vein jolts in the monk's neck as he waits outside the town's monastery gates, imagining the donation that would have plugged the most urgent of his debts. This big-head little chief evidently thought a no-show was a good show. Chaura drops the prayer scroll he had prepared for the chief's daughter's wedding into a puddle where a back-flipped beetle is drowning and allows a grin to spread about his face. 'We shall see about that.' He grinds the sole of his sandal down on the scroll, and closing his eyes he spits three times.

Back at the bridal house, the astrology line has been left dangling on the seventh floor. Mrs Po Duong is descending. Down the stairs she goes, down past her son's empty room on the fifth floor, catching her breath and descending again. Down and down once more, crashing through the door into Lila's bedroom, and blundering against the mosquito drapes like a bloated ghost.

'The moon!' she pants. 'Oh Lila, ma chérie, the sun dawdles in the dark side of the heavens, and a deceitful moon comes sneaking. It is come to bring ruination upon us all.'

'I see,' Lila says quietly.

'Would that you could, my daughter, for I will soon be proved right.'

The Valley of Love

After all this, the Duongs make it to the church on time.

Yes, the guests tolerate a Catholic Mass (the one unassailable condition set by the mother of the bride). Yes, the bride looks exquisite (French lace acquired through a private source in Saigon), and no, she does not use her cane today but leans upon her father's arm. Yes, there are only two (insignificant) cancelees from the list of sixty-five notables and Very Important Personages. Yes, that (peculiar) son is skulking somewhere. And yes and yes, and oh yes yes yes, the groom's tailor has surpassed all expectations, delivering up a suit which every one of the two hundred guests agrees has concealed the extra limb artfully in the lining with minimal bulking and a pretty orchid buttonhole.

Mass is done with by twelve o'clock, and for the moment all is well. The spring sky is still as drear as ditch water, but while the moon remains absent Mrs Duong, for one, will chew her crackers quietly and refrain from disrupting proceedings. Her husband, ignorant of Mr Duma's weather predictions and psychologically impervious to any such mumbo-jumbery, bestows his megawatt grin on all and sundry, but most of all on his exquisite daughter.

'Hurrah!' shout the crowds loitering on the drive outside the cathedral. 'Hurrah! A fertile and prosperous life to you both!'

The rice is thrown, and now it is the groom who leads his wife with every appearance of care to the pink-wheeled pony trap. Beneath the blossomed branches of the cherry trees and to the toots of happy car horns, they trot through town to the Valley of Love for the official photographs.

An unfortunate incident occurs at the lakeside. Scenting fresh union, three Valley cowboys lope up on their ponies, pistols cocked, lassoes whirling, offering their photographic presence for a suitable fee.

The police chief blows his emergency whistle thrice. Junior officers in wedding suits charge out from the crowd to corral the cowboys in a discreet corner.

'Do you not know?' The police chief's breath steams up the ponies' nostrils. 'That man over there is People's Party Commissar Nao. Heading for Hanoi no less. He also happens to be my most beloved son-in-law. This capering, capitalist nonsense of yours may be well and good for spendthrift Southern tourists, but to come sniffing about a man of stature, a man who bears the inheritance of foreign aggression upon his very person, I'm sorry, boys, but you disgrace your ancestral homes. Report with your paperwork to the station on Monday. Eleven a.m. sharpish. Go. Get away now, please.'

The cowboys wheel off and head for the safety of the pedalo park on the far shore. Duong turns, instant megawatty. 'Son-in-Law, my profound apologies. Shall we start with a happy record for the People's Party? Where is that photographer man? Who has brought Uncle Ho?'

By twelve-forty the Party's most notable notables are arranged in hierarchical tiers in front of the rhododendron pots by the lake. Along with three reproductions of Ho Chi Minh, the photographer has thoughtfully provided an assortment of wooden blocks. Duong selects a six-inch mount and clambers up next to his daughter, whom the photographer has swivelled towards Uncle Ho's portrait, placing her palm on the top edge of the gilt frame. On the other side of the portrait, Lila's husband peeks shyly across at his beautiful wife.

'Smile please,' the photographer says. The notables smile. Click. Click click.

'Most important of the Very Important Personages up next,' the photographer says. 'Smile please.' Click. Click click.

It is not until arrangements are being made for the family snap that it begins to happen. The photographer notices first, plucking at a scab on his skull and attempting to reset his light meter. 'Curious,' he says, squinting at the darkening lace on Lila's dress. 'Most unusual for this time of year. Never known anything like it myself.'

But his insignificant voice goes unheard. The notables and VIPs and other guests are busy with the first trays of sweet-meats to arrive from the Frog and Lake Café. Piles of plum dumplings and mulberry candies, towers of pork buns and delicate egg rolls. Such a spread, it is said by the notables, licking their fingers, that it bodes well for the feast to come.

Unusually, Mrs Duong is not to be found among the sweetmeats. She has located her son loitering by the trap ponies and is coaxing him towards the rhododendron pots. The chief, who is keen to avoid his son, for reasons to be addressed another time, is manoeuvring himself paternally towards the groom's thin shoulder for the family snap. And Lila, designated Bride of the Year, is squeezing her thighs together and wondering why all the sparrows, swans and chattering finches seem to have suddenly lost their voices or flown away.

'Come along, photographer, let's have less of your artistry,' Duong chides merrily to the man click-clicking his light meter and shaking the shady folds of Lila's dress. 'Shouldn't take a moment to beautify five bodies.'

But it does take more than a moment. In fact, it won't be happening at all.

Because light is draining from the sky.

'Remarkable, most remarkable,' says the photographer, abandoning his light meter. 'Chief Duong, begging your pardon, but I'm thinking a flash extension will be required.'

'Hurry the man up, will you?' Exhausted by a morning on her feet, Mrs Duong gives her husband's belly a poke. 'This flish-flashing is nonsense, I tell you. Who's ever heard of using a lightbulb outside in the middle of the—' Realising she can barely see the face of her little husband, Mrs Duong shuts up and cranes her neck to assess the heavens.

And Po Duong's pelican jaw drops to let out a howl, one which is long enough for Party members to lick off their fingers and turn and tsk tsk the chief's crazy fat burden of a wife, and loud enough for the trap ponies to shiver in their traces, and deep enough to set three babies screaming.

'Deceitful, smothering moon!' Mrs Duong howls. 'Didn't I tell you, Lila, this was foretold?'

Sure enough, at a minute to one o'clock, a creamy disc is beginning to slide over the sun. Within five minutes it is black as night.

In this darkness three things happen. The mass of moon-blinded guests topple onto each other. The bride receives a sour-scented lip-bruising kiss. And the sound of gunshot boom-booms through the Valley of Love.

Magnetism

Your GLOBAL ADVENTURER recommends . . .

DALAT, the diamond that dazzles in the Central Highlands crown

Known as the city of eternal spring, this former hill station boasts verdant pine forests, cascading waterfalls, remnants of French colonial charm and some of the most thrilling, forward-thinking hospitality Vietnam has to offer (to see our XXX report on *The New Universe* – follow this link – adults only!). If your heart wasn't broken sampling the delights of the *Universe* the night before (and the delights really are delicious, gentlemen!!), round off your trip with a visit to honeymooning hotspot and municipal monument to kitsch, *The Valley of Love*. Don't leave without getting snapped with the world-famous Dalat Cowboys (John Wayne eat your heart out!!!). Dalat in three? An Absolute Gem.

N.B. *GLOBAL WAR ADVENTURERS* will be disappointed to discover bullets are thin on the ground in the town itself. Other than the Tet Offensive, Dalat served mainly as a R&R destination for Military top brass from the rigours of the Central Highlands

Campaign – and who would not want to R&R in this town's temperate climes??? Despair not: it's easy to pick up a tour from any one of the Travel Agencies to nearby Buon Ma Thuot for a very satisfactory 'Blood and Battlefield' experience.

Three of the best . . . tearooms
Waterfall restaurant, Sing Son Waterfalls (tel. 608 3943) Take your tea 'on the rocks' beside some of the most spectacular rock formations in the Highlands. A geologist's wet dream.
The Unfolded Lotus, 164 Victory Rise (tel. 606 8878) Animal lovers will love getting down and dirty with the resident chimps. For everyone else there are the delights of Chef/Proprietor Man Chu's sublime pastries.
Frog and Lake Café, The Valley of Love (no phone). Run by eccentric Mr Han and his five delightful daughters. Get on the right side of Father Han, gentlemen, ask to see his Yoda impression. But *don't* mention the war!

On this night-gobbled day of wedding belles and whizzing bullets, a day some say was long destined for doom, a Global Adventurer will come to find himself embroiled in proceedings.

If he was to be woken from his slumbers in the bedroom of the Frog and Lake Café and informed of this in advance, it is unlikely the news would have surprised him. For freelance Asian blog correspondent Jules Chretien Bone is a man to whom Big Things happen. Magnetic is how he would have to describe himself. Simply magnetic.

Downstairs in the washroom of the Frog and Lake,

eldest sister Bai Han is describing the journalist somewhat differently, as she has been doing for much of the morning, while holding back the hair of her younger sister, who is on her knees vomiting into a pail.

'Son of a giant's turd,' Bai is hissing in her sister's ear. 'So he could not keep his snake out of action? I'll make it missing in action. One snip of the shears should do it.'

Bai is answered by a wild scream from the bedroom above.

'Poor Jules,' her sister says, spitting into the bucket, 'another nightmare.'

Bai hands her a cloth to wipe her lips. 'It was feeling sorry for him that got you into this mess in the first place.'

'Please, Mummy, I can pull it out myself,' the foreigner wails above them. 'Please Mummy, it hurts, oh it hurts, oh you'll ruin your pretty dress. Don't ruin your pretty dress, Mummy.'

Bai gives her sister a meaningful stare.

The folding door of the washroom slams back. A half-plucked goose enters, beak first. 'Where is it?'

'Hello, Papa.'

'Where is this filth hiding itself?' The goose goes plunging about the corners of the room, brandished in the old man's hands like a bayonet. 'Let the GI reveal itself and I will fillet its flesh and fry its intestines.'

'I think he went outside. Try the rose beds, Papa.'

Bai watches her father spin round and rush out of the café on spindled legs. She tries not to think of the two hundred mouths requiring sweetmeats deluxe in a few hours' time, business that is desperately required. Behind her Mai retches into the bucket. Bai rubs her sister's back, and sighs. 'You would have thought this family might have learned something about foreign involvement in the past forty years. Please God, Papa never finds out what's happened to you, Mai. For all our sakes.' She sighs again. 'Though how we prevent this, I don't know.'

Upstairs, JC, as Jules Chretien Bone prefers to be known, wakes to discover he is not strapped to a dental chair in Woking, that his Parisian-born unhappily married mother and her dental clogs are nowhere in sight, and that the blood that was gushing from his molar is in reality nothing more threatening than a dribble of drool on the bed sheet.

He reaches beneath the pillow for his laptop. Opens the diary page:

Mummy again. Sour milk in smoothie or dodgy cheese sarnie?

Take it up with old man Han.

He considers the flashing cursor for a moment and then switches screens to continue on a half-written document:

Handcuffed to the electrified bedstead, Frank Doonaghan grinned. He had taken the worst the Red Guards could throw at him – and he had survived. Shaking back the curls of his leonine hair, he dislocated his wrists and slid himself free. His grin grew wide. Today it would be the Commies who would discover they just couldn't take any more.

JC pauses to lean back and allow his own curls to tickle the blades of his shoulders. *Leonine.* It was a great word. Out of nowhere. Inspired. And if that wasn't the sign of a true writer, Mummy, what was? Nearly sixty words down in, what has it been, a minute, maybe two? He is on a roll. He is on fire. It won't take more than a couple of weeks to finish off *The Mercenary's Tale*, a post-modern masterpiece of McNabism. The question is where to do it. The clattering has started up in the kitchen downstairs, and it isn't even ten-thirty. These people have no idea of the conditions needed for art to flourish. No idea at all.

'You wait, sir,' Bai shouts to the Englishman, who has appeared demanding coffee and omelette, and complaining, if she has understood him correctly, about the noise. She turns back to the goose she is dismembering in the kitchen sink.

'Chill, little lady, no hurry, just as long as it's soon.' JC settles himself pleasantly against the doorframe, where he can watch the three youngest Han girls mincing garlic and chillies and ginger into metal bowls. Such dolls, the Vietnamese. Fragile as little china dolls. Maybe Frank Doonaghan could take a little East-West loving – soften things up in between the action. It wasn't as if he hadn't done the research for it, JC thinks. 'Hey, where's my lovely Mai?'

'Mai sick.' Bai severs the bird's feet. 'Head not lift from bucket all morning.'

'Oh, that's rotten.' A journalist does not travel as extensively in Asia as JC has without becoming sensitive to the suffering of its people. 'I hope it's not catching.'

Bai rips the wings off the goose. 'Sick yesterday morning also.'

'Poor darling. If she needs the marvels of Western medicine – Imodium, aspirin, melatonin – I'm her man.'

'Yesterday yesterday morning also. Could not stand smell of kitchen.'

'I think you mean the day *before* yesterday.' JC is always happy to help out where phrasebooks fear to tread.

'Yesterday yesterday yesterday morning also. Non-stop sickness, sir.'

'Sounds like we should be steering clear of Mai.'

'Yes, you clear off.'

The tiny figure of six-year-old Su Han slips through the doorway. 'Mr?' she tugs lightly on JC's jeans. 'Egg.'

'Hey there, doll face, are you trying to tell me my omelette's ready?' Utterly adorable this one. JC crouches down and tucks her hair behind her ear. 'How old are you anyway, poppet?'

Bai's cleaver descends on the bird's neck. 'Not yet seven.' Whatever these people promised to write about the café in their foreign guides, it was not worth it. Nothing was worth this. 'Yes, sir, your egg is all cooked. For my sister Mai, we try young guava, if it is not too late.'

JC goes for a stroll through the park after breakfast, so the girls can do his room properly. He takes his laptop, because you can't be too careful, even in lockable rooms, and in any case he might be assailed by further inspiration for *The Mercenary's Tale*. Six months; that was the deal with Mummy, six months doing his *Global Adventurer* blog (byline: 'Bone up with Bone!') and then dental school. But that was before he was struck with the inspiration for *The Mercenary's Tale*. And that was nearly a year ago. Not that a time limit can be put on art. Still, a couple more weeks in the café in the park – if he can bear the racket, and if Mummy will wire the funds – and then he can head home, skint but manuscripted to the max. As Frank Doonaghan might say: no problemo, mate.

Although, of course, there is a problem.

It might be chance, or perhaps it is simply his extraordinary magnetism at work, but while he is thrashing out a trail through the magnolia woods, contemplating the allocation of movie rights, JC finds himself stopping in his tracks. His attention is drawn to a wedding party fidgeting by the lake below. A second later Jules 'JC' Bone is striding, then sprinting out of the trees. He is swerving past cowboys and ponies and careering down the grassy slope. For along with his own undeniable powers of attraction, JC would have to claim something of an eye for the ladies, and standing like a Grecian statue among the guests is a gorgeous bride. Indeed, his own mother aside, it is possible that this girl is the most perfect piece of flesh JC has laid eyes on – he thinks about it for a second – ever.

He skids down onto flat lawn and rolls to take cover in a rose bed.

'Damn it all,' he curses, peering between budding branches. For in the passion of his descent, he has neglected to remember what brides are commonly paired with: his Venus is glued to the arm of a lump-fronted weakling.

Clearly an urgent rescue mission is called for.

What would Frank Doonaghan advise? Tear gas? Snipe the villain? Or set up a M40 grenade launch and take them all out. Boom. Frank would not need medics; he would revive the girl himself, mouth to mouth, once he'd carried her to safety.

JC pops his head up for a number count, and pops down.

Alternatively, given the overwhelming numbers set against JC, Frank might recommend waiting for nightfall and cover of darkness. The Viets were a notoriously tricky lot, despite their size. JC didn't need Frank to tell him that.

But most curiously, as JC disentangles his leonine curls from rose thorns and settles to his vigil in the compost, he notices the air around him is indeed darkening. In the middle of the day.

Remarkable.

It is as if the sky itself is bending to his magnetic will.

Time of Death: One Twenty-Three

High above the Valley of Love the moon releases its solar stranglehold. The eclipse has lasted for just fifteen minutes. As the cathedral bell chimes the quarter, a fat yellow sun is shining down on the wedding party. Except now there will be no party. For the day's second dawn reveals the groom slumped lump forward on the gilt-framed photograph of Ho Chi Minh.

'Man down!' Dalat's horrified police chief gasps, grabbing at his son-in-law's legs and turning to the crowd with eyes desperate for assistance.

But the wedding guests, who seconds before were toppled in sociable piles, are now rising and backing away, straightening hairpieces and shoving neighbours with sharpened elbows. Someone has ruined their day after only one tray of sweetmeats has been served. Somewhere within these most noted of notables prowls the primest of suspects.

'Stand back!' Chief Duong cries at the retreating crowd, hauling Commissar Nao onto his back. 'The man is injured, he needs air.'

From her viewpoint among pot shards and rhododendron roots, where she lies unable or unwilling to rise, Mrs Duong lets out a hoot. 'He's more than injured, husband! I can see his brains bubbling from here.'

Duong seizes the green-socked ankle of a retreating traffic officer. 'You! Stop dithering. Get down here and check his pulse.'

'Waste of time, husband.'

'That's an order, boy.' Duong drags the traffic policeman onto his knees in front of the groom, whose forehead is hinged open like a soft-boiled egg.

'Come on, boy, quick sharp with you. A speedy procedure is a successful procedure.'

The policeman swallows and reaches a finger for Commissar Nao's jugular. 'Nothing there, Chief.'

'Of course there's something there.' The chief's voice seems to be tightening in his throat. 'Life doesn't run out just like that, you know. Try again.'

'Sorry, Chief, not a murmur.'

Duong leaps to his feet and blows his whistle at the gawping crowd. 'Who knows Resuscitational Strategies? Sergeant Yung, where in Ho's name are you? You attended the Saving Friend, Sparing Foe Academy course, yes?'

Three rows back a moustachioed face nods glumly. Duong's long-time deputy sergeant is a desk man, always has been. 'I'm not the best with blood, Chief, if you remember. I failed the course. Three consecutive attempts.'

'Well, you can make amends now.'

'Yes, Chief.' Yung looks around miserably just in case a younger stronger-stomached sort of man – a non-desk man – might jump in to save the day.

'Sergeant Yung! Time is of the essence.'

'Yes, Chief.' Resigned to his ill fortune, Yung shuffles forward and squats down, averting his gaze from the grey dribble of brain that is worming from the nose of the eminent groom. The sergeant begins to tug at Commissar

Nao's jacket buttons, breathing through his mouth, as sensible Mrs Yung has always advised if he ever felt in danger of hyperventilating.

'His ghost will not thank you for this spacial invasion.'

Yung looks to the splayed and soily mass of Mrs Duong. She crunches on a prawn cracker and winks. 'It will not, Yung, my dear. In a public place too.'

Duong crouches close to Yung's ear. 'Since when has my wife been your superior, Sergeant?' He finds his own jacket could do with a little loosening. 'Look to my son-in-law.'

Yung does not look. Mrs Yung also advises this. He fumbles for the hooks on the medical corset that has been revealed beneath Commissar Nao's shirt.

And now the crowd, for so these notables will henceforth be known, starts to return. A horde of murmuring curiosity, it inches forward. Just enough to get a decent view so that something can be salvaged from this sweetmeat-spoiled suspicion-smeared day. Just close enough so they can tell their friends and families how they were there the moment the worst-kept secret in the Central Highlands was revealed. How they will never forget – not even in the hour they leave this world – how many black-nailed fingers they saw sprouting from Party Commissar Nao's extra arm.

Except what comes flopping out is not an arm.

It is a tree.

Specifically, it is a twisted dwarf juniper sapling, about the length of a baby's thigh, rooted in a bag of soil, its trunk and limbs bound tightly in white string.

A dozen onlookers groan and retopple down. Three babies restart screaming.

'A bonsai!' Mrs Duong hoots, appreciative as ever of

top-notch lunacy. 'That's the secret to his triple-cork-screwed conifer commendation at the Spring Flower Festival right there, folks! Nurtured at the breast!'

Fang Duong, younger brother of the erstwhile Bride of the Year, hugs his sister tight. They are sitting in the pink-wheeled pony trap, where he has led her to escape the goggling at her brain-spotted gown. So the man was fond of junipers, he thinks. You would have coped, Sis. Just another eccentricity to throw in the family pot. Fang's sigh is almost audible. He kisses Lila's cheek and takes up the reins.

Lila says nothing as she is carted off. She is biting her bottom lip and recalling an incident that appears to have gone unnoticed by all around. She is thinking about the mouth that assaulted her the moment before the gun was fired. It had been no matrimonial mushing of tongues, she is sure of that. The kiss had an alien pong to it. A sweatiness. She can still taste its damp stain on her lips.

She folds her arms. 'So tell me, Fang, am I a widow?'

Fang looks over his shoulder to where Sergeant Yung is pummelling both fists and now his forehead on Commissar Nao's chest. He turns back and squeezes Lila's wrist.

'The poor man,' she says. 'But still,' she ponders practically, after allowing a respectable pause to elapse, 'if there is a bright side to all this, it does mean I have time to revise my pressure points before the course starts next Monday.'

'Well?' Chief Duong pants. 'Have you completed it?'

'Chief?' Yung swallows down bile.

'The resuscitation, Sergeant!'

'Begging your pardon, Chief, but the heart has stopped.'

'Then restart it at once.'

'Begging your pardon again, Chief, but it won't work.'

'Of course it will. That's why they teach you these techniques, Yung!'

'Yes, Chief.' Yung blows on his sore knuckles and straddles the groom.

The chief supervises intently. 'Excellent work, Yung. A little more to the left, further to the right. Hit that spot again. Faster! Lower! Excellent! Again!'

But the chief's optimism is to no avail. A violet bruise is flowering on the commissar's chest. Sergeant Yung bows his head. Sweat meanders down the threads of his moustache. He consults his watch. 'Time of death, one twenty-three.'

Standing over his stiffening son-in-law, the little police chief shakes his head in disbelief. He looks away to the road that climbs the valley. Sirens screaming, an ambulance is speeding towards them, passing a pink-wheeled trap in which his daughter is being driven away.

His beautiful daughter.

And for a moment the crowd, who are starting to disperse before unpleasant questions begin to be raised, pauses to wonder whether they have in fact got two tragedies for the price of one. Because with a gasp and a buckling of knees, and a faint cry which sounds a little like 'repayment plan', Dalat's very own chief of police and miscreant management is keeling sideways.

Unconscious before he lands, Chief Duong is ill-disposed to appreciate the one stroke of luck he has been delivered on this unfortunate day: his fall is cushioned by his chuckling wife.

Clause 46cii

'No, I will not see him.'

'Yes, Chief.'

'A disgraceful waste of police time, Sergeant.'

'Apologies, Chief. Only he's asking about your daughter, Chief.'

Duong's thumb trembles on the intercom switch. It is a muggy Monday morning, more humid than is usual in the city of eternal spring. A whole day has passed since the commissar's murder and he is starting to feel the heat. 'My daughter will not see him either. What in Ho's name does he want with my daughter?'

'He asks to respectfully remind you that he is a journalist, Chief. European. French or British. Both, I think. He seems unsure.'

'And?'

'Says it's a story, Chief, the wedding. Human interest – doomed love.'

'Tell him my only interest is in finding the sick mind behind the wanton murder of an upstanding provincial leader. Tell Mr European this. Tell him to keep his big nose – I presume he has one of those?'

'Yes, Chief. Hooked and leftward leaning.'

'Well, tell him he can keep it out of our town's business.

His visa – check it out, yes? And get the fans on please, Yung. My brain is steaming up in here.'

In the chief of police's small-windowed office – comprising statutorily: one filing cabinet, one formica desk, two swivel chairs, one framed portrait of Ho Chi Minh, one metal wastebin and one chief – situated behind the main investigation area on the first floor of the two-storey police station, located adjacent to a roundabout and the famous Petit Eiffel tower, the ceiling fan clicks on. Desiccated flies and clots of plaster whirl down onto the chief's writing pad, obscuring a short list of non-notable wedding guest names under the heading 'Potentially Murderous Characters?' and a doodle of a water buffalo in mid-gallop.

The chief pats his brow and tries not to look out the window at the roundabout, where there isn't much room for a statue anyway and planning permission would probably be problematic, even for a short policeman. He feels the eyes of Uncle Ho upon him. Middle aged, military attired, the Great Leader smiles down from his frame on the wall opposite. It is the same reproduction as the print that had to be doused in the lake to rinse off the commissar's brains.

Duong flicks a fly off the writing pad and turns to a fresh sheet.

Official investigation into the death of Commissar Bao Nao he writes.

Photographer? he writes.

Suspicious? he writes.

Is Uncle Ho significant?

Is suspicion significant?

Almost half a side of paper is nicely full. He presses

the intercom and orders a bowl of shrimp-tail porridge and a cold beer from Man Chu's.

Halfway through his brunch he is disturbed by a waft of eucalyptus slithering under the door into his office, followed by a swift rat-a-tat on the woodwork. Before Duong has a chance to reiterate that he is indisposed, a figure, chopstick thin, is stalking in.

'Oh, it's you, Jimn.' His upstarted fast-tracked deputy. Hanoi-trained and hotfooted here. He holds out a brown file, sporting that peculiar lip-shrinking smile of his, the one that stretched his skin so taut a man didn't need reminding of the skull that sat beneath. 'Everything all right, Deputy?'

Slimn Jimn pulls his pale gaze from the chief's congealing bowl and a pressed linen handkerchief from his jacket's outer pocket. From an inner pocket he removes a medicine bottle, applies its contents to the handkerchief and snorts sharply up his left nostril. 'Regarding developments in the Nao murder case, there are none, Chief. Developments would be greatly assisted by the commencement of witness interviews, a forensic investigation of the victim's abode and DNA analysis of the crime scene, Chief. That is not to mention the autopsy, the initiation of computerised background checks on wedding guests, and so forth and so on. I have fifteen officers outside, ready and awaiting green-lighting from management. Sitting around and consuming noodles, Chief. Sitting and eating and drinking, also betting on the cows since Sunday, Chief.'

Duong sucks his spoon thoughtfully. 'Well, that's good, Jimn. Readiness is good. Like a soaring hawk, isn't it? Ever ready for the field mouse's first move.'

'A governmental statistic, Chief – eighty-three per cent

of murders are solved in the first forty-eight hours. A good trail is a warm trail, Chief.'

Barely sprouted his last crop of acne and after a man's job. 'Well now, Jimn my boy, it seems I may have to remind you of the wisdom of our great Uncle during the Da Nang campaign in '69, long before you were born, of course, "The best of trails is a carefully planned trail. Otherwise" – and this bit's the clever bit, Jimn – "how would we know where to go?" Now isn't that just lovely advice?'

Jimn places the file on the desk. 'Already it's been forty-two hours, Chief. The window of opportunity is closing, clouding blue-sky thinking and disabling a fire-fighting response. With this in mind I have initiated background checks of all wedding attendees, including the victim, on the National Criminal Database.'

'The victim?' Duong sniffs. 'A most exemplary member of the Party, Jimn. Hanoi-bound. The highest level of the Interior. A spotless socialistic record.' Duong sniffs again. Jimn's confounded eucalyptus must be making his nose run. 'Criminals, you say? At my daughter's wedding? I don't mind telling you I'm completely flummoxed by this, Jimn. It seems so unlikely.'

'Unlikely but one hundred per cent factually correct in at least one case.'

'Well, be that as it may, Jimn, I don't recall authorising any checks.'

'You didn't, Chief, I self-authorised.'

'You self-authorised?'

'Yes, Chief, in accordance with edict 461 from Policing HQ. "Self-authorisation of action by deputies is permitted when there may be reason to believe their senior officers have become unduly incapacitated."'

'I do not notice myself becoming incapacitated, Jimn.'

'By grief.'

'*Grief?*'

'It would only be natural, Chief. Some interesting data was outputted from the searches.'

Duong tries to deflect the sudden vision of being outputted to the paddy fields now his Hanoi-bound son-in-law lay two floors down in the basement morgue.

Jimn watches his boss shake his head and dab at a shrimp dribble on his tie. Jimn applies his handkerchief to his right nostril. 'I believe this case must be especially painful for you, Chief. Given your intimate domestic involvement.'

'Now just hold it there, Jimn – my what?'

'Your daughter married him. You were standing right by him at the moment of death. There was no one else between you and the victim, Chief.'

'Uncle Ho in Hanoi, man, you're not suggesting—'

'I am merely proposing that it might be more appropriate if I took over responsibility for the case. Standard Proximity Protocol.'

'Standard what?'

'Eighty-eight per cent of victims know their killers, Chief.'

'I very much dislike—'

The telephone on the desk begins to ring. An outside line.

'Your insinuations, Jimn. I dislike them very much.'

'Chief?'

'Yes, Jimn?'

'I believe that is the phone, Chief.'

'That is correct, Jimn. Answer it, would you?'

'It's the district superintendent.'

Duong quickly shovels the last porridgy shrimp tail

onto his spoon and into his mouth, shaking his head. 'I'm indisposed.'

He watches Jimn enjoy a rapid conversation and a joke or two before the handset is replaced. 'Old navy colleague of my father's.'

Duong pulls the telephone back across the desk. 'Will that be all?'

'Just the time frame on initiation of leads – crime scene, victim's house etc. The super was asking after progress.'

Duong beams suddenly. 'But he didn't mention this protocol proximity what not, did he, Jimn?'

'Not as yet, Chief, no.'

'Well then,' Duong beams up at his young deputy's disappointed face, 'I think you'll find everything is quite safe with me.'

The intercom buzzes.

Duong beams down gratefully at the flashing light.

'Hello, Sergeant Yung. No, you're not disturbing me at all. Really? How very peculiar. You may as well send them in, Sergeant.'

'Catch up later, yes, Deputy Jimn? Have a most important lead. Best handled alone. Sure you understand. Keep the men on standby, yes? Instruct them to turn on computers, sharpen pencils, squat some thrusts. Plenty of preparatory activities while awaiting further orders.' Duong catches the eye of wise Uncle Ho on the wall. 'We humans are not so evolved from the humble ant, Jimn. I hope they at least taught you that in cadet school. Societal busyness makes for societal happiness, yes? Let's have spring rolls all round.'

He hears the clinking before they appear. Three of them waddling in with their chaps and spurs, twisting their ridiculous hats in their hands. Duong looks up at Uncle Ho and shares a swallowed smile.

'Come along, stand here in front of the desk.' Duong flicks over a fresh page of his notepad. 'Identification?'

They give their names falteringly, and Chief Duong writes them in for the sake of convenience as Cowboys One, Two and Three. He fixes them in his gaze. 'Now, tell me straight, boys, who sent you?'

The cowboys look at the floor.

'Come on, come on. I will not bite your heads off for it. The greatest conversations begin with a single word.'

'Sir, you required us to attend,' Cowboy Three mutters, 'so here we are.'

'I did?'

'Yes, sir!' Cowboy One clicks his heels together. 'Are we in trouble, sir?'

Chief Duong stares at them perplexed. 'Why on earth would I do that? Do you know the deceased, is that it?'

'No, sir.'

'His family?'

'No, sir.'

'My family?'

'No, sir.'

'You're sure?'

'Yes, sir.'

'Well then, do you have grudges of any kind against the deceased, the family of the deceased, or my family?'

'No, sir.'

'Not even a small one? One you may have forgotten about?'

'No, sir.'

'Hmmm. Real guns, are they?'

'Oh no, sir, not real at all,' Cowboy Two ventures. 'Water pistols. From the market, sir.'

'Very well.' Chief Duong strikes an official line through Cowboys One, Two and Three. He considers the boys' jingle-jangle costumes. It would have been of as much use to bring the ponies in for questioning. Then a thought – the sort for which he is famous in the force – suddenly occurs to him. 'You were by the pedalo swans, yes? Across the lake? Mounted, yes? Good view, I expect.'

'Oh yes, sir, you get excellent views on horseback, sir,' Cowboy Three replies. 'The finest.'

'Ha!' Chief Duong's sudden smile dazzles the cowboys. 'Ha!' His genius – that surely no Hanoi hotshot school could teach – has not deserted him.

'Sergeant Yung!' he buzzes the intercom. 'My genius has not deserted me! Stickers, if you would, Yung. No, not any kind of stickers, red ones and green ones. And glue, Sergeant, dabbing glue. A cardboard sheet. And beers for my guests.'

Duong scrapes together the fan-fallen flies and plaster clumps into a small mound on his desk. He adds a handful of drawing pins, three cloves of garlic and a scoop of paperclips. Then he returns his attention to the cowboys. 'Now that we're done with the formalities I can reveal the real reason I asked you here.' He points to the dusty pile and lowers his voice. 'Highly confidential, boys, hunker round and listen up. I need you to imagine this desk as the Valley of Love, and that Valley as a battlefield, yes? Imagine the sky darkening, as indeed it does in the heat of battle. Black smoke hangs everywhere, stinking of iron and cordite and blood. It's noisy too, thunderously noisy. You never get a second's peace in war, boys. Or if you do, then you know you're really in for it, I can tell you. BOOM! BANG! Artillery hammers the earth, smashing it inside out. BOOM! BANG! Men fly up into the air. Men fall. Screaming, they fall. Like monkeys, boys, that's how they scream when they fall.'

After a few seconds, Cowboy One clears his throat quietly.

Chief Duong blinks and looks up. 'Quite right, son. You young men weren't invited here to listen to an old soldier's stories. So, where were we?'

Cowboy One hesitates. 'On a battlefield, sir?'

'Excellent, yes, we're pretending we're in the thick of battle. And in this dreadful place, a general calls out, "Scouts! Get me my scouts!"' Duong bounces back on his chair, spins around and pinions the cowboys in his brilliant beam. 'Well?'

'Sir?'

'It's quite simple. I am the general and you boys are my scouts. First, we shall build a replica plan of the park, and once we have done that you will recreate exactly what you saw from your mounted positions on the far side of the lake. You will indicate the precise positions of the wedding guests just before the eclipse and the moment of murder. Ah – excellent, Yung, come in.'

Yung deposits the cardboard, stickers, glue and beers on the desk. Duong continues. 'So, boys, take this fragment of bluebottle here. Let us name this fly Party Commissar Nao. The intimate wedding party – family and the like – you can code with green stickers, boys, and the VIPs will be red. You may begin.'

After three hours and twelve cold beers, the cardboard sheet is a rash of red and green, with additional flies,

43

topographical paperclips and explanatory biro scrawls. With the phone off the hook and his sandals hanging from his toes, Chief Duong is beginning to enjoy himself, when Sergeant Yung enters again and salutes shakily.

'So sorry to disturb you, Chief, when genius is afoot. But the superintendent has been calling. Thrice. Also,' Yung advances hesitantly, 'this arrived for you, Chief.' He places an envelope on the desk. It is addressed 'To the Chief of Police with commiserations for your family's recent loss.' Yung lowers his voice. 'It is pink, Chief. The envelope is pink.'

'I can see that.'

'Hand delivered by a minority boy.'

The stalks of Duong's eyebrows spring up. 'A minority boy?'

'Yes, Chief.'

'Clothed?'

'Minimally, Chief. Is everything all right, Chief?'

'Naturally, Yung.' Duong rips open the pink envelope without reading the address, to show how all right everything is.

A bullet thuds down on the replica park, crushing the bluebottle.

'Mother save me!' Yung exclaims. 'You don't think that's the actual – I mean, you don't think it should go to ballistics, do you, Chief?'

Duong forces out a thin smile. He picks up the bullet and rolls it between his fingers. 'Wrong calibre. This is an old machine-gun bullet, Soviet manufacture, MP40, if I'm not mistaken. Also, Yung, it is unspent.' Duong frowns, feeling a rough scratch on the polished metal. 'Magnifier, Yung, if you would.'

'Is it a clue to the Commissar's murder, Chief?'

Duong goes to the window. Through the lens he sees a number has been etched around the bullet's circumference. *46cii*.

He glances to Uncle Ho, who looks undecided.

He twists the bullet round and round. Then for the second time in one day, as only ever happens on the rarest of occasions, his genius reasserts itself. 'Ha!' he cries, returning to his desk and yanking on the bottom drawer. 'Ha! Ha! Ha!'

'Ha!' Yung shouts, marvelling once again and with some relief at the ways in which his boss's genius works, even with pink envelopes.

'Ha!' Cowboy One shouts, enjoying the dregs of his third beer.

But before Cowboys Two and Three can join the general exaltation, a gassy gasp rises from the chief as he rifles through the bottom drawer. For here it is, typed neatly on the eighth sheet of a pink-paper contract: clause 46cii.

In the event of the occurrence of a hitherto unforeseen act of God, or an unfortunate act of death, full repayment of the five hundred dollar loan from Uncle Duc Mei to Mr Hung Duong is due with ten per cent costs. Failure to repay this amount within four days will evoke clause 47i.

For a few moments there is nothing to be heard from the drawer but rustling.

Yung knocks politely on the desk top. 'Begging your pardon, Chief. Just hoping everything is all right and no assistance is required, Chief.'

Duong emerges very slowly from the desk drawer, with a second sheet of pink paper and a glazed expression. 'Forty,' he gasps, 'seven.'

'I see,' Yung says, although he doesn't quite. He is not unaware of the significance of pink paper in the police station, being the man tasked with shepherding wild-eyed fathers and wailing husbands into the chief's office. But to imagine that the chief himself had got involved with Mei? It was impossible. A ludicrous idea. Perhaps he should offer Mrs Yung's favourite solution to such an outlandish turn of events – there must have been some mix-up of addresses.

Suddenly his boss is lurching for the wastebin.

'Chief Duong?' Yung's face swims close. 'Do you require me to call upon the station physician?'

Duong looks up helplessly as a shoal of half-digested shrimp shoots into the bin on waves of frothy beer.

'I'm going for the physician, Chief.' Yung turns for the door with a resolve that surprises even him.

'No physician,' Duong whispers. 'Food poisoning. Just a touch. All better now.'

'I don't know,' Yung says, eyeing the pink envelope on the desk and worrying the strings of his moustache. 'I don't know at all.'

The cowboys twiddle their beer bottles and inspect their spurred feet.

Duong mops his mouth and tries to redirect his thoughts from forty-sixes and -sevens. Uncle Ho looks on sympathetically. *What is a storm but an opportunity for the pine and the cypress to show their strength and stability.* Yes, Ho was right, as he always was. A man must be strong.

'Listen,' Duong says to his anxious-eyed deputy, 'pop

these cowboys outside somewhere, and I'll be frank with you. We have no secrets in these walls, do we?'

'Oh no, Chief. Thank you, Chief.'

When his loyal deputy returns, bringing a stomach-settling lager, he finds the chief much fortified.

'Excellent work, Yung. Now, as you probably already guessed, this note is simply a communication – albeit in a dramatic form – from the businessman Duc Mei. No, it's really quite all right, Yung, he is merely notifying me in advance of the required repayment of a minor loan, and the possible transferral of – well, the transferral of ownership of an asset, if I am unable to pay him back.'

'Oh Chief. Oh Chief. Oh that's terrible, Chief.'

'Please don't alarm yourself, Yung, it does no good for the bodily systems. As I say, a reasonable business request, and the asset in question is entirely safe. Entirely. It is simply a matter of returning the loan. Which, of course, is very straightforward.'

'It is?'

Duong calculates. The banks would have been shut on Saturday, and Commissar Nao surely hadn't had long enough to spend the dowry before the wedding. And the extra ten per cent could be sourced from any pawnbroker. Perhaps in exchange for a few of his wife's old vases.

'It is. To return to important matters, please instruct Deputy Jimn to cordon off the entrance to Commissar Nao's house at once. Under no circumstances is anyone to enter it.'

There is plenty of time, until the end of tomorrow in fact, to find the cash. Which has to be in the house. All the time in the world. Duong can picture it right now, the green block sitting in the blue plastic bag – possibly with that busy cockroach still running about inside – somewhere in the commissar's home. Possibly in a modern aluminium filing cabinet. Probably in the bottom drawer.

He beams at Yung. 'What could go wrong, Yung? What we mustn't do is lose sight of the investigation, yes? Therefore the cowboys will now accompany me to the lake, where we shall pin down once and for all that man responsible for the commissar's murder. Following this, I will personally supervise a search of the victim's abode. You see, Yung, each of the businesses of life must be run like a trusted motorcycle part – when everything is serviced to schedule, what can ever go wrong?'

'Well, there is something, Chief. Two things, actually. Man Chu, the seafood restaurateur, left a message. He sounded distressed and begged a return call. And Chief, some terrible news last night – most upsetting for the superintendent, Chief. He said you must phone him as a priority, he says it is a direct order, whether you say you are indisposed or not – the MLA has struck again.'

The Reigate Rambo

Chief Duong is not alone in the world in experiencing the stomach-flipping fear that is so large a part of fatherhood. At this very moment as the police chief rips a pink envelope into pieces over a wastebin, another man half a world away sits with his wife in the front room of their terraced home in Reigate, England, stroking the ears on a photograph of their sixteen-year-old daughter. 'Gracie baby,' this man is saying, 'we love you, honey. Gracie baby, please come home.'

With a chorus of clicks and purrs, the room flashes white. In the fireplace a scrum of photographers resets and refocuses.

'We're not angry with you, Grace.' A carrot cake trembles on a tea plate on this mother's knee. 'We just want you home, Gracie, please come home.'

To look at these parents, there would seem to be no obvious link to armed robbery overseas. Mrs Marsden teaches Self-Expression through Ceramics at Dorking Halls two evenings a week, and Mr M heads up Reigate Comprehensive's geography department. They support social economic policies, local composting schemes and the CND. As Mr Marsden is explaining to the reporters, their two sons have secured white-collar employment, settled marriages and steps on property ladders. Darling

49

Emma, Grace's elder sister, is trying to decide between a career in the Anglican priesthood and a degree in mental health provision. The carer in the family, darling Emma.

'And Grace?' a reporter enquires, popping up from behind the sofa.

'More tea, anyone?' Mrs Marsden says unhappily.

The journalists demur. They stretch and shift and discreetly yawn. Disks are fed into the jaws of black video cameras. A woman darts forward and, with a move that is both a pat and a push, lands a newspaper article on Mrs Marsden's lap. Taken from a tabloid Sunday supplement, the page shows a blurred image of a chunky figure in battle fatigues and balaclava. The caption reads:

THE REIGATE RAMBO!
POSSIBLE FIRST SIGHTING OF MISSING SURREY SCHOOLGIRL TURNED JUNGLE GUERRILLA?

Mrs Marsden strokes the black print of the blurred balaclava, which is bowed by a pair of pushy ears. She closes her eyes and bites her lip.

Producers raise eyebrows at cameramen. Fingers slip to Record buttons in the nick of time.

A tear drops from Mr Marsden's left eye into his beard. 'We just want to know, where did we go wrong?'

But Mr and Mrs Marsden may never get it, that top-of-the-list parental Christmas gift, the ducking diving magic bullet called exoneration. For a quick rummage in the Marsden family closet reveals at least one possible explanation for this shocking turn of events. An old one but, psychologically speaking, a good one: elder sister, darling Emma's asthma. And Mr M does not need his

Year Eleven geopolitical top set to remind him what chaos may spring from a single cause.

The diagnosis of darling Emma's asthma at the age of eight heralded a new law in the Marsden household: no pets allowed. It was applied with immediate effect, with one particularly ruthless effect: ten-year-old tabby, Mr Sludge, was rehomed forthwith.

Was this it? Was this the moment the cell of militancy split in Gracie's five-year-old mind? The day her dear tom was scraped off her bed and carted away in a cardboard box. Was this all it took? For while her brothers received tanks of stick insects and dust-free rainbow iguanas for their birthdays, young Grace's replacement for the warm weight of a cat on her duvet was merely a laminated panda poster and biannual updates from a zoo in Chengdu.

But in Mr and Mrs Marsden's remembrance little Gracie never seemed to complain. She threw herself into bamboo cultivation, minor league rugby and moderate vegetarianism. She seemed to develop adequately. She acquired pink hair briefly, and a boy she held hands with. In fact, for years she appeared the very model of a modern teenager and displayed not the slightest hint of rifle-toting, lip-curling Sylvester Stallonery. But a trigger? A tipping point? Mr and Mrs Marsden ask themselves night after night in the empty house. There must have been something more than an evicted old tom to set her off.

'Is this about the ears?' he asks his wife. 'Was I wrong to forbid the pinning-back operation when she asked for it and you said yes to her? Should you have insisted? Should I have agreed?'

But if it's blame he's seeking, magic-bullet hunting Mr Marsden, he could do worse than try Mr Fisher, the family dentist, whose overzealous bracework had thirteen-year-old Grace unable to sleep one night and fidgeting beneath her Mr Sludge-less duvet. Flicking back and forth through her WWF update magazine, Grace had come across an unassuming appeal in the back pages.

Save the caged snub-nosed monkeys of Asia.
From ten pounds a month.
Contact PO Box 986574331.

If grumpy Mr Fisher had not been thinking about his wife's latest tango partner, and had attended to a girl's winces and put his pliers aside, it is probable such a meek request from a magazine's back pages would have gone unheeded. Grace's life would have slipped down an alternative track. But such speculation is meaningless, for no clock can be turned back to the night after the dentist had done his worst. The night when Gracie, fighting the throbbing of her canines, read the back pages into the early hours. The night Grace Marsden was summoned.

'Save the snub-nosed monkeys,' thirteen-year-old Grace yawned, her head nodding over the picture of a monkey stretching a beseeching arm between bars. 'The caged snub-nosed monkeys of Asia.'

Her eyelids fluttered low. Grace swayed on the threshold of sleep.

At this moment the caged monkey opened its mouth and began to speak. 'Save us, Grace Marsden. Help us out, would you, Gracie, it's such a tight fit in here.'

Grace's head nodded onto her chest and she fell asleep. And then they pounced.

Pouring through the open door of her dream came

snub-nosed monkeys – red-headed, lion-maned, albino. They bent the bars of their cages and leapt onto jungle tracks, cackling and cartwheeling, tumbling and hopping and whooping. 'Gracie M,' they cried, 'you have set us free!'

The ranks of liberated monkeys grew. A black baboon stopped the bus he was driving and jumped out with a shining trumpet to take the lead. The numbers multiplied to a legion strong. The baboon tootled and the snub-nosed masses rose up on their toes and began to march to his tune. They goose-stepped over the skin of seas and the sand of deserts, up remote mountain summits and across rush-hour streets. They bestrode the Himalayas and the Alps, the Seine and the Channel. They paraded clockwise around the M25 from Kent to Surrey, through Reigate's one-way system and up Waterloo Crescent to the reclaimed oak front door of the Marsdens' residence. There the black baboon tootled one last time and the ranks fell silent, marching on the spot beneath Grace's bedroom window.

From this night on Grace's every dream was invaded by monkeys. Her hair grew whippy as a tail. Her palms sprouted thick calluses, which the family doctor diagnosed as hormone warts but she knew to be stigmata, her mark of co-suffering with the oppressed. Grace dropped the boy's hand she had been holding and took up Saturday work and Sunday too.

Then one Monday she failed to appear in the kitchen for muesli before school.

The report into the latest attack by the self-styled Monkey Liberation Army pings onto a laptop screen on a kitchen table beside butterfly killing jars and bonsai-trimming wheels, ten thousand kilometres to the east of Reigate. It makes for grim reading.

02:43 *Victim awakens to the sound of shattering glass below.*

02:45 *Victim runs down to restaurant to investigate.*

02:47 *Victim confronted by masked intruder armed with pistol. Intruder described as 160–170 cm in height, of stocky build. Intruder does not speak. Intruder forces victim to sit facing the back wall reading aloud from propaganda leaflet – the same material as in other attacks – of poor grammatical quality and bombastic ideological content.*

02:55 *Intruder saws through bars of baboon cage with a locally manufactured hacksaw – matching previous descriptions.*

03:10 *Impervious to victim's explanations that baboon is old, domesticated and requires medication, intruder attaches baboon to a length of rope and removes to an unknown destination.*

03:15 *Victim contacts police.*

In the kitchen of Dalat's chief superintendent, a Painted Jezebel shivers and expires in a killing jar. A fist crashes down on a table. It could spell trouble this report, big trouble. That much is clear.

In the office of the chief of police and miscreant management, where a little chief of police is putting on his jacket to head to a lake, the intercom begins to buzz.

'On my way out, Yung. Hold all calls.'

'Yes, Chief. Only a thousand apologies, Chief, but the

superintendent is on the line again. He will not be re-diverted again, Chief. He is threatening to come down and get his hands on you himself he says, Chief. I'm so sorry, Chief.'

Duong sighs. He presses down on a beansprout that is coming unstuck on the edge of the replica lake. Though he is a modest man, he has to admit the topographical resemblance is remarkable. 'Very well. Put him through.'

He beams at the receiver with the best of intentions and holds it away from his ear. 'Good afternoon, Chief Superintendent.'

A snarl slithers down the line. 'I take it you've read this, Duong.'

'Begging your pardon, sir, read what?' Duong assesses the grouping around the bluebottle. Perhaps his own sticker should be larger. The scale is not yet perfect.

'Heavens, man, the monkey people, what else? Binh Linh's dumpling emporium was attacked last night. What is that now – ten incidents?'

'I think it is seven actually, sir. We have encountered two cases of common vandalism and one of mistaken identity.'

'Never mind about the details, Duong.'

'Apologies, sir.'

'And don't interrupt when I'm speaking – speaking about something highly important, Duong, and totally Top Secret.'

'Yes, sir.'

'Right. Yes, you might as well be told now, I suppose – big things are about to happen round these parts, Duong. Huge, in fact. Very beneficial for those in at the off, if you catch my drift.'

'Sir?'

'Heavens, man, I'm talking money, *dollar* money. *Overseas investment* money. The world turns, Duong. Bygones are bygone and Foreign Foes become Comrades in Commerce, Buddies in Business. The world turns, Duong, and big things happen to those who turn with it.'

Duong swivels his chair away from Uncle Ho's steady gaze.

'You hear me, Duong?'

'Whatever you say, sir.'

'So, this monkey business, I don't mind telling you it's proving upsetting for our new Comrades in Commerce. Most upsetting. And we don't like to upset our friends, do we, Duong?'

'No, sir.'

'You understand the importance of playing nicely with friends.'

'Yes, sir.'

'On a new local playground our friends are going to build in the area.'

'I see, sir. Very good, sir.'

'Look, Duong, the fact is our Business Buddies are getting twitchy. They don't understand how things work with us. Cultural differences, let us call it. Gorillas, they say, could be Cambodian guerrillas next. Not good international PR, they warn me. Could be easier to set up their business in a calmer spot, they hint. Perhaps a coastal spot. This is what they are saying. This is what they are threatening, Duong.'

There is a pause while the superintendent coughs out his spleen.

'Are you well, sir?'

'Never mind me, Duong. It's you I'm worried about. I don't mind telling you I'm beginning to question whether you are the man for the job. Whether a younger, hungrier sort of man might not have cleaned up this monkey mess two weeks ago.'

'But it is my job, sir,' Duong says in a small voice. 'I mean, chief of provincial policing is my job and it has been for some time.'

'Well, if you want to keep your job, damn well do it. Get yourself over to Binh Linh's pronto and take a look. Right now, you hear me, Duong?'

'I hear you, sir. Right now. Only, sir, what about Commissar Nao? First-degree murder of a prominent civic figure.'

'Damn it, man. For the last time, the MLA is your top priority. I want results. Today, Duong. Today.'

Duong wistfully swivels a paperclip around on the park plan. As he does, a curious burbling noise begins to leak from the phone.

'Say, you were up close, weren't you?'

'Sir?'

'Heavens, your daughter's wedding, Duong. Got a good look, did you?'

'Begging your pardon, sir?'

'The juniper, man! The juniper that he was feeding at the breast!'

'With all respect, I'm not sure he was actually feeding—'

'Explains rather a lot, don't you think? Not playing fair in my book, all that undercover suckling. If everyone gave their bonsai crops round-the-clock care, I should imagine the Festival results would have turned out some-what differently these past seven years.'

'Yes, sir.'

'Let that be a lesson – never trust a man you've not seen naked, Duong.'

'No, sir.'

'You may be interested to hear I've asked the judging committee to commence a retrospective enquiry into the past seven finals. The Flower Festival doesn't like cheats, Duong, not even dead ones.'

'No, sir.'

'Throws this year's Spring Bonsai Freestyle Formation wide open, of course.'

'Yes, sir.'

'By the way, wasn't Nao tipped to be the next Party man on the National Police Advancement board?' With a damp chuckle the line goes dead.

The Legendary Lady Professionally Known as Hot Chocolatie

'You are drunk. My naughty monkey soldier boy has gotten himself all drunked up,' a low voice growls down a hot ear. 'For this there will be punishment.'

In a padded candlelit cell, a head is shoved deep into crimson cushions and cuffed wrists are jerked up behind a bare back. The cushions emit a whimper; it seems the restraints have been wrenched a notch tighter than strictly necessary – could it be the lady is out of sorts tonight? 'Present yourself to me. Raise high the ass.'

Two moons of a police chief's bottom wiggle upwards with an anticipatory shiver. It has been a long day.

Binh Linh's loss had touched the police chief's heart. It hadn't been a pretty discovery, the dumpling emporium owner curled up inside the baboonless cage in a tangle of Gola-Cola bunting, weeping into the triangled faces of international soccer star Sam Porcini.

'Grief kidnaps a man's dignity,' Duong had observed for the edification of the younger constables on the investigating team, before crawling between the sawn-off bars to coax the old man out.

'Never underestimate the consequences of the loss of a treasured friend,' Duong had further observed, patting the old man who, now liberated, was clinging to him like a baby chimp.

'One that needs daily medication for his arteries,' Binh sobbed.

Duong held him to his chest in a comforting embrace and promised a memo in the morning to the municipal zookeeper. Something along the lines of: 'Send your sparest baboon or other ape-ish animal special delivery to Comrade Linh forthwith.' For Duong was happy to explain to the emporium that a wise chief enjoyed sharing the benefits of his provincial position with all.

After this he requested Binh cook up a batch of his finest pork knuckle dumplings, and open a litre or so of rice wine to wash them down. 'Old-style care of the community policing,' he assured the constables tucking in around the table. 'We take time with victims. Get them straight back into their comfort zones doing what they do best. Could someone pass the fish sauce?'

During the early part of a second litre of wine and a second serving of dumplings, when Duong believed it was still unwise to leave the old man on his own, even though the constables had long since been dismissed to their families, he felt able to confess to the restaurateur – not withstanding Binh Linh's loss – that if he ever became superintendent, he wouldn't get so worked up about the Monkey Liberation Army. Whatever these so-called Comrades in Commerce might demand, a true man stood firm in his conviction. Firm as a mangrove against the tide. Yes, he said, polishing off the wine jar in a toast to Binh Linh's baboon, he wouldn't ever be swept out to a foreign sea. Of such nationalistic fortitude were statues surely made.

After a palate-cleansing lager, Duong had bid Binh Linh farewell and stepped outside, somewhat surprised to discover that in the course of his investigation the day had dissolved into a very dark night. He engaged the Hero full throttle and with the chorus of the 'Peasant Girl's Lament' on his lips, he set off weaving down route sixty-six for home.

Less than three kilometres separated him from a peppermint house when he happened to glance left and catch sight of a pink neon globe throbbing invitingly through the rubber plantation. The Hero obligingly braked at once, so as not to miss the turning. And why not? Duong agreed, for even though he hadn't quite made it to a park to pinpoint a murderer, or to a dead groom's house to recoup a dowry, or to a forest to catch some monkey thieves, it had been a hard day and the pressures on a police chief were many.

In suite seventeen at the New Universe Entertainment Palace a sharpened silver nail rakes seams in pimpled flesh. 'Naughty drunked-up boys need whipping good. Here I think, and also here, here and here I will strike. Hottie's muscles are turbocharged tonight. Full of P M Tension.'

'Speak to me in French. Call me mon chéri. Mon cher petit soldat de singe.'

'Quiet!' A stiff crop of dried buffalo hide comes whistling down.

The buttocks flinch. The cushions gasp.

'I will decide what I call this naughty boy.' *Thwack.*

The cushions whimper, 'Apologies.'

'Raise higher the ass!' *Thwack.*

'I'm truly sorry.'

Thwack. Thwack. Thwack. 'I should think so. You are more than a naughty boy. You are a bad little man wanting this foreign-language filth spread on Choccie's pretty tongue.'

'I am I am I am. I am very bad.'

Thwack. Thwack. Thwack.

'You are too noisy also.'

The crop dangles above striped and quivering buttocks.

'You are a too noisy monkey soldier boy who gives his Choccie a headache, and possibly also Moonduck in the adjoining suite.'

The legendary lady professionally known as Hot Choco-latie clambers off the satin bedsheet and wiggles her bulk out of a sequinned G-string. Yanked back by a blindfold, a head emerges from the cushions, fluffy and gasping as a hungry chick. 'Maybe this will give poor Choccie some peace.' Plump fingers roll up panties and plug up a mouth with a spangled ball. A head is shoved back down.

'Now I am rested and still dissatisfied with my mood, I will see what this drunked-up, dirty-mouthed monkey soldier boy can take. Raise high the ass.'

A reinvigorated chief of police winces his way across New Universe's crowded dance floor. The club is busier tonight than Chief Duong has ever seen it. Around the dancers on the podiums businessmen cluster tighter than mating toads. The walls between two karaoke booths have broken down under the weight of warbling. The blackjack queues are ten bodies deep. Duong limps to the bar, pausing only to watch Kong, the mighty mountain gorilla, being cheered through one hundred press-ups by admirers crammed around his cage.

'On the house, Chief,' bartender Giau shouts, slapping down a glass and sloshing it half full of Mekong. 'First drink on the house. All members. One night only.' Scarfed in Gola-Cola bunting, Giau tosses the triangle faces of Scunthorpe striker Sam Porcini over his shoulder and nods to the far corner of the club in explanation.

Duong turns to look. Two bouncers guard a red cordon. Behind this a dark-skinned boy stands sentry with a machine gun, and behind him, on a raised dais, a stuffed albino tigress tilts her jaw in a deathless snarl. On the big cat's back a tiny white-suited figure is draining the juice from a young coconut and rasping his bottom back and forward along the animal's spine.

Giau shouts to Duong above the roaring music. 'Uncle Mei has big plans.'

'Civically approved ones, I hope,' Duong says with an attempt at a smile.

Giau refills the policeman's glass and leans closer over the bar. 'They say there's a new shipment arriving any day, Chief. Dream Team they are being called. New suites have already been soundproofed. The dungeon suite is most high-tech spec. Taiwanese design – all mod cons and very roomy.' Giau pours himself a glass and winks. 'And not just cheap Cambodian imports this time, Chief. Rumour has it that the flowers of Vietnam are being harvested.'

Duong stares at the winking barman.

'And the best news of all, Chief,' Giau tips his whiskied words right into Duong's ear, 'is that a local crop is promised too.'

Duong's knees wobble. He grips the bar. 'I'm sorry, Giau, I think I misheard you.'

'I said a local crop is being gathered. Just imagine it. What about Mrs Le, the Third District tailor's wife – her husband's got quite a gambling loan outstanding, I hear. Silly fool. Still, one man's loss and all that.' Giau raises his glass to knock against the chief's. 'Just imagine the sweet taste of that, Chief. Chief?'

The little policeman has vanished.

'Chief? Where are you going?' the barman shouts into the crowd. 'You've left your drink. And I forgot to mention, the pastry and seafood chef is here and looking for you. He says it's urgent.'

But Duong does not hear a word of this. Seized by a quake in his bowels he has waddled himself into the conveniences as fast as he is able.

Which is how Dalat's most celebrated cook comes to find the town's police chief drooping over the sink, dripping with water and avoiding the mirror. Beneath the fluorescent ceiling light a gecko clucks alarm.

Expressing his deepest regrets for interrupting the police chief's private latrinal reflections, Man Chu tiptoes across the tiled and puddled floor.

'Terrible news about your son-in-law,' the chef begins. 'May I offer my sincerest condolences for the tragedy on Saturday.'

Chief Duong nods and turns away from the sink.

'Sincerest,' says the town's foremost sculptor in suet, a chef whose fish-filleting fingers are rumoured to be touched by the Divine.

'Thank you,' the police chief says, heading for the door.

'Don't mention it,' the chef replies.

'Well then, goodnight,' the police chief says, opening the door.

'Chief?' Man Chu shrieks at the policeman's departing back. 'I must speak to you, Chief.'

The gecko clucks. Duong turns slowly round. 'Tell me, Chu, have you heard anything about the flowers of Vietnam?'

'Chrysanthemum?' the chef offers. 'An excellent digestive.'

Duong nods miserably and steps outside.

So this restaurateur of renown – a man with a perfect palate, a thriving catering business, a minor investment in coffee beans and, as it happens, a domestic crisis of his own – can think of no other course of action but to lunge forward and grab the police chief's sandals.

'Man Chu?' Duong looks down with some surprise at this impediment to his exit. 'You too have suffered a terrible tragedy?'

'Mr Duong – Chief, I cannot take it any longer,' the baker sobs. 'My marriage is in the gravest danger. I regret to inform you that I must be returning your son.'

Creative Techniques for Information Extraction

Sending Fang to work at Man Chu's restaurant had been Duong's idea.

'Seafood,' he had explained to his wife's back just two weeks before as he dusted off cracker fragments and mounted the marital bed, 'the middle way and certain to fix him.'

The mound beneath the dragonfruit-print blanket provided no response, but Duong had been certain this was the answer. He settled himself along his edge of the mattress, removing a shrimpy eyeball that had glued itself to his spine. 'What's more, the boy can live on site. A perfect solution.'

Duong often felt certain of solutions. What he was less able to put his finger on in this instance was the precise cause of his son's malady. He had his private suspicions, but scientific verification remained pending.

Looking at the family photographs Mrs Duong had long ago nailed to the bedroom wall above her vases, it was clear the boy's childhood had advanced normally enough. Birth. A holiday at the Cu Chi Comrades' Museum. A family shot at Po's niece's funeral in Saigon a week before the gravel-truck accident (possibly the last time they had been anywhere as a family), Duong's long-service award ceremony in Hanoi (just him and Fang on that occasion). And the day of completion on the additional three storeys of the townhouse, prior to peppermint painting. No clues anywhere there.

Of course, Fang had always disliked meat. And, of course, that couldn't be regarded in itself as a crime. Rather, it was a simple misfortune: a malfunctioning palate. He would, the doctor had said when the six-year-old was presented for urgent diagnostic inspection, soon grow out of it.

But Fang hadn't.

Instead, more alarming abnormalities began to rear up through the boy's adolescence: an aversion to firearms; a pet rat under the bed; a craving for soya bean puddings.

'Perhaps he will make a monk,' the doctor said. 'I wouldn't worry.'

But Duong did. He tried as best he could to engage Fang with gruesome war stories, secret policing missions and Central Highland camping expeditions. Until finally the day came when he could no longer avoid the heartbreaking truth: there was something seriously wrong with his son.

This was over three years ago, in a dreary November when the chief was spending seven days a week and as many nights wrestling with the slippery 'Rubber Slasher' case. Moonlit sap thieves were bleeding dry the state-owned plantations in the province, and Duong was under some superintending heat to produce results. He had returned from his investigative labours one night to find the peppermint front door open and two long kerbs of rolled sheets stretching back into the gloom of the narrow reception room. The only light came from the flickering electric candle on the ancestors' shrine.

'Hello?' Duong said, peering into the darkness.

'Evening, Daddy, be careful please. Keep the lights off and don't take another step.'

Duong could just about make out the shady aspect of a thirteen-year-old boy crouched at the far end of the rolled sheets. 'Is there something wrong, son?'

'Go round the back please, Daddy.'

Duong frowned at the marble floor in front of his sandals. It appeared to be twitching.

'The floor appears to be twitching, son.'

'Isn't it marvellous, Daddy? I have gathered here scorpions, woodlice, stick insects and ants – including soldier, jungle and honey ants. And four species of beetle – dung, horned, stag and sticklebacked, also jumping, lynx and wolf spiders, some common centipedes, two cicadas and seven caramel cockroaches.'

'And?' his father said warily. 'And now, son?'

'Now I'm funnelling them outside. Isn't it wonderful, Daddy? They're all going to be free.'

Duong's own feelings of wonder came later. His immediate response was swift.

Stamp. Stamp. Stamp. Stamp. He despatched those pests he could with his sandal soles and the remainder with Mega Marvel Fly Exterminator.

Fang was sent to wash out the sheets.

'How did this happen, my dear? How can it be with this boy of ours?' Duong had asked of his wife on clambering aboard the mahogany bed the night of the incident. He shunted himself close to her, it being in that era when – despite the recent gravel-truck tragedy – the marital bond was still tightly knotted and cordially coated. 'Is our parenting policy not up to scratch?'

Po turned to face him – it being in that time when she was still able to manoeuvre a full one hundred and eighty degrees, and still keen to do so. She licked a finger to flatten the tendrils of her husband's anxious brows. 'It is his time of life, mon chéri, nothing more.' This was when she still bought off the peg and combed out her hair, before the television went on and the cream cake and noodles pulley was installed on the outside back wall, and all further pepperminting plans ceased. 'You mustn't worry yourself, mon petit soldat, it will pass. My elder brother turned peculiar at that age. Bubbled up with pus spots and believed himself immortal. Enjoyed public nakedness too. Fang has the Diems' creativity in his veins.'

Duong chivalrously ignored this allusion to his Southern in-laws' lunacy. 'But Sergeant Yung's grandson is out rifle training with the National Youth every Sunday, and Doctor Thoc's boys are kung fu crazy. How is that? I picked up my first rifle at fourteen and I was proud, Po. How is that?' Avoiding the peculiarly thin-browed stare of his son in the walled photographs, Duong wriggled down under the sheets and clasped his wife's warmth to him. 'Do you know what I think, darling? It was a mistake to say yes to rhythmic dance lessons, and this "no meat for me, thank you" was bound to stunt his masculinic growth.'

His wife coaxed her husband's head up to her own and she kissed along his bushy brows. 'Hush, mon mari. Leave tomorrow's cares in the care of tomorrow. Close your eyes and cuddle up close.' And she began one of her tales of an ancient dragon-slaying king, for she always did know how to soothe him.

But beneath his shuttered eyelids Duong's mind drifted

away from fire-breathing reptiles and gallant warriors and meandered into the usual nightmare of trenches and traps and explosions. And when his mind finally ran away from an old war it began shuffling events closer to home. Whichever way he dealt things it didn't look good. 'Where is the man in the boy?' he mumbled, turning over and over in his sleep. 'How will he defend himself if he won't pick up a gun? Must toughen up. Must rubberise, vulcanise, strengthen, yes.'

Duong woke the next day and prioritised. He solved the Rubber Slasher case super-quick with well-placed non-lethal mantraps. He turned down all but the most urgent of policing business and booked a brief vacation. He would concentrate on the re-education of his only son.

All stops were pulled out.

'Nothing is too much for my only son,' he shouted above the cough of the Hero. It was day one. Art was on the agenda. 'Your mother tells me you like theatrical nonsense, all this make-believe operatic nonsense, yes?' He was driving his son out west past the new-built coffee villas in their fragrant white-blossomed gardens. They were heading to Farmer Fu Yan's poultry smallholding. 'Today, son, I will present to you one hundred per cent genuine real-life drama in the greatest show of all.'

Farmer Yan greeted them in the yard with a kitchen clock and a bamboo basket crammed with chickens. After a blast from the policeman's whistle and a nod to the clock, he popped apart the vertebrae on thirty-eight birds in sixty seconds.

'Outstanding work,' Duong said, applauding and bowing. 'I officially declare you have broken the regional speed record. You are the fastest strangler in the west.

Many provincial congratulations.' He gave Farmer Yan a certificate to prove it and selected a hen from the pile at their feet for Fang to have a go gizzarding at home.

The second day Duong devoted to science. Specifically, the application of physics in the arena of information extraction. 'Your father is a moderniser,' he explained to his son, leading him out to the privacy of his lean-to, 'a man at the forefront of innovation. You must never be afraid to innovate, Fang.' From the bottom drawer of the filing cabinet he pulled out his trusted and somewhat dusty professional manual: *Creative Truths in Provincial Policing* – a gift from his father at his passing-out ceremony – regrettably long since out of print. He scraped a dried ant off the opening page of chapter four, 'Creative Techniques for Information Extraction'. 'A little motto I like here, son – innovate or die. Also, don't tell your mother what we are about to do.'

Duong skimmed through the chapter and proceeded to demonstrate the classical electrical techniques with a cattle prod and a bucket of damp dead bullfrogs. 'See the spark of life, son? See how it leaps in them? Perhaps it will not be long before we humans can plug in like a television and recharge forever. Your wrist please, son.' Duong applied the current once to Fang and twice on himself. 'Harmless, yes? Most neurologically invigorating, I think you'll agree.'

Duong disappeared behind the filing cabinet and dragged out a black box with a row of switches and dials on the top. He beamed at his son. 'Hidden in here is power enough for half a street when fully charged.' Using a metal crocodile clip Duong attached a lead from the box to a steel manacle. 'Conduction is the name of the game. Your wrist again please, son.'

Fang offered his slim wrist to the manacle and did his father proud: the box buzzed, his arm flew up in the air, but he did not shed a tear.

'Heroic blood flows in you from somewhere,' Duong sighed, wiping at his eyes. 'Perhaps your maternal grandmother. Now, let us up the voltage, my boy. How high shall we go?'

'As high as you want, Daddy,' his young son bravely replied.

'The academics are now complete,' Duong announced at an early breakfast they were taking on the third and final day. 'But all theory is useless without application. Today is a day for action. Today, man or mousiness will be revealed.' They went outside and Duong mounted the Hero. 'Reputations die hard, and mousy reputations die hardest of all. Up you come, my boy, and hold on tight.'

Chief Duong set an eastern course. Their target was the coastal village of Mui Ne. For a small fee and the overlooking of a minor traffic offence, Mrs Nguyen of Nguyen's Top Quality Skins for International Exportation would kindly allow Fang to get blood on his hands for the first time in his life by spearing a crocodile or two.

The route took them through the heart of Dalat's splendid forests. Drenched by dawn rain, the white pines and weeping pines dripped their perfume over the road. And now the sun, climbing high and hot above the canopies, was tempting adders and earthworms and leeches and all kinds of wriggling life to come sliding out of the orange forest mud to bask on the steamy tarmac.

On the back of the Hero, thirteen-year-old Fang Duong clung to his father's anorak. Head down, his eyes fixed on the bike's front tyre, his lips began to move. In Duong's mirror it looked at first like a prayer. But it was not that. Fang was counting. As the Hero carved up spray on the wet road, Fang was recording every life that was squashed or sliced under the wheel. Every death, slow or sudden, Fang numbered and silently mourned.

A yellow dog loped across the road and Duong swerved to avoid it. 'See the bitch run to her babies?' he yelled over his shoulder. 'Tastiest meat there is if you get it young enough.' Duong slowed the bike to point to the three pups in the ditch, their tails whirling as they suckled. 'There's endless debate about the best recipe. I remember an old Delta aunt of mine swore by a tenderising drowning and ten turns on the spit. Whereas your grandmother – now, she can cook a dog, by Ho she can – she says the only way is to hang and cure the meat for a month and stir fry it with shredded ginger. You hungry? What do you say we stop off on the way back and pick up that runt on the left. Ripe-looking belly on it.'

But Fang wasn't listening. During his father's discourse he recorded the crushing of five newts, twelve maggots and a young vole. As his father drove over the head of a black viper Fang turned his eyes away. He stared up into the hard blue sky, glowering at the burning sun, willing his pupils to sizzle and fail.

Which was when a most curious thing happened. But not to Fang's eyes.

His ears popped. The beeswax plugs that he had inserted to stopper the sound of his father's voice for the last three days shot into the air.

His ears crackled.

They snapped.

Fang's eardrums exploded with the force of a thousand Tet firecrackers.

Static tore down his tubes. A torrent of noise ripped the nerves of his body.

'Help,' Fang mouthed. 'I am drowning in sound. Help me, Daddy.' He clutched his father's anorak, sensing his brain short-circuiting but powerless to prevent it. 'Help me help me help me.'

Only days later would he begin to understand the remarkable transformation that was happening to him. A transformation that would remain unverified by any medical institution but that Fang himself knew to be real. The reality he recognised was this: his hearing was being retuned to the sounds of the forest. The gasp and groan of each and every half-mulched creature assailed him in a multiphonic symphony.

Too much for a brain of only thirteen years' development, the world turned black and three seconds later Fang had fallen off the bike.

'Selective mutism.' This was the label attached to Fang by the consultant psychologist in the assessment room. Though no bones were broken, Fang was still in hospital two weeks after the fall. 'There is nothing physically wrong with him, he is simply choosing not to speak. It often follows incidents of trauma, though a moped accident on an empty road is unusual. Would you say he's a sensitive sort?'

Chief and Mrs Duong looked to their son. They squeezed the bones of each other's hands. 'Doctor, for how many days does this last?'

'It has been known to continue for a month or two.

One chap I had never spoke again, although that was an extreme case.'

Chief Duong reached for the tissue box. 'My son, what has happened? You know how we love you. Why are you doing this to our family?'

Fang reached for his bedside pad and pen and wrote: *Can I trouble you for a banana soy shake?*

The little chief turned away and howled.

His wife did not cry, but as she rose from the bedside she discovered scalpy clumps of hair clutched in her fists. Blood spotted the shoulders of her dress.

'Tell me, doctor,' Duong enquired in a low voice in the corridor, 'have you heard of the benefits of electricity in cases such as these?'

The psychologist smiled kindly. 'I believe shock therapies were popular in Moscow for a while. But it is not something we like to recommend here. Old-fashioned values are our way. All you need is love, isn't it? Love is all you need.'

Released back into the bosom of his family, Fang returned silently to school. He developed a calligraphy that delighted his teachers and began to translate written English and Mandarin with a facility the language master pronounced 'uncanny'. At the age of fifteen he was nominated to represent the province at the Ceremony of Praise and Reward for Gifted Students in Hanoi. He did so silently. A sixth family photograph – of Fang and his father – was nailed to the bedroom wall. At weekends he disappeared into the forest for hours. In the evenings he sat at the desk in his bedroom listening to the rats under the bed (he had two now), silently compiling a thesis on rodent communication systems. He showed this to no one. He told no one about his new powers of understanding. He suspected he would never be believed.

His father locked his policing manual in the filing cabinet's bottom drawer. His parents tiptoed around the possible causes of this second tragedy. One afflicted child was enough for any family (and neither parent needed reminding how Lila's accident had happened). They burned incense in the sand of their ancestors' shrine, made offerings at the temple and lit candles in the cathedral. They maintained public unity and parental pride. They avoided all talk of doom.

But each silent day that passed in the peppermint house, hope was being eroded. And each night beneath the blanket of their comforting words, blame snuck in. The knot between them loosened.

Insomnia plagued Po now. Each night she chewed down towers of fried crackers, watching her husband's bushy brows twitch in dreams beside her. And as she watched she thought she began to spy something rising from his pores. Something vapid and unknown. Something alien. Who is this man? she began to ask of the fan and the bed and the mosquitoes flip-flopping in the net. What kind of father would electrically shake his own son? Why could this parent not hold on to his child on a moped going around a bend? Po lay sleepless, chewing up crackers and waiting for answers that didn't come.

Over the months blame began to chisel a seam between the two bodies on the bed. The couple greeted each other at breakfast like hotel strangers. Po dispatched her affections elsewhere: to the constancy of rice noodles and Man Chu's gateaux; to the unafflicted joy of television medical dramas and the secret promise of the bathtub. She ordered in a seven-storey rainproof pulley and a lock for the bedroom door. She took a hammer to her favourite vases and then took to bed. She built blubberous barricades.

Duong's refuge was his work. In the manner of one bereaved, he removed the pre-pepperminting family photograph from its nail on the bedroom wall and placed it on his desk at work.

'Such misfortune, Chief,' one of his officers commiserated.

'Incredible. Two terrible accidents in the same family, Chief,' another added.

'How unkind are the stars.'

'What a strong-chinned boy,' a third said. 'Ho in Hanoi, how like his mother he is!'

Duong took to staring at this family photograph for hours, staring at the boy who towered above his father with eyebrows sleek as tar. A boy who shied away from smiling megawatty at the camera, who turned his face from bowls of nutritious goat or chicken stew.

How like his mother.

Was it only inevitable that Duong began to wonder?

Could it be? he wondered. Could there be something in it? He observed his wife at night as she snored. Could she have been bothered? he wondered. And if so, with whom?

Time had moved on since the publication of *Creative Truths*. These days there were tests easily available to a chief of police, tests that would tell him the absolute truth. It was simple enough to collect a hair here, a fingernail there. He bagged these samples and locked them in the middle drawer of his filing cabinet, accumulating, labelling, preparing for an appropriate date when some tipping point had tipped.

77

So the peppermint house descended into its own selective mutism. In the shock of this second tragedy, Lila, beautiful pragmatic first-afflicted Lila, grew almost unnoticed into her womanhood: practising pressure points in her bedroom; shaking out the gloss of her mother's gift of hair; beaming her father's extraordinary smile at walls and windows alike. And learning to take good care of herself.

Please Do Not Feed Richard Nixon

Man Chu had taken on sixteen-year-old Fang most reluctantly. He could see the benefits in having a mute employee. But a certified lunatic? With cleavers around? And boiling pans and griddle plates? And gas and glass and knives? Was he mad? Mrs Chu thought so.

'Most regrettably, my wife's cousin's children are coming to work at the restaurant. Three of them, from the coast,' he told Duong when he was summoned to the station and confronted with the police chief's plan for Fang. 'Triplets. Cannot be divvied up. Impending typhoon necessitates their accommodation inland. My deepest regrets but I think it is not possible to squeeze in another.' Man Chu's floury fingers scuttled about the tuft of his beard. 'With respect, perhaps you might consider employment less taxing for the boy. I hear there may be a vacancy in the tea plantations.'

Duong slurped the last flap of chicken skin from the bowl of noodle soup the chef had brought. 'This really is quite delicious. You have surpassed yourself, Chef.' He drained the bowl and rose from his chair with a belch. 'Do excuse me. I must make a little room for those pastries I see you've been kind enough to bring.' The chief nodded at the chef and squeezed himself out from behind his desk, knocking a brown file to the floor as he passed.

Alone in the office Man Chu packed away the bowl

and shook out a cloth to mop the chief's desk of spills. What an idea! How he'd had to think on his feet! He sighed and bent down to pick up the file the chief had dropped.

Report into allegations of bacterial contamination in local eating establishments, he read. *Security level: medium. Action: immediate.*

With a glance at the door the chief opened the file and scanned the list of restaurants. His floury fingers began to tremble.

Sandals were slapping back up the corridor. Man Chu had just enough time to close the file, jump back and attempt a watery smile as the door opened. 'Chief, you would not believe it, wonderful news! My wife has just called here in a panic – incredible, I know. Two of the triplets are struck very low, the third looks also succumbable. Some form of dysentery. It appears I am requiring a trainee to commence immediately.'

On Fang's first morning, Man Chu sat him down at a table in the empty restaurant. It was not seafood that the boy would be set to. A lunatic with pliers and pincers, skewers and scalpels? Also boiling water and oil and far too much rope around? 'Uncle Ho in Hanoi,' Mrs Chu had said, 'no no no!' She took herself off to the coastal cousins before the unfortunate's arrival.

Man Chu poured Fang a glass of Gola-Cola and laid down the law, not unkindly. Hours from six to eleven p.m. – pot washing. Eleven p.m. to four a.m. – bread baking. Four to six a.m. – starching of cloths, laying of tables. Six-thirty a.m. – breakfast and bed. 'No need to bother customers, unless in a medical emergency, OK, son?'

Fang tried to keep his eyes respectfully on Mr Chu as the chef moved on to workplace health and safety protocol, but he found himself getting distracted.

'Two parrots sitting on a perch, one says to the other, "Smells a bit fishy round here." Hear about the cow that wanted to cross the road? Needed to get to the udder side. Two elephants fell off a cliff. Boom boom.'

Something somewhere was telling terrible jokes.

'What do you call a deer with no eyes? No eyed deer. What do you call a deer with no eyes and no legs? Are you listening, Jackie, only you've got your eyes closed? Still no eyed deer.'

It sounded like a chimpanzee.

Mr Chu began to summarise Mrs Chu's management ethos, drawing looping floury circles on the tablecloth. Fang thought it safe to look round.

In the glass tanks against the far wall beneath a framed print of Halong Bay and a poster of Scunthorpe striker Sam Porcini netting a Championship goal, a shrimp was complaining of stomach cramp and a crab was teaching her daughter how to roll a sand ball. A school of whitebait was performing long division.

'Fifteen supper species,' Man Chu said proudly, looking up and following the boy's gaze. 'Delivered daily from Nha Trang. Goat too, snake and porcupine some days. Whatever the customer wants he gets. New economic policy. Mrs Chu's idea.'

Fang nodded politely.

What sad eyes, Man Chu thought. 'As I was saying, here we are one happy family, son. It's about much more than fine pastry and fresh seafood. Are you hungry? No? Come then, I'll show you where you're living.'

Fang followed Chef Chu past the pastry display case piled high with baguettes and doughnuts, mung bean mooncakes and waffles, and featuring a seven-tiered pink wedding cake. The jokes were getting louder. 'Hey, Jackie, I saw this ape chatting up a cheetah. I thought, he's trying to pull a fast one. Did you hear the one about the seal who walked into a club. A *club*, Jackie, a CLUB!'

It was a chimpanzee. Bald headed and fat bellied, lounging in a lacquered cage by the door to the toilets. A cigarette dangling from its hand, it was shrieking smoky laughter at its own jokes. A handwritten sign on the wall above the cage read 'Please do not feed Richard Nixon'. Across the way a second cage contained a smaller sleeker full-haired chimpanzee named 'Jackie O'. She was sitting in the lotus position looking down her nose at her stomach.

Man Chu handed Richard Nixon a bottle of Gola-Cola through the bars. 'Dicky is an addict. First it was nicotine. Now this caffeinated sewage. Terrible for his teeth and the expense of it is crazy. Five bottles a day or he screams without stopping. Between you and me I blame my wife. She weaned him on the stuff.'

Behind the chef, the chimp named Jackie O appeared to raise her eyes and refocus.

'Shall we proceed?' the chef said.

The back corridor was dim and smelled of stewed bones. A cockroach bustled between Fang's sandals, shiny as a cough lozenge. 'Welcome, welcome, an honour to have you here. Heard so much about you, young man. Quite the town celebrity. We're planning a full reception committee tonight, but must be getting along now – nest to sweep, kids to feed, never stops, you know how it is.'

The beetle shimmied up the wall and disappeared inside a loose electrical socket.

'And here we are.' Man Chu ushered Fang into a tiny windowless room. 'Home. I'm sure you'll make it quite cosy. There's a toilet pan and bedding roll in the closet, and I might even have a spare Gola poster or two somewhere.'

Fang held his breath against the smell of grease and looked around. Next to the closet was a steel sink, piled high with dishes. Beneath it were two buckets and a grumbling flea colony.

'There are some pots from last night. Mrs Chu thought it might be a good idea to get you into the swing of things, but take your time. No hurry is no worry here. The bakery's through the other side. Once you've mastered yeast there will be so much more you can learn.' Preferably by then, as Mrs Chu told her husband later, in another establishment. 'I'll bring you some tea and sticky rice cake, and once you're settled we'll teach you the secret of baking the finest bread in Dalat.' Man Chu rubbed his beard, patted Fang on the shoulder and left, quietly locking the door behind him.

At first the chef was beside himself. Glasses shone spotless, tables set fair, and the loaves – oh the loaves! They rose golden as sunlight and melted on the tongue like snowflakes on water.

'This was a masterstroke of mine,' he told his wife on the telephone, summoning her back to town. 'The boy has holy fingers. We have been sold out of bread every day this week.'

Mrs Chu heard her husband out and agreed to return. In truth, she was never happy leaving him alone for long.

Curly whirly artistry in icing was all well and good; however, sound financial planning and staff management required a woman's brain. Without her the business – she was well aware, and willing to state publicly – could fall apart overnight.

As indeed it almost would. Because on the weekend before Mrs Chu was due to board the bus back home, her husband made a fatal error. It happened just eight days after the boy's arrival, and his mistake was simply this: he left the scullery door unlocked.

If the truth were told – and definitely not to Mrs Chu – it was not a mistake at all but an act of kindness to the boy who gave him golden loaves. For the chef's five years of post-war re-education in a high-wired camp had taught him not only bread-making from the basest ingredients, but also the effects of incarceration on a sensitive mind. 'Besides,' he imagined explaining to his wife, 'there is clearly no one about at night for the boy to harm.'

That very night, as Man Chu slept soundly upstairs and loaves puffed and billowed in the oven, Fang took a break from the dirty pots. He opened the unlocked scullery door and listened. In the restaurant Richard Nixon was grinding his teeth in his sleep. From the yard Fang could hear a goat complaining about its insomnia, chickens fussing over dirty feathers, and three pigs debating the existence of some kind of higher intelligence, possibly, it was mooted, a boar.

Fang felt his way down the corridor to the kitchen and switched on the light.

Above the refrigerator's hum he could just make out a genteel voice. 'Darling, would you mind awfully shifting your spine? Just a fraction to the left would be absolutely super.'

Fang looked down and saw a pail crammed with lobsters.

He did not hesitate. Helping himself to a bicycle in the yard, he balanced the pail on the handlebars and pedalled off through the sleeping town to the lake at the Valley of Love. Fishing was prohibited there.

In the restaurant oven forgotten loaves burst and blackened.

A night later three kilos of clams went missing from the larder. The morning after that a white goose was spotted flapping up route twenty to the north.

'I am afraid I have to lock the door on you – security precautions – a goose is loose,' Man Chu told Fang the following day when the boy returned from his sister's wedding. The chef tugged at his beard. 'I'm not pointing the finger, I'm just saying no one is safe. Perhaps the thief may be after you next.' Man Chu knew it must have been the chief's silent son behind the clam theft, at the very least; there was no other explanation. But he couldn't quite believe it. Not with those soft eyes.

His returned wife, however, insisted he speak to Chief Duong forthwith. She re-repaired to her cousins until such time as the lunatic was removed from the premises. Otherwise, she said, her next trip would be to the civic divorce courts for a Stage One Separation Order.

Most maritally perturbed, Man Chu agreed to speak to the chief without delay. In his heart he was reluctant, for he had felt strangely soothed by the boy's mute presence. Yes, his wife was right as always; this charity would ruin them if it was allowed to continue.

A Code Red Situation

Having revealed his intentions to Chief Duong's sandals in the New Universe toilets, Man Chu comes home. He is resolved to release the boy in the morning, after the breakfast rush and just before he telephones Mrs Chu to re-return for a joyful marital reunion.

It is long after midnight when he arrives back at the Unfolded Lotus. As he enters the restaurant, the chef notices the air smells of something strange. After checking the boy's door is locked and nothing is burning in the kitchen, he creeps upstairs to bed. But inside the scullery Fang is not sleeping, nor is he washing pots. He is standing by the door, still as a panther, waiting for the sound of water to clatter down a bathroom waste pipe, for the springs on a mattress to hiccup and sigh: it is the scent of revolution that fills the air.

Five minutes pass. Ten. Fifteen. Fang's heart pounds but he does not make a move.

After twenty minutes a cockroach slinks under the door, its hindlegs clicking rapidly. 'Code green, sir. The Chu is in REM sleep pattern and heading deeper. Monitors are in position. All clear to proceed.'

Fang feeds a key into the lock, forged at the ironmongers from a dough-baked cast on the morning of his sister's wedding. He heads first to the yard and opens the gate to the pigsty. A female dwarf hog steps out huffing nervously, followed by a large white razorbacked male. Next Fang unlocks the hencoop and then unfetters the goat. Since the goose escaped the yard gate has been bolted and padlocked. Fang herds the livestock through the corridor to the restaurant. He turns his attention to the bolts on the chimpanzee cages.

The female bounds out at once, stretching her long arms towards the ceiling. 'I salute the sun,' she cries, sweeping in a bow to the floor. 'And this human, I salute him too. Six years it's been in that box with only lotus positions and zen mantras to keep a primate sane. Dicky, come on out. You don't know what you're missing.'

But the bald chimp is hanging back in his cage, shaking a cigarette out of a packet and glowering at Fang. 'Expecting a joke, is he? Somersault or two? Thinks this is some kind of twenty-four-hour circus, does he?'

The female lunges into proud warrior pose. 'Don't sulk, Dicky. It's marvellous out here. Even the air feels fresher.'

Dicky blows a smoke ring in Fang's direction. 'Of course it's no circus. Right now is my down time, and I'll thank that human to respect it. I'm an artiste not a sodding machine. We have rights you know. And while we're at it, can someone tell those chunks of pork to stop staring. They're probably diseased. Don't suppose the human considered that before he brought them into a food consumption area.'

'Stand back, coming in for landing!' A cockroach emerges from the ceiling light socket, shimmies down the bulb and drops onto Fang's head. 'Twitching of limbs has been observed on the bed, sir. Departure from REM-patterning suspected. Monitoring team reports hypnic jerks.'

Fang glances at the stairs to the Chus' sleeping quarters and then looks back at the chimpanzee stubbing out its cigarette and making a big show of being unable to get back to sleep. He takes a green bottle of Gola-Cola from a crate behind the bar and waves it in front of the open cage.

The chimp darts out and snatches the bottle. 'Don't mind if I do.' Fang shuts the cage behind him, but before he can persuade Dicky to the front door the chimp clambers onto a table and bows to the assembled animals. 'All right folks, we're up and running. A few reminders – no sweet wrappers, chit-chat, backchat or fighting in the aisles. So, ladies and gentlemen, there's this chicken walks into a restaurant, asks for a shrimp salad, easy on the papaya. The waiter says, "Sorry, we don't serve food in here." Speaking of birds, anyone wondering how you get a fat chick into bed? Anyone? Jackie? No? So let me tell you it's a piece of—'

The punchline is lost under a sudden enormous roar.

For a moment it seems to the shocked assembly that the waves of a mighty tsunami are breaking onto the restaurant floor. Fang spins round to see the front window collapse in a hail of glass.

'Cake,' Dicky whimpers, jumping off the table and running for his cage. 'Piece of cake.'

For a second or perhaps two no one makes a move.

The animals stare, petrified by a beam of white light that dazzles from the black night beyond. A heavy object is dislodging what remains of the glass. A shape is grunting in the darkness.

The female hog whines. The razorbacked male dives into the pastry display case. The hens hustle under the seafood tanks. The goat jumps onto the bar. Dicky and Jackie retreat behind the toilet door. Only Fang remains standing as the last shards of glass tinkle onto tables and chairs around him. His knees are wobbling, but his heart is strong.

The cockroach on Fang's head begins to click its legs. 'Alien body invading the safe zone. I repeat, an alien body is invading the safe zone. Please clarify contingency plan for alien invasion. Troops prepare for contingency action.'

But Fang has no contingency.

Fang is staring at the sturdy balaclava and combat-clad figure as it deals a final blow to the glass with the butt of a rifle and climbs inside the restaurant. The figure switches off a headtorch and advances.

Fang retreats a single shuffled step.

A second cockroach plummets from the ceiling light onto his head. It races down to his ear. 'Urgent. We have a code red situation. The Chu is on the move. Repeat transmission: the Chu is on the move. Evacuate immediately.'

But Fang doesn't.

'Repeat transmission – we have a code red situation. Evacuate immediately. Red for danger, sir. Red for imminent and immense danger, if you remember, sir.'

Fang doesn't even nod. He is still staring at the intruder as it crunches towards him.

It is short and vaguely feminine. Its balaclava bulges at the ears. 'Freeze!' it shouts in a foreign voice – English – some sort of high-pitched English. 'Hands on your head and no monkey business.'

Fang is transfixed by the intruder's tiny grey eyes: bloodshot, red-rimmed and – something else. There is something else in those eyes. What is it?

'Freeze I said!' The intruder jabs the rifle at Fang's chest. 'Hands on your head, monkey-torturer. I'm not telling you again. It's disgusting, you should be ashamed of yourself.'

Fang unravels the foreign words.

The person wants to rescue the chimpanzees. He would laugh if he could. Instead a smile bursts from him. He cannot control it. He does not understand it. But sure as a stun gun, a beam of a million megawatts shoots from his face.

The balaclava is zapped, and a pair of cumbersome ears sizzle in the heat of a full body blush.

'Blimey.' The intruder turns away to shield her eyes. 'Crikey.' The replica rifle wobbles in her hands. For yes, the intruder is female. She is, in fact, no other than Grace Marsden, aka the Reigate Rambo, a long way from her Surrey home.

Grace feels her brow with a grubby finger. Is she sickening? Could it be malaria or dengue fever? She hadn't had time for the jabs. She shivers and turns back to face the brilliant smile of this soft-eyed boy, this time taking in the sight of a goat skidding about on the bar, a pig polishing off a seven-tiered pink cake and a pyjama-clad man bounding down the stairs into the restaurant like a giant grasshopper. Except that no grasshopper Grace has ever seen screams like a soul in hell and waggles a gigantic glistening machete.

'Jesus, Mary and Joseph,' Grace says, her replica rifle clattering to the floor, all her bones melting to milk. 'This doesn't look good.'

Fang turns and his beaming smile vanishes: the machete is whistling towards him.

'TRAITOR!' the chef screams.

'Duck!' Grace shouts.

Fang ducks. The machete slices into the seat of a chair.

Sixty cockroaches plunge from the ceiling. 'Code RED!' they scream. 'All units in the vicinity of Victory Rise report to the Unfolded Lotus. Immediate backup – repeat – immediate backup required.'

But Fang isn't waiting for backup. He is grabbing the intruder's hand and racing for the smashed window.

Swept off her feet, Grace does not protest.

Together they leap into a moon-bright night.

And watching the machete being yanked out of a chair by their irate owner, the restaurant animals decide collectively, speedily and without demur that it might be in their interests to run along too.

The Great Orchestra of Life

They don't stop running until they are deep in the pines on Robin Hill, eight kilometres west of Dalat. Fang checks behind him. The chimpanzees are the only animals to have lasted the distance. Behind the monkey liberator's headtorch they trudge up the steep track in silence, cable cars hanging above them like boulders in the night sky.

'Here we are then,' the person says in English, suddenly vanishing into a bramble thicket to the left of the track. 'This way please.'

Fang follows through dense bushes into a clearing, where six small snub-nosed monkeys and an old black baboon are sprawled around a dying fire.

'They are free to go now they're liberated. I don't want you to think I'm keeping them here by force,' the person says, turning off the torch. The balaclava is removed. A girl, Fang sees, of course it is. A Western girl who is trying her best not to look at him.

The black baboon comes running and the girl bends to hug him. 'Only they don't seem to be that good at it – taking care of themselves and what have you.' She kisses the baboon's head and opens her rucksack, pulling out paper bags of nuts and seeds and avocados and strawberries. 'I shop at the market most days. They do get through rather a lot. It's the fresh stuff they like best. To tell you the truth, I'm starting to run out of money. I didn't really budget for the aftercare. Pretty stupid of me, you're probably thinking.'

Fang is silent.

Grace realises she is jabbering on and in English. She busies herself with the rucksack zips. 'Gosh. Sorry. Welcome, anyway. It's not much but it's home for now.'

Fang looks behind him. Only the female chimpanzee – Jackie O – has made it into the clearing. He hears her trying to coax Tricky Dicky through the bushes with talk of warm fires and avocados. Eventually she reaches back with a long arm and the protesting form of the bald chimp is hauled bumping through the thorns.

'Gracious me,' Fang hears Jackie O saying, 'if I'm not mistaken that's a black baboon over there. Technically speaking, he's not black at all, of course, apart from the soles of his feet. Chacma, I understand the species is called. African in origin, I believe.'

'But that's impossible,' Dicky replies. 'How could I let this happen?'

'Sadly it's not, in this day and age,' Jackie says. 'Non-native species can be kidnapped and crated and removed from their environment faster than you can say return ticket to Beijing, cargo class please. Don't blame yourself – what could we do? You remember our youth, don't you, in the Saigon zoo? How Mother said we were from somewhere far far away. Began with a C, I believe.'

'It's a total disaster. I'm such a fool.'

'It is. Perhaps we too grew up in Africa. The glories of the savannah. Imagine it, living freely, at one with the flora and fauna.'

'Jackie,' Dicky is patting himself down. 'Oh Jackie, please listen. Something dreadful's happened.'

'All over the world, Dicky, my love. Every hour of every day.'

'No, right here, Jackie, right now. I forgot my fags. I would have brought them if I'd known we were going to be dragged this far. But what with those panicking humans and all the pandemonium of leaving. Oh God, Jackie, there's nothing for it, you'll have to go back for them.'

Jackie turns her attention to the snub-nosed monkeys. 'Of course, the snub-nosed is at least indigenous. I'm hoping they'll know a bit about the area. What do you think, then? Shall we go and be sociable? Look, they've got a bag of strawberries. I bet they'd love to hear a joke or two.'

'You'll have to go back, Jackie. You don't want me to die, do you, because that's what'll happen if I don't get them. I won't be able to breathe and I'll die horribly. You don't want me to die horribly, do you, Jackie?'

The female bares her teeth brightly and saunters off towards the fire.

'Oh, that's nice. Leave me all alone, why don't you? Leave me all alone to die. I can feel my chest tightening already.' Dicky spits on the ground and heaves out a wheezing cough, which drags on for a minute or two and ends in a whimper. There is no obvious sign of response from Jackie. Spitting and muttering, he limps off towards the fire.

The foreign girl is still rummaging in her rucksack. Fang goes over to her.

She looks up at him and smiles. A blush shoots straight to her cheeks. 'Good work tonight,' she says, pulling out a sheet of paper and striking a line through a word on a list. 'Nine down. Only the biggie left, then we're all done in Dalat.'

Fang nods. He doesn't quite understand and the girl isn't offering any more information. She has pulled a nit comb from a back pocket and is sat with the black baboon, setting about its belly hair very intently. American, Fang wonders, looking at the blotches of broken mosquito bites on her pale arms, or English? Either way, she is a long way from home. He will have to find some mountain aloe for those bites. He wishes he could tell her not to scratch them.

Grace feels the eyes of this boy on her, and her cheeks heat up in some kind of response. Pavlovian – is that it? That's what her GCSE psychology teacher would say. But what is she responding to, and what does she want from him? She steals a glance – not at his face, just his shoes or something safe. Concentrate, she tells herself. Look serious. She frowns at the baboon's belly, remembering she must be serious about lice – or at least look as though she is. And for a few seconds she does very well. Then she sneaks another peek and meets the boy's eyes. Crash. Bang. Wallop. Damn. Her cheeks have bloomed instant fuchsia. 'Damn damn bloody damnation,' she whispers to herself, taking liberties with language not afforded her in Waterloo Crescent. 'This is not supposed to happen. Certainly, definitely, absolutely not.' Grace takes a moment and qualifies that last thought: whatever 'this' is. She yanks on a fluffy snag. The baboon yelps.

'Sorry,' Grace says to the baboon. Sod it, she says to herself. This is ridiculous. Will you just look at him.

So she does.

'Grace Marsden,' she says, tapping the nit comb against her chest, resisting the desire to waft it to cool the fire in her cheeks. 'My name is Grace.'

And she is delighted to discover that on gazing into those soft eyes she doesn't spontaneously combust, as her RE teacher warned was possible in underage emotional extremis.

The boy looks back with a smile and his mouth shapes a soundless word.

'Grace,' Grace says again slowly, 'from England. Surrey actually. Reigate to be precise. Historically a market town but now it's called the commuter belt.'

Silently the boy repeats the word.

'No problem whatsoever,' Grace says. 'My voice goes all the time. Must be the humidity. Phew, this fire is making me hot.' Which, she thinks, is another stupid thing to say. If the boy can't understand her – and why should he? – she might as well be jabbering away in chimp speak, like the bald one shrieking non-stop at the snub-noseds right now. 'Pheweeeee,' she says, wafting the nit comb at her cheeks. Then remembering she'd decided against this stupid wafting, she says sorry and wipes the nit comb on her trousers and turns to the baboon's snagged shoulders with zeal.

Fang sits by the fire and pokes it to life. He is drawn to watch this girl's every move in a way he does not understand. He tries once again to speak, to drag out a voice to give her his name. But there is not so much as a whisper in his throat.

In the last three years he has become a loner; skirting his shadow round his classmates' shouted soccer games or lounging with the ants and lizards in the almond trees. He believed he'd never minded this, never worried about sitting as dumb as his ink pot in the schoolroom. After her accident, his sister had said to him in her pragmatic way, 'I'm fine really, Fang, you know you can't have everything in life.' So what, then, if he was more of a ghost than a real person, drifting quietly in a world of noisy humans, all of them oblivious to the great orchestra of life around them. Really he should look on humans with pity for what they did not know, for the secret music they would never hear. He had considered himself lucky, so very lucky.

But now? Well, now Fang glances through the flames at this Grace Marsden from somewhere in England and finds he does mind. A lot. He finds there are things he wants to say. What they are exactly he isn't too sure. But speak he knows he must, or he will lose something. Something he doesn't want to lose. Though he has no idea what it is. Fang shoves a log deeper into the fire. He finds he is feeling confused.

The girl is talking again, her eyes on the baboon. 'I guess you don't speak English. Because I have to tell you my Vietnamese is practically totally non-existent. Sorry. Do you want a leaflet, by the way? It's been printed in Vietnamese, and explains pretty much everything I'm trying to achieve. No? Well, anyway, I just wanted to say thanks for your help back there. Much appreciated.'

Not a problem, thinks Fang. He closes his eyes and tells himself that it really isn't any sort of problem at all. Tells himself what psychologists and speech therapists have long given up telling him: that whenever he chooses to, he can talk.

'Are you feeling OK?'

He opens his eyes. The English girl – Grace – is frowning at him. 'Do you need some food?' She makes an eating motion. Then giggles. Then says 'Sorry'. She seems to like this word a lot. She has a wisp of baboon hair stuck between her front teeth.

And it seems he is choosing right now, because his finger is pointing at Grace's mouth and his own mouth is opening, and from somewhere inside him a voice quieter than a moth in the breeze, and for that matter in English, is saying out loud, 'Hair.'

'Hair,' he is saying and pointing. 'Hair – teeth – there.'

'God, how disgusting of me.'

She heard him.

She definitely heard him.

She heard and understood and answered. And now she is blushing and despatching her thumb into her mouth.

At this visible cause and effect, this communication received and acted on, Fang feels something surge in his veins as surely as if he has been jolted by his father's black box.

'Hair,' he says. 'Teeth,' he says louder.

'Nose,' Grace says, pointing at her own.

'Hair, teeth, nose,' Fang says. Fang is laughing.

Anything, he tells himself. I can say anything at all.

He is laughing. A laugh so loud he feels it rushing up his throat and down his ears all at once. Has he forgotten what laughing is like? Perhaps. He could forget about most things looking at this red-cheeked girl.

'My name is Fang Duong,' he says in a giddy rush of schoolroom English. 'I live in Dalat. I am nearly seventeen years old.'

Grace's returning smile is not without its own sizzling charge. 'It's very nice to meet you, Fang.' And she offers her hand to him in the Western way.

As his skin touches hers Grace feels her blood boil hotter than school pipes in summer. 'Crikey O Reilly,' she breathes. 'Jesus, Mary and Joseph, so this is it. This is really and truly it.' And being a long way from Surrey censors she whistles 'Bloody hell!' for good measure.

Applause breaks out around the campfire, where the primates have been enjoying the humans' performance. Now the female chimpanzee offers the observation that this mating ritual is highly touching, and the body language is possibly indicative of a monogamous pairing, or at least an attempt at it. 'Humans,' she sighs, 'are an overambitious species.'

The six snub-nosed monkeys confer among themselves and chorus their wholehearted agreement. The old black baboon, who is chewing on a pecan nut and remembering a dumpling recipe that was once made specially for him, wipes a tear from his eye. It is left to Tricky Dicky to temper the general rapture with a personal recollection. As he discovered to his cost, courtesy of a minx of a zoo chimp called Celeste, and as he now shares with the camp, 'The course of true love runs a lot more trickily in reality than many an ape might hope.'

And as everyone settles down for the night, another word of caution must be added: things could get trickier still if the lovers are outlawed from every town and village in the country. As within hours these two humans will be. For somewhere in the air above their heads a message is sprinting towards an email inbox. It is carrying a super-intending order to do just that.

A Curse Upon Their Children

'Where am I?' the police chief shouts through a loudhailer.

'Where am I?' the valley whines back. 'Where am I?'

Standing in the middle of Love Lake, Duong winces. The water is tickling his welted buttocks. He squints into thick fog.

It is dawn again in Dalat. Arriving with a dollop of smog from sunnier cities and drenching a canopy of pines beneath which a fugitive band is breakfasting. It is pouring through a shattered window, where a chef lies sobbing in glass shards and icing. And it is dumping on a police chief's plans in a lake. Unwelcome dawn.

'Where am I?' Duong calls out again.

'Where am I?' the valley replies. 'Where am I?'

There is a distant jangling sound and then a faint cry. 'Here, sir! You're over here.'

'Indicate position. Repeat, indicate your position.'

A stetson floats in the foggy distance.

Aha! Due east! Duong consults the cardboard replica park that is being held above water by Cowboy Three. He strikes a cross through the sticker marked Police Chief and conclusively eliminates himself from enquiries.

'Excellent work, Cowboy Two. Where I was standing is a mere one metre from the victim's terminal position, yes? Wave please, Cowboy One. Excellent work. The pathologist has stated that the entry wound indicates the fatal bullet was fired from a range approximating—' Duong peers beneath the replica for a scrawled note, '—thirty-five metres and from a south-easterly aspect.'

'Easterly aspect,' the valley agrees.

'Cowboy One, maintain the victim's terminal position at the rhododendrons. Cowboy Two, consult your compass and proceed in a south-easterly aspect for thirty-five metres.'

The distant stetsons dance in the mist.

'We shall pinpoint the culprit in a trice,' the police chief informs Cowboy Three. Scooping up water he splashes his face and feels rather cheered. For what is life – as the chief likes to ask miscreants at interrogational low points – what is life without hope?

Returning in a state of some anxiety from New Universe, Duong had bolted the doors and checked on his daughter on the third floor before ascending to his edge of the marital bed. After a buffalo-stuffed and telephone-interrupted sixty minutes of insomnia, he had aborted the idea of sleep, salted his buttock welts in the bathroom and descended seven floors to sit on the toilet in the lean-to, a place where he could be assured of achieving his most productive thinking. Here the chief unplugged the persistent telephone, consumed two refreshing cans of lager and drew up an anxiety-dispelling three-step plan on his notepad.

Step One: solve Commissar Nao's murder in the park.
Step Two: locate dollar dowry, return loan in full and destroy pink contract.
Step Three: celebrate prompt success of steps one and two with Binh Linh's ground pork and mushroom dumplings.

Lila smiled down approvingly at her father from her pre-gravel-truck photograph on the filing cabinet. He was right, it was a good plan. Although a better plan would involve the swapping of steps one and two. But then there were Deputy Jimn's eager computers to think about – and Deputy Jimn himself, if Duong was honest about it. Besides, he had not reached the current heights of his profession by letting murderers run amok for a second longer than was ever necessary. No, a delay was neither professionally nor morally advisable. And now it was clearly written down on paper – a strategy he was always willing his young constables to adopt – Duong could see there was plenty of time to return the money to Mei. Even if, in some unforeseen event, he ran behind schedule on step one, Mei, as a prospering businessman, would no doubt be most open to the benefits of extending the loan terms for a few extra hours or days (step four?). He would understand.

Duong gazed at his three steps with satisfaction and doodled a tiny civic statue in the bottom corner of the pad. (It was always tricky to know what to do with the arms. Raised in salutation, they looked too grand. Hanging loose, they were far too passive for a man of action. Maybe they needed a prop. Binoculars or a pair of civic handcuffs perhaps. No doubt the sculptor would have some ideas.) Following this, he re-salted his welts and returned to his side of the mahogany bed, where he slept dreamlessly for two hours before plugging in the telephone to call the cowboys and proceed to Love Lake to greet the disappointing dawn.

'Begging your pardon, sir, but why are we standing in the lake?' Cowboy Three mumbles, shivering.

'The view, son. Three hundred and sixty degree. From here no overturnable stone will remain unseen.' And indeed the fog does seem to be lifting, revealing the ghostly stetsons to be perched on solid human heads. Duong can make out three brown ponies tethered to the rhododendrons, and a short way up the drive, the Frog and Lake Café, which has been boarded up following old man Han's suicide on the afternoon of the murder. Duong shakes his head. Han had been mad as a hot-hoofed mule, of course, but his death was a tragic waste of culinary talent. Not to mention the secondary tragedy of the five daughters left behind. The daughters that had since been rumoured to have . . . Duong raises his loudhailer and returns promptly to the matter in hand. 'Cowboy Two, secure your position.'

A red balloon begins to rise through the mist.

'Begging your pardon, sir, but I think I'm being bitten.' Cowboy Three dolefully lifts his heel, to which a grey shrimp is clinging.

'Curious, a freshwater species no doubt. Now put it down please and pay attention as we proceed to step one subsection B, elimination of suspects – ouch!' Duong feels a sharp pinch on his left buttock and a flash of spangled panties clouds his vision. He reaches into the water and pulls out a lobster, two strips of police trouser clamped in its claws. He throws the lobster onto the shore. It will do for lunch.

'Begging your pardon, sir,' Cowboy Three says, 'only there's someone heading this way.'

'Another of your John Wayne gang?'

'No, sir, I think he's after you.'

Sure enough, on the distant drive a tiny figure is waving wildly and hurrying in the direction of the lake.

'Cease and desist from further movement.' Duong is calm on the loudhailer. 'A police investigation is in progress. You are out of bounds and damaging vital evidence. I repeat – stop where you are. This is your final warning.'

The figure continues to advance.

'You have exceeded your final warning.' Duong allows his voice to grow stern. 'Take one more step and you will be arrested.'

The figure breaks into a lumbering run.

Exasperated, Duong drops the loudhailer and raises his binoculars. 'Uncle Ho in Hanoi, it's Sergeant Yung!' Duong drops the binoculars and raises the loudhailer. 'Slow down, Sergeant, the wise sloth digests his breakfast gently. This sloshing speed is no good for the internal organs in a man your age.'

But the sergeant continues his charge down the slope. Only when he reaches the lake's edge do his sandals effect a skidding brake.

'Thank Ho for that,' Duong mutters.

'Chief Duong, sir!' Yung is waving with both arms. 'I have orders from the superintendent – he has been trying to reach you on the telephone all night. You are to return to the station immediately. It's the monkey people.'

'Monkey people?' the loudhailer screeches in retort. 'Still with that nonsense? Well, I'm going to ask you something, so think carefully, Sergeant. I'm going to ask you which is more civically important – catching the cold-blooded murderer of a groom at his own wedding or locating a harmless ape thief? I think we both know the answer to that. Now you will return yourself to the station, and the superintendent will have to wait.' Duong drops the loudhailer, satisfied. Sometimes it is necessary for a man to stand firm against the wind when conviction carries him forward.

Except, what is this? Yung isn't for turning. He appears to be testing the water with a toe. He is removing his sandals and now his socks. He is rolling up his trousers and he is wading into the lake. 'A thousand apologies for this interruption when genius is at work, Chief. But it is your son. MLA involvement is witness-confirmed.'

Deputy Jimn doesn't bother to rise when Duong drips into the office. 'Please,' he motions with his eucalyptus-scented handkerchief to the spread of newspaper on the floor, 'no need to ruin the linoleum.'

Duong squelches obediently to the indicated spot and hazards a joke. 'Just wondering what you're doing in my chair, Jimn. Something I haven't been told?'

'Yes.' Jimn raises a pale palm to block further communication and dials a local number on the phone. He smiles lipless at the mouthpiece. 'I have him here, sir.'

The receiver is held out to Duong.

'Look here, Duong,' it is the district superintendent on the line, 'no pleasant way to say this, so I shan't bother. I'm putting you on suspension. You were asked to sort out the MLA business, what with our Comrades in Commerce breathing down my neck, and you didn't. Naturally, I did wonder what reason there might be for such blatant insubordination, and now I find your son's involved. Highly interesting, wouldn't you agree?'

'My son? With all respect, that's impossible. I mean, sir, you know he's a—'

'Heinous criminal? Not right in the head and just been outlawed from every state, town and village in the country?

No, don't interrupt me, Duong. Jimn'll keep your seat warm while we catch the bugger and his gang. And we will catch him, Duong. Rising star is young Jimn, in the ninety-eighth percentile of his graduating cohort. Nothing to worry about, just the man for your job. Good heavens, there goes a Paris Peacock. Phung, my darling, fetch the butterfly net!'

The line goes dead.

Slimn Jimn inhales on his handkerchief and spins Duong's chair full circle. 'Top-notch shock absorption. A Germanic reproduction, I would hazard.'

Duong avoids the disappointment in Uncle Ho's wall-hung gaze. He avoids the pre-pepperminting family photo-graph on the desk. He sniffs. It must be the eucalyptus making his eyes water. 'I should point out my son hasn't spoken to me in three years, if that's—'

'Please,' the pale palm rises, 'save the excuses for the interviewing team. One hundred per cent of excuses are made to interviewing teams.' Stepping neatly round the desk, Jimn taps official sympathy onto his ex-boss's shoulder with two fingertips. 'Yung will pack your personal items onto the moped. You may wait in reception.'

Jimn opens the door. 'No need to call in, we know where to find you.'

A tearful Sergeant Yung escorts a shaky-legged chief from the building. 'Mrs Yung says to me to say to you, you need anything you phone me,' he wails and flees inside.

The station door slams shut. Duong considers his moped in a daze. A small cardboard box of personal possessions has been bound onto the shelf behind the seat. Wedged between the tie ropes is a pink envelope. It is addressed to him.

Duong pulls out the envelope and opens it.

He gasps. A greeting card floats to the gutter.

Duong stares at the card as though it isn't a lovely sepia photo of his Lila on her wedding day at all, but a primed grenade. He sinks to read the message printed inside.

Best wishes for a happy and prosperous future!
Notification of revised schedule:
clause 47 effective from 12:00 today.
(Refer to clause 165iii for further information.)

Anyone now observing this suspended chief of police might be forgiven for thinking the man to be a drunk. He staggers and keels as if he were standing not on a civic pavement but on a ship's deck in a perfect storm. 'My silkworm,' he cries. 'My beautiful silkworm!'

Given the location it is perhaps inevitable that word of the ex-chief's performance is soon relayed to the station. A filing clerk is despatched promptly by acting Chief Jimn to calm the commotion that has troops goggling at windows while crimes are awaiting solutions.

'Sir?' The clerk touches Duong lightly on the sleeve. 'Acting Chief Jimn requires me to inform you that there is no licence for public theatricals on this stretch of pavement. The acting chief requests immediate confirmation you are on your way.'

But the ex-chief's gaze is stuck on the sepia image of his daughter. 'Twelve o'clock,' he whispers, 'revised schedule.'

'No, it's coming up to ten, sir.'

'Two hours!' Duong howls. 'I need more time!'

The clerk looks at the pavement. In truth, he is beginning to feel a little embarrassed for the ex-chief, who he has always thought a decent enough boss, even with that fat mad Frenchy-loving wife and plague of family sorrows hanging over him. 'I'm very sorry, sir, but acting Chief Jimn has no more time to give. You must move on or face immediate arrest.' He picks up the card. 'Such a pretty girl. She your daughter, sir?'

Duong stares at the card.

'Tragic, sir, absolutely tragic what happened to her husband. How is she coping?'

Duong stares at the man, who is taking him by the shoulder and steering him towards the bike.

'I expect you'll be wanting to go home and see her. It'll be nice to do some things together, now you have a little free time. Got your keys, sir?'

'I have no time,' Duong says as he is sat on the moped, staring at the tarmac. The helmet is buckled under his chin. The footstand kicked away. 'I have not attended to my daughter.'

'Come now, sir. I'm sure every father feels that. It's only a natural part of parenting, my wife tells me – we fathers like to drum up a sense of guilt.'

Duong raises his gaze and looks the clerk in the eye. 'I have failed my daughter.'

'If you say so, sir. You know best.' The clerk turns the key, revs and releases the throttle. 'You drive carefully, sir. Mind how you go.' He leaps back as the suspended police chief wobbles away.

Three times the moped loops the roundabout, oblivious to blasting car horns and the screams of cyclists. In fact, it is beginning to seem to the clerk that the Hero might circumnavigate the central flower bed for all eternity, but then the sound of the cathedral bell striking ten produces a sudden transformation in the driver. His back straightens and the moped lurches to the left. With a growl of the throttle it swings off in the direction of the governmental district, a puff of diesel in its wake.

Lovely Lila has indeed been neglected a while. Lovely pragmatic Lila, who returned to a peppermint house after a wedding and emptied a trunk of betel-stained sanitary towels. Who built a fire in the backyard and threw a brain-blotted dress on it to burn. Who is standing at the foot of her mother's mahogany bed with a letter in her hand as her father races the clock. Who is quietly weeping.

Her mother is not weeping. Her mother is splayed on the marital mattress shredding family photographs with her teeth. On the dome of her belly a pyre is building. Strands of grey hair and scalp, noodles and shrimp crackers, and photographic fragments are piling high. The past is being minced into confetti.

'Daughter, may you never remarry.' Mrs Duong spits out a corner of a negative imprinted with the image of the rough cotton ao dai her mother-in-law had stitched for her own wedding thirty years before. 'Doom is all these men bring upon their wives and children. First, your terrible affliction happens to us, and now your brother's trouble. Now him *twice*. C'est ça. I mean, look at you. Look at Fang. My children have been cursed, Lila. C'est vrai. This man, this Hung Duong and myself – this North and South never should have united. From it comes only,' she pauses to unpick a strip of negative from her molars, 'doom.' Fat fingers fiddle for a few strands of hair and then yank. 'Better, child, you had remained unborn.'

Hearing the familiar ripping sound Lila moves around

the bed to her mother's feet. 'Hush, Maman, I was well enough to start with, was I not?' Dropping the letter on the bedsheet, Lila takes her mother's right sole and presses a knuckle into the crease of the heart-line. 'Sometimes accidents just happen, do they not? At least we know Fang is alive and healthy. Why don't you close your eyes and tell me one of your stories. Tell me the story of the minstrel prince and his hermit sister – the woman who grew too wise to bear the ways of the world.'

But Po's eyes are predatory. She considers then dismisses smashing the last of the glazed vases in the cabinet against the wall. There are no more photos to destroy. Her gaze alights on the letter – composed in dancing calligraphy and delivered to the seventh-storey window by a mountain pigeon – that Lila has left within easy reach. She takes it up and in a funereal baritone she reads it aloud.

Dearest Mother

I have joined the MLA to save our primate cousins from wrongful imprisonment at the hands of humans. To prevent the family becoming implicated I will not be in touch for a while. Please don't worry about me. Give Lila a kiss and apologise to Father for the embarrassment. I will resume contact when we have achieved our goals in the Highlands.

Your son, Fang.

Mrs Duong opens her mouth and folds in the letter. She chews up her son's words, swallowing them down with a mouthful of cold noodle soup and a slice of coconut pie. 'Go,' she shakes her heel from her daughter's grasp. 'Chop down the pulley ropes and send for the stone masons. With their cement and bricks they will seal me in. This is how it shall be ended.'

Collapsing back against the pillows she shuts her eyes. 'Go. Do this last thing for your mother who loved you. Go, Lila, I cannot look upon you again. With their union your parents have brought a curse upon their children. Blame us, ma chérie. Your doom is all our fault.'

The Way of the Bonsai

It is something of a disappointment, his son-in-law's house. No more than two storeys high and built from old-style colonial brown bricks. It is unpainted and unenhanced with satellite dishes or aerials of any kind. The shutters are flaking on the windows and in the broken guttering a flock of sparrows has set up home. Were it not for the police cordon flapping at the gate, Duong would think it a policing error to match this hovel to that eminent man.

He makes his way through the front yard, shaking his head and stumbling over the tangle of white binding string that trails from stunted bonsai trees potted everywhere; string that criss-crosses the beaten ground like the web of a monstrous spider; a web that would have been nothing short of a deathtrap for a blind daughter. What was he thinking, wanting to send Lila here?

He does not know. And anyway, there is no time now to think. There is not even time to be shocked at the state of the interior reception room, a space that has no obvious coffee tables or soft seating areas for eminent provincial party receptions, but contains four trestle beds of black soil and white germinating shoots and a mushroomy pong. There is time only to note the lack of any sort of bureau or filing cabinet or blue plastic bag. A district away, the cathedral bell chimes eleven. Duong hurries into the kitchen. Nothing here, not even a bottled lager in the refrigerator for refreshment.

On the first floor he encounters one window – open to the air, thankfully – and some evidence of human existence: sink, single bed, wardrobe and china wall-clock. Also, one framed photograph of last spring's Flower Festival Freestyle Bonsai Final. The award chairman is shaking Commissar Nao's hand in front of an exquisite miniaturised Yellow River mountain scene with miniature juniper, conifer and yews rooted magically to a miniature granite mountain. Miniature hermit monks pray in candlelit caves at the summit, and miniature peasant figures fish for carp in a turquoise lake at the base. Standing next to the commissar and casting a shadow over him, the towering bulk of the police superintendent holds up his silver-medal-winning Rare Butterflies Glued on a Seashell Encrusted Chrysan-themum display as he glowers at the camera. Duong checks behind the photograph: nothing. He scours the room. Still no sign of a safe-storing bureau. No filing cabinet for important paperwork. No evidence of a blue plastic bag. The other two rooms are bare. The bathroom is bare. What kind of man was this? What kind of eminent official had no bathroom soap? Where was the necessary paper trail to show the direction of this man's life? And – although it wasn't really the point now – what exactly had Duong been planning to let his daughter in for?

The china wall-clock strikes the quarter.

The chief's knee joints loosen. Sweat springs in the bushes of his brows. There had been three hours between delivery of the plastic bag to this address and the wedding. The dollars could not possibly be anywhere else, could they? They could not, he tells himself, sternly re-penning his thoughts within appropriate bounds. They could not.

The sight out of the bathroom window of a small roof terrace reignites confidence in the police chief's heart. At the end of the terrace is a small glasshouse.

It is a jungle inside. The chief fights his way through orchids tumbling from terracotta pots, star lilies, tiger lilies, canna lilies, dwarf mango trees, lemon trees, jasmine, honeybees, shovels, sacks of goat droppings, and fern root. He squeezes past a wheelbarrow, and just as panic is beginning to balloon in his heart he sees it against the wall: hope in the form of a pine chest of drawers.

Sweat drips steadily off the police chief's nose as he rifles inside. The bottom drawer is stuffed with staples and screws and string. The middle drawer, he sees with approval, contains a manual, *The Way of the Bonsai – how to zen up your life*. Beneath this is a sheaf of architectural drawings and real estate details of a garden centre called Bonsai Bonanza in Pleiku.

Bonsai Bonanza? Duong pauses in his mission to wipe sweat from his face. Commissar Nao was planning to buy a *garden centre* with the dowry gift? He bats away a bee and extends his considerations a moment. Had Nao not been intending to head to Hanoi to do great things in the Interior Ministry and sit on National Police Advancement Boards after all?

Duong shakes his head. He shakes it again to rid his ears of the sound of a police siren whining down a distant street. Now is not the time to be drawn into speculation on the disappointments of sons-in-law. Duong pulls out the top drawer, and sitting silently, like it was waiting for him all along, is a shoebox marked **Confidential**. 'Merciful

Ho!' he exclaims to the lilies and the orchids and the bees. 'Here we have it for sure!'

But the chief might have been somewhat hasty in his assessment. For unhelpfully the box contains no slim green block. There is not even a blue plastic bag. There are only documents. Some in Vietnamese, stamped with government seals, others typed in English, embossed with green bottle-shaped logos. There are several carbon copies of a letter Commissar Nao himself has sent, stamped HIGHLY CONFIDENTIAL.

Duong is running short of time, he knows this. But a policeman's curiosity, as he likes to tell the station youngsters, is a tap that should never be turned off. So he unfolds one of the copies of Commissar Nao's letters.

From: The Office of People's Party Commissar Nao
To: The District Chief Superintendent, Central Highlands Police Dept

Dear Superintendent

I regret to inform you I will not be able to accede to the proposal you have submitted on behalf of Gola-Cola Inc. for the following reasons:

1. *You may not be aware but the site proposed for industrial development forms part of a nature reserve where sixteen species of indigenous bluebell (and accompanying fauna) devastated during our country's conflict have recently begun to return.*
2. *The site is sacred to the local minority population*

of Ma tribe who have been settled on the land
since records began.

3. *The corporation whose interests you say you repre-*
   sent . . .

Duong reads through two pages of 'unethical' and 'un-Vietnamese' concerns. The letter concludes:

I am returning the 'donation', as you choose to
call it, in full. If these G-C Inc. development plans
are halted pending an extensive and public enquiry,
I shall refrain from raising this attempted bribery
during the summer's National Police Advancement
Board.

I end with salutations and the words of our great
Uncle: 'The forest is more precious than gold. We
must learn how to protect it.'

Sincerely yours
Comrade Nao

PS Commiserations on the silver medal in the
Southern Provinces Freestyle Final. I did enjoy your
moth-festooned glitter-wrapped apricot blossom.

The delicate carbon copy quivers in Duong's hands as surely as if the commissar's ghost had floated through the glasshouse walls to breathe his disdain upon it. Could it be possible? Could it be believed? Was this the reason his son-in-law had met his end, because of the *superintendent's* plans, the big things about to happen?

Duong's heart is leaping like a frog on hot coals. Calm

down, he says aloud. He reminds himself that the super had declined to attend the wedding. But that wasn't to say he wouldn't have means to exert his dark desire from a distance. And Duong has fought on the frontline of crime for long enough to know that whatever is formed in the stomach of desire usually gets regurgitated in some sort of civically untoward action. 'Where there are criminal wills,' he mutters to himself, 'there are always criminal ways.' And the super is known to be possessed of a formidable will.

Duong's head is spinning. He needs air. And he needs to find the dollars.

He rushes from the glasshouse into a world of noise.

Police sirens are bellowing in the street below the roof terrace. Eager police dogs are yelping. Duong thrusts the carbon copies down his trousers and dives behind a tub of camellias.

'Just selecting blossoms for my son-in-law's funeral,' he says when he is discovered, removed and taken downstairs.

'This is an unexpected surprise, Ex-Chief.' Glowing in the germinating dark of the reception room, acting Chief Jimn is wiping his fingers of black soil. A whining spaniel scratches at a leather briefcase at Jimn's feet.

Duong holds out a fistful of camellias. 'My daughter requested I come and fetch some flowers. A romantic child, I could not deny her this in her grief.'

Jimn's lips retreat from his smile. 'Naturally. My own wife is – how would you say – sentimental?' He sneezes into the creases of his handkerchief. 'These blasted pollinators.' A pale palm is extended. 'If you wouldn't mind.'

Duong places his official skeleton key upon it.

'I will ask a member of the search team to transport a

floral selection to your home. The blooms may as well die there as here.' Slimn's slim fingers click. A constable appears and salutes. 'Escort Mr Duong to his moped.'

For the second time that morning Duong finds himself on the street as a door slams behind him. Up above grey clouds stifle the sky. He kick-starts the Hero and is spotted with rain.

Pity if you will, this suspended police chief driving away without a single dollar on his person, with inky incriminations bleeding into his buttocks as a cathedral clock strikes noon. Pity this father who takes a turning past a decomposing hummingbird and accelerates down shady roads to scurry up a long drive to beg for time. Pity him because it is already too late. Uncle Mei is out on important business.

The Dream Team Menu

YOUR GLOBAL ADVENTURER
RECOMMENDS . . .

NEW UNIVERSE (unsignposted: follow the pink neon globe, 2km east of Dalat on Route 66). An indication of just how far modern Vietnam has come, this exclusive gentlemen's club offers the finest French cuisine, a stellar array of Podium dancers, Karaoke classics in private booths, and for those who like their Global Adventuring hands-on, an extensive and accommodating 'massage service'. But fear not, Gents, here you needn't abandon your ethics at the door. Applying modern Socialist principles to the oldest profession in the world, NEW UNIVERSE represents a revolution in the global pleasure tourism industry. More than twenty girls (HIV tested on a weekly basis) have been rescued from village poverty by the owner. The business is operated as a Fair Trade co-operative with all the lovely ladies (and they truly are lovely!) receiving a cut of the takings. Communities across Asia benefit from the money the girls send home, and every afternoon the girls receive schooling in cottage crafts useful for life after the Universe. There we have it, Gents, guilt-free pleasure guaranteed!!!

*Top Tip 1: Ask to see the Special Services
catalogue.*

*Top Tip 2: Be safe: use European condoms.
In one reviewer's experience Asian
products are not designed for the
girth of the Western male.*

JCB

'What do you think?'

'We need this condom business?'

'I think it helps. After all, we are a responsible travel publication, readers expect this kind of information.'

Reclining on the albino tigress on the VIP platform in the empty club, Uncle Mei pinches his silk loincloth and frowns. 'Does not make us Vietnamese men appear – what is this expression used by my old Yankee brothers in arms – lacking?'

'Good lord, no.' Global Adventurer Jules Chretien Bone wobbles earnestly forward on a snout-down stuffed warthog. 'Advice. Reassurance. Readers love all that. Frees them up to try new experiences and experiment in safety.'

'If you are sure.'

'I am, sir.'

Mei rubs his stump along the tiger's rump. 'If you are sure, you may proceed.' He hands back the printed sheet and looks at his watch. He is waiting for news.

JC also waits. He looks around. It is very quiet in the empty club. Everything is sleeping but for the gorilla in his cage on the dance floor. The gorilla is performing star jumps.

'Thank you,' JC says.

'You are welcome.'

Mei looks at his watch and turns his attention to a loose thread dangling from his loincloth.

JC witnesses the unravelling of a metre of silk hem. In the black distance someone is starting up a Hoover. JC scratches the warthog's neck. Finally he emits a small cough. 'Excuse me, sir.'

Mei snaps off the thread between gold teeth.

'I was just wondering, Mr Mei, about the research.'

Mei reties his loincloth in a double bow with long fingers. Fingers rumoured to be too long for a man born of human parents.

'The necessary research – as we agreed.'

Mei looks up from his loins, fixing JC with a murky stare.

'For the article? We did agree it, Mr Mei, I promise you we did. Business is business, you remember you said.'

For a moment JC thinks the club is surrounded by hyenas. But no, it appears it is only Mei having a laugh – a sudden loud laugh, at him.

'Indeed it is, young man, you are right, you are right.' He whistles into the darkness.

A dark-skinned boy in a camouflage loincloth materialises on the platform and presents JC with a heavy ring-bound file entitled 'The Dream Team Menu'.

'Thank you, God,' Jules whispers.

'My pleasure, Mr Bone.' Mei leans over and taps the cover. 'I recommend you select from Uncle's A Team. First section. These are one hundred per cent tried and tested. Multi-purposed, fully-functional and up to speed. You might also consider the B Team – vaccinated and fully-insured etcetera, only awaiting advanced training. If there is one of interest to you it is possible to fast-track and make operational by tomorrow. But a warning, Mr Bone, some specialised skill sets may be lacking.'

Mr Bone barely hears him. Mr Bone is lifting laminated page after page of photographed female flesh, passing old, young, obese, anorexic bodies. One girl has light down all over her body. Another is short-haired and slim as a boy. Mr Bone's fingers hover over some kind of double-jointed acrobat. 'This is incredible, Mr Mei. What an amazing collection you have.'

'All one hundred per cent natural construction. No artificial inflation anywhere in the Central Highlands.'

'You must be very proud. It's so well organised. It's incredible actually. I mean, you actually have vital statistics and specialisations and running costs and full service history. I mean—' rather unbelievably, JC finds himself lost for words. 'I mean – wow – awesome, spectacular. I mean, I think I've died, Mr Mei, I really think I've died and gone to heaven.'

Mei scratches his rump and looks at his watch.

JC flips over the divider and into the B Team Menu. Where he encounters five familiar faces. His fingers skid on the laminate. 'Christ,' he says, 'Jesus.'

'Some have called me both in gratitude it is true, Mr Bone.'

'But these look just like the daughters from—'

'Indeed, Mr Bone, the Frog and Lake Café. You know of them?'

'Not well. Not much at all really. Hardly. Perhaps in passing.'

'Interesting. Well, Mr Bone, since the tragic self-killing

of Mr Han and his unfortunate outstanding debt to me, I take on their care. These sisters I offer as group package. Like your Nolan Sisters or Sister Sledge. We are family, I've got all my sisters with me. Very hot property. This one here is – how you say – growing,' Mei's hands curve out a round bump in front of his belly. 'That is hot property also, if you like? Some Western men can't get enough of this.' Gold throbs in his grin. 'Ready in five days for first client encounter.'

'Christ,' JC says, his own hands involuntarily shaping his own bump in the air, his mind drawn back to a hasty exit from a valley café while a group of wailing sisters knelt around the body of an old man. 'You don't mean? I mean, seriously, Mr Mei, you're not telling me she's—'

'Yes.'

'Jesus.'

'Ha ha! You are interested!'

'I'm not really looking for a group deal.' JC's hands flip on as fast as they can, speedily surfing the Bs, passing goofy, toothless, permed and bald ladies, two schoolgirls, identical twins, a redhead and a hermaphrodite. They hurdle a cardboard divider away from the Han sisters and into a third section. Where the valves in his heart contract.

Her. It is her.

'Ah. The C Team – delivery pending. Mr Bone, you have strayed too far.'

'Her. I want her. This one, Mr Mei.'

'No, no, no, Mr Bone, this will not do. We are special friends. Buddies. Close as family. Closer. You will call me Uncle.'

'Her, Uncle. Give me her.'

'Show me,' Mei says. 'Ah.'

It is, of course, Lila. In her lace wedding dress. In the rhododendrons. A rope of black hair coiled on her head; the tiniest beauty spot touching her top lip; her sightless eyes seeming to stare right down the lens, right into the cavities of JC's heart.

Mei assesses the Englishman's finger stabbing the laminate. His eyes measure up the cut of the boy's linen shirt, the hand-stitched calfskin shoes, the titanium non-ticking of his diver's watch. 'Mr Bone, I regret that—'

'Uncle Mei, I need that woman.'

'—regret that one is most highly sought after. Not for freebie-jeebie journalist's quick pleasing. She is export quality. She is not part of—'

'Uncle Mei, I don't think you understand, I must have that woman.'

'—not part of our New Universe and Global Adventurer freebie deal. Perhaps this one in the Bs. The spectacles come off, no worries. Similar skill set – myopic and exceptional stayer.'

'No. The other one. I tell you I want the other one!'

'Mr Bone, she is—'

'I have to have her – give me the other one!'

'—most expensive, Mr Bone. The other one is most expensive. Will make long-term export deal only. Certificate pending.'

'How much, then? Long-term export, how much?'

Rasp rasp rasp. Mei scrapes thoughtfully along the tigress. Rasp rasp rasp. He smiles green-eyed and avuncular at the manicured boy with the titanium watch and the hand-stitched calfskin shoes. 'Permanent package deal, marriage licence and all papers attached – two thousand five hundred US dollars. Ten per cent holding deposit within twenty-four hours. Full balance to be paid cash on delivery in five days' time.'

'Deal.'

But where is this girl who is to make two men so very happy? Where is Lila? Is it just possible she is still safely stowed at home?

The chief – for let us continue to so name him during this difficult period – has returned from the locked gates of Paradise Plantation to the peppermint townhouse, where he notices, with a sob of relief, no signs of disturbance at the front door. In the hallway the ash from an incense stick is still warm in the ancestral sand tray, and there is a cooling pot of jasmine tea in the kitchen. But as Duong mounts silent floor after floor, calling for his silkworm, telling himself some popping out has merely been done, a dread fear takes hold of his ankles and weights his steps with lead.

Lila's room is tidy, her clothes are stored away. In her bathroom, a toothbrush lies waiting for her popping back. Above the bed the rolled mosquito net has no more and no fewer insects dying in it than before. But there by the window is the cane she never leaves home without. Dread surges up and kicks the police chief in the back of his knees.

He staggers up the stairs to the top floor. The door to the marital bedroom is locked. The television is off. There is no sound of chewing. 'Po, my darling,' he coos through the keyhole. 'Sorry to disturb. Have you seen our Lila today, by any chance?'

Silence.

He rattles the door handle. 'Hello? Po, darling, hello?' The door does not give.

He begins to knock, gently at first, then with increasing panic. 'Po, my darling, do let me in. It's very important. It's about our daughter. Have you seen Lila? Do let me in at once.' He begins to shunt the woodwork with his shoulder. 'Po, I know you're in there. Where is Lila? Answer me, Po!'

The room makes no response. Very well. Grim-faced, the chief turns and hurries downstairs. The time has come for drastic measures. From his safe box in the top drawer of the filing cabinet he takes his spare skeleton key.

'Po, darling,' he pants, readdressing the keyhole, 'just to inform you I am applying a master key, after which I shall be entering. Do excuse the imposition.'

But before he can turn the handle, and to his great surprise, his wife blasts out of the door. To his greater surprise she is wielding a hatchet.

For a second or perhaps two, husband and wife are united in an ear-popping scream.

Mrs Duong is the first to shut up. She needs to concentrate. She swings the hatchet high and drives with severing intent at her husband's neck.

Duong swerves. The blade strikes the doorframe. Po yanks it out and lunges again. 'Aaaaaahhhhhhhhhhhh!' she cries.

'Argggggghhhhhhhhhh!' her husband replies.

And this time the blade connects, chipping a slice off her spouse's right ear. Red drops splatter the landing walls, the detached half-inch of flesh salchows sausagey in the air and Po whoops delight. She hauls the hatchet above her head for another go.

Seizing his chance, Duong scarpers.

And for the first time in two years, in an achievement that in other circumstances would be cause for family celebration and perhaps a photograph, his monumental wife – in whooping pursuit – makes it down seven floors and beyond the front door without once stopping to catch her breath. Having got this far she doesn't pause, she chases her little husband to the end of the road and around the corner. It is only when they pass the butcher's in the next street that witnesses attest to Mrs Duong's pace starting to slow. Her whoops turn to warbles. Her head lolls. She attempts to hoist a heel on the kerb.

The hatchet falls to earth by the tripe display and a second later Mrs Duong follows, imploding like a detonated tower into the dust.

The ambulance crew say there is no need to restrain her. Four of them and the butcher's assistant manage to scoop her up and press most of her into a wheelchair. The butcher comes through the gathering crowd to assist in hoisting the chair into the ambulance. 'Extreme trauma,' the chief paramedic announces. 'Any reason you can think of?' he asks the police chief. 'Mrs Duong, can you hear us?' the paramedic asks.

Po's head hangs over the first of her chins.

'Mrs Duong, hello?' he says. 'Mrs Po Duong?'

Between her lips frogspawn bubbles inflate and pop.

Mrs Duong has lopped off a good wedge of her husband's right ear and it is dripping blood. Yet, as evening creeps up on this busiest of days, the chief has no time for paramedical ministrations. As his wife is driven away, he climbs once more upon his moped to roar down shady roads and up a long plantation drive.

'I have come for my daughter,' he bellows, peeping the Hero's horn at the dark-skinned guard standing in the shadows of the verandah with an M16 rifle. 'Put down your pop gun and bring her out at once.'

The figure does not move.

Mosquitoes land to inflate on Duong's ear.

He gropes for his regulation service pistol in his trouser pocket. It is slippy with blood. 'Son, do not play games with me.' Is it his imagination or can he hear sobbing from that lighted window high above? 'I am your civically appointed police chief, yes. Do not force me into an action which I may later regret.'

The boy shrugs. 'Ex is what I hear. Thrown out with the rubbish. As for regrettable actions, I think you've already managed plenty of those.'

Duong lurches from his moped and rushes up the marble steps. 'Lila!' he howls at the window. 'Daddy is here. Everything will be all right now, my silkworm. Come home to me, LILA LILA LILA!'

'Ex-Chief Duong?' a second gun-slung boy materialises in the mansion's bright doorway. 'Please don't wail, you'll disturb the cats. Follow me, and do try not to drip on the zebras.'

Duong is led into a cavernous hall that smells of hide and is carpeted with a hundred zebra skins. Suspended from the rafters are flocks of red-headed vultures and short-toed eagles clutching burning candles between stiffened claws. Moon bears and mongooses, foxes and muntjacs, warty pigs, golden jackals and tapirs form a glass-eyed guard of honour on either side of the room. If Duong was on a sight-seeing trip he might marvel at the woolly mammoth kneeling in the corner. But he is not, and he only has eyes for what is directly ahead of him – a recumbent giant panda and a small loinclothed figure lolling against its belly singing a Western song into a microphone attached to a machine.

'Welcome, Ex-Police Chief, my old friend. You arrive noisily and unannounced. Nevertheless, would you care to join me for a chorus with the Supremes? I have it in translation?'

Duong darts forward and falls to his knees at the panda's feet. 'There has been a terrible mistake, an appalling misunderstanding, Mr Mei. My daughter was taken from my home before I had a chance to pay you.'

'"Baby Love" is their finest, of course. Do you know it, Ex-Chief?'

'My daughter, Mr Mei—'

But his words are drowned by a burst of foreign music and foreign female voices and Mr Mei's own voice raised in some sort of harmony.

A hand nudges Duong with a tissue. 'For your ear, you are dripping onto the zebras.'

'Such a perfect duration for a song – three minutes and three seconds. Popular music – a great gift from the Yankees to the world, don't you agree? My platoon leader's favourite. Oklahoma Joey. He had a talent for the soprano parts.'

'Mr Mei, my daughter—'

'You have come for a drink, Mr Duong? Or some needlework, perhaps? My boys are highly dextrous and I see you have taken a nasty nick. Harmony remains in your household I hope?'

'Gracious Mr Mei,' Duong addresses his words to the lowest of the panda's black-nailed paws, 'I require nothing but my daughter.'

Mei is stabbing at buttons on his machine. 'Would you care to join in "Stop! In the Name of Love"? I also have the Vietnamese translation. Although the original is superior.'

'Mr Mei, please, I have your money.'

Mei stops stabbing and looks up, smiling wide and golden. 'Well, why didn't you say so! Hand it over, then.'

'I mean, I will have the money very soon, sir.'

'Ah.'

'In no time at all, sir. Just as soon as we sell up, yes. You see the commissar's property is now Lila's, and it's a very fine property, old style but full of potential. If you give me a pen and paper I will sign over six hundred – no, make it six hundred and fifty dollars – to be transferred to you just as soon as Commissar Nao's estate is finalised. Which will be just as soon as the murder investigation is concluded, which shouldn't be long. Not long at all, because I have the clearest of leads to the culprit.'

'You do?'

'Yes, sir. Then I will transfer over seven hundred dollars, a round seven hundred for the inconvenience of this smallest of delays. Only I require a little more time. I had a heavy workload today. Just a little more time, sir.'

Mei hoots and gives the little police chief's speech a patter of long-fingered applause. 'Well said, Mr Duong. What man would not like to have more time? Oklahoma Joey would have liked more time before BOOM! he bought it. I myself would relish being twenty again. Mistakes to enjoy making once more. Eight hundred dollars you say?'

'But Ho in Hanoi I am a fool! I meant eight hundred of course.' Duong kowtows to the panda's paw. 'Yes yes yes, eight hundred dollars – no problem, sir!'

'Perhaps you could find another fifty, or say a hundred, to make it a round nine? My lucky number.'

This poor little police chief – his ear weeping and his smile flickering at the weakest of wattage – what can he do? 'Yes,' he mumbles, 'nine.'

And just as if he has made a puppet dance upon his finger, Mei explodes with delighted laughter. 'Good game! Good game!' He dabs at his wet eyes. 'Forgive me, Ex-Chief, I tease you. Forgive me this little amusement for a bored businessman. Nine hundred? Of course you could never find that. You have not consulted Clause Seventy-Two.'

'Seventy-Two?' the little chief croaks.

'Allow me to assist. On assumption of Clause Forty-Seven – transferral of female assets – Clause Seventy-Two takes effect concurrently. It's all there in the small print, Ex-Chief. Regrettably, after an act of God or death etcetera etcetera, and I quote, "All the female's hitherto owned assets come into the lender's possession."'

'The lender?'

'Me.'

'You?'

'Naturally. My sympathies, Mr Duong, but the law is the law and Commissar Nao's house is now mine. For what that dump is worth. As for you rustling up nine hundred dollars, you will forgive my bluntness, but any self-respecting moneylender would probably sell their own daughter before they gave you anything. After all, where is even your most basic of salaries now?'

A sudden dizziness sweeps through Duong. It may be that his ear injury is affecting his balance. It is certainly affecting his voice – he can no longer seem to find air in his throat.

Mei pinches an itch in his loincloth. 'But you know what I think, Ex-Chief? This is a bad business. You sold your daughter and you sold her cheap. Nine hundred? She is worth three times as much. Current export price is three thousand US. So, Mr Duong, if you cannot deliver this much in five days' time, I will take the export price for your daughter. Then it will be bye-bye Vietnam, bye-bye Lila.' Engulfed in a fresh wave of hilarity, Mei screams so hard he drops his microphone and rolls off the panda.

Just in time, as it happens, to soften the fall of his guest.

Night has long darkened the hill town when a moped exits a plantation drive and takes a road south of Dalat. In the gutters along the moon-shadowed tarmac cats brawl over chicken carcasses and sugarcane pulp. Lights from solitary lean-tos prick the sky, but the road is deserted. For who but the crazed or the criminal would be about their business at this late hour?

The peaks of Lying Lady Mountain blacken the horizon. In the near distance the ribbed tin roofs of the Ma tribe's shanty settlement wink at the stars. Rain begins to fall, softly soaking into the hunch of the bike rider's shoulders, streaming down his visor. But he does not turn back. Nor for that matter does he consider the road ahead. He is staring down at the Hero's front wheel.

Here perhaps? The moped sidles towards the smoke

drifting from the Ma shacks. Or maybe here, where high hoardings crowd the road. Where a government notice tells of shanty clearances to come, of new business partnership with new Comrades in Commerce. Here, by the billboards projecting a mighty new factory staffed by waving throngs. This is far from peppermint paintwork and police station roundabouts, and daughters trapped inside great white prisons.

Or would over there do instead? There, where the tarmac peters into mud, where shadowy dogs eye the road from their ditches.

But as has happened so often during this longest of days, it is not this man that decides it. No, it is the moped that lurches beneath him. It chokes and stalls for want of fuel.

So here it will be, then. Yes, here will do. It is as good a place as any.

Dalat's sometime chief of police lays the Hero down in the thick broom grass, where it might be taken up by some lucky soul. He leaves the key inside his helmet, along with his identity card. He knows what the traffic police say about these cases, and Hung Duong is not an inconsiderate man. He steps back out onto the tarmac and into a pothole, one that is just large enough for a small policeman to arrange himself in and await the wheels of a passing truck.

He curls himself up like a worm. Damp gravel grinds at his back. Mud seeps into the welts on his buttocks and onto the words on a carbon-copied letter. He tries to herd his thoughts from stolen daughters, insane wives and long-lost sons. He will find a constellation in the sky. He will find Scorpio, as his mother taught him, and look on that. One sting. It will be over soon enough. There will be no statues.

But at the close of this most miserable of days, rain-clouds shroud the heavens. Galaxies are dying unobserved and not one speck of a collapsing star penetrates the fog to comfort this damp little human. Duong turns over in search of a hint of moon. For he is not a fussy man; any light will do.

And this is how and why and precisely when a miracle might be said to happen. Duong finds himself staring up at two blue haloes twinkling in the rain. He shuts his eyes then opens them slowly. The haloes remain, sparkling sapphire at him. But Chief Duong is a man of the world not the heavens; even in extremis he will not be seduced by any of the superstitions favoured by his Southern wife. He looks hard at the haloes and the logical explanation becomes clear: it is simply an advertising billboard. The blue haloes are nothing more than two neon irises lighting up the gargantuan face of British footballer Sam Porcini. A bottle of green liquid is glued to his lips. A speech bubble bursts from his mouth, spouting excitable English words:

DRINK GOLA-COLA WITH STEALTH
FOR INCREASE IN YOUR WEALTH!

A banner tacked across the colossus's chin announces in Vietnamese:

GOLA-COLA INC. IS PROUD TO PRESENT –
SCUNTHORPE UNITED AND ENGLAND STAR
STRIKER SAM PORCINI
ON TOUR TO RADIO HCMC, SAIGON,
THURSDAY 18TH APRIL!

Beneath Duong the pothole begins to tremble. A heavy

vehicle is making its way down from the mountains.

But despite himself and his current plans, Duong finds he is sitting up. He is thinking hard. There is just one day left before this footballer's arrival in Saigon.

Could it be possible?

The heavy vehicle's beams blast over the bumps of Lying Lady's toes and begin a dazzling descent through the rain. The pothole begins to shudder.

One day.

Would it be achievable?

The vehicle crashes onto the plains with a roar and starts to accelerate.

Duong looks up into the steady blue light of Sam Porcini's neon eyes.

And finds salvation.

Five seconds later, oblivious to the grin that is blooming megawatty in the broom grass on the verge, a lorry thunders through a small pothole on the road and roars away into the night.

Orchidee

'Two weeks,' Hot Chocolatie is telling them, 'this is how long your induction will take, unless fast-tracking is required. Each of you will acquire a basic skill set and will be accorded a specialisation in line with your physical USP, any natural aptitude observed in training, and whatever add-ons are requested by your purchaser – should one come forward. We are a can-do organisation.'

There is a sudden sob from the front row.

Hot Chocolatie smiles brightly in its direction. She looks around the narrow attic room. 'I know it seems a lot to take in right now, but don't worry, the basic principles are straightforward and easily achieved. And do remember, most girls discover joy somewhere down the line. Ours is a giving profession. A vocation, some say. Let us remember our motto – service with smiles.'

There are fifteen girls starting this Wednesday, each clothed in a simple red ao dai, each with her hair pulled back from her soap-scrubbed face. They kneel on the floor, their backs to a grilled window, their silent faces turned towards their instructress who, perspiring in a peach PVC catsuit, is handing out questionnaires.

Hot Chocolatie's gaze is approving. She and Moonduck have been overstretched lately, and these are fine additions. Strong. And the five sisters in the front row possess a pleasing peasant look that is coming back into vogue, a look exemplified by the almond-eyed lovely with the growing belly. They will be a popular choice with those who can afford a package deal. 'If you remain non-export, you will receive board and lodgings and five per cent of your earnings right up until the loss of your first tooth. Do not worry, this may take many years, and there are ways of preventing this occurrence.' Hot Chocolatie smiles plastic-toothed and maternal at the almond-eyed girl. 'There are ways of preventing most occurrences.'

With squeaks of protesting PVC she proceeds along the front row, breaking the chain of hands gripping hands. The youngest Han girl's mouth falls open, and in a moment she is crying great gulping tears, as heavy as a monsoon.

'Dear little flower, you will please listen carefully to me.' The artiste known to intimates as Hottie C acts quickly, crouching and gripping the girl's chin between star-spangled nails, swiping away her tears before she sets the others off. 'You do not lose four sisters today, but gain many more. Each girl in this room is henceforth your kin, as she is mine. We are lucky. It is a wonderful gift, sisterhood, a bonus of our ancient profession.' Hottie digs down between her breasts and exhumes a damp tissue. 'Hush your tears and clear this pretty nose, child. All sisters will please note – henceforth we prioritise physical presentation. We are on twenty-four-hour watch. It will not do for us to have mucus or any other substance leaking out from where it shouldn't when it shouldn't. We will be holding a fluids seminar on day three, so let us move along now. Your little sister here has raised the first lesson of the morning, let us applaud her for that. Your sister has reminded us that from this moment on we forget the past. It is worthless, the life we had before and the sorrows that brought us to this sanctuary. Throw away useless memories, my sisters. Shrug them off like dead and done-for skin. Emerge like the butterfly and begin life anew.'

Hottie C gently releases little Su Han's chin and pauses to stare at the grilled window. 'Stepping outside today's scheduled programme for a moment, sisters, I'd like to share an elder's wisdom. If I've learned anything from my own seventeen years in service, and the girls I've watched coming through, it is that there are those who make every effort to adapt – girls who learn to love their vocation such as it is, who find a way to put the joy into joyless,' Chocolatie fixes each and every one of her fifteen charges with a smile of plastic-toothed warning, 'and then there are those poor souls who don't. That is all that can be said for them.' She smiles meaningfully down each of the rows. 'Wonderful. We will now share a ten-second embrace of sisterhood.'

The sightless girl, kneeling still as a statue in the second row, she is one to take the breath away. There is such harmony in her features, strength in the jaw and softness in that drape of hair. She alone has not shed a tear since her arrival. And her smile – that smile bestowed blind but fulsome towards the crying Han child – it is nothing short of dazzling. Chocolatie senses some familiarity within that beam. She also knows better than to ask questions about Mr Mei's acquisitions. Besides, it is unlikely an article of this quality will remain in the depot for long.

Once Hot Chocolatie has clasped each girl to her bosom, she claps her hands. 'Wonderful, now we are become as close as full-blood family we will move on with the induction into our exciting new life. Each of us will participate in a naming ceremony. Very exciting, a gift to keep forever. You, blind beauty, will come first. The rest of you can start filling in your prior experience forms while waiting. As much detail as possible, please – dates, durations, numbers, frequency. I'd like to draw your attention to the comments section. Please detail any positive feedback you've previously received. Don't worry if some of the terms seem baffling, or even if you're still hymenetically sealed – I have no doubt within a couple of days you'll have caught up. This afternoon our introductory seminar will be on the charms of the female tongue. I think you'll enjoy it. Come, blind beauty, we will start with you. Lean upon my arm.'

In the great hall zebra skins bristle under Lila's feet.

'The Englishman has fair judgement,' a man's voice booms down on her. Uncle Mei is mounted on an elephant calf, wheeled in while a blood-stained panda is being dry-cleaned. 'In the flesh you do not disappoint. Take off your clothes.'

Lila's chin jerks up. 'I will not. I don't know who you think you are but I require you to take me back to my parents' house immediately. As I am fed up of repeating to your lackeys, I have a place reserved for me on a reflexology course commencing in five days' time.'

'Indeed? Well, that will be useful. Tootsie-twiddlers always go down well with clients.'

For a moment Lila thinks she is surrounded by screeching hyenas, then the noise fades.

Mei raises a pair of binoculars. 'Take off your clothes.'

Lila's chin does not drop an inch. 'There has obviously

been some kind of mix-up, which I am confident my father is currently endeavouring to rectify. You will return me to my home at once. This is the last time I will make such a polite request. Though I do not enjoy mentioning this, for your own sake you should know my father is Dalat's chief of police. He is highly experienced in managing miscreants and—'

'Your father is foolish and greedy. He sold you to me.'

'He would never do that!' Lila's retort bounces off the rafters. 'Never!'

'For a bargain price.'

'You are a liar!'

Mei clicks the focus on his binoculars. 'I do not have the time to assist acquisitions in their swallowing of unpalatable truths. You can believe what you choose, Tootsie, it's all the same to me.'

Lila takes this moment to spit volubly onto the zebras.

Hot Chocolatie's nails grip sisterly on her arm. 'I have tried to speak to her of new beginnings, Uncle.' Poor little police chief, she thinks, placing the girl's beam at last. That it should come to this for him. 'She is yet to make appropriate adjustments. However, I am confident that by the end of our two-week course she will be fully induced.'

Lila spits again.

Mei's binoculars swoop over Lila's body. 'We do not have two weeks, not with this one. Listen up, Tootsie, you would do well to attend to your instructress. You will submit quietly to today's necessary procedure, or you will not. It's all the same to me. If your wisdom is as big as your mouth you will not struggle. You will understand that this is nothing more than the first step to a financially useful life.' Mei's fingers snap twice. 'Proceed.'

Lila gasps. Someone has grasped her without a warning sound or smell and is pinning her wrists behind her back. Cold metal is sliding under the tunic of her ao dai with a slow steady snipping.

Lila kicks out. A third pair of hands cage her ankles tight.

Fabric is falling away from her body.

As the scissors start on her trousers Lila raises her chin high, and then higher. She jams her kneebones together and begins to count slowly.

Rasping his rear on the elephant calf, Mei clicks his binoculars and chuckles. 'I do admire a fighter, however hopeless the cause. When you are ready, boys, commence with the positions.'

Lila is dragged to the wall. Her arms are spread against it. A button on a camera is pressed. Click. Her legs are spread. Click click. Her nipples are iced. Click. Click click.

'Excellent,' Mei says. 'Let's see the profile.'

Lila is turned ninety degrees. The camera click click clicks.

There is only one problem; it seems the clenched jaw will not lower.

'Stubborn as a starved dog, this one,' Mei chuckles. 'Still, these Englishmen are said to be fond of their animals.'

Several attempts are made to haul down the jaw. Blood is drawn from a vein, gums are prodded and hair roots drag-combed for lice. Thermometers monitor, tapes measure, and callipers pinch perfect ratios.

This done, three pairs of hands pull on the jaw. Still it does not shift.

A discussion is had with the figure astride the baby elephant.

On the grounds that the jaw's elevation might pass as a single flaw, thus emphasising the overall perfection of the face, the matter is dropped. Lila's chin remains tilted to the ceiling as she silently counts out her resistance.

Click click click. Clickclickclickclickclickclickclickclickclick.

Feet hurry the film off to the Quick-Time printing shop.

'Summon the ink artist,' Mei calls out. 'I have decided.'

Orchidee: this is what Mei names her. He does not want to market this one on her common-as-rice blindness, but on the exquisite structure of her face and the satin softness of her skin. 'Like the goddess of the mountain lakes, it's as if she has been fed a diet of honeycomb,' he explains later that afternoon, in excellent English in a shady corner of New Universe, rasping an itch along a tigress's spine.

'Orchidee,' an English voice sighs on a nearby warthog, stroking the laminated photograph of a slender tattooed ankle. 'What a perfect goddess you are, my Orchidee.' Lips pucker up against the inky name that is sandwiched between the Paradise Plantation crest and a bar code. An Adam's apple joggles uncontrollably in the shadows.

The club is quiet. In its cage on the darkened floor the mountain gorilla is performing push-ups.

'Mr Bone.'

'Yes, my darling,' the enraptured Englishman sighs.

'Mr Bone!' Mei claps his hands sharply. 'As agreed, I require a deposit of ten per cent today, or regrettably—'

'No problem! None whatsoever!' JC ferrets in a money belt under his shirt and pulls out a fold of dollars. 'Here it is. The full two-fifty. Take it please.'

Mei clicks his fingers for a torch and counts the money twice, then tucks the notes into his loincloth. He smiles golden and most avuncular at JC. 'You will see in the brochure that all health and virginity is currently being checked out. Contracts are being drawn up, fully inclusive of VAT pricing. These will include particulars of age and ownership, information pack on natural talents and temperament, fully-witnessed marriage certificate, list of personal history details and preferences for immigration interrogation, should one arise, and Uncle Mei's no-questions-asked thirty per cent money-back guarantee. Though I must tell you, this refund has not been called on once. Uncle Mei holds one hundred per cent consumer satisfaction rating.'

JC's Adam's apple struggles to keep up. 'Goodness, there's rather a lot of paperwork, isn't there? I mean, I thought maybe it was just, you know, hand over a few quid and then, you know,' he strokes the photographed ankle bone wistfully, 'Bob's your uncle.'

'Uncle Mei is a proper uncle to you. With export it does not do to be slapdash. Your interests are included in this. Now, Mr Bone, I will mention latest Taiwanese technology. Five years in the future a bar-coding tattoo on ankle skin is old news. A chip under the skin is the modern way of tracking goods. In five years you will never have to worry again where she is day or night. I will include for you, my journalist friend, a special certificate. Bring Mrs Bone back in five years for no-quibble, charge-free implanting. One hundred per cent freebie-jeebie special offer for special friend.'

'I'm honoured.'

'Certainly. In the meantime your uncle advises you to

consider safe storage for some weeks prior to export. Perhaps a honeymooning holiday while visa application is in process. As we old men say here, "A woman's brain is that of a bird – always seeking to fly. But the man who keeps her leg tied on a rope is wise-headed indeed." I am not sure of the exact translation.'

JC reconsiders the photographed ankle. So utterly fragile. Utterly breakable-looking. 'Are you saying there may be difficulties?'

Mei chuckles. 'Adjustments, Mr Bone, adjustments, as in every marriage. It would be my suggestion that you find what we call a Getting to Know You place. Perhaps you should be looking for a location where transport is not happening regularly. I can recommend, if required?'

JC runs his thumb along the feathery creases on Orchidee's heel and up the rise of the ankle bone. He clears his throat and leans towards the tigress. 'Um, you mentioned specialisations. Just curious – any idea what they might be?'

'Ha ha ha. Good question, Mr Bone. From what I have seen this girl possesses talent for most things. This blindness gives other senses added sparkle. She has received one hundred and three per cent Can-Do rating in her latest assessment. Imagine that, Mr Bone.'

JC imagines.

'I think of blinding some of the other girls to achieve same.' Saliva shimmers in Mei's golden smile. 'You are a lucky man, Mr Bone, four thousand dollars is a bargain price from Uncle Mei. We will make fast-track with her professional skill set for you.'

'Excuse me. Did you just say *four* thousand dollars?'

'As we agreed yesterday.'

'Christ, right. We did?'

'You have a problem?'

JC considers this exquisite girl's exquisite ankle, thinking of her blind skill set, her added sparkle, her one hundred and three per cent Can-Do rating. Briefly, he thinks of another painful call to his mother. Was it drugs? Was that why he needed all this money, she had wanted to know yesterday. Was he being honest with her? 'No. No, Uncle, there's no problem at all. Somewhere quiet, you say, for honeymooning?'

Uncle Mei opens his arms expansively. 'Young love requires privacy's cloak.'

'Certainly.'

'You say you are a journalist, so you want adventure place, Mr Bone? Real adventure. Man's adventure.'

'Certainly, Uncle. I am a real man.'

Mei shakes his head. 'I don't know.' In the black distance someone is mopping. The caged gorilla is shadow-boxing the bucket. 'I don't know. Maybe Vietnamese adventure proves too tough for you.'

JC attempts to shuffle himself taller on the warthog. 'Now, Mr Mei, you should know there's very little that scares me, really very little indeed. You see, my mother was always of the opinion that—'

Mei's sudden wolf whistle interrupts him.

Out of the darkness three boys appear.

'Mnong warriors, Mr Bone. Strongest tribe on the dragon's spine.'

'Dragons?'

'The Highlands, Mr Bone. No foreigners go to these mountains.'

'They don't?'

'Foreigners are cowards.'

'Perhaps not all of us. You see, my mother—'

'Cowards all. Even Oklahoma Joey in the end.'

'Oklahoma Joey?'

'Cried for his mummy. Cried like a baby girl.'

'Right.'

'But these boys,' Mei slaps the muscled belly of the nearest boy, 'they are ready for war.'

'Gosh.'

'It is ancient warrior land, Mr Bone.'

'Right you are.'

'Before you and your Americans attempted imperial invasion,' Mei ignores JC's squeak of protest, 'before this, the backbone of the dragon was the hunting ground of our noblest warlords. After the work of your Agent Orange the poisoned soil grew no life. Since then some say the tribes grow strange ways.' Mei grabs a boy by the neck and knocks on his forehead. 'Not right here.'

The English Adam's apple wobbles. 'I see.'

Mei releases the boy and beckons JC into the darkness between them. His breath is sour as curds. 'They are human-flesh eaters, it is said. These boys? I doubt it. Prefer pork.'

'Right,' the Englishman retreats. 'Pork.'

'This is the question, my journalist friend. Do you have a real man's courage or are you feeling as cowardly as your English custard?'

'Actually, I'm not too fond of—'

'Quiet please. Think, Mr Bone, this is one-off offer only.' Mei turns to the Mnong boys and asks in Vietnamese, 'Is the construction of the Minority People's Tourist and Spa Complex completed yet?'

'Sort of,' one of the boys says. 'The external walls are nearly done.'

'Excellent,' Mei says.

'I'm not afraid,' JC says. 'I'm not afraid of anything, me.'

'Good job. We can arrange exclusive three-week honeymoon package with warrior tribe. Unique experience. Full board. Special price to you of six hundred dollars plus VAT. But no guarantee that if you wander off you won't be caught for dinner.' Mei's laughter surges into the darkness on waves of putrid breath.

Happily, here it is necessary to leave murky dealings in the dark and return to the right side of the law. To be precise about the location – to the small office of Dalat's acting chief of police, because dramatic things are about to happen.

Just an hour after a meeting concludes in a shady corner of a nightclub, a telephone on the acting chief's desk begins to ring.

A fan of green notes freezes in the air. Narrow loafers leap off a desk. The telephone handset is snatched up by thin fingers. 'But that's terrible news, sir. Certainly, sir. Tonight, under cover of darkness. Fifty officers, dogs and marksmen, sir.' The sure-suspension chair gives a squeak as a body springs from it to stand to attention. 'Failure is not our option either, sir. Thank you, sir, and a very good evening to the wife.'

The handset is replaced. A thin smile creeps back from thin lips and a pale hand drops a fan of green notes into an open briefcase. A match is struck and tossed into a metal wastebin.

Inside the bin a blue plastic bag curls and starts to melt. Flames race along the bag's seam, where a cockroach has recently birthed forty young. Most of the newborns are consumed instantly. The mother scrambles up the side of the bin with two infants clinging to her shell. She leaps from the inferno into the only cover around – an open briefcase on the floor.

The fire in the bin subsides. The briefcase snaps shut. It is swept off the floor and swung out of the office, accompanied by a jaunty whistle and a whiff of eucalyptus.

It is a sad little incident this, and seemingly inconsequential, and there is no time now to dwell on what has been lost and what gained, and by whom. There is only time to fly west with the day's dying sun, past a thin peppermint house where a cattle prod is being charged, beyond the civic asylum where a new inmate's head is being shaved, and high above a grilled window where a blind beauty is refusing to join in a chorus of sisterly weeping. It is time to leave the fading sun warming the ironwork, and venture where it cannot go: deep beneath the forest canopy where a ragtag army is on the move.

Everyone Wants to Be an Alpha

'Crikey, we were lucky to get out of that alive,' Grace says, sliding to the ground. 'I never want an experience like that, never ever again in my entire life.' She and Fang are hiding in a mulberry thicket at the base of Robin Hill. 'Just need a five-minute breather,' Grace mutters, curling up on the ground and closing her eyes, 'then we should push on for camp before the light fades.'

Fang watches her. It was a long run from the club. A terrifying run. Grace looks exhausted, her face grey as the dusk, her clothes tatty and worn. Fang watches her and wishes for a moment he could swap his super-tuned ears for some useful powers – the sort that humans understand; powers that could conjure, say, a chocolate bar from his pocket, the foreign type she craves. He would present it to her for services to animals at a little ceremony by the campfire. Maybe the monkeys would applaud – the snub-noseds seemed to like doing that. He would like to see her face when he gave it to her. He would like to see her smile. 'Didn't you know I have special powers?' he would say to her.

He smiles. 'You did it,' he tells her softly. 'You freed all the captive primates in Dalat.'

'We did it,' Grace yawns, her eyes closed.

'Mostly you.'

She smiles and shakes her head. 'Those boys with the machine guns, how did they miss us?'

'Perhaps they didn't want to hit us.'

'That would be a nice thought.'

He likes this in her. Her desire to see the best in people. 'Perhaps it was him they didn't want to hit, not us.'

'That would still be nice of them.'

He smiles. 'I suppose it would.'

'Is he still with us?'

Fang turns and looks back. The magnificent mountain gorilla they have liberated is sat on a tree trunk a short way back on the track, buffing his pink nails on his magnificent ebony chest. His eyeballs seem to glow in the darkening sky. 'I should go and say hello.'

Grace closes her eyes and settles back down. It makes her smile – Fang makes her smile – the way he grunts and hoots with the animals, for all the world as though he is Doctor Dolittle. 'Each to their own,' she yawns. In a moment she is snoring.

'Good evening, gorilla,' Fang says, heading back down the track, chattering his teeth and knocking on his chest in his best approximation of simian speech patterns. 'My name is Fang.'

The gorilla looks above, around and behind him.

'It's me,' Fang says, approaching, 'me talking.'

'My good man, that is quite impossible.' The gorilla is holding out his nails and studying the shine on them. 'Your species does not have the neurological capacity for an advanced level of motor-verbal communication. It's a well-established fact. And all that chattering with your teeth is causing you to drool excessively. Not a good look in any male. Calm it down, there's a fellow.'

Fang stops dead. The snub-nosed monkeys had been far more polite about his attempts to communicate.

'That's better, my man. A word of advice – I'd keep my distance, if I were you. I could take off your head with one twist of my fingertips. I can run at you twice as fast as you can run away. And were we to connect in combat, you should know I have more than fifteen times your body strength. I am warning you now, the fight would not be a fair one.'

'But I don't mean you any harm.'

'Of course you don't.' The gorilla's eyebrows twitch with languid amusement. 'That's what your sort always say. And then you bring out the nets or blow your little darts at us. What's your method going to be, my man, have you decided?'

Fang is starting to feel slightly despondent. 'We only wanted to set you free.'

'You will excuse me if I find that a little hard to believe.'

'It's true. We don't want to kill anyone.'

'No one?'

'No.'

'Good heavens, my man, how are you going to survive in this world with an attitude like that?'

Fang stares glumly at his feet, thinking of the bullets that so narrowly missed them less than an hour ago.

'Well, no harm done on this occasion, we all have our growing up to do.' To Fang's surprise the gorilla has sauntered up the track on two feet and is standing over him, perfectly balanced, tapping him on the shoulder. 'Chin up, my man. You need to get some steel in these bones if you want to make an Alpha.'

Fang thinks uncomfortably of his father. Was it really

not possible to be a man and also be, well, kind to things? 'Do I want to be an Alpha?'

'Dear boy, everyone wants to be an Alpha.' The gorilla is offering his hand. 'But I'm afraid I've no time now for private tuition. It's been splendid meeting you, but I'll say cheerio. Nothing personal, only I'm a tad randy as it happens, being cooped up for so long. You're a red-blooded male from the look of you. Sure you understand, needs to be met and so forth.'

Fang is about to express his doubts. He's about to try and say, 'I'm not sure where you'll find female mountain gorillas round these parts,' when he hears a crashing sound in the thicket and Grace shouting. 'Fang! Quick! Look down the hill!'

A distant caterpillar of lighted circles is crawling up the hillside.

'Cars, Fang. Must be twenty of them at least. We're being followed.'

The acting chief of police (Dalat and Central Highlands province) locks his jeep, folds back his shirtsleeves and switches on his headtorch. He looks up at the dark densely forested hill track, surveys his map and calls the dog handlers to him. 'They went that way. Synchronise time-pieces and unleash the hounds in a one hundred and eighty degree arc, maintaining radio contact.' And being a man trained in the motivational arts, he pins the search team in his bright white glare to add, 'I will personally reward the successful trapper with a one-dollar bill. Go. The window of opportunity is open to you all, and failing to jump through it is not an option.'

* * *

'Marvellous. That's just marvellous,' Tricky Dicky spits when Fang and Grace rush into the camp and wake it with their unfortunate news. 'Here we go again. Run run run. These humans clearly had no idea what they were getting us into with their daredevil antics. If they'd taken a moment they might have realised that kidnapping an eminent celebrity such as myself was bound to have terrible repercussions. I was only saying to Jackie—'

A smooth low growl from the edge of the clearing interrupts him. 'With the greatest respect, Chimp, I believe it was the theft of my good self that provoked this dramatic pursuit. It's inevitable when you're worth your weight in gold. I don't think we've been introduced.' For the benefit of the predominantly female gathering tittering into their hands, rather than the balding chimpanzee hogging the fire and attempting to light a cigarette he's made from leaves and grass, the gorilla raises himself on his two magnificently developed legs and emits a low roar. 'Good evening, all. The name is Kong, King Kong. You are fortunate enough to see before you a prime example of an original silver-backed mountain gorilla. Alpha class, in case you thought you were dreaming, ladies.'

The snub-nosed monkeys titter.

'Alpha class and in prime position on the extinct register.'

'The stink register more like.' Dicky coughs. 'Don't know why the humans bothered kidnapping you.'

'We did not kidnap anyone,' Fang protests. 'It was a rescue mission.'

'I'm afraid that's rather a question of semantics,' Jackie O says, pulling her heel into a half lotus and trying to withhold her gaze from the mighty silver thighs cavorting about the clearing. 'You humans may choose to believe you are a force of liberation. Other primates may choose to disagree. We may question your subspecies' right to keep fellow family members captive in the first place. Thus we may reject this alleged liberation from a prior-enslaving cousin. You also need to consider the responsibilities that accompany any alleged liberation. Perhaps you might translate for your female accomplice there – a few green bananas and a fire at night are not enough.'

'Well said, that pretty lady!' The gorilla drops onto his knuckles and swings close to Jackie O, his ebony nipples flickering splendidly with reflected firelight.

'Goodness,' Jackie O murmurs, her eyes drawn helplessly to those splendid nipples.

'Fang,' Grace says, 'we have to go. Now.'

But before Fang can answer, there is an incident at the fire. 'You keep your hands off my sister,' Tricky Dicky shrieks, and charges at the gorilla.

The gorilla raises an amused eyebrow, extends an arm and intercepts Dicky's punch, scooping him up with one hand and holding him flailing above the ground.

'I'm terribly sorry,' Jackie murmers into the ebony ear, 'he's not usually like this. There's a lot of cold turkey going on.'

'That's quite understood, little lady, the weaker members of the team often have their problems adjusting. He'll settle down in a moment and accept his place.'

Jackie sighs. She has just sighted the gorilla's glorious belly button.

'Fang!' Grace tugs on his sleeve. 'Did you hear that?'

It comes from deep in the forest, a howling snarling frenzy.

'Please, would you mind delaying whatever it is you want to discuss?' Fang urges the camp. 'We must go at once.'

'Go?' Jackie's eyes flutter from the gorilla's glorious belly button to his majestic biceps, which are beginning to quiver under the strain of dangling Dicky above the forest floor. 'But where would the humans have us go? One cannot run forever. Besides which, Dicky and I are still recovering. My soles are shot to pieces.'

'Poor little lady, may I see?'

'No!' Dicky snarls.

'No!' Fang shouts. 'Unless you want to be torn apart by dogs.'

'Dogs?' the snub-noseds chorus and shiver.

'Dogs?' Dicky shrinks in horror.

He is answered by an echoing howl. And then a mighty roar from the gorilla as he drops the chimpanzee and raises himself up on his mighty legs. 'Fear not, cowardly chimp and assorted other apefolk, canines shall not cow us! Extinguish lights, fires and smoking materials, fall in single file and follow me!'

At once the camp is abandoned and this loose association of assorted apefolk plunges into the thickets of bamboo and bramble, the howls of dogs driving them on. In the dark the undergrowth is treacherous. The apes stumble and bump on ill-conditioned and cage-softened feet.

'Halt!' the gorilla shouts suddenly from the front. 'Nice and slow please, no pushing and shoving, there's nothing to see.' The monkeys skid into a pile behind him.

He beckons Fang to him. 'They're gaining on us. Our scent's everywhere. We'll never make it on foot.'

'I see.'

'Well?'

'I'm afraid I don't really know what to suggest.'

'I suspected as much.'

'I'm sorry. I suppose we should admit defeat. Go quietly, so nobody gets hurt, that sort of thing.'

'Good heavens, man, are you suggesting we turn ourselves in?'

'Well—'

'Back into captivity? Back to a life of humiliation and degradation? *That*'s your solution? And you want to be an Alpha? Well, well.'

'I never said I wanted—'

'You want us to resume a life of physical privation and untold mental stress? *That*'s your suggestion? Dear, dear me.' The gorilla shakes his head, striding back and forth. 'You're going to need more work than I thought.'

Fang looks at his feet. 'I'm afraid I can't see another way.'

The gorilla spins and charges at a pine trunk. In three bounds he is swinging his great bulk from a creaking branch above them. 'There is always another way! Assorted apefolk ascend the pines! Ascend or face certain death!'

All around Fang and Grace, the apes – grumbling but obedient to the gorilla's instruction – wander to the trees and begin uncertainly to climb.

'I guess they're leaving us,' Grace says quietly, watching the black baboon shunt himself laboriously up a trunk.

Fang takes her hand. 'It's better this way. It's what we wanted, isn't it? I suppose we'd better get ready to face the consequences.'

'We can at least put the dogs off the scent,' Grace says. 'Muddy the tracks.'

They turn away.

There is a thunderous crash onto the ground behind them. 'Where the devil do you think you're going?'

'Just,' Fang says, 'well, just—'

'No man gets left behind. Not on my watch.'

Before either of them know what is happening, Fang and Grace are being hoisted onto the back of the mighty gorilla.

'Humans, cling on, old baboon at the back, keep up.'

And together the assorted apefolk ascend to the forest canopy and swing out under the moon, just, in fact, as if they were born to it.

'How do you make a baby gorilla float?' Dicky hoots, leaping at the crown of a tall mahogany. 'Take your foot off its head. So, a lorry of turtles crashes into a cartload of terrapins. What a turtle disaster. *Turtle* disaster, anybody?'

Gradually the sound of dogs begins to fade in the night.

After what seems an age the gorilla lets out a roar. 'Apefolk, halt.'

The weary monkeys hang in the canopy gazing at the stars and listening to owls hunting and porcupine and boar rooting far below. They have been travelling so long that the edges of the eastern sky are blurred with orange.

'Apefolk, descend.'

Gratefully the travellers slide, slip and tumble to the ground. Grace climbs from the gorilla's shoulders to consult her compass by torchlight.

'West,' the gorilla says, tapping the instrument approvingly.

'West, he said,' Fang tells Grace.

Despite her tiredness, Grace starts to giggle.

'What?'

Fang smiles that irradiating smile at her, right into her bones, so Grace cannot help but giggle some more. She giggles until tears run from her sore eyes. 'I've gone and fallen for a boy who thinks he's Doctor Dolittle.' Giggling, she topples backwards with her rucksack into a clump of fern. Within seconds she is snoring.

Fang looks around for something to cover her.

'Goodness, no no no, my man!' The gorilla stares with undiluted horror. 'Are you entirely clueless?'

'I'm sorry?'

'Have you done any outward bound training? Any sort at all?'

Fang looks at his feet.

'I thought not. Dear boy, you cannot possibly let her sleep here.'

'But she's exhausted.'

'It's uncleared, for goodness sake. It'll be crawling with scorpions, snakes and the like. Not to mention porcupine. Besides which, once a man's down it's damned difficult to get him up again alive. Damned difficult. Done any leadership training, have you? Any sort at all? Good lord.'

The gorilla marches over to look at Grace. 'She's far gone now, and I can tell you from personal experience, it's a damned difficult job to wake a female once she's gone off like that.'

Hastily Fang starts prodding the forest floor around Grace for snakes, scorpions, porcupines and the like. 'Actually, I don't think either of us can keep up this pace for long.'

'That's pretty evident. So what's the plan of action, my man?'

Fang looks down and keeps on prodding.

'Dear, dear me,' the gorilla says.

'It wasn't,' Fang hesitates, 'planned.'

'Even a performing chimp could see that.'

Fang says nothing. Suddenly he has no idea quite how all this came about: the machetes in restaurant chairs, the howling police dogs, the fugitive life, the trouble he's causing his father again.

Something is tapping on his elbow. 'Excuse me, please.'

Fang looks down. It is one of the snub-nosed monkeys – the golden-headed one. 'My aunts and cousins and I have been talking things through, and we thought, all things considered, we'd very much like to head for Laos now. My grandmother lives out that way – or she did, as best we remember. Only the thing is,' the monkey pauses, delicately nibbling the rim off a fingernail, 'I'm rather ashamed to say, but none of us is quite sure how to get there. So we were wondering whether you might be able to assist.'

'Laos?' Fang says, looking at the gorilla.

'Wonderful country. Heaven on earth, my man, heaven on earth.'

'You know of it?'

'Heard tell from my mother before she passed on. Tragic what happened to her, of course. Dear woman. Such a tragedy.' The gorilla clears his throat. 'All water under the bridge now, my man. And Laos is supposed to be a very convenient place for lying low, if you get my drift. Very laissez-faire. Great ones for Buddhism, I believe. As for the ladies – ooh la la! Had a couple on the podium at New

Universe. Very tasty-looking, I can tell you. Did an eye-watering turn with peeled lychees. Quite extraordinary.'

The little snub-nosed coughs.

'But the thing is,' Fang returns them to the subject, 'I have no idea how to get to Laos, and we're running out of money. And if the police are hunting us we'll have to give towns a wide berth and,' he looks down at the mosquitoes hovering like a stack of tiny aircraft above the ferns, 'and I'm not sure whether Grace is up to it. She's not exactly used to this kind of life.'

'Head west, my man. Just as you're doing.'

'But that's—'

'Over the dragon's spine, through one or two uncleared minefields, past the odd hostile tribe. Almost as fearsome a terrain as Cambodia,' the gorilla shudders, 'and you really wouldn't want to go there.'

'Oh well,' the snub-nosed says, with a delicate shrug of disappointment. 'Perhaps another time, then.'

'What you really need is a local guide,' the gorilla continues. 'Someone who knows this sort of terrain.'

'Someone who knows,' Fang murmurs, remembering all the jungle survival strategies his father had tried to teach him when he was a child. Hadn't his war been out this way, out on the dragon's spine? Wasn't that what all those bedtime stories were about? He feels his chest tighten unexpectedly. His father would know what to do.

The gorilla raps on Fang's forehead. 'Anyone home? I was just saying, you need someone who knows the territory like the back of his hand.'

'Yes, I suppose you're right.'

'Without a guide you really wouldn't stand a chance. There is always China. You could try for up there. Rather a long journey north, and possibly not so welcoming on arrival. But even there, without a guide I'm afraid you're doomed.'

'Doomed?'

'As are those of us apes who find this re-naturalisation process challenging. Pardon me for echoing that delightful lady chimp's words, but it's another of those things you really might have thought about before setting off on this gung-ho and rather self-indulgent adventure of yours.'

Fang nods. 'You're right. I am very sorry for all this, Kong, I apologise.' He crouches to the tiny snub-nosed. 'Sorry for not thinking things through.'

The gorilla pats Fang heavily on the shoulder. 'Quite. However, chin up, my man, it's just possible you may be in luck.'

'Sorry, Baboon,' Fang says, 'sorry Dicky, sorry Jackie O.'

'All right, my man, these things can be overdone.'

'Sorry.'

'Do listen up. I said you may be in luck.' The gorilla lowers his voice. 'It could be we have a guide within our very midst. One of the greatest.'

'Where? No one has claimed any knowledge of the region.'

'Right here, my man!' the gorilla bellows, leaping up to beat a samba on his magnificent ebony chest.

The gorilla licks his thumb and holds it high in the air. 'And I can tell you we're heading in quite the wrong direction. North is what we need. Baboon – wake up. Chimp – stub it out. Apefolk and assorted brethren, fall in double time. Quick march everyone, follow me!' He scoops Grace into his arms and charges into the under-growth.

'But wait,' Fang calls as the monkeys vanish from sight, 'I haven't even asked Grace if she wants to go to Laos. She could get into serious trouble for it.'

The reply comes booming from deep in the forest. 'My dear boy, this little lump would follow you anywhere on earth. Now do come along.'

Fang doesn't have to feel the blush rising in him to hope that, in this matter at least, the gorilla might be speaking some truth.

The Central Highlands People's Asylum for the Insane

At dawn, with disappointment, Slimn Jimn calls off the dogs.

We have succeeded in cleansing the district of this despicable gang, he types in his email report to the chief superintendent, after a small cup of black coffee and the removal of price labels from a pair of Italian-import snake-skin loafers. *I led my men in giving chase through the night. The outlaws have been driven far away. Concurrently I initiated a no-stone-unturned survey of Dalat eating establishments and I can confirm a one hundred per cent lack of ape species therein. Therefore I deduce the MLA will never again plague the town. I respectfully suggest this case is categorised as 'no longer actionable within provincial jurisdiction' and is therefore closed. I humbly recommend myself for the Valiant Conduct Medal for exemplary leadership shown during the pursuit through treacherous terrain and into extended overtime.*

No outlaws apprehended as ordered. Displeased, is the superintending reply.

It is followed some minutes later by a second email: *As are our Comrades in Commerce. Reflects lack of local control. You will prioritise deployment of all available manpower on street patrols and roadblocks. Maintain a visible presence. Increase arrest quota. Prepare riot officers for Ma tribe eviction to commence at 06:00 hours on Saturday.*

This is followed by a superintending afterthought: *Commissar Nao murder enquiry to proceed with medium status.*

Followed by a signing-off with an example of exemplary leadership: *Do not displease me further.*

The superintendent returns to his butterfly killing jars.

Acting Chief Jimn tries his Italian loafers for size.

Oblivious to both his ex-deputy's new purchases and the great strides being made in his ex-boss's provincial development plans, Duong is to be found on this Thursday morning driving out of town in his as yet unsuspended official black jeep. While his ex-boss euthanises a Chocolate Albatross and his ex-deputy waterproofs his toecaps, Duong is heading south on route twenty through dawn mists at the start of a momentous day.

This is a day of Duong's own making. Whatever obligations drive him on, the day will be shaped entirely by his own decisions; let us be very clear about that. Once this day gets going it will alter not only his life and his family's, but that of his ex-boss and his ex-deputy and many others; in fact, many more than can ever be named. It is going to be that sort of day.

But it does not do to get too far ahead of events, nor too far ahead of Chief Duong as he turns the jeep onto route twenty. Better perhaps to simply observe him whistling as he stops a couple of kilometres south of Dalat, just beyond a small pothole in the road and just in front of the shanty shacks of the Ma tribe's settlement. Beneath a pair of giant neon footballing eyes, officers at a police roadblock are waving him down.

Duong is still whistling as he winds down his window. 'What's all this about then, Truyen?' he calls to the constable manning the bollards. 'Deputy Jimn working you to death before the sun's even up? After another runaway monkey, is he?'

'Eviction preparation, Chief.' The constable points to the government billboard with its announcement of impending construction. 'Civic calm and law and order are required before the settlement relocation begins on Saturday.'

Duong beams at the giant footballer's billboard face delighting in its draught of Gola-Cola. He beams at the constable. 'Well, that's excellent news, Truyen.' He is looking, if truth were told, every inch unbothered with the efficiency of the policing taking place without him. 'Excellent work, yes.' He unscrews his travel flask and offers the young man a tot of warming rice spirit. Which is regretfully declined in accordance with new rules.

Duong beams at the schoolgirl portrait of Lila he has taken from the wall of the lean-to and sellotaped to the dashboard, and restarts the engine.

'Just a moment, Chief – my apologies – *Mr* Duong,' the constable blushes. 'Please state your destination, if you would.'

'Excuse me?'

'Orders. From the new chief, sir,' the constable mumbles into his boots, 'for the record. Everyone leaving the town limits must state their destination.'

'I see.' Duong thinks very carefully. 'Well then, Constable Truyen, I am paying a visit to my mother. I shall be taking route twenty-seven west.'

'Very good, sir.' The constable records. 'Thank you, sir.'
'Not at all. May I?'

'By all means, sir. Enjoy your trip and best wishes to your mother.'

The constable's ex-boss drives off with a farewell toot, looking every inch the vacationer and nothing at all like a man whose wife is rumoured to have been locked up for her own safety, whose influential son-in-law has been murdered, whose son is a wanted fugitive, and whose job has been snatched from under him. So the young constable will say with a bemused shake of his head to station colleagues later that day when his long shift is over. Old-school mettle, must be.

In truth, there is much about the policeman's analysis that is accurate, and it will surprise no one who knows him that in time young Truyen will go on to head a major criminal investigation unit. But it is Ex-Chief Duong not the constable who is this story's concern. The ex-chief who is currently driving past the turn-off to route twenty-seven (west) and continuing along highway twenty (south) with the chorus of an old Red marching song on his lips.

> Advancing toward Saigon, we sweep away all
>   enemies
> Heading toward the delta, we advance toward
>   the city
> On the way, we hear our mothers are waiting
> Advance forward to liberate Saigon!

Curious behaviour indeed, but it must not be forgotten that this is a man who revels in action, who is happiest looking neither too far ahead nor behind, and since he picked himself out of a pothole, Duong has been busy: faxing carbon copies of letters to Hanoi government offices, purchasing rope, sacking, and bottled water, laminating three A4 double-sided cards, recharging a battery box and a cattle prod. He has been rereading a long-abandoned policing manual and meticulously writing his to-do list.

This morning he has already consumed two omelettes and rigorously evacuated his bowels (an indication of impending success if ever there was one), thus completing two items on his to-do list prior to even leaving the front door. And at his journey's end adoring arms await him, and if he is in luck, the finest chicken broth in all Vietnam. What reason can there be not to sing?

But before accompanying this cheery police chief any further south, it is only proper for us to make a short detour off the main road to call in at the Central Highlands People's Asylum for the Insane. The detour will be short, because the asylum is not a place anyone would care to spend much time in, unless one didn't actually care.

Just how much the asylum's latest arrival does not care, the registrar, clever Doctor Mung, is currently trying to ascertain. The steel furniture is bolted down and the temperature is turned up high in the reception room – higher than might be comfortable for the body in order to aid the mind in arriving at a swift appreciation of how and exactly why it finds itself in a place of hard edges and reflective surfaces.

Doctor Mung approves. Hiding from reality is what has made these people ill in the first place. Although the clever doctor acknowledges to himself that the patient sitting across from him today would be a hard one to hide anywhere.

'So, Mrs Duong, how are we feeling?'

Sweating freely onto the interviewing table and spilling over the two stools required to accommodate her, the patient makes no response. She is engrossed in drawing a line around the reflection of the doctor's head on the table with the club of her left hand. Which has been bandaged to prevent further incidents of self-harm.

Composed but not entirely sentient = first impression Doctor Mung records in neat pencil on a blank sheet in the admission file.

'Do you know *Romance on the Wards*, doctor?' the patient enquires of his table-top reflection, her voice far deeper than he expected and inflected with an Old Saigonese decadence.

He writes down *Old Saigon = decadence* and shakes his head. 'I can't say I do, Mrs Duong.'

'A pity. It would almost have been like watching you on television, if you could have done some of the lines.' She begins to hum the drama's theme tune.

Malign influence = television Mung writes. Since the virulent – there was no other way to think of it – invasion of this so-called entertainment medium into Vietnamese homes, the People's Department for Citizens' Moral and Social Well-Being had recorded a fourteen per cent increase in violent crimes. Mung glances at the plasters on the woman's shaved scalp: also an eleven per cent rise in incidents of self-harm. With his own three young children to protect, Doctor Mung will be adding his name to the list of physicians petitioning for a curfew on broadcasting hours.

He presses his palms together and leans towards the patient. He does not believe she poses any threat to strangers. 'Tell me, Mrs Duong, does the television talk to you?'

The patient rubs blobs of sweat into the reflection of the doctor's hands.

Craving for physical intimacy Doctor Mung writes. 'Does the television tell you to do bad things?'

'I miss the television. I also miss shrimp crackers. Please fetch me shrimp crackers at once.'

Gluttony = oral substitute for emotional fulfilment Doctor Mung notes neatly. Since the arrival of convenience foods in Dalat obesity levels have shot up two hundred and forty-four per cent. Doctor Mung glances at the lean figure of Ho Chi Minh in his brass frame on the wall. Not in *his* day. This is why Doctor Mung's own children pursue rigorous exercise routines, consume traditional cuisine and have their weight monitored three times a week. They will not end up in here.

'I see from your notes you are a Catholic, Mrs Duong.'

'That would depend, Doctor. I pray to the Holy Trinity on a Sunday. The Goddess of Mercy gets some sort of offering on Tuesdays. Wednesday I generally spend in the bath. Thor has been accorded Thursdays, and Phoebus Saturdays. Although I should tell you I'm thinking of swapping those two round. Phoebus isn't really working out on the weekend.'

'That's quite a range, Mrs Duong. Do you hold faith with any particular one of them?'

'Did you say whether this place does shrimp crackers?'

'That's not really my area of expertise, Mrs Duong.'

'Call me Delia, if you would.'

Delia? He checks her notes: *Po (Poonana) Duong.*

Identity = crisis he loops a circle back to the word *television*.

'Could you find out?'

'I'm sorry?'

'About the shrimp crackers.'

Doctor Mung feels the time has come to be straight. 'Mrs Duong, you do understand why you were brought here?'

A wave of grey falls down the patient's face. She emits one loud cry, such as a birthing buffalo might make.

Buffalo Doctor Mung writes in the ensuing silence.

'Mrs Duong, I will repeat the question. It requires an answer before any discussion of foodstuffs is undertaken. Do you understand the reason for your incarceration here?'

'Absolutely, doctor. My husband tortured our son into mutism and sold our daughter into some form of slavery. Added to which, the stars have been very bad for this family for a while.'

Mung's sigh is louder than even he anticipated.

Delusional. Consider anti-hallucinogenic medication. Possible candidate for cell radicalisation trial.

As a concession, he rubs out her given name on her notes and replaces it with *Delia*. Then another thought comes to him.

Schedule her in with Bung this afternoon?

Two hundred kilometres to the south of Dalat's asylum, a black jeep turns off the highway onto a track to a shrimp farm. It drives until it is no longer visible from the main road and then pulls over. The driver unscrews the blue government number plates on the jeep. He replaces them with a pair of civilian white ones, in accordance with a to-do numbered three on a notepad. He consults to-do four and continues on foot to the farm café to take an early lunch. It is all going very well so far.

Chief Duong takes a table in the shade of a mango grove and dines on caramelised shrimp and boiled rice. Into the distance workers are sifting the shrimp beds with their netted paddles beneath a hot blue sky. Chief Duong sits back and observes happily as his lunch settles. And as so often happens to him during the digestive process, he finds his imagination inflamed by inspiration. He opens his notepad.

To-do 28: Become Shrimp Farmer!
Farm to be named EMPEROR PRAWN FARM!

After all, when this nonsense has blown over, when Lila and Po are safely home and the business with Fang is cleared up one way or another, when he has been civically reinstated at his desk, there will still be certain realities to face. Like the truth, that no man can fight crime forever, and in the Central Highlands province statutorily not beyond sixty-five years of age. For a man who will have come into a small sum of money, what a perfect retirement plan a shrimp farm would be! The likelihood of civic statues might be diminished, but then no man should expect to get everything he desires in life. Besides, a small statue could surely be erected at the entrance to the farm, if the land was his. Nothing grand, simply a welcoming figure – possibly carved from mahogany – arms outstretched in warm greeting. And a small painted sign beneath: *Farmer Duong welcomes you . . .*

Farmer Duong. It has such a wholesome ring to it.

Continuing his contemplations whilst taking a trip to the café latrine (to-do five), Duong is shocked to recall how a man with such a profitable future ahead of him could have toyed so wantonly with self-destruction. How close he came! Sudden tears of relief sprinkle the latrine floor. How lucky he is.

Returning to the jeep, he tests the charge on the cattle prod (to-do six) and then gets back in the front. He kisses Lila on her pretty forehead and checks the city map. He knows just where to park. He applies his aviator sunglasses and devotes himself to the last part of the drive down to Saigon – a mere ninety kilometres – with renewed zeal and the jilted husband's libretto from *The Fishwife's Lament*. Yes, it is all going very well indeed.

Good Morning, Vietnam!

Beneath a fizzing yellow sun, a bottle-green limousine glides out of the Mekong Hilton Golf and Spa Resort and turns towards Saigon, and to Radio HCMC in the heart of the city. Behind tinted glass Scunthorpe striker and England international Sam Porcini is reading aloud from a blog called *Global Adventurer* and rehearsing his Vietnamese hellos. An orange-skinned white-haired man sitting opposite is fiddling with the air conditioning.

'Put a sock in it, Sammy, there's a good kiddo.' The man turns the dial to max. 'We need to go through the schedule. And no cock-ups today if you don't mind, son.'

Sam Porcini looks at the man, who has taken out a tortoiseshell comb and is scraping it through his hair. If Sam concentrates he can hear it rasping against Tone's skull, dislodging flakes of dead scalp. He's got six weeks of this.

The air conditioning current picks up a clot of dandruff from Tone's comb, twirls it like a snowflake and deposits it on the strapping on Sam's left ankle. The ankle that has him out of the rest of this season and shipped to Asia. The ankle that may as well have a shackle around it, turning him into Gola-Cola's performing monkey for six weeks. Sam wonders how you say that in Vietnamese. He thinks about asking the chauffeur. He'd always liked languages at school. 'Is the Virgil in your blood, darling,' his mother liked to say, swearing to a direct line of descent from the Capitoline Hill in Ancient Rome to a sandwich shop in Hackney. She'd be getting up about now, he thinks. Starting early with the bread deliveries and the simmering of stock pans, apron on, up on her stool to reach the stove with ease. Sam smiles. 'What's that you say, Tone?'

'I said no cock-ups, Superman? Think you can manage that today?'

Like Sam had wanted that girl to jump at him from the balcony of the Hong Kong Sheraton. Like he was supposed to let her fall onto the tarmac and brain herself.

Tony Thirsthead tucks the comb in his top pocket and pulls his hair back into a ponytail. 'You hear me, kiddo?'

Sam touches his brow in mock salute. 'I will stay on message, sir! Smile at all sponsors, sir! Evade falling females by the nearest fire exit, sir! Do everything my earpiece tells me, sir!'

He immediately feels sick and turns away to stare out the window at the flower sellers and the shoeshine boys, at the cane juice carts and the noodle street stalls. At all the people who aren't locked inside an airless green cage. People who are just people, not circus monkeys. He wonders if he dare ask the driver to stop. He'd like to get out for a walk, just a walk on the streets. He can't remember the last time he'd walked alone on a street. 'All higher brain-functioning switched off, sir!'

Thirsthead doesn't raise an eyebrow. Privately, he thinks it's like keeping racehorses, this business of his, repre- senting coltish clowns. Three or four good seasons he gets out of them, with a half-decent sponsorship deal along the way if he's lucky, then there's usually some kind of leg injury and it's curtains. It remains to be seen whether

Porcini's torn ligaments will be the end of him. Thirsthead watches the footballer press the button to electronically unwind the window, ruining the system, letting in all that stink and noise and filth. He reaches across and presses the button to wind the window back up. 'Security hazard, Sammy.'

Too clever by half, this Sammy Porcini. First the A levels, now this Open University nutrition degree nonsense he's got himself embroiled with. 'Brains in boots is the best place for them,' Tone likes to tell his boys. 'You pay me to do the thinking.' Brains anywhere else was, well, special needs. Tone watches Sam opening an ice-cold Gola-Cola, pouring its bubbling green liquid into a bucket on the car floor and refilling the bottle with plain water. 'You need to get yourself a wife, pal.'

'I hate this shit,' Sam says, returning his attention to the Saigon streets. Two kids are scrapping over a green can. 'Remind me, Tone, why we went with a company that sells gut-rot to kids. Do you know what I think, Tone?'

'Sammy kiddo, I'm the one paid to think.'

'I think if we went up into space and looked back down at Earth, all that green you can see everywhere wouldn't be trees and grass and stuff, it would be their plastic crap lying about polluting everything. Remind me again why we had to take this deal?'

Tony Thirsthead finds his own reflection in the window and counts out each of his bank account balances in soothing single digits. Except for the attitude, Porcini was a marketing dream: twelve goals in ten internationals, last year's league player of the year; a Desert Orchid of a footballer. The sort that only came around once in an agent's career. Worth the blood-pressure pills. 'Because of the millions it makes us (you moron),' he snaps back. 'If you don't want them, there's plenty of poor buggers who'll bite your hand off for them. Now get your earpiece in, and can we please start talking about the effing schedule.'

On the street outside the radio station the crowd is crammed closer than paws in a pickle jar. Hot breath and hammering heartbeats and more hush than a thousand humans might normally manage. There is no room to raise tea flasks for those who have waited behind the cordon since dawn. There is no space for a quick faint in the broiling heat. There is simply a heaving murmuring organism of two thousand eyes fixed on the end of the road, every one of them willing the snout of a bottle-green limousine to creep into view.

Is it any wonder, then, that later in the day, when the Saigonese police begin their investigations, no one recalls anything untoward? No one recalls a small sun-glassed figure with bulging pockets squirming his way beyond the cordon of Mr Vong's Big Strong Boys Brigade onto the red carpet. The crowd's two thousand eyes seek nothing but a glimpse of superstar; no one will remember this insignificant little figure, no one at all.

Chief Duong joins the VIP queue on the red carpet and straightens his suit. He checks his pockets: top left – smoke canister, bottom left – goggles and face mask; top right – identity card and service pistol, bottom right – foldaway cattle prod. He runs through to-do items eight to eighteen in his head and waits his turn to approach the entrance, where a PR girl in a bottle-green football strip is ticking names off a list. Above the girl's head someone has hung a portrait of the great Uncle, and next to this a poster of Sam Porcini. They are united by a garland of yellow chrysanthemums. Surely a sign of success if ever one was needed.

'Next VIP.'

Duong clears his throat, throws back his shoulders and walks up. 'Good day,' he thrusts his fake identity card forward, 'Commissar Linh from Nha Trang Province.'

'Greetings, Commissar,' the PR girl murmurs, looking down her list.

'The Culture Ministry insisted I be present.'

'Yes, of course, Commissar. But that's odd,' the girl's finger is dangling over the Ls, 'I don't see you down here.'

'You don't?' Duong affects cheery but authoritative surprise.

'No. There are definitely no Linhs anywhere here.'

'Never mind. As I say, the ministry insisted.'

The girl looks through the rest of her sheets, a frown wriggling her brow.

These lists were prepared weeks ago. Perhaps you could call the ministry and ask them to send through authorisation?'

'Wishing you no further disrespect, do you not think the ministry has far more important matters to attend to than a brief visit from a foreign footballer?'

The girl's frown deepens. 'This is strange, we've three in already from the ministry.'

Duong laughs away this unfortunate news. 'Come now, you're not telling me a clerical error is going to cause trouble between us.'

The girl smiles tightly and lays down her pen. 'Mr Linh—'

'Commissar Linh, please.'

'Mr Linh, I am afraid I cannot help you. The strictest of orders. You are not on my list. As you can see,' she indicates the building behind her, already clogged with bodies, 'fire regulation policy.'

'Yes but really, miss, I am not such a big man—'

'You could be Mr Porcini himself, but if you're not on my list . . .'

'Miss—'

'I'm sorry. Next VIP, please.'

Duong turns away in a daze as a man barges past and is in a second later. A bouncer picks Duong up and places him beyond the bounds of Mr Vong's red rope.

Just like that it is over.

How quickly he has failed.

Chief Duong stands for a moment, stunned, inside the throbbing crowd. Slowly he begins to fight his way back through the bodies, irrelevant as a ghost at a party. He shuffles off down the street and does not look back.

The party goes on without him, of course. The red carpet is cleared and swept this way and that. Carpet freshener is applied. A thousand green bottle-shaped balloons stream from the building and shimmy along in the city's hot air. The introductory bars of 'We Will Rock You' send a sizzle of nerves down the street. The snout of a green limousine is sighted at last, causing a single shudder and gasp in the crowd. The car pulls up to the radio station and a rear passenger door swings open. And finally it happens – bouncing on the toes grown men have been known to weep over, Sam Porcini touches down in Saigon.

Seeming to give no thought to his weak ankle, Scunthorpe's star striker bounds along the inner cordon of Mr Vong's

Big Strong Boys, waving at the tinkers wobbling on their ladders, and the I-Speak-Your-Weight boys leaping off their scales. He gavottes and cabrioles and bows and waves and blows kisses at the ticketless masses as if he might perform for them forever. But soon – too soon he is pulled inside the building by an orange-faced white-haired man. Sam sprints with unmatchable grace past the mob of VIP attendees and soars onto the Gola-Cola podium.

The orange-faced white-haired man assumes a position in a dark corner. He speaks into his lapel. On the podium Sam touches his ear and nods. Drums rumble. Plumes of dry ice hiss. A spotlight transfixes him in limelight as gassy green bubbles pop in the air above him. Sam waves Vs of peace around the room. It seems, VIPs will later say, he is enjoying his first trip to the East. 'Good morning,' he shouts in Vietnamese. 'Good morning, Vietnam!'

Chief Duong hears the roar of the crowd as he stumbles round to the alley behind the radio station. It had seemed such a perfect location to park the car. Methodically, in accordance with no to-do on his list, he empties his pockets into the boot, laying his tools down neatly one by one.

It is only when he climbs back into the driver's seat and finds Lila's photograph waiting patiently for him on the dashboard that he begins to sob. Holding the memory of his child to his chest, listening to the roaring screaming happy people inside the radio station, he drops his head and he sobs and sobs and sobs. Because tears are all he has left.

A Proper Clinical Observation

Mr Bung (Dip. Hyp.) the Lyons-trained post-Freudian hypnotherapist stares at the snoring shaven-headed woman in front of him, watching her chins vibrate against her bosom. Mr Bung wipes his wet palms on a tissue and, without taking his eyes off the patient, doodles a watermelon on his pad. It is always a shame, he thinks, society's denigration of the larger lady: the personification of plenitude; the ambassadress of abundance; the first lady of fecundity.

Mr Bung expels a small ball of mucus from his throat into the tissue. 'Excellent. Let's get the ball rolling, Delia. Please describe to me where you think you are.'

The patient snores.

'Come along, Delia. Wakey-wakey, this is work time, lady,' the Lyons-trained hypnotist urges with a prod to one of the soft and splendid knees exposed beneath the hospital smock.

This seems to do the trick because the woman begins to moan.

'That's a start, Delia,' the hypnotist says as she moans on. It is long and rumbling and the only thing Mr Bung can think to equate it to is the noise of a birthing buffalo. Perhaps she has sunk deeper than he planned? Perhaps she has slipped through a species gateway. Hadn't the

Hypnotrix© instructor hinted as much could happen in extreme cases? Mr Bung gives the knee a second poke. 'That's enough now, Delia, it's not very ladylike, is it?'

There is no cessation of the moan.

Mr Bung swallows down mucus and leans in. He grips the patient's head and tilts it back against the chair. Mr Bung circles a mole on her cheek. It is very smooth. 'Delia, this is your doctor *commanding* you to cease this unpleasant moaning. After three counts he is *commanding* you to open your eyes and tell him where you are. Three and two and one. Eyes wide open.'

He has done it! It has happened – he could clap his hands for joy, were they not comfortably pressing into soft knees right now – the patient's eyelids are creaking open!

'Whee,' she says, 'whee, whee, whee.'

'Excellent!' Mr Bung peers into the sludgy gaze. 'That's really excellent, Delia. And now you will tell your dear and patient doctor where you are. He has already asked you twice.'

A high helium giggle, then 'Whee, splash, splashy splash splash.'

'Excellent. You're swimming.' Mr Bung ducks to avoid a sudden flail of arms. 'You're in the municipal baths? Or the lake, perhaps? In a bathing suit? Or are you skinny-dipping, I wonder? Naughty girl, I think you are, aren't you?' Mr Bung avails himself of a second tissue. 'While you're bobbing about so beautifully, Delia, I think perhaps you'll find you'd like to introduce yourself properly.'

And what a sugar-sweet smile of girlish submission she gives him! 'Je suis l'atome de Delia.'

An *atom*? But the course instructor had said nothing

on this! Regression and past lives, certainly, but psycho-*physiological* reductions of the personality were surely incredibly rare. Certainly there was no mention of atomic theory in the manual they had been given. Mr Bung is not entirely sure what it means anyway. He avails himself of a third tissue and takes a calming sip of artichoke tea. He sits back in his armchair to enable a proper clinical observation. 'An atom, you say? Aren't they very small?'

'Whee,' she giggles happily at him, 'whee whee.'

A remarkable thing the human mind, *this* human mind.

Mr Bung continues to observe the patient for some time, pausing only to relieve himself of further mucus clumps and wipe his dampening hands.

When his tissue box is empty he gets up and treats himself to a walk around the patient in order to observe her immensity from every angle. Returning to his seat he leans and presses his forefinger into her soft smooth forehead. 'The doctor is talking directly to Delia now, who I know is in there, somewhere inside the atom. Delia, when I remove my finger you will drift away into the deepest of sleeps.'

Mr Bung admires the instant toppling of the head, the sagging of the breasts. He lifts a wrist and drops it – delighting in how it bounces on the patient's thigh. He rolls off a hospital sock and pinches a toe – she does not flinch! Mr Bung sits back in his chair taking a steadying sip of tea. What a subject. Textbook. Exceptional really.

'Delia,' he says. 'Delia Delia Delia.' This name of hers that does not match the one on her identity card. 'Who are you?'

And an idea, the tiniest germ of something suddenly

sprouts in his mind. The hypnotist rubs his hands on his trousers and takes up his pencil and pad.

Outside the asylum's barred windows the bruised sky darkens as evening sets in. The hypnotist turns the desk lamp on. His entranced patient is illuminated, as statuesque in her own way as the Golden Buddha of the Zen monastery. She is surely just as magnificent.

Urgently the hypnotist begins to scribble.

Delivered Up, As If on a Plate
With Noodles

Night is beginning to seep into the pit of the mountain valleys as a black jeep turns west of Dalat onto route twenty-seven, the unmetalled track that creeps like a worm into the heart of the Central Highlands.

There has been no noise from the boot for an hour now.

Chief Duong casts a grateful smile into the rear-view mirror, thinking of the boy swaddled in a bedsheet back there. The boy who had simply landed in his lap. There was no other way of putting it. Duong had needed him and the boy had come.

One day he will tell the story. One day sitting in the afternoon shade at Emperor Prawn Farm watching the workers sifting busily, with Lila's children playing in the sand around him. After all, it has occurred to him, once today is done he will be able to buy his daughter any husband she wishes and possibly – Duong's smile broadens – possibly her sight back too. What a miracle that would be. And not just a miracle but an aid – the greatest of aids perhaps – in the process of marital thawing. If such a thing was still possible (and not that Po was entirely innocent herself in the matter of the gravel truck, of course, but he would let that go). On this happy future day, probably over a shellfish supper, he will tell the grandchildren the story of how Sam Porcini came to stay. Maybe Sam could marry Lila himself. Such things are not beyond the realms of possibility. Not with a daughter as beautiful as his Lila. Overcome with happy futures, Chief Duong does not know whether to cry or sing. It is a testament to his talents that he manages to do both and keep the car on the track.

As he sat in his jeep, the sudden bang inside the radio station had sounded no more exciting to the chief than a blown gasket or a gas canister popping somewhere. Duong hadn't given the noise a second thought. Although it is strange to think this now he is motoring along so joyfully, but at the time his forehead was pressed against the steering wheel. At the time, he was thinking of potholes.

So he hadn't seen him coming – the boy, his yellow hair flopping as he sprinted from the radio station's fire exit. He hadn't heard the screams from the building, nor noticed the sound of the jeep's door slamming as the boy leaped into the back.

It was the voice he noticed first, foreign and persistent, drilling into his miserable consciousness. The voice that kept on and on urgently. Duong's head turned before he was aware of it, and he discovered him sitting there, delivered up as if on a plate with noodles: the British footballer.

Duong rubbed his wet eyes dry as he took in the vision. Rubbed the pink-faced blue-eyed apparition into reality. Slowly Duong began to smile at this boy, who was sitting in the back gesticulating, shouting, urging him to do something with the car. Pointing at the key and the wheel. And from a shaky and disbelieving start it had grown and grown, this smile of Duong's, until even the boy in the back had to shield his eyes, because it seemed quite simply as if every supernova in every galaxy was simultaneously exploding over central Saigon.

Duong smiled at the boy and locked the doors and started the engine. It had been that simple. He drove steadily, unsuspiciously, and with some singing, out of the city limits. He hadn't looked back.

The jeep churns on through orange mud. In the darkness the arable hills of strawberry and avocado farms and tea and coffee plantations have given way to thick bamboo forests, and rising above them the potassium-stripped spikes of the dragon's backbone. For an hour Duong has encountered not so much as a goat. He turns the headlights to full beam and yawns. A fruit bat streaks past the window, scooping up firefly clouds. Far off in the forest a baboon or a monkey is hooting. As the jeep growls around another summit Duong's exhaustion mingles with a familiar bliss: he is coming home.

The Finest Dish Is Incomplete Without a Dash of Fermented Fish Sauce

A half moon hangs over a Highland lake, its reflection a knuckle of bone on the black water. In the lilies at the shoreline, fishing canoes lie still as sarcophagi. In these dead hours of night, the small settlement of thatched longhouses between the lake and the forest stands grey and silent but for the shuffling of animals under the wooden stilts, or the clunking of a late-night ladle in a rum jar.

Inside a rotting longhouse that remains as it was built, close to the water and far from the eyes of village life, a sickle-backed figure bats away from her ear the spectral breath of her husband, and throws a toad into a hissing basket. She shakes out a bedding roll next to the fire plate. Shrunken into her decrepitude, Mrs Poonana Duong is shorter now than the village children. Her vision is cloudy, her skin snags on her bones and crackles to the touch. But her ears are strong. Age has not yet made off with her hearing, and certainly it will never steal away with her recognition of the hum of a 1998 Suzuki two-litre fuel injection engine – such as she is sure she is hearing now.

The old woman hauls herself from her bedding roll and hobbles to the door, turning her best ear to the east. Perhaps she is imagining it once again. But the village dogs are out and barking in the direction of the road. This time, surely, she is not mistaken. Giddiness floods her veins: it has been so long.

What to do? Relight the fire – he must have some warmth from the night's chill. Clean the waste from the hut – it will never do to receive him like this. Change her clothes – or he will think she is already three years in the tomb! She turns up the lamp and lets out a cry – the pisspot! Sloshing it out on the steps, she can already see pinpricks of light puncturing the distant forest. 'Quiet!' she hisses to the snakes in the baskets. 'Get off me!' she snarls to the ghost of her husband hovering by her throat.

If only there were time to light the fire, but there isn't. There is just time enough to hide the pisspot and sweep the floor and brush down her skirts, because the Suzuki is entering the village. It is crawling along the village track. In a matter of minutes the planked steps are shaking, and with a shout of 'Mother Prawn, it is I!' her one surviving son is flinging back the door, home at last, every plump cell of him.

The old woman lowers her head and charges.

'My piglet runt, my emperor prawnlet, my leftover lump no sickness or foreigners will ever take away. I knew he would come while his mummy was still in the world. Husband, where do you hide yourself? I see you skulking there behind the rum jars. You shall not have this one too, you hear? You shall not take him away.'

Duong straightens himself from the maternal impact and bends to extract the skull that is boring into his belly. Where once were scents of cardamom and fresh split peppercorns now remains only urine and the sweetness of decay. 'Let me look at you, Mummy.'

But Mrs Duong is already jumping back. Her hands are slapping her son's cheeks, her knuckles are digging for flesh on his hips. Her fingers are frisking down chins. 'But how thin he has become!' A blackened thumb jabs his jugular. 'But how weak and watery this pulse is!'

And now comes disgust, spat onto the planks at Duong's feet with a legendary ferocity that, along with a serrated shovel, once kept off five pillaging GIs for three days. 'Pah! That stinking Southern madam! That so-called wife I said to throw away! Two children, no more, she gives, and look how she is starving Mummy's piglet. Starving him to death. Didn't I say she would take all Mummy's piglet's truffles all for her greedy self. Didn't I tell my piglet so? Pah! But Mummy is wasting time!' The old woman scuttles off to haul a blackened pot onto the brazier above the fire slab. 'Mummy must lay a fire. Mummy's son is being murdered alive by those said to care for him and Mummy is wasting time. She must wring a chicken and blood a toad. He will have his special soup. And then the Emperor Prawn will tell his Mother Prawn how life passes in the city with his children and with that – pah pah pah!' Poonana spits out a daughter-in-law into the cooking pot. 'He will stay some days to recover his strength. I have a pig ripe and ready for the knife. We'll soon stretch that stomach of his. Come, come, sit.' She kicks up a pile of rags on the floor. A harvest mouse makes a run for a hole in the wall.

Duong has not moved from the entrance. He is keeping an eye out the door. 'Actually, Mummy, I need your help with a Top Secret Policing Mission. Some soup would be nice but don't bother with the pig – I am afraid to say my Secret Mission necessitates my return to Dalat at dawn.'

His mother's hands bat away this nonsense. She lights a bundle of twigs under the cauldron and hangs the paraffin lamp on its stand. In the firelight jars of pickled crows and rats glow amber. Bunches of drying herbs grow shadows tall as trees.

'Perhaps a little crow wine,' Duong concedes, heading outside. 'I'll be back in a moment, Mummy, I have a present to fetch you.'

Poonana stops her bustling to watch her son leave. His face is puffy. A sign of something out of sorts. And that pulse!

'That weak and watery pulse!' her husband hisses in her ear.

'You be quiet, Mr I-know-nothing-but-I-can't-stop-talking!'

'You try and make me, hag-wife.'

'Pah!' she says, slapping the air behind her. A fresh rattlesnake will be restorative. Something to encourage the appetite. But first she will kill a hen, the one that has not been pushing out so many eggs of late.

Mrs Duong's grip is no longer strong and the bird's claws are still spasming against her skirts when the hut's steps shudder for a second time.

The shock of what she sees almost does for her.

In the entrance stands her son. But behind and towering high above him, filling every inch of air to the rafters, is nothing less than a monstrous quivering grub.

The old woman shrieks. Her hands fly up to shield her eyes. The hen's skull smashes on the floor. 'Aie aie aie,' she cries, peeking behind a thumb for confirmation. 'This so-called son brings a monster into his mother's home.'

Duong tugs gently on the rope tied around the waist

of the cocooned creature. 'Mummy, may I introduce Mr Porcini. He's a footballer from England and I'd like him to be your guest for a day or two. Mr Sam Porcini, please be acquainted with Mrs Poonana Duong.'

Sam has spent several hours wondering whether, in the back of his mind, he'd known the black jeep parked behind the radio station wasn't a security vehicle, and if so, why he had jumped in. And when he thought about it, hadn't he also recognised on some subconscious level that the sudden bang in the building wasn't in all probability a bomb or a gun but simply something exploding in the kitchen. A gas canister maybe. So, really, the crowd's screams shouldn't have set him off. But they had. Tone had shouted, 'Threat level one!' And like a dipped sheep he'd leaped off the podium and legged it out the fire escape. And then he'd jumped into the car in the alley, his heart pounding with dumb excitement. *He had jumped into the car.* Just like a sheep.

So, frankly, Sam concluded, as he lay swaddled in the boot as the car drove interminably on, quite frankly he'd just become an accessory to his own abduction. 'Not feeling so smart now, are we, kiddo?' Thirsthead popped into his head to say, God help him. And he'd need help now, poor old Tone, letting the performing monkey slip his chain. Despite the insulation tape sealing his mouth, Sam feels an overwhelming urge to laugh.

'Better safe than sorry.' That was the motto presented on PowerPoint at the pre-tour briefing by the Gola-Cola International Talent Manager, Sherry-Sioux Ballou, one of those American women sculpted entirely from peroxide and cartilage.

'Sammy honey,' she had said, flashing black-lashed violet eyes at him, 'you may see yourself as a simple footballer and an East London Italian immigrant mother's son, and that's real cute and very marketable. But to me, honey, you are so much more precious than that. To me,' a red-clawed hand gripped Sam's thigh and the violet eyes hardened to amethyst splinters, 'you are no less precious than an Old Master picked up at an auction, a Picasso or a Van Gogh, say. You are my *Sunflowers*, honey.' The PowerPoint screen clicked through several Old Masters to scenes of blindfolded hostages, guns jammed against their skulls. Ms Ballou's claws were sinking into his skin. 'And gee, Sammy, I guess you understand that if a lady's gone to all the effort of buying herself some *Sunflowers*, she'd sure like to keep them safe.'

Sam had wondered whether Sherry-Sioux knew this was the exact repeat of a lecture she'd given him two years before, when she'd popped by during the blood tests at the insurance medical. If he remembered correctly, and he generally did, her eyes had been jade on that occasion.

'Asia's a crazy old place, honey. Sure, we'll have you on twenty-four-hour security detail. Sure, you won't take a shit without us knowing about it. But you hear danger – you run. You smell danger – you run. Get out, get out, as fast as you can – *keep the* Sunflowers *safe from the kidnap man*.'

In the boot Sam shivered. He *had* just run away from danger, hadn't he? So in a way he was following the correct protocol. Perhaps it wasn't totally his fault. Perhaps getting kidnapped was simply circumstantial bad luck. Tone was probably taking his magnifying glass to the liability clause on the Gola-Cola contract right now.

But still – the car. Why had he got in the car?

His mother had always warned him his lust for adventure would land him in trouble. 'Marco Polo's ghost walks your veins,' she'd say when she was feeling sentimental about it. And 'You're just like your good-for-bloody-nothing, vanished-down-a-crack-in-the-crazy-paving, so-called father,' when she was not.

Sam felt a stab of guilt. His mother would be beside herself when she found out what had happened to him. She'd never taken to Sherry-Sioux Ballou or her global plans. Thoughtless. He'd been stupid and thoughtless – just like his good-for-nothing father. Sam tried to kick at the door. Stupid and thoughtless, and now thoroughly stuck.

And this got Sam to thinking about the moment he could kid himself no longer that they were just taking the long route back to the hotel. The moment the driver had pulled over with nothing but paddy fields in sight, produced a pistol and turned it on Sam in the back seat.

'Good morning,' the man had said in English, then gave him a thumbs up and pointed to the boot. He showed him a photograph of a pretty schoolgirl, as if in explanation. God, Sam hoped the man wasn't into that sort of thing.

The man had helped Sam into the boot with a big smile. But then, as kidnappers go, this one had just been handed rather a lucky break. And it was an undeniable fact that Sam hadn't struggled, but had shown further accessorisation by slipping on the handcuffs as requested while the man bound his ankles. The man had given him a drink of water and stuffed a pillow under his head before patting him on the shoulder and taping over his mouth. All in all, the initial signs weren't too bad.

Careful, Sam thought. If he wasn't careful he'd be

succumbing to Stockholm syndrome straight away. He began to mull over the repercussions. This was not exactly how he'd envisaged his career ending up when he'd first gone to the under-seven kickabouts on Hackney Marshes of a Sunday. It was probably best not to think about the repercussions. So he tried to figure out what the girl in the photograph had to do with all this; perhaps it was something to do with Gola-Cola rotting her teeth, some kind of revenge for that. And while he was deciding if he had it within him to inflict violence if it came to it, like his grandfather in the Puglian Resistance, if his mother could be believed, or whether he'd be better off directing his brain to something comforting, like running through the nutritional content of a few family recipes – spaghetti and meatballs or the legendary Porcini panini coronation chicken mix, perhaps – while he was thinking all this, Sam finally dozed off.

Duong helps the boy down to the floor and props him against a post. 'Relax,' he says in Vietnamese, patting the boy's head, hooded in a dragonfruit print pillowcase, and tying the rope around the post. He pats him again. 'Do not mind the noise, it is only my mother.'

Mrs Duong is undoubtedly making quite a ruckus. She is charging around the longhouse looking for her shovel. She is screaming and bouncing up and down on the boards. She is gnashing what remains of her teeth.

Beneath the pillowcase Sam begins hurriedly breaking down the nutritional content of baked ziti with low-fat parmesan. Under no circumstances, he tells himself, pay any attention to whatever kerfuffle is going on out there. It's probably best that you can't see.

He is probably right about that because Mrs Duong has found her shovel behind the snake baskets and is making a sprint for the boy. Duong intercepts, grabbing her arms. 'The Westerner is young,' he pants, trying to waltz his mother back along the hut, 'also very very VIP. Do not frighten him, Mummy.'

Mrs Duong spits on the floor. 'A Westerner is inside? My Emperor Prawn brings his Mother Prawn a Westerner? Is it a GI like the ones that took all my bravest sons? My silly youngest son brings a GI to kill off his mummy and kill himself too.' She drops the shovel. She wonders what might be achieved by a quick sideways sling of a frying pan. 'Are you in league with your father?'

'What? No. Listen, Mummy, this one doesn't want to harm us.'

'Pah.'

'Also, Mummy, he is to stay alive at all times.'

'Pah!' Poonana ducks from her son's grip and races for a scythe hanging on the wall by the crow jars.

'The boy is helping me out.'

She darts forward and is body blocked by her son.

'He is, Mummy. We must remember he is VIP.'

'Pah.'

'He is a special VIP friend of the family.'

'Pah.' Mrs Duong feints left, feints right and makes it past her son. She raises the scythe above the cocooned footballer.

'Mummy, stop! Do you want me to put him back in the car and drive away?'

The scythe wobbles.

'Because I will, Mummy, I will if I have to!'

'Show it me.'

'Alive, Mummy. This one stays alive.'

'Let me see.'

'Promise me. Otherwise I say goodbye Mummy and I don't come back.'

'Pah.'

'I mean it, Mummy. Not ever. Drop the scythe.'

Mrs Duong gives the smallest of shrugs – which is as much of a submission as this formidable woman has ever been known to make. She lays the scythe on the floor.

Duong eases the pillowcase from the boy's head.

Fluffy yellow hair and berry-bright cheeks appear. And despite the advancement in her years and the shock of old traumas resurfacing in the past ten minutes, Mrs Duong gasps with delight. 'A cuckoo! Just like a baby cuckoo!' Mrs Duong claps her hands. 'Did you see what he did, son? Did you see how he blinked! Do you see the size of this enormous head he has!' She hovers close, a black thumb trembling near Sam's nose. 'The size of all of him!' Sitting down, the Westerner is almost as tall as Mrs Duong. Suddenly he sneezes and she is compelled to giggle. 'Can I touch him?'

'Policing business, Mummy. He is here under the greatest level of secrecy.' Duong wipes Sam's nose with a tissue. 'He is our honoured guest.' The boy looks not much older than Fang. Meatier though. Fang is finer-boned, thinks Duong, registering with a moment's surprise his satisfaction with this realisation about his fugitive son. He pinches the boy's cheek paternally. 'So, Mummy, I was wondering whether Mr Porcini might be your honoured guest for a day or two?'

'He has a mangrove root for a nose. Can I touch it?'

'Well, Mummy? He will be good company for you.'

Mrs Duong cackles happily. 'I tell you your father will not like it.'

While Mrs Duong puts the soup on, Duong makes three trips to the car to fetch her guest's necessities. Poonana is squeezing a bulltoad's bile into the cauldron when Duong returns with a black box. It has grown hot inside the long-house. Duong unwraps the sheets from the boy's body. To look at him now in his skimpy green shorts, Duong cannot think how this boy managed to make so many millions by running around on grass. *Football?* That counted for nothing in this Highland place. How many of those big football Americans had he seen crying and dying in these hills? Duong shakes his head and puts a bottle of lager into the boy's manacled hands. 'Good morning,' he says in English.

'Good morning, Vietnam,' Sam says in Vietnamese, drinking steadily, concentrating on the taste and doing his best to ignore the black box that has been placed in front of him. Concentrating on hops and barley and not the wires from the box that the kidnapper is unwinding and clipping to his manacles. 'Good morning, Vietnam.' Why hadn't he learned more Vietnamese? Why had he got in the car?

'Supper is ready,' Poonana says. 'He looks anaemic, so I've chopped in a young adder.'

Duong sets to his bowl with enthusiasm. It is the most delicious of soups – the sourness of the toad bile slices through the silken chicken, the softness of the rice cushions the adder's muscular flesh. Duong takes a second bowl, eating quickly and in silence. He lays down his chopsticks and drains the remaining liquid in one gulp. 'That was the most balanced of soups, Mummy. I feel quite restored.'

But the boy has not touched his bowl.

'He's not touching his bowl,' Poonana says.

'No, Mummy, he isn't.'

He really isn't. Sam has screwed his eyes shut. He has abandoned all ziti calculations and contemplations of barley and he is willing himself back to the most comforting place of all: a muggy sandwich shop just after school; a mother's hug and a bowl of minestrone waiting on the stove for him.

'The toad's bile is best taken warm.' Poonana removes the ladle from the cauldron. 'Perhaps he does not know how to eat with sticks. I will feed him.'

'No, Mummy, wait. His eyes are closed. He could be praying.'

'Pah! Your wife is the praying sort and look where that got her. Fat, they say. Fat as your house is tall is what I hear! Not that I am ever invited to this house of yours. Full of Southern fancies is what I hear.'

Duong refrains from entering an unwinnable debate. He turns to the footballer, who is staring at the bowl, his berry-bright cheeks paling. 'You are a big boy, yes? Like the mountain bear you must eat to keep up your strength. My mother makes the finest soup in the world. Watch me.' He lifts his own bowl and slurps out the dregs with a big smile. 'Easier than suckling on a wet breast, yes?'

The boy makes no move.

Duong repeats the demonstration.

Still the required response is not forthcoming. Poonana has been highly respectful to her guest, but the two prized hen's feet bob in the boy's broth untouched.

Duong finishes a third bowl, taking his time, as provincial policing manuals advise a wise man to do when faced with unpleasant but necessary decisions.

Duong lays down his bowl and wipes his mouth and hands. He has decided. 'OK, Mummy, once we set a plan of action we do not deviate until resolutions are resolved. This is the first rule of man management – follow through.' From his briefcase Duong extracts three laminated cards, which a Scottish suspected drug smuggler has kindly translated for him. 'Watch closely, Mummy. I will be firm but fair. This will be an example of how to proceed if insubordination occurs during your VIP guest's stay.'

Duong reads the Vietnamese on each card and then selects one. This he places at the boy's feet and turns over to the English translation:

TAKE A DUMP IN THE BUCKET IF REQUIRED
EAT / DRINK PLEASE, THIS SHITE IS GOOD FOR
   YOU
UP THE RANGERS.

With a sob the footballer looks down into his congealing bowl. Duong smiles encouragingly and presents a second card:

DO AS YOU ARE BLEEDING WELL ASKED, MATE
I MEAN YOU NO HARM
UP THE RANGERS.

The chicken feet remain untouched.

'You see what I'm doing, Mummy, I'm giving our guest a chance, yes? In the policing manual it is called take-up time. Time to consider before acting. Because it is very important he takes responsibility for his actions.'

But although Duong sees the boy is beginning to weep

with the effect of considering the bowl, he is showing no sign of progressing to action. Duong wishes he had more cards to express the necessity of eating. 'Nutrition is a man's best friend,' he tells the boy and pinches a calf muscle as evidence. 'Come along, my mountain bear.' He smiles and gives the first card another tap.

But the boy just hangs his head.

'OK, Mummy, after take-up time it is important to understand the consequences of choice, yes? Mr Porcini has chosen not to eat, as invited. But Mr Porcini must also be helped to learn to make the right choices. Sometimes it is necessary to help people in this way.' With a friendly nod to the boy Duong inserts a car battery into the black box. He flicks a switch and the box begins to hum. He presents the third card to the footballer.

IT IS A SHORT SHARP SHOCK
IT WILL NOT HAVE A LASTING IMPACT ON
   YOUR CAREER
UP THE RANGERS.

Sam reads the card and jerks himself back from the man with his box. 'Please, no. Please no, I'll do or say anything you want, but please, no.'

Duong reaches and pats him on the cheek. 'Hush, Mr Porcini, there's no need to get upset, no need at all.' Not one hour in the Highlands, he thinks, this one wouldn't last one hour. 'A brief education, that is all this is. I will make it very brief. In life there is always some unpleasantness – the finest dish is incomplete without a dash of fermented fish sauce, is it not? My own dear son withstood it magnificently, you know. And I'll tell you in confidence, a certain lady I know tells me some people rather like it.'

But, of course, the boy doesn't understand him. The boy is crying.

'Please don't cry. This is only necessary because of my Lila. That is the only reason why we must do this. I know you are not a miscreant. Truth be told, I am not behaving totally inside the bounds of the law myself. And I offer you apologies for this. But it is for Lila. If you knew her you would understand.' Duong wipes the boy's tears and then wipes his own face too. He gives a thumbs up and returns to the box, resolved to proceed as quickly and kindly as possible.

'Watch me closely, Mummy. Three pulses, this is all that is needed.' He checks the batteries. 'Up for on with the main lever, then you flick the smaller switch and count two seconds. Watch me and count.'

Duong flicks the switch up. The boy stiffens. He flicks it down. The boy slumps. 'That's all there is to it. Have a go, Mummy, quickly while he is still dazed.'

Poonana cackles with delight at the magic that makes the boy dance to the flick of her finger. Blood floods into the chambers of her old heart.

'Down, Mummy! Flick it down!' Duong forces her finger from the box. 'That was far too long. You must be most careful with the dosage. Two seconds, no more. Always remember that this is our VIP guest. Also remember Mr Porcini is a Westerner. Most likely he has been brought up the soft way with no experience of steeling the self. In addition, there is limited life in the batteries.'

Poonana watches her son coax the boy back into a sitting position. 'A marvel,' she giggles, her crow-bright eyes dancing. She pays no attention to her husband, who is splashing in the cauldron behind her and spitting in her ear. She is beyond such petty matrimonial teasing. She is transfixed by the twitch in the boy's pale thighs, and the clouds clearing from the blue of his eyes. 'Such magical movement of the flesh.'

'Electricity, Mummy. One hundred per cent natural. Now, the important thing is reinforcement. That is how we learn. Bring him a fresh bowl of soup.'

Poonana claps her hands. 'How eager he is!'

For sure enough, Sam Porcini's trembling hands are sloshing the bowl up to his lips. He is chomping on claws and gulping down gristle, his eyes clamped closed. He is gagging and swallowing and chewing again.

'Better than the rubber-tyre rubbish these Westerners eat. We will probably return him twice as healthy to his home.' Duong rubs Sam's back as he drains the bowl. 'You see what I'm doing now, Mummy? It is always important to demonstrate your pleasure when compliance is achieved.'

Poonana snatches up the empty bowl and returns to the cauldron to fill it. 'But he is so big, he must eat more.'

Sam bursts into tears.

'Enough, Mummy.' Duong sits down next to the boy and puts his arm around as much of the vast shoulders as he can reach. 'He is probably just overtired from the journey. Save the rest for his breakfast. Now please brew up your valerian stew, the strongest you have. This will be the kindest way to transport him.'

Duong gives the boy's yellow hair a paternal kiss. 'Don't worry, you'll have a lovely holiday, I promise you. When you are a father you will understand how necessary all this is. Perhaps one day I will ask my own son to write to you and explain. He is most proficient in your language, my son. Always top of the class.'

Poonana sighs to see this fluffy-headed cuckoo in her little son's embrace. 'He is so big,' she sighs. 'For how many days may I keep him?'

An hour later, having obediently drunk a honeyed sleeping draught, Sam Porcini is re-bound inside a dragonfruit print cocoon. With the old woman taking up the rope, and Duong steering the boy's swaying body, they totter to the edge of the lake. The night sky is paling and a rumbling frog chorus clambers onto grey lily pads to observe this curious sight. Duong lays the footballer along the length of a wide canoe and packs the necessary equipment around him. Soon enough, snug beneath his sheet, the boy begins to snore. Duong sits with the lantern at the stern and Poonana stands at the bow and takes up the long oar. They set out across the lake for the far shore and the island known locally, and with some trepidation, as the Island of the Dead.

The Island of the Dead

News of Sam Porcini's disappearance travels the globe in seismic shockwaves.

'Good morning, Vietnam!' the Scunthorpe striker bellows on a billion television screens, his arms raised in salutation. 'Good morning, Vietnam,' he cries as a small bang is heard somewhere off camera and an orange-faced white-haired man shouts into a lapel. Sam Porcini puts his hand to his ear and is seen – last seen – jumping from the podium and racing out of a back door.

Biggest mystery since Lord Lucan! British tabloids screech in black-topped special editions. *Priceless Porcini vanishes into thin air!*

My terrorist fears: exclusive interview with Porcini agent, Tony Thirsthead.

He did it for love and he's not coming back! Psychic Peg gives her predictions on the runaway footballer.

'I will do everything within my powers to find out what has happened to Sam,' a Scunthorpe-scarfed British Prime Minister announces, exiting a Middle East press conference to hold an emergency media briefing. 'This is my number-one priority. People of Britain, please stay calm.'

But fans are hurling themselves onto locked Scunthorpe stadium gates. Civic community services begin twenty-four-hour counselling shifts. Celebrity magazines are spinning into memorial meltdown.

And Sam? Far from the pandemonium, about ten thousand kilometres away, in fact, on a small cemetery island known locally as the Island of the Dead and uninhabited by the living for this very reason, Sam is snoozing. A red sun rolls up through dawn mists and warms his face as he rocks peacefully in a canoe by the shore, stalked by curious cormorants and guarded by a sickle-backed old woman.

Some fifty metres inland, a little police chief is standing in waist-high grass in front of a stilted tomb house with a bottle of lager and a plastic bag. He has been standing in front of the unopened hatch for some minutes. He has been reminding himself it is not necessary to be nervous about what he is about to do. Not necessary at all.

Sweat starts to plop from his bushy brows as he reaches for the handle on the hatch. All he has to do is open it. That is all. Technically, it constitutes part of to-do twenty-eight – the last on his list for the day. Technically, this last to-do constitutes a cause for celebration. But Duong is beginning to realise to-do twenty-eight has many parts – a far worse action must follow the opening of the hatch. Better, perhaps, not to think about that now. Concentrate on beginning to-do twenty-eight. Ends are harder to stop, the policing manual advises, once beginnings are begun.

So he does it. He opens the hatch.

'Hello, Daddy,' he says.

Squat within a circle of creamy bones on the corpse-board, a cobwebbed skull stares back and makes no reply.

Not that it can, Duong reminds himself. Nevertheless, on eyeing the remnants of no less a personage than the village chieftain – a fearsome man whose mysterious death in his prime still had loose tongues clucking – Duong's heart grows fluttery as a bird in a box. 'Apologies I do not bring whisky, Daddy.' He twists the cap off the lager and places the bottle next to a dusty Gola-Cola can in the far corner of the corpseboard. He watches the bottle.

Nothing happens.

Not that it would. Duong banishes his mother's superstitions and focuses on the nobility of the reason behind what he is about to do. 'Forgive me, Daddy, but this is for your granddaughter. I know you never met her, but I think you would have got on if you had.' Duong clears his throat and shakes open the plastic bag. 'It is only a temporary procedure.'

He hesitates.

A millipede is weaving through the skull's nasal cavities.

Duong reminds himself of his own identity, no longer the family runt but a resting police chief, a man of considerable – if temporarily suspended – provincial status, soon to be well monied and in time possibly in possession of a thriving shrimp farm, if not a statue. He shakes out the plastic bag and stretches a hand for the tiniest toe bone.

The skull's empty sockets stare back.

Old Chieftain Duong, it was said, could outstare the moon.

'You still dithering?' Duong is delivered of a dig in the ribs. 'My city son is afraid of his father's scrap ends! Stand aside. And you, you old bully,' Poonana swipes a hand at the air behind her ear, 'you can shut up. I've been waiting to do this for years.'

She grabs the skull and blows it clean of insects and

dumps it in Duong's bag. Handfuls of bones clatter in behind. 'There, done.'

Not for nothing had the chieftain and his wife been considered well matched.

The bag of bones is dumped in the long grass beneath the stilted tomb. The lager bottle – declared 'a useful pisspot' and 'wasted on that bully's ghost' – is drained dry. Following this, Sam Porcini is rolled up the shore and hoisted with some effort onto the corpseboard and unwrapped from his dragonfruit bedding. Far away in valerian dreams his left toe nudges a ball past the Leyton Orient's under-tens' goalie. A finger uncurls and points to a long-ago spectators' stand where a man lifts a polystyrene cup in proud acknowledgement.

Duong smiles fondly and fetches the batteries and black box. He loops rope through Sam's handcuffs and ties it to the post behind the boy's head. He makes adjustments for comfort, loosening the cuffs on Sam's wrists, and stuffing the pillowcase beneath his head with armfuls of soft grass. Finally, he removes the emerald boots from the footballer's big feet. A grubby sock slips off Sam's left foot and Duong gasps. He has been honoured with a rare sight: webs of skin join each one of the footballer's toes. And because curiosity is a tap a policeman cannot turn off, Duong checks the right foot, which is equally impeded.

A little embarrassed for this superstar – for some reason his son's own elegant arched insteps dance into mind – Duong lifts Sam's manacled hands to tuck the dragonfruit sheet around him. 'Sleep well, my froggy-footed boy. Have the best of dreams under the roof of a thousand stars.'

Poonana joins her son, and for a moment the Duongs stare at their guest asleep in the family tomb.

'He looks content.'

'He fits right in.' Poonana pinches the tip of a toe poking up under the sheet. 'Valerian is good for dreams.'

Duong consults his notepad for any additional instructions he has written down. He reminds his mother how to operate the black box. 'Mummy, listen carefully, you must return to check him tonight, but not before. We do not need any neighbours asking questions of you during the day. Mr Porcini is your super-secret VIP guest, so you speak of him to no one. Understand?'

'Pah, no one in the village speaks to their Snake Mother any more. Even for their medicines they send the children.'

'No one?' Duong frowns filially.

'Excepting your father. Can't shut him up.'

Duong adds a twenty-ninth to-do to his pad to remind himself when everything is over to clear up the issue of his mother's care. The peppermint townhouse had never been welcoming. But perhaps in a roomy shrimp farm on a big plot of land, where there might be space for a whole separate wing . . .

'In this instance, silence is helpful. When you return tonight you switch on the box, yes? This is imperative – he is strong, you do this first. We do not want him breaking free and running around the island lost and unhappy. You wake him politely and you give him the bucket to use. You might wash him a little, that would be nice for him, freshening. You show him the cards and feed him a bowl of rice soup – kill your fattest cockerel for today's supper, these sporting types need a lot of meat. Do not worry about the expense, I will bring more birds when I come back. You give him a drink of water and then you spoon him full of valerian paste. You leave when he is asleep, you return tomorrow morning before he awakes – we do not want him feeling lonely – and you repeat the procedure. I will return for him tomorrow night.'

'Sporting types,' Poonana murmurs, pinching the webbing between two toes.

'Require plenty of meat, Mummy.' Duong glances out at the rising sun. 'I must return to Dalat, there are Top Secret things to be attended to. I will return tomorrow night. Gently, Mummy, gently with the pinching. And please remember, his body is not used to electricity. It is last resort only, yes?'

Poonana scores her thumbnail down the footballer's left sole. 'It is so soft.'

'Mummy?'

'Son?'

'Did you hear what I said?'

'So big this boy. So big and soft.'

How Much Should a Man Want?

Chief Duong makes good time on the return journey. The hours fly by, preoccupied as he is by a single question: exactly how much ransom money should he demand?

In his notepad the costs add up like this:

Purchase of Lila's safe return	3,000 American dollars
Assorted outstanding wedding expenses	860,000 dong (40 dollars)
Three hens for Mummy	300,000 dong (14 dollars)

And that, he reflects, is pretty much it. Or it had been before overseas eye operations and retirement shrimp farms came creeping into his calculations. To be quickly joined by thoughts of the medical necessities required for a wife's return to mental health. In addition to all this, Duong has begun to mull over the costs involved in locating a lost son and purchasing pots of paint for the unpepperminted back wall – to celebrate the achievement of all the above.

And as if these significant spending schemes aren't enough, the police chief now finds himself beset by desires for unnecessary fancies, such as an internal dumbwaiter to cheer up his wife (if she is ever returned home), a new vinyl seat for the Hero, and a leather notepad case for himself. It is most peculiar that these items are trivialities he has never contemplated before, yet now they are in his head they seem not to want to leave. It is very hard, thinks Duong, to dig out dug-in ants. The essence of the dilemma, he realises, is this: how much can a man ask for without turning into a capitalist greedy pig? How much should a man want?

By lunchtime, still wrestling with the philosophy of desire, Duong is back home and most surprised to discover Sergeant Yung skipping about the peppermint doorstep in a public display of overexcitement.

'You are resummoned, Chief!' Yung blurts before Duong has even one foot out of the jeep. He flings himself at his boss. 'Isn't it wonderful? I think they want you back!'

Duong peels himself away from his subordinate's embrace before the butcher spots them and jumps to infelicitous conclusions. He remembers carbon-copied letters faxed to Hanoi offices. 'They do?'

'The superintendent requires you urgently. Couldn't reach you on the telephone, so he sent me to find you.'

'I was vacationing,' Duong indicates the jeep's muddy wheels, 'in the west.'

'How lovely, Chief. Oh Chief, you don't think – I mean, you heard the news on the tannoys out west, didn't you? You don't think the superintendent wants you back for – oh Chief,' Yung's eyes gleam with undiminished loyalty and two blobs of glaucoma, 'oh Chief—'

'Sergeant, you will please spit out whatever is choking you.'

'Yes, Chief. Sorry, Chief. It's the missing footballer, Chief.'

'Hmmmm,' Duong straightens his spine and allows himself a smile at the thought – rather delicious – of chasing his own tail. 'It's on the news, is it?'

'Everywhere, Chief. A catastrophe, Chief.'

'Well, I won't deny that my detection skills are among the highest in the Highlands. To create the sharpest of knives it takes many a strike on an old stone, isn't that what they say, Sergeant?'

'Oh certainly, Chief!'

'Hmmmm.' Duong peers at his notepad. He scribbles some calculations. He has forty-eight hours to source the money and deliver it to Mei: a tight but achievable schedule. And returning to work will be a perfect alibi. He beams at Yung and glances up at Lila's window. It will not be long before his silkworm is home safe and sound. Never to be lost again. 'I must take a shower and avail myself of a brief nap. After this I shall drive to the station on the Hero. If you would be so kind, you might arrange for the deskboy to come and give the jeep a scrub out with the mortuary disinfectant. Transported a couple of pigs for my mother, got a little stinky back there.'

'At once, Chief!' Yung salutes and applies himself joyfully to his radio.

Duong enters his home with a happy whistle, pausing to pluck a splinter from a hatchet job to the doorframe. There may just be time to call in at the asylum en route to the station. There are dumbwaiters to be discussed.

Though it has only been a matter of three days, Chief Duong is welcomed back to work with a round of relieved applause. 'Beers for all!' he shouts before striding manfully into his office, where a thin voice is muttering 'So unfair' and a superintending growl is answering 'Agreed, but I assure you this is the safest way to keep an eye – ah, good afternoon, Duong, about time.'

'First-class suspension,' Slimn Jimn springs out of Duong's chair with a gust of eucalyptus, 'not to mention outstanding air-bubble levitational assistance and hydraulic fluid injection.'

Duong places his small box of belongings on the floor.

'Shut the door, there's a fellow,' the superintendent rumbles. He is sprawled in a plastic-wrapped brand-new armchair next to an unfamiliar chrysanthemum bonsai beneath Uncle Ho's old portrait.

Duong squeezes himself past Jimn to resume his seat behind his desk. His feet dangle at the new setting. On the wall Uncle Ho smiles warm and welcoming. The super stares at Duong as though he wants to kill him.

'It's nice to be back,' Duong hazards into the silence.

'I suppose it is for you,' the super growls, shaking his head.

Slimn Jimn blows his nose into his handkerchief. Duong thinks he can make out the smothered words 'So injust'.

'I'll get straight to the point, Duong. Jimn here has done an excellent job of tying up your son-in-law's murder.'

Duong starts in the chair with a squeak. 'He has?'

'He has.'

'I have.'

'Oh.' Duong is thinking uneasily of indications of corruption levelled against the superintendent. Of carbon-copied letters faxed to Hanoi. 'May I enquire who you believe responsible?'

'You may not,' the super says. 'In my book, you've done rather too much enquiring into the wrong sort of business.

However, if Jimn is feeling generous he may offer to explain.'

Jimn sniffs into his handkerchief. 'It is not a matter of having a "belief" about a possible perpetrator, as you put it, there is one hundred per cent *proof*. It was disappointingly easy. I deduced it would be solved most economically by the application of ballistic theory. It was the café owner – old man Han. His prints were all over the firearm discovered at the scene, and although the actual bullet has not been recovered, the weapon and the nature of the brain wound had a one hundred per cent correlation.'

'Old man Han?'

'Indeed.'

'The *café owner*?'

'Indeed.'

'But *Han*?'

'One of the sustaining joys of provincial crime-fighting is the locating of hitherto unexpected hotbeds of criminality in the community. I believe there is a chapter in the latest *Socialist Policing* magazine on just this subject. A modern investigator does not presume that because a man has no criminal record he also has no criminal intent. Twenty per cent of all crimes are virgin acts.'

'But a motive?' Duong cannot shake the thought of carbon-copied letters in governmental in-trays. Letters thick with motive. He avoids the super, whose stare is boring into his skull. 'You're lacking a motive against Han, Jimn.'

'A motive is meaningless in four per cent of all murder cases.'

'But Han used his rifle to kill himself, so naturally his fingerprints would be on it.'

'That's enough, Duong!' There is a thud of a superintending fist on the armchair. 'I don't want to hear another word from you. Goddammit, you've done more than enough.' The super is standing and snarling and quite red in the face. 'I intend to mention this only once. Once, because it is such disloyal and damned despicable behaviour that it wounds me to the core to speak of it. There have been accusations – below board and totally unfounded, little short of lies – that were faxed to Hanoi in a cowardly, anonymous report. Near lies that threw a switch on the track of certain business transactions. Near lies that have required an inordinate amount of sweet-talking on my part to facilitate the restoration of transactions to their rightful track.'

Duong finds himself staring at his desk.

'I wish to make it clear that in return for *not* seeking the desperate snitch who forwarded these allegations to Hanoi – with a local fax number, I might add – I expect all disloyalty to cease. Commissar Nao is dead. He was a sanctimonious meddler, a dinosaur who failed to adapt to modern times. Not to mention he was an out-and-out bonsai cheat. A cheat,' the super thumps the desk, 'who was shot by a man crazy as a thirsty parrot. Case closed.' The super thuds down into the armchair and turns his scowl on the chrysanthemum while regaining his superintending equanimity.

'Perfectly expressed, sir,' Jimn sniffs. 'If I may say so.'

Duong stares at the desk and says nothing.

'Jimn has done rather well,' the super continues. 'I expect I shall be recommending him for a medal of some sort. Though I should say we've had no luck capturing the MLA. They're off the radar now. No word from your son?'

Jimn snorts. 'He wouldn't admit it if he had.'

Duong watches Jimn's slim fingers fold the white silk handkerchief. He thinks of Fang. Also delicately fingered. As well as brave under the application of electricity. And hopefully surviving somewhere in the Highlands. Duong, who has had cause to surprise himself over the past day recalling the finer points of his son, turns proudly to the pong of eucalyptus. 'You're right, Jimn. I don't think I would.'

'Well, as luck would have it for you, Duong, I'm not a man to bear grudges,' the super snarls, 'I've never been that. You're back for a reason. And the reason is, I see the bigger picture not the small worm that wants to eat through it. But let's be clear how I like my worms. How do I like my worms, Duong?'

'I don't know, sir.'

'Under foot, Duong.'

'I see, sir.'

'Crushable at any second.'

'Yes, sir.'

'So, Duong, unfortunately you're back. As to the reason for this meeting, I've decided that Jimn here is to keep his promotion to the position of police chief, as you are most generously being permitted to return to yours. It is most good of Jimn to agree to this.'

'Thank you, sir.'

'The fact is, we are entering a period of great provincial activity and I must be focused on the bigger picture, the big things that are about to happen. And I must have my best man with me on that, Jimn.'

'Thank you, sir.'

'Chief Jimn will lead Operation Green Bottle – the eviction of the Ma slum settlement tomorrow – with the main cohort of men and resources. You, Duong, can pick up any policing slack.' With a show of magnanimity the super unclenches his fists. 'Job share. It is the true socialist way.'

Duong's voice is small. 'Is there anything I should attend to?'

The super gives a snigger. 'I believe there's a Western footballer gone missing. Hanoi's at a loss. All departments in the region have been asked to contribute investigative manpower. I suggest you concentrate on that.'

And now it is Duong's turn, at last, to smile. He is glad of the chair's suspending support for he has grown suddenly giddy. Dollars are spinning down in front of him like leaves in a monsoon wind. Dollars are riding up and down in a shiny dumbwaiter. Shrimp are swimming in dollars. Lila is dancing in dollars.

'Sergeant Yung will constitute your team. I'm sure Hanoi will issue a directive at some point.' The super levers himself out of the armchair and waddles to the door. 'Good day, Duong. Don't forget what happens to worms. Slimn, let's consult on Operation Green Bottle at my place tonight. Seven all right with you? The wife will rustle something up.'

Slimn Jimn slides out behind the super. 'Don't worry about my statutory claims to the co-office, Co-Chief. I shall base myself in the open seating area with my men. If it's all the same to you, I'll pop back for the bonsai. Studies show greenery is integral to the fostering of a tranquil working community. Cerebral processing efficiency has been known to rise three hundred per cent.'

Duong is still swinging his legs and beaming vacantly at Uncle Ho when Jimn returns. Beneath a doodle of a little stilted hut, a note on the pad reads: *Estimated cost of speech therapy for rediscovered son?*

As Jimn removes the chrysanthemum something is triggered in Duong's dollar-dazed mind. There is nothing to be lost now in asking. 'Say, you didn't happen across any large quantities of American money when you searched Commissar Nao's home, did you? Nothing in the glasshouse or up a chimney? A blue plastic bag, perhaps?'

'Ah yes,' Jimn freezes behind the delicate yellow blossoms. 'Commissar Nao, you say. Dollars? Ah no. No. Nothing at all.' He licks his thin lips. 'Why do you ask?'

'No reason.' Duong gets up to help with the door.

'Listen, Duong,' Slimn Jimn hesitates, 'no hard feelings? You know, me and the super and the big thing we're working on?'

'Good heavens no.' Duong grabs his co-chief's hand and shakes it in a haze of happy benevolence. 'Mighty fine watch you have there.'

Jimn's pale face pinkens in two spots. 'Isn't it? Genuine imported Seiko. Water-resistant to five hundred metres. Compass. Calculator. GPS patent pending. A present to myself re. the promotion. Hire purchase of course.'

Duong beams. 'Very nice indeed.' Not one of his thoughts, as he shuts the door behind his co-chief, is on the man's expensive wristwear or its financial origins, but rather Duong is considering a bowl of Man Chu's beef noodle soup, followed by a final calculation or two. And then there is a phone line to be scrambled and an important telephone call to be made.

Not An Easy Calling

'Why are you crying, Delia?'

'They have closed the university. Time of war, they say. I cannot go to study, and if I cannot study I will not be awarded my doctorate. I have just this final year. Without my doctorate all my research will mean nothing. I need to complete my studies. Please don't close the university, please, not for six months.'

'But how old are you now, Delia, twenty-six? Might you not want to marry and have children before it's too late? That would be something. An achievement. Some say the greatest achievement, the most important gift a woman can give her family, and also her country.'

Delia raises her jaw and snorts. 'Look at my country – see how left hand fights with right. This is no place in which to bring new life. And look at me,' she shakes her shorn head, 'see the size of my bones. See this jaw my father says is too strong for the weakness of men. No, I am happy with my vases.'

'But your hair, Delia. I think you have beautiful hair, do you not?'

Delia's hand reaches for a twist of black she imagines to hang behind her. 'My hair shines like first-spun treacle, my father says. It is free as a cormorant's feathers on a windy day, my father says.' She falters in her speech. Tears glisten on her eyelashes. 'Go, Papa, I beg you.'

'Where, Delia?'

'Paris, of course. Professor Lechevre has sent the visa and the letter of employment. He is waiting for you. The university is waiting for you. You must leave now. Go, Papa, I beg you.'

A damp palm pats a soft knee. A mucus throat is cleared. 'This is your doctor speaking, Delia, not your father. Do try not to confuse us.' A warning the hypnotist has had to repeat several times. 'Tell me what your father is saying to you.'

The patient weeps. 'He will not go. I beg you, Papa, you know how I beg you, but you will not go. You are not too old for a new home. How many others have been given this chance, Papa? Every day the message comes from Paris, "Leave now before the flights close." They send tickets and franc bonds too. For Professor Diem is world expert in pre-classical archaeology. They say the position is waiting at the Sorbonne. There is only you who can fill it.' The patient stares at the hypnotist, her eyes blazing. 'But you say, "I am Vietnamese. I grew from this soil I dig. Your mother and your brothers are buried under this soil. What is Paris to me?" It is life, Papa.'

'Excellent, really lovely, Delia.' Mr Bung takes a sip of artichoke tea and checks his watch. Two hours unbroken trance state. 'Marvellous work. We'll take a break.' He leans forward to push a fingertip into his patient's fore-head. 'Float away from this unhappy time. I am going to mop up your tears. If you feel me touching you it will only serve to relax you further and send you deeper and so on and so forth.'

Mr Bung observes the patient slipping into doughy tranquillity, and wipes his hands. Two hours, he recalls, was the instructor's recommended mental max. But with a subconscious the calibre of this one? He allows himself a sigh of admiration. He shakes the dregs of the teapot and wonders about his own stamina, recalling the many sacrifices he has made in the name of healing.

'You were much more bearable as a crap teacher,' the ex-Mrs Bung had grumbled when he first raised the idea of a correspondence course, as offered by the International University of Past Life Healing (correspondence address, PO Box 3645, Alabama, USA). It had been during that awkward month when the unfortunate and entirely unproven incident with the tenth-grader came to the attention of the school authorities. 'It's a pity,' his sour-tongued wife added, 'that your hands have a past life of their own.'

When Mr Bung returned from his ten-day Hypnotrix© training course in Lyons, his wife had already run off with an incense manufacturer from Pleiku. All because she was unable to handle his newly discovered hypnotic talents, he said. She said his suspect behaviour with teenage girls aside, the incense manufacturer had a sound financial future and hadn't squandered the family savings on crackpot courses that taught dirty men how to dominate women's minds.

Which proved how little his wife knew about the healing vocation.

'Jealousy,' he had told her.

'Inappropriate boundaries,' she had replied.

Mr Bung sighs as he considers his patient. It is not an easy calling, the caring profession. He lays a sympathetic palm on the broad expanse of Delia's thigh. 'If you hear me leaving, do not panic. I am only going to refresh my artichoke leaves. Then we will be perfectly placed to continue.'

The Finest Left Toes in the World

'Ten million dollars!' Yung screams, bursting into the chief of police's office and banging the door against the plastic-wrapped armchair Duong has not had a chance to remove.

'Goal!' Duong's head jerks up from a soccer magazine he'd opened in a show of research, only to drop off almost immediately. 'Sergeant Yung,' he says, pulling himself together, and peeling a damp footballing fact from his cheek, 'you will not enter the office of a senior officer unannounced.'

Yung is hopping from one foot to another. Duong shares Mrs Yung's concern for the nervous stress his sergeant allows his body to endure. 'Sincerest apologies, Chief, but the intercom was off. And the telephone.'

Duong rises and replugs the wires. 'Energy conservation is a necessary pursuit, Sergeant, much beloved of our great Uncle, who was ahead of his time. Now of what are you wishing to inform me with such undue energy?'

'Ten million dollars is the ransom demand from the bastard greedy abductor of the footballer, excuse the strength of my language, Chief. Must be some Southern stinking capitalist type – no disrespect to your wife, Chief. Or possibly Chinese.' Pasty at the best of times, Yung's face appears to have mildewed. 'It's terrible news, Chief. Who on earth has ten million dollars?'

'Isn't this all getting a little out of hand, Ho help us?'

Ho smiles down and Duong smiles at Yung. 'I doubt very much the sum mentioned was anything as grand as that, Sergeant. Not for a footballer. You have misheard.'

'Not just any footballer, Chief. One with the finest left toes in the world. One whose league penalty record has stood unblemished for four years, whose courage in last year's cup final remains unsurpassed – scoring the winning goal with a shin splint *and* a dislocated thumb. Oh Chief—'

'Yung, you will please desist from hyperventilation in the office. Sit down on that thing there and calm yourself, there's a good man. This excessive excitement does no good for the digestive functions in a man your age. Think of the grandchildren.'

'But the Party Secretariat is assembling for a broadcast, Chief.'

'For a *footballer*?'

'Yes, Chief.'

'A *foreign* footballer?'

'Yes, Chief.'

'How extraordinary.'

'He is most extraordinary, Chief. Those toes.'

Yung witnesses no inclination in his boss to rise. He hesitates, respectful for the mysterious ways in which the chief's genius works. Yung remembers how the chief had once caught the Phan Rang strangler by such a non-interventionist approach. Three weeks Chief Duong sat behind his desk insisting on a total news blackout as a monster wrung the necks of eighty-four canaries. It had ended only when the strangler wound a length of aviary wire around his own neck. What kind of world was it, he wrote in his suicide note, if no one was bothered about songbirds any more?

But this time? The eyes of the world are on Vietnam, and it is just conceivable, Yung thinks, that the bastard greedy abductor hasn't incarcerated the footballer in a city hellhole, as the papers speculated, but has secreted him in a Central Highland cave or jungle lair. Sam is alone, desperate and most assuredly missing out on key pre-season physiotherapy for his injured ankle. Yung blinks back tears. 'Perhaps we shouldn't miss the broadcast, Chief?'

'It's hardly going to point us to the criminal.'

'With the deepest respect to your genius, Chief, I was thinking of watching it for background research. Your recent holiday has perhaps left some residual unawareness of the fever of feeling flushing the nation.'

The chief flicks through the thirty-page profile of the footballer in the magazine. According to an interview with Mrs Porcini, Sam's favourite dish is something called coronation chicken. An imperial recipe, but Duong wonders whether his own mother could give it a go, to help the boy feel at home. 'I suppose you may be right, Sergeant. It might prove interesting.' He makes a note and rises. 'Very well, lead on. And please don't *run*, Sergeant. I've told you how it confuses the intestines.'

To Duong's eyes it appears every business on Victory Rise has relocated to the Unfolded Lotus for the broadcast from the television set on the pastry display case. Cheers erupt as Hung Duong, co-chief of police, and Thuc Yung, sergeant, lifelong Scunthorpe United fan and dedicated Police Veterans League team left winger, squeeze through the throng to front-row seats, and a free coffee pot. News of Duong's assignment has raced through town.

'All this for a footballer?' he says.

'Such national unity of passion,' Yung sighs. 'Is it not wonderful?'

His boss does not reply. Nor does he take his front-row seat but moves close to the screen, on which a woman wearing a black lace veil is weeping into the bread she is buttering. A caption explains this woman is Comrade Porcini's mother and the owner of a thriving catering establishment in London.

Silence falls in the Unfolded Lotus as the programme cuts to three men in their eighth decades sitting brittle-backed at a baize-covered table, a gold-starred flag and gilt portrait of Ho Chi Minh on the wall behind. On the table are typed briefs, microphones and three glasses of green liquid. The central figure, Nguyen Dai, Interior Minister, and tipped for the top job on the occasion of the President's demise, takes a wincing sip of Gola-Cola and picks up his typed speech.

'The People's Government of the Socialist Republic of Vietnam reacts with regret to the news that British foot-baller Porcini has been abducted. Our nation enjoys strong ties with the British people, and this will continue. The People's Republic of Vietnam remains a welcoming place for international commerce.'

The screen cuts to a female presenter, who informs the nation of the ransom demand made to the British Consulate in Saigon. Ten million dollars is to be sourced within twenty-four hours.

Yung nods, satisfied with this confirmation. His boss, however, is gripping the glass front of the display case with bloodless nails.

Man Chu approaches with a fresh pot of coffee and a stack of rice buns. He is sporting a necklace of Sam Porcini Gola-Cola bunting. 'For the man who is going to catch this bastard greedy abductor. The best beans from Buon Ma Thuot.'

In lacquered cages by the toilets, two baby macaques hoot.

But Chief Duong is not drinking the best beans. He is not acknowledging the cheers of the crowd nor the owner's latest pets. Without a word to Yung, without so much as a finger on a flake of pastry, he has turned and is crashing through the tables. He is making a beeline for the street.

'Wait for me!' Yung cries. He has been watching the arrival on the television screen of a block-jawed American face, sporting a Gola-Cola cap and two brilliant strips of teeth. Yung grabs a sticky bun. 'The chief has no time to eat when genius is afoot!' he shouts proudly, before pursuing Duong outside.

He finds his boss clinging to a lamp post, with sagging knees and the look of a man who has just been unexpectedly drenched.

'Chief? I brought you a bun.'

'Excellent, thank you, Yung.'

'It is still warm, Chief. Is everything all right, Chief?'

His boss has slid a further few inches down the lamp post.

'So, when should we start after this bastard greedy abductor, Chief?' Yung holds out the bun. 'Can you believe the greed of him?'

His boss does not even sniff the bun's edges.

'Chief, do you require a hand?' Yung leans in. 'Only there's people watching.'

Duong glances at the gathering crowd. He hauls himself back up the lamp post. 'I am perfectly well, thank you, Sergeant. I am merely squat thrusting – a necessary physical exercise routine for the over-fifties. I recommend it.'

'Certainly, Chief.'

'Also, I suspect there has been some sort of communication error concerning the amount of money requested. Therefore, your reference to the abductor's greed may not be entirely appropriate, yes? I suspect the person responsible for borrowing this footballer is essentially a man of honour who may have fallen into unfortunate financial difficulties, yes. But, overall, he is upstanding and caring. Just a hunch I have.' Duong releases the lamp post carefully. 'We shall start our investigation with you going back to Man Chu's and ordering me a bowl of chicken noodle soup. Make sure it contains two fresh-boiled thighs. Wait as it is prepared. It should stew for at least fifteen minutes.'

'But, Chief—'

'Right away, Yung.'

Yung sighs and respectfully salutes his boss's departing back. The investigation would perhaps proceed like the case of the Mysteriously Materialising Ostrich Steaks. The chief's commitment to sampling all the region's meat imports (he acquired eight extra kilos of weight and an allergic reaction in the process) had been instrumental in tracing three hundred shipments of the smuggled delicacy all the way back to Vientiane. He hurries into the restaurant in time to enjoy a replay of the footballer's vanishing act. Still, the loyal sergeant takes comfort in one thing –

once the great Chief Duong is properly fed just about anything will be possible.

Alone in his office with the plastic-wrapped armchair jammed against the door, Duong takes out the line-scrambling device from the filing cabinet and connects it between the phone socket on the wall and the handset on his desk. He unplugs the intercom and switches the fan to max. He unwraps a strawberry candy, and as a final precautionary measure he grasps his windpipe and pinches firmly. Then he dials the number of the British Consulate in Saigon.

'I have just witnessed a broadcasting error,' Duong informs a trainee in Visa Affairs. 'Mr Porcini's release will cost ten *thousand* dollars, as stated in my previous call. I am not a greedy capitalist sort and I do not expect to have to clarify the amount again. Ten *thousand* dollars is all I require. I will call tomorrow morning to confirm delivery arrangements. You will please ensure information is corrected in all future television broadcasts.' He crunches the candy noisily. 'This is not a hoax. I know about the toes.'

A Solemn Pledge

'Yowsers, Mike, we've just heard that *twenty* million dollars has been demanded by a source that the Vietnamese government and my own corporation believe to be genuine. Yes, Mike, you heard me right. *Twenty* million. That's a one hundred per cent inflation since yesterday.'

On CBS *Breaking News* a block-jawed man with a strip-light smile stands in front of a frothy vista of popping green Gola-Cola logos and skipping Asian children. He nods and re-forms his expression into a frown. 'Gee, Mike, yes is the simple answer to that. Yes, as a responsible multinational trading organisation, and yes as a family company with a great love for the Vietnamese nation, a great sympathy for the British people, and the greatest respect for the genius of a human being as gifted as young Sam, Gola-Cola International intends to shoulder the full financial burden for the cost of bringing him home alive. To this end, Gola-Cola is seeking to make funds immediately available.'

The man nods. His finger stabs conviction at the viewer. 'Mike. Let me assure you and every one of the billions of viewers out there, as I assured Sam's dear mother Angelita just two hours ago, that I, Bradley Burdock the Third, CEO of Gola-Cola International, will get this boy out alive. That is my solemn pledge. Thank you, Mike. And can I just add that my prayers and the prayers of Gola-Cola's Global Team are with Sam, wherever he might be. God bless.'

Digging for Kings

Abductions and other necessary unpleasantness aside, Chief Duong has had a better than average couple of days. So why spoil it for him by announcing news of this further deployment of misinformation by a mighty multinational that is swinging like a wrecking ball towards his plans? Why alarm him further by revealing the bleeping secret a purple-eyed passenger harbours in her hand luggage beneath her goose-down first-class bed as she skims the clouds above the Pacific Ocean?

No, let the chief whistle his way home from work on his Hero. Let him stop at the asylum with a wrap of roses, where he is denied access because therapy, it seems, is still in progress, and let him take himself home to bed.

He needs his rest because tomorrow is going to be a big day. There's no point waking him with night fears of multi-million-dollar disasters, nor with premonitions of disturbing events on the Island of the Dead. The chief sleeps soundly and dreams of seeing daughters and speaking sons and imagines himself a monkey soldier boy, wrapped up in a young wife's embrace.

While the chief dreams, others in the town are hard at work. Two kilometres away, the lights in a small annexe to the district asylum are on. Therapy, indeed, is still in progress.

Having poured himself a glass of artichoke tea Mr Bung is resettled comfortably in his chair. He raises the glass to his lips, blowing a cooling ripple on the amber surface. Slumped in front of him the patient, Delia Duong, awaits his will.

Mr Bung unwraps a beef and peanut spring roll and consumes it thoughtfully. He wonders what the record for sustaining a trance might be. He wonders which institution, if not the Alabama Past Life University then surely some other illustrious American establishment, would provide grants for the physician talented enough to achieve it. He licks his fingers and exhales happily. 'Delia, my dear,' he whispers, leaning to plunge his palms into the patient's fine knees, 'let us press ahead on our travels. Whither shall we sail now?'

Immediately the patient hunches forward. Her fingers curl to shovels and she begins to scoop at the air, vigorous as a dog in sand.

Mr Bung retreats to a safer distance. 'Careful, Delia.'

The patient's black pupils fix on Bung regally. Regally? Yes, Mr Bung thinks, the woman grows most regal. 'I am always careful when digging for kings.'

'We have no kings in our land, Delia.'

The patient flashes him a lightning look of scorn. 'Are you telling me you know nothing of the Van Lang? The first Viet dynasty, founded in 2879 BC? You have never seen a bronze drum? Did they teach you nothing at school, boy?'

On this occasion Mr Bung allows the slur to pass. 'If you say so, Delia. Seeing as you think you know so much, perhaps you could tell me what year it is now.'

'It is 1972. You really should know that.'

'Of course it is.'

Delia tosses back imaginary black hair and lowers her voice. 'If you promise not to blab, boy, I will let you into a secret.'

Mr Bung wipes his hands on a tissue.

'Well?'

'I promise.'

'On your ancestors' tombs?'

'On my wife's.'

'Very well.' The patient leans close and conspiratorial. 'There is an undiscovered citadel where the greatest of the Van Lang kings were laid to rest with the spoils of their Empire. Everyone assumes they travelled no further south than Phu Tho, but I have a primary text that indicates otherwise. After all, why has no one unearthed a single tomb? Bronze sun drums and spearheads are common as coffee beans, but the intimacies of casket or corpse pit are nowhere to be found. I have been camping here for three weeks. The ancient texts my father left me say this is where the kings are entombed. I am about to discover their resting place on the Highland plateau, and the world will pause in its warring and be amazed.'

Mr Bung coughs a mucus clot into his tissue. 'That's very interesting, Delia.' And in a way he thinks it is. He wishes he had the course manual to hand. He is clearly witnessing the patient's arrival at some kind of junction between her memory and her imagination. 'It's 1972, you say, and whereabouts are you exactly?'

She laughs. Coming from such a heap of a body it is startling – girlish and merry as a mynah. 'I'm not falling for that one! I cannot reveal the location, otherwise you or others might come and plunder what is not yours to find. But I will say my tent is under a banyan tree by a lake and that I am not far from Buon Ma Thuot, although I am not bothered by them.'

'By whom?'

'Just the soldiers – the Minh and the SVA and their Yankees.' She laughs. 'They're all here.'

'And how did you get here, Delia?'

'I walked.'

Remarkable. Mr Bung sips his tea while he considers how to proceed. 'We are telling the truth, aren't we, Delia? We know to tell the doctor the truth. You walked over three hundred kilometres from Saigon to Buon Ma Thuot? During the war?'

'It is not so difficult. A woman alone is not suspicious if her head is down and she is weeping. There are lots of weeping women on the roads, not all can be Cong guerrillas or Yankee-pregnated whores.'

'So why are you crying, Delia?'

Her chin jerks away from him.

'I was only attempting to soothe you.'

'Don't.'

'Don't?'

'No.'

Resistance, Mr Bung thinks with satisfaction, her first sign of resistance. He is surely nearing the nub.

'Ow!' the patient flinches further away. 'Ow, stop, that is jabbing me.'

'But I'm not touching you, Delia.'

'Lay it down at once!' she cries in a gruff Northern accent. 'Lay down the shovel! Lay it down, I say, and stand up slowly or I will be forced to fire.'

'Who is saying this, Delia, this "stand up" business? Who is here now?'

The patient makes no response.

'The doctor has asked you a question, Delia.'

Mr Bung clicks his fingers in front of the patient's eyes. 'Where are you, Delia?'

A Pretty Girl's Sigh Is Sweeter Than Honey

But Delia is far gone from her doctor. She has wriggled down a wormhole of memory and out the other side, and in this place the rising sun is making it hard to see. But there, in a rustling banana palm by the lake, she thinks she spots a monkey.

She hoots. 'But silly me, you're not a monkey at all! You only look like one, with your too bushy eyebrows on that too big head under that too big hat.'

A short figure emerges, rifle first, from the fronds of the palm. 'Lay down your weapon,' it is saying with what appears to be a nervous and certainly a most incongruous grin. 'I shall not tell you again.'

'Hey, monkey-soldier boy, that grin is too big for you!'

'Get up out of the mud, madam. Drop the shovel and stand up. Raise your hands above your head.'

'Even that gun is too big for you!'

'You will not joke please, madam.'

'If you don't mind me saying,' Delia is no longer smiling, 'you have seen too little of life to be walking around with a gun and a grin that are both too big for you. Why don't you run off back to school and let me finish my dig in peace. Or,' she adds levelly, 'kill me quick, if you'd prefer.'

The soldier boy slaps a mosquito against his chest, his look instantly perplexed. He aims the rifle at Delia's heart. 'May I remind you, madam, that my cartridge is loaded. Choose your words with care.'

'Do you know how to use that thing? Only you're waving it around rather freely. And by the way, it's still "miss" with me.'

'Very well, miss, you are under arrest. You are out at dawn, no doubt permitless, in a Viet Minh controlled zone. I have the authority to shoot on the spot for such transgressions.'

'I'm sure you do.'

'Please don't interrupt, miss. From your accent I can tell you are some sort of spy for the imperial-loving Southerners.'

'You make a fair deduction. Proceed. Fire away. I shall not resist.' Delia Diem opens her arms wide as if in welcome. 'Shall I locate my heart for you? It might make things easier.'

The boy's eyebrows leap up. Such a skinny thing, with a head round as an onion bulb and that galactic grin he can't seem to control. 'Why don't you do that, then.'

Delia cages her fingers around the steady thump-thump of her heart. 'Just here should do it.'

He steps his sandals into a secure firing position and raises the rifle.

'Wait. What's that?'

'What?'

'What rifle have you got there – automatic or manual?'

'Manual M40 106 millimetre. Recoilless.'

'Make it three shots here and finish me off there,' she points to her forehead. 'Equidistant to each eye, just to be certain.'

The boy nods.

'Wait,' Delia says again. 'You'd better come closer, that barrel is wobbling all over the place. You have done this before, haven't you?'

'Of course I have.'

'You look a little young for it, that's all.'

'I'm not. I'm the second oldest in my platoon.'

'I'm sure you are. But tell you what, I'll hold the tip of the rifle against my chest for the first shot to make certain you get a good one in, then you can fire away and it really won't matter if you miss a few. A good opener, that's the thing.'

The boy blinks miserably. 'Shut up, madam.'

'Miss. My apologies. Go ahead.' Delia closes her eyes and waits, feeling the heat of the sun warm her skin and a calmness seep into her veins. Her thoughts drift to her father as he was found in his study, the Van Lang bronze dagger he'd used fallen on half-completed French immigration documents on the floor. She waits, listening to a parakeet chittering in the banyan and the crack-crack of a distant gun's retort. After a few seconds she opens an eye to squint at the boy. 'Take as long as you want,' she says pleasantly and shuts her eye again. This time her mind wanders to her brothers. She wonders which clearings they are rotting in. She wonders whether Thuc's gold crucifix will ever be discovered. Will it remain knotted around a rib or collarbone? Will it be dug up by a girl in two thousand years' time? She opens an eye. 'Will you leave me here?'

'What?'

'I'm just wondering, will you leave me here just as you found me? I mean, you won't attempt to move me afterwards?'

'I expect I wouldn't bother.'

'Good.' She shuts her eye and allows herself a smile at the thought of her bones lying in the mud with the ancient kings. Papa would have liked that. 'Ready whenever you are.' She waits for the blackness to collapse her. Like a star, she thinks. Like becoming her own black hole.

'Ow.' A sudden scratching pain at her heart. Surely that wasn't it?

'Ow.' It didn't feel like a bullet. Has she been grazed by a bayonet? The pain could not be so puny.

She opens both eyes. The sunlight is blotching the view but the soldier boy is definitely still there. As is she – being jabbed in the ribs by a rifle butt.

'You are very lucky, miss. I have decided not to execute you after all. Instead you will come with me.'

Delia considers the boy as he solidifies in the hard blue light. He can be no more than sixteen. Seventeen at most. Three years younger than her brother had been. 'Look, I understand this might be difficult for you but if you don't shoot me now you'll probably regret it later.'

The boy shakes his head.

'I know *I'll* regret it. Please. Listen, I'm sorry if I was rude. Sometimes I speak out of turn. It's a very bad habit for a woman, so my mother always told me. I promise I won't say another word.'

'Apologies, but no. I order you to come with me.'

Delia finds herself dropping to her knees in the warm mud. 'I'll make it easier for you. I'll turn away if you like. Or shall I lie down? I know I said one between the eyes but I'm not so fussed – you could just go wild and pepper my back or my skull. Either way, I promise neither I nor my spirit or whatever it is you believe in, well, I promise we won't hold it against you.'

'No.'

'Please.' Delia falls forward clutching the rubber straps of his sandals. 'Please, sir, I beg of you. I'll really beg if you want. I have some cane rum in my sack, if that would swing it?'

'Shut up!' the boy screams suddenly. 'Shut up!' He staggers backwards and discharges his cartridge into the banana palm. 'And get up. You will come with me. I am a lieutenant, you must comply.'

Delia looks up at him. He is swiping hot tears away. Her blood begins to quicken. It might be caused by some sort of maternal hormone perhaps, or simply the heat of the sun. Whatever it is that takes a hold of her she lowers her chin. 'You're right,' she says softly, 'I should not ask you to do the task that remains for me alone. I apologise. Wipe your eyes and lead on where you choose. I will follow you.'

The storms of war ravage Vietnam. The country rages. It turns on itself like a rabid dog. And a Saigon archaeology student, Delia Diem, finds herself caught within the cauldron of the Central Highlands campaign. She finds herself living with a platoon of Viet Minh, led by one Lieutenant Hung Duong. She finds herself there and she does not leave, for there is no place else for her to go.

'You are not my prisoner,' the little lieutenant informs her a few weeks after her arrival, as she pounds rice husks against a boulder for the platoon's supper. 'You will feel free to depart at any time.'

Delia does not look up from her thrashing.

The lieutenant squats beside her, gathering up the grains.

He waits for her to stop, to push back her black drape of hair and look at him. 'But we both know you are Saigonese,' he says quietly, as she continues her work. 'I should inform you that yesterday we were given orders to shoot Southern women in this zone. Naturally, only where necessary – where spying is suspected or family guilt involved.' A rosy blush colours his cheeks. 'I understand this execution business is neither this way nor that with you, however—'

Delia lays down her husks and pushes back her hair to consider this little floppy-hatted Northerner who is plucking at his sandal straps and avoiding her eyes.

'—However, I could be your protector, if you wish it. I will not attach any strings to you. I will simply say you are acting as our scout, yes? It would not be uncommon, women are being used in such ways everywhere. If you wish it, I will vouch for you.'

Delia lifts her chin slightly.

Lieutenant Duong is not certain what level of accord this signifies. He decides to plunge on regardless. 'But in return I would ask that you do me one thing.'

Delia watches him disappear into the bamboo thicket that is to be their shelter for the night. He returns carrying a thick leather-bound tome. It is her *Viet Dynasty: The Foundation of a Nation, Volume I* – the one book of her father's she had taken from that terrible study, the one thing she could not bear to leave behind. The little lieutenant offers it to her now with an uncertain grin and a blush. 'Please, miss, you will teach me to read.'

The soldier is a quick learner. Wherever they stop to camp Delia pours water on the ground and with a stick draws alphabets in the soupy dirt. Doggedly, Lieutenant

Duong works to decipher her muddy proverbs: all cats are grey in the night-time, a chained buffalo does not enjoy grazing, old foxes want no tutors. In time, he writes his own for her to read: the dead erect no gravestones, even a leech falls when sated, a pretty girl's sigh is sweeter than honey.

His nights she fills with stories. As mortars pummel the ground and phosphorus flames blind the sky, as the mountains burn rancid and the darkness moans with the slow dying, Delia whispers to the little lieutenant tales of their country's past.

This soldier boy likes the adventures of heroes best of all. 'Tell me again,' he begs bashfully, rocking his hammock towards hers, 'tell me that story of the seven warrior kings. I will start it for you. There was once a dragon that laid seven eggs.'

A year passes. To the members of this Highland platoon it begins to seem as if hell is theirs to inhabit forever. Then the nearby town of Kon Tum falls to the Northern Army. Pleiku follows. The tide is turning, some say. Most, like Duong, say nothing. The little lieutenant, grown a little taller, is placed with a battalion to attack a suburb of the Southern stronghold of Buon Ma Thuot. He is promoted to captain. The battle for the town is pitiless. The captain's friends die, sometimes one by one, sometimes five or ten at a time. It is during this period he hears word that all three of his brothers have been killed. But throughout, Captain Duong survives without a wound.

'You must be my talisman, miss,' he tells Delia one morning as she strips a handful of water hyacinths into the cauldron. 'When you are with me my life is safe.'

Delia gouges a maggot from a root. 'But surely this is only half a life you speak of having. How could it be anything but half? We are but the leftovers after so many loved ones have gone. You may feel the weight of your body as normal, I grant you, your limbs and so forth are an indication of physical substance, but I tell you this is merely the weight of an empty flask, or the barnacled shell of an oyster scraped of its pulsing flesh. The precious purpose is gone.'

Captain Duong ponders the perfection of her allusions. He beams at her, thin white hairs twitching in his bushy brows, and he dares a reply. 'Well, perhaps our two shell halves have been glued together, yes, miss? Perhaps this is how we are still living. Our two separate shell halves are re-hinged as one.'

Delia Diem looks down into the soup and makes no response.

Soon enough campaign calendars tell of another year come. This one named 1975, for those still counting or naming. It is in this year that the stronghold of Buon Ma Thuot falls to the Northern forces. Like a city of sand, it is said, crumbling with one sweep of a new tide.

'The Southern Army is a snake whose head has been severed,' the little captain confides to Delia as his platoon sets up camp in the deserted town. 'The body thrashes hither and thither but its purpose is gone. It will be over soon enough. You will see, miss. Saigon will fall and then all this craziness will stop. Now we have taken the heart of the country, the rest of the body must follow.'

'How your proverbs are coming on,' she replies and attends to the cauldron on the fire.

To Call It Love Would Be Unnecessary

It takes two months for the captain's prediction to be realised. In April the Southern government concedes. Abruptly this most uncivil of wars is over and the stitching together of a torn country begins. For his loyal services in defending the Motherland, Captain Duong is asked to relocate from his Red Delta home in the North to the Central Highlands. The new government needs dependable people to assist in the re-education of Southern troops captured in the region. Camps are being set up for this purpose in the hills around Dalat. His parents are granted papers to relocate from their Delta village's barren soil to this fertile land to be closer to their only surviving son. Plantations are reassigned, villages reconstructed: his family is indeed most fortunate, the little captain is informed. They are given a longhouse and hens. The Duongs will surely prosper.

'We will fill the Highlands with dependable people,' Duong tells Delia as they begin the long hike from Buon Ma Thuot to Dalat, where he is to begin his civic reassignment. 'Assimilation. Education in socialism. New economic policies. This is how we shall all become Viet together.'

Delia Diem shifts her backpack and says nothing. She is thinking of her home among the tamarind trees in the university district of Saigon. Of the study where her father was discovered broken as his shards of ancient pot and glass. She wonders what purpose an archaeologist could ever have in this bombed-out land.

A year later, released from the army, twenty-one-year-old Hung Duong, with a little help from Miss Delia Diem, passes the requirements for joining the town's new police force. Thirty-year-old Delia Diem, with a lot of help from Constable Duong, has found employment in the kitchen of the hospital canteen. He has also found her lodgings in the Young Female Socialist Workers' boarding house, even though she is no longer young and with an accent like hers they do not talk about her socialism.

'So, miss,' Duong says, laying down his binoculars in the wooden sentry post above the marketplace. As has become her habit over the weeks of their new life, Delia has brought him lunch. Today, a luxury – an omelette roll made with a real egg, with fresh black pepper. 'It has been four years, this companionship of ours.'

'Indeed.'

'Four years since you went looking for kings.'

'Yes.'

'And found me.' He can joke about it now, that meeting by a muddy lake.

Behind her veil of hair and despite herself and the morning she has spent washing pots in the canteen, Delia finds she is also smiling.

'Four years,' he grins.

Delia looks through her hair at the little policeman who is swinging his legs on his high stool. He has not taken one bite of the roll. 'It is best eaten warm. The egg.'

'The thing is, miss, we need to think about what you are to do.'

'To do? But no one has complained about my work of late. I am always on time. I keep my head down. I try to be polite. I know someone spoke to the supervisor of my Southern arrogance, but there are characteristics in the manner in which I was raised that I truly cannot help. I will try harder to stay silent if that is required.'

'No, no, it is not that. Please do not worry yourself there. It is not that.'

'It is not?'

'Listen, miss,' his grin is awkward. 'It is my chief. To put it simply, he is asking questions. This comradeship, he says, needs tidying up. Either that or clearing out. Whatever, there is to be no more Southern capitalist craziness here. There is to be neat filing and new socialist harmony.'

Delia twists a strand of hair between cracked and swollen fingers. Not for the first time she wonders at the life she seems to be living in this Highland town with its flower gardens and foreign-built villas on pine-cloaked hills. She wonders if anyone gets to choose their life. Whether it would have been possible at some point for her to have chosen differently.

She hands Duong a napkin.

'Thank you, miss.' The little policeman is trying to avoid staring at her hair, spinning between her fingertips like silk stretched for the loom. He looks for support to the print of Ho Chi Minh sellotaped to the back wall of the booth. 'The thing is, with this new job of mine I could make life a lot easier. For you, I mean. I seem to be doing all right and,' he picks up the egg roll and fiddles with it, 'and I know you are an old maid now, and Southern of course, but I don't really mind.'

'It will go cold – the roll.'

'Apologies.' He stuffs the roll into his mouth. 'So I'm telling you I could marry you. I mean, if you wish it.'

'I'm sorry?'

Duong chews rapidly and swallows. 'I could marry you.'

Delia starts. She looks to this little man with bulges in his cheeks, who is trying to grin that grin that always took her by surprise, that always seemed in its simple beam to light up the blackest crevice inside her, if only for a second.

'I really don't mind at all.' Duong stuffs his mouth with the rest of the roll.

Delia turns away, spinning hair between her fingers. She looks out the small window at the marketplace below, at the fish traders tossing shrimp into paniers, bludgeoning eels on wet slates. 'It is true what you say. I am an old maid with no family to be found in Saigon. There is no university to take in my old-world ways.' It is also true, she admits to herself, that she has not felt despair tug at her heels for some weeks now. She has not woken with blackness waltzing her veins to terror and her limbs towards knives or ropes. More than once she has glanced up and seen the sun above the clouds. And she has smiled.

She turns and looks at the little policeman gobbling his egg roll and trying to grin. And her heart fills with fondness.

'Naturally, if I am to marry you,' he says, 'if I am to do this thing for you, I am afraid there is something I must ask of you in return. You can be Delia no longer. I am afraid that colonial name is no good to you or me or anyone now. You must demonstrate you are with the Minh and our great Uncle, all honour upon his resting soul. I offer all regrets to your ancestral family and wish all honour upon their resting souls, but if we are to build a new life together then Delia Diem must be gone with the Southern losers, yes?'

Delia's fingers cease their spinning.

'I've been thinking,' Duong continues, 'how about Po? It was the name of my grandmother. It is also a shortening of the name of my heroic mother. It would sit very well on you. After all,' he reaches for a proverb to seal the matter, 'rice is simply named yet it fed our army's victory. Will you take it, please?'

Delia's fingers tighten on a twist of hair. What choice, she wonders, does anyone ever have with anything really? Her fingers yank and the roots rip away. A pleasing pain tingles her scalp.

'Po, you say? All right then, I suppose. I accept.'

'So this is it!' Mr Bung exhales, spellbound by his patient's revelation. 'This is the provenance of her hated name. The shovelling at the lake is her life's great turning point. From that meeting all else has blossomed!' Wiping his palms he attacks his neglected pad. *We go tomorrow!*

The patient's eyes open and consider the scribbling hypnotist coolly. 'I had decided to submit to life a while longer, doctor, so I did what I must do. To call it love would be unnecessary. The South was closed to me. My family was lost. I did what I must do. This little man, he was not so bad.' She allows herself a remembered smile. 'Of course, I never did find the ancient kings. And now I would like some shrimp crackers, if you would be kind enough to arrange it. I find I am rather ravenous.'

Even a King Must Step a Shoe in Mud Some Day

Despite his best efforts, Yung has crashed into his chief's office and burst into tears for the second day in a row. 'Is he all right, Chief? They better not be ill-treating him. How can they demand this twenty million? They must be drug barons or Chinese warlords. These sorts are probably willing to torture the boy. Oh twenty million! Oh Uncle Ho! Oh, what will Scunthorpe do next season if they break his toes?'

'Calm yourself, Sergeant, of course Sam's toes are fine.' Duong looks up from a notepad full of possible plans. It is seven in the morning of a very important day. Already too late in the day on this very important day to be dealt such a shattering blow by a subordinate. 'Now tell me again and slowly, Yung. Did I hear you say *twenty* million? Which of the station's jokers told you that?'

'I wish it were not so, Chief,' the sergeant wails, 'but it is.'

'Will you place your hand on the frame of the portrait of our great leader and swear to the truth of this?'

'It's on the news, Chief. It's all over the national news.'

Duong lays down his pencil and considers the possibilities. Either the message is not getting through or he has a speech impediment no one has ever told him about. 'Stand still, Yung, and repeat after me, without hysteria please, "Sam Porcini is receiving first-class Vietnamese hospitality."'

'Sam Porcini is receiving first-class Vietnamese hospitality.'

'And this, "The man responsible is probably a man of honour, possibly fallen into financial difficulties, but most definitely upstanding and caring."'

'The man is honourable but possibly difficult and most definitely upstanding and caring.'

It seems it is his message that is not getting through.

Duong ponders the conundrum in a doodle of a football on his notepad while Yung bursts into a fresh bout of tears. 'All respect to you, Chief, but I don't know how you can say these things, I really don't.'

'Maintain your dignity in the workplace, Yung.'

'I can't, Chief.'

Duong hurries round the desk and slaps his sergeant twice on the cheeks and once on the forehead in accordance with the management chapter in *Creative Truths in Provincial Policing*. 'Dignity is as essential to a man as his own skin. Furthermore, as I am sure Mrs Yung will agree, histrionics play havoc with the bowels. In Ho's name, no more histrionics please.'

Chief Duong massages his own unquiet belly and thinks hard. 'Sergeant Yung,' he says eventually, 'I am required to attend a convention of Provincial Policing Policies in Saigon this afternoon. We shall be sharing information and strategic planning on this very subject. I have a private phone call to make and then I must hit the road.'

Yung nods disconsolately, drying his cheeks with the tips of his moustache. 'And me, Chief?'

Duong weighs up the intelligence of the man. Unlike his erstwhile deputy and recently promoted co-chief,

Duong has always preferred to avoid the employment of bright sparks in the office. 'Too many sparks and the whole place will go up in flames,' he likes to say. 'And then where will civic calm, Hanoi's policing policies and Dalat's miscreant management be?' Today he is confident that this policy will pay dividends. 'This morning I shall be requiring you to attend to the Ma settlement clearance, under Co-Chief Jimn.'

Yung's moustache starts to tremble. For the past twenty-four hours, while the footballer has been languishing in some hellhole awaiting rescue, Yung's boss has set him to a variety of seemingly pointless tasks: optical and speech therapist research, dumbwaiter quotes, and now this slum clearance work, of all things. Yesterday one of the officers was savaged in the line of duty by his own dog. 'But, Chief—'

'A crucial aspect of the investigation, Sergeant.' Duong moves to the office door. He peers out, slams it shut and beckons Yung to him. 'I need you to watch Co-Chief Jimn all day. Record when he arrives, when he leaves, who he speaks to, what is said.'

Yung's eyes bulge. 'You don't mean—'

'Seen the new watch? The snakeskin loafers? The silk handkerchiefs?' Duong's smile is dazzling. 'Which government employee has that kind of money all of a sudden?'

Overwhelmed by the reconfirmation of his boss's genius, Sergeant Yung exits the room like a sleepwalker floating into a sugar-spun dream. Chief Duong wedges the new armchair against the door, scrambles the phone line and dials a number in search of an answer to a twenty-million-dollar question.

* * *

'The the the there is a problem.' In Saigon the unluckiest of work-experience boys in the British Consulate's visa department stammers into the microphone.

'Excuse me?' Beneath the clucking of the ceiling fan and the hiss of the line-scrambling box, Chief Duong is not sure he has heard the boy correctly. He pinches his nostrils and pops a sour plum in his mouth. 'Repeat communication, please.'

'I'm most terribly sorry but G G G Gola-Cola does not have the money yet.'

'But we agreed I would collect the money today.'

'Er. Regret to say so, sir, but no.'

'It seems they are playing for time. Time I do not have.' The truth is out before Duong realises. Then he realises how good it sounds. 'Nor time that Sam has,' he adds as fiercely as a man can with a plum stone wedged between molars.

'An in in in insurance stipulation, sir.' The work-experience boy reads the sweaty note the Vietnamese head of the multinational investigation team has shoved at him, trying to ignore the terror that is galloping like a hunted boar through his brain. 'G G G G G G G Gola-Cola International's insurers are regretful but they will not cover the cost of the kidnap without evidence of Mr Porcini's continuing good health. Best business practice they s s say.'

'But I want to hand him back tonight. And I only want ten thousand dollars for him.'

'Well well well well yes,' the boy agrees, for in his extremely limited experience of ransom demands, it does sound reasonable. He is delivered of a sound slap to the back of the head. 'One moment, sir,' he reads from a second note flung at him.

Duong takes a moment. He pats down his brows and comforts his stomach. He has pressing family commitments and these people are playing for time. He looks to Uncle Ho, for if truth be told he could take a little inspiration, but for a moment, in the Great Leader's place, it seems a stuffed panda stares back. They are playing with *Lila*'s time.

And in this moment a penny drops: this stinks of a trap. He has not been a greedy man, and who would turn down his terms otherwise? Could this mean they are getting close? Is it *he* and not Jimn who is actually under Yung's surveillance? Is Yung brighter than he looks?

Duong spits out the plum stone.

Bugging devices! They could be anywhere! They could have been installed during Slimn Jimn's brief tenure. The chief drops the phone and leaps from his seat. The plastic-wrapped armchair that Jimn has not removed! He rushes to upend the cushions. Nothing. He yanks out the back and feels behind it. Nothing.

But a crocodile that is not spied from the surface may very well be lurking beneath. Duong turns to Uncle Ho with a whimper. No signs of bugs behind the canvas. Nothing in the frame but Ho and his serenely soothing smile. Ho is right as ever – panic is what they want from him: he must keep his head. Very well. Even a king must step a shoe in mud some day: it is time to play dirty.

He returns to his chair, tucks the handset under his chin and pops another sour plum in his mouth. With his left hand he increases the pinch on his nose and with his right he chops at his larynx to produce a ferocious gargle. 'Hello? You seem to forget I hold the life of this boy in the palm of my hand and yet you wish to play games with me. If his life is of so little worth to you, what value does it have for me? If Gola-Cola requires evidence of Mr Porcini's continued existence, I am happy to oblige. I shall take a knife to the footballer's toes and slice away the unnecessary skin between them, every flip and flap. I may even tear off pieces with my teeth, yes?' Duong chews noisily on the plum. He looks up. Ho smiles serenely back. 'Where shall I mail the bits?'

In the visa applications room at the British Consulate, the work-experience boy pulls off his headset and races from the room and also the building, never to return to diplomatic work again. The government interpreter relays the information to the assembly of foreign detectives and bigwigs. 'They are going to chop Mr Porcini's feet into bits and pieces. Then they will start on the rest of him.'

The air in the room slows. The British Metropolitan Police's Special Head of Project Porcini turns with a look of revulsion towards the Gola-Cola Public Relations repre-sentative. The Scunthorpe United Director jumps to his feet and smashes his fists on the desk. The Communications Director of the British FA gasps and yanks at a knot on his tie he imagines to be choking him. Tony Thirsthead rubs his face so hard orange comes off on his hands. 'Shergar,' he moans, 'all over again.'

In his office Duong pops a lychee sherbet in his mouth. 'Hello?' he says to the phone. 'Anybody there? Very well, if this is how you value the boy, which foot shall I start snipping?'

The interpreter interprets into English.

The Vietnamese Chief Investigating Officer slumps on the desk, muttering of national doom.

Tony Thirsthead screams 'No!' and lunges for the phone headset.

The Gola-Cola representative shouts 'Stop!' and tackles Thirsthead's ankles.

The Scunthorpe United man roars 'Bloody Yank, this is all your fault!' and swings for the Gola-Cola man's chest.

All three crash backwards into the visas pending filing cabinet.

The Metropolitan Head of Project Porcini – who is a rugger man and considers football an overpaid game for girls – sighs and picks up the headset. He clamps it about the interpreter's ears and writes a note:

Another moment please, putting you on hold.

A few seconds later and a few thousand kilometres away, a cellphone tinkles to life in the executive tip of the top of a bottle-shaped green glass skyscraper. Bradley Burdock the Third, CEO of Gola-Cola International, spins round from his stratospheric blue view. 'Good morning, Vietnam.'

'Mr Burdock, sir, they're threatening to slice and dice the boy if we don't stop messing around,' the Gola-Cola PR man pants down the line. 'There's some disagreement here over how to proceed.'

'Get me a speaker phone on Sherry-Sioux,' Bradley yells at a secretary hovering in the darkness at the far end of his vast office.

'Yo, Sherry-Sioux,' he says. 'How d'you fancy popping up to the one hundred and fourth for a little crisis management get-to thingy?'

'Shucks, Bradley, nothing I'd like more, but I'm on vacation,' a faint female voice replies.

'Ha ha. That sure is kinda funny, Ms Ballou. I'll see you in five.'

'Well, that could be difficult, Bradley. I'm not sure the other passengers would appreciate me asking the pilot to three-sixty when we're halfway across the Pacific.'

Bradley Burdock the Third watches a pigeon fly at the window and plummet.

'You still there, Bradley?'

'Jesus, Sherry-Sioux. Are you effing kidding me?'

'The line's getting awful faint. I may be losing you.'

'Oh sweet Jesus.' He spins back to the vast and empty office, to the Warhol Cola bottles on the walls, to the vanishing silhouette of a secretary. His voice drops to a whimper. 'Jeez, Sherry-Sioux. What am I supposed to do?'

On a trans-Pacific flight that is beginning its descent into Saigon, a purple-eyed passenger opens her handbag and admires a green beeping light in its depths. She smiles contentedly at her reflection in the window. 'Hang on in there would you, Brad? And go easy on your language to a lady of the Christian persuasion. Unlikely they'll go for the toes immediately. Not in their interest. Squeeze another day out of it. Get yourself back on all the national networks. Then go European. Then worldwide. I've left you some VT packages on charity projects in Asia. Get those smiley kiddies out to the stations and get yourself tearful about it. Saline drops, Brad. And while you're at it, go pleasure yourself with these sweet numbers – in the past two days brand consumption is up seven hundred and forty per cent. Brand recognition is at nine hundred and climbing higher. Heading for the clouds, if we hold on. Right now you're more famous than the sweet lord himself, Bradley.'

Bradley sniffs, sucking on his thumb. 'I am?'

'Hardball, Bradley. One more day. Say, you want me to put a call in to these kidnap cowboys?'

'Gee, Sherry-Sioux, I don't know. Life feels awful lonely up here, you know.'

'Toughen up those nuts of yours, Bradley. I've gotta go now, but I'll catch you in a couple of days.'

'Sherry-Sioux?' Bradley Burdock the Third says. 'SHERRY-SIOUX?' he screams. He stares at vast empty office. 'Son of a – she's gone.'

The corporation's decision to delay payment again is relayed by the Gola-Cola representative to the man from the British FA, who passes on the bad news to Scunthorpe United and Tony Thirsthead, who turns sobbing towards the shoulder of the Metropolitan Head of Project Porcini, who writes a further note:

We understand your frustration but there is nothing we can do; we require an extra twenty-four hours to clear the insurance issues and raise unmarked bills. I give you my word, give us another day and we will ask no more. Please do not harm Sam, it is not in anyone's interests to do so.

Which is interpreted to the Vietnamese Head of Investigation and reluctantly agreed and subsequently relayed down a scrambled line to a small police office in Dalat. Where a clock is doodled on a notepad. A twenty-four-hour delay pushes Chief Duong to the final hour of the fifth day of his deal with Mei. His last chance for Lila. And then there are the practicalities to think about. The footballer will have to spend another day in the company of his mother. Duong makes a note: *To do – purchase additional hen for Mummy.*

He sucks hard on the sherbet and addresses the phone. 'I want the cash ready for collection by midday tomorrow. This is the last of my accommodations, yes? After this the toes get it and the boy will follow. And as we're playing it your way, you can deliver up the full ten million. I am not a greedy man but I believe the amount was your suggestion.'

Chief Duong flicks the switch on the scrambler box, cutting the line. Has he really just demanded ten million dollars? He spits the lychee sherbet into the wastebin; he finds he has rather lost his appetite.

A Revolutionary Device

A few hours after a phone line is reconnected in a little police chief's office, a purple-eyed guest travelling under the name Staff Sergeant Ballou checks in at the Saigon Majestic Hotel, some three hundred kilometres to the south of Dalat. She heads straight to the roof terrace bar that overlooks the brown churn of the vast Mekong River. Ignoring the view, she orders a whisky sour and lights a cigarette.

And now she turns her attention to her handbag, removing a silver handset the size and weight of a walkie-talkie. She extends an antenna and studies a green light pulsing on a screen. She blows a smoke ring at a butterfly on a bougainvillea and watches the pulsing light, and she smiles. How true her poor mama's words: things always have a habit of righting themselves.

It was three years ago in March that Sherry-Sioux had been approached. Representing a German firm, Kapital-Secure©, an enterprising ex-Stasi named Doctor Kunz had written to her with a simple proposition.

Dear Successful Executive – the letter began –
*Like a loving parent always fretting about their child,
so the diligent Executive is constantly worrying about
the whereabouts of their most valued possessions . . .*

The letter enclosed a photograph of a Supreme Champion Lilac Persian called Minky, and the glowing endorsement of Minky's owner – a Mrs Bahn from Munich – who had the microchipped tomcat tracked and returned safely after he was stolen during the Milan Oriental Convention.

> . . . *here at KapitalSecure© we were inspired by Mrs Bahn to invent a revolutionary device guaranteed to take the stress out of human capital ownership.*

Doctor Kunz's proposed extension of the Minky concept was simple. All the anxious executive had to do was call in the sponsored film or sports star for their annual medical. Under the auspices of blood testing, KapitalSecure© would implant a minute GPS tracking device in the shoulder muscle, and he promised – *You will never lose sight of your money. No more sleepless nights!*

The product came Stasi-certified and with a lifetime guarantee. It seemed an idea with potential to a sharp-shooting executive at Gola-Cola, newly promoted to Head of International Talent Management at the unprecedented age of twenty-eight – and just two years out of the army.

Sherry-Sioux took the letter to the very top.

'You've got a fine pair of balls on you, young lady,' Bradley Burdock the First said, whirring his wheelchair round the race track he had installed in the very tip of the top of the bottle-green tower he had built up from nothing but a fifty-dollar loan sixty years before. 'The good lord himself didn't make no finer stuff than balls.'

'Are you saying I have your blessing, sir?'

'Sure you have my blessing, sweetheart, you go give this thing a whirl.' Bradley Burdock the First rolled his chair up a small ramp and whooshed down the side into a slalom. Spinning left, he braked an inch from Sherry-Sioux's Jimmy Choos. 'Who knows, sweetheart, with balls like yours, perhaps someday you'll be taking up this seat of mine when the big man above calls me home.'

As it happened, the big man was swift in responding. Within a week of the implant being secretly injected into Gola-Cola's stable of thirty stars, Bradley Burdock the First keeled over from a coronary mid-chicane.

As it also happened, in a remarkable double-signing for the Almighty, a day later Doctor Kunz caught a toecap under a Munich tram and did not re-emerge in one piece.

In the space of forty-eight hours, a thrusting green-eyed executive had been left with a silver handset and a bitter taste in her mouth as she watched Bradley Burdock the Third leap-frogging fifteen layers of management to bounce from the mail room into his grandfather's throne in the tip of the top of the bottled tower. The braces weren't even off his teeth.

On the terrace of the Majestic, purple-eyed Sherry-Sioux knocks back her whisky sour. Within twenty-four hours Bradley Burdock will have withered away, exposed by all sorts of nasty revelations. Thinking of balls, what did Mama like to say? There is only so long a woman can keep a man's balls in the air before they drop. Come to think of it, Sherry-Sioux smiles, it won't be long before Brad's balls land clean off in her hand.

Dusk is darkening the busy Mekong and riverside adverts cast their neon stains into the murk. A cross-river ferry roars. Sherry-Sioux sniffs rising vapours of diesel, spice and sewage, and briefly wonders how this poetic moment might be translated onto celluloid; the lone heroine alone in the East. She considers insisting on co-directorial rights. Then a pulsing green light on the handset draws her back to the business at hand: the footballer.

She pulls up the *Global Adventurer* blog page on her phone. A picture appears of some ghastly goofing Englishman in a pith helmet with a godawful byline: 'Bone up with JC Bone!'. She cross-references the location on the handset with the blog's area map of the Highlands. She flashes a fan of dollars in the air. A waiter stops in his tracks.

'Speakee English, honey? One hundred American dollars all yours once you source me a chauffeured aircon jeep ready to depart here at dawn. I'll also require a semi-automatic firearm – Chinese real deal only, no Taiwanese repros. Cartridges not bullets, comprendez? Also a large-scale topographical relief map of the Highlands, south of this here place – Buon Ma Thuot, right? And you can fetch me a double refill of this poison while you're at it. Make it pronto, tonto.'

Few Achievements Are Won Without Great Suffering

As whisky sundowners are sipped on Saigon terraces, a battered sedan taxi is chugging through the Highlands. It is making its way to Buon Ma Thuot, Vietnam's unprepossessing coffee capital some four hundred kilometres to the north.

'I'd like you to think hard, Delia,' the eminent hypnotist Mr Bung says, the stony road bouncing him close to his patient on the back seat. 'Do you have any inkling why I commandeered this taxi, or why we might be heading this way?'

The patient turns her blindfolded head towards the last rays of the sun bleeding through the window. She does not answer the hypnotist.

'Excellent,' Mr Bung says, 'that's just how your doctor likes it.'

The taxi has poor suspension. Mr Bung cannot help but note how the patient's breasts jostle in the brassiere the asylum has supplied. The dietician's plan has worked wonders for Delia's initial weight loss, but any further shrinkage would be purely in accordance with current fashions and entirely without consideration for the woman's emotional needs. In Mr Bung's experience – and he is now reflecting personally as well as professionally – the more a woman consumes, the more she is able to give of herself to others. And if that isn't a woman's greatest asset Mr Bung is hard pushed to think what is.

He lays his hand therapeutically on his patient's bouncing thigh, just below her hospital smock and just above the pad of her magnificent knee.

'I'd rather you didn't do that, doctor.'

'How your confidence has come on, my dear!'

'Your hand, doctor.'

Mr Bung swiftly relocates his fingers to a position next to the patient on the vinyl seat. He glances at her face, the heat of that regal gaze – a gaze he has come to admire so much! – is scorching through the blindfold. 'Just think how impossible this trip would have been two days ago. What giant strides you have made since then!'

Delia says nothing. Her blindfolded gaze is redirected towards Mr Bung's little finger, which has found its way up the side of her thigh.

'You must steel yourself,' the hypnotist counsels. 'Tomorrow's treatment may be painful for you. Few achievements are won without great suffering. However, you can rest assured I am here with you and for you. I will not desert you.'

'Your finger, Mr Bung?'

'A sign of comfort, Delia, nothing more. Sometimes the therapeutic need for the blindfold upsets patients.' Mr Bung re-employs his finger in excavating wax deposits in his ear.

They spend the night in the military hospital in a western suburb of town. Once Delia is assisted onto the bed her blindfold is loosened by a nursing student eager to see the hypnotist's powers in action. Mr Bung does not allow the blindfold to be fully removed. Therapeutic focus and complete disorientation must be maintained at all times. She can thank him in full-sighted rapture tomorrow.

Mr Bung goes on to explain to the nurse that he has never encountered a subject the calibre of this one. If he succeeds tomorrow he will surely rewrite the course of medical hypnosis and definitely receive dollar funding, if not from the Past Life University in Alabama, USA, then certainly from some other illustrious American institute. Mr Bung has no problem with foreign financial recompense. 'After all,' he tells the nurse, 'they lost our war.'

As the nurse observes closely, Mr Bung asks Delia to sit up and listen to him very carefully.

'Is that really necessary?' Delia finds she is quite comfortable lying back listening to the tooting of scooters on the street outside.

Mr Bung conceals his surprise with a chuckle. 'Naturally, some pre-catatonic resistance is to be expected,' he whispers to the nurse, 'but it is easily overcome. You will observe.' He addresses himself sternly to the patient's left ear. 'Delia, you are sick in the head and you will only get better if you do exactly as your doctor tells you. You are feeling very tired.'

'Am I?'

'You are.'

'I don't feel that tired.'

'Do not fight it, Delia. You are weary and terribly drained. With every second that passes your limbs are getting heavier.'

'I suppose it has been a long journey.'

'You are too exhausted to speak.'

'If you say so,' she yawns.

'But even though you are aching with desire for sleep, aching more and more with every passing second, you will sit up for the doctor and listen carefully.' He turns to the nurse. 'Few physicians attempt a hypnotic induction without eye contact, but then few are lucky enough to train with the great Lyons behaviourists. I have no such fears, as you will observe. Delia! Sit up!'

'Sorry, too tired.'

Mr Bung smiles brightly at the young nurse – pretty enough, if one could forgive her those buck teeth, and Mr Bung is a forgiving man. 'You're too tired to speak, but there's nothing wrong with your hearing, Delia. You will sit up now.'

'I'll try, doctor, but it's really quite difficult.' Delia's words are falling away from her in a surprising slur. 'I'm really quite done in.'

'Excellent, yes, that's exactly what I wanted,' Mr Bung says. 'Some assistance with the patient please, nurse.'

The nurse hauls Delia's bulk into a sitting position.

'Delia, you are feeling much too drained to bother with another word. In fact, you might not speak for a day or two, we shall decide about that later. Right now you'll find you want to sleep for many hours.'

Delia is feeling much too drained to answer.

'Soon you will sleep, Delia. Concentrate on my voice and wait for release from your conscious agony. Keep an eye on the bed legs, if you would, nurse, and stand well back.'

Mr Bung releases his grip on Delia's shoulders and stands back. 'Five!' he points to her blindfolded eyes. 'Sleep is coming. Four! You yearn for release. Three! Your body is a lead weight dropping into the ocean! Two! – wait for it, wait for it, Delia,' Mr Bung dances in close in front of his swaying patient. 'One! And–' he flicks his thumb against the patient's forehead, 'sleep!'

Delia crashes back against the mattress.

The pretty nurse gasps.

After applauding for a few moments, the nurse accepts the doctor's offer of raising a wrist. She marvels as the arm drops down and slack fingers graze the lino.

Mr Bung relieves himself of further mucus and replaces Delia's arm on her chest. He pulls up the bed bars. Given the beetling resistance that has snuck into her brain, he will take no risks tonight. He will make this preparation perfect. Deep. He will send her deeper than she has ever gone before. When it is all over tomorrow it will not only be Alabama but the woman herself who will honour him. He might even rename her in his turn. That would be most fitting.

A voice whispers in the dark waters where Delia finds herself floating. Obediently she shrinks to the tiniest of atoms and slips away to bob on the vastest of oceans.

There she does not attend to a syrupy giggle asking, 'So what can you do with her now, doctor?' She does not buckle under the application of Mr Bung's seated weight to her stiffened raised leg, or cry out as needles kebab her cheeks and a lit match dances under her palm.

Nor for that matter is she aware of the coincidence of her location, which is fewer than thirty kilometres due north of her mother-in-law's village, a place she has not visited since a wedding day thirty years before. It is a distance that neither daughter nor mother-in-law has ever sought to narrow.

If a kind voice had revealed any of this information to

her it is doubtful Delia would sleep so soundly. But as a half-moon swells in the sky she drifts on her dark ocean. As Mr Bung traces a candle's flame across her unflinching soles, and as a student nurse wheels out a rack of syringes to practise extractions from willing veins, Delia drifts happily, unaware how her body is employed. Unaware how close she lies to her husband's mother's home, where another captive is laid out beneath the fattening moon.

The Gift of Electricity

On the Island of the Dead, just thirty kilometres due south of Buon Ma Thuot, Sam Porcini lies on a corpse-board lost in a valerian dream. He cannot find his way out of it. He is not even sure where it begins. He can do nothing but endure its circling, ceaseless as clouds round the Earth.

Sam stands at the penalty spot for the last kick of the match in the semi-finals of the East London Under-Tens Cup. He knows he should be focused on a point in the south stand twenty metres behind the top-left corner of the net. This is where his coach has instructed him to aim for. But Sam isn't looking through the net's left corner. He is watching a blond-haired man in the east stand who is shifting on his feet, sipping from a polystyrene cup, a small space like an air bubble between him and the regular supporters. This man is distracting Sam as he steps up to the ball, because he looks so real. He looks like a photograph come to life. Sam knows this is impossible, but he looks so absolutely perfectly like he is made from Sam's own flesh and blood.

His penalty kick is ambling and easily trapped by the Leyton keeper. In the west stand the Leyton supporters roar their victory. Sam doesn't hear them. He is turning his back to the goal and shrugging off his teammates' commiserations, because all he can see is the east stand, where the man who surely isn't a stranger is staring at him with a terrible smile on his face, the smile of someone, Sam thinks, whose insides are being eaten by an unseen worm. Sam begins to run across the pitch towards him.

Beside Sam's slack body an old woman shuffles about. Having propped open the hatch of the tomb to let in the moonlight and checked the wires running to a black box, Mrs Poonana Duong is inching back the sheet covering the boy's toes. 'What can be the harm, husband?' she turns to ask the air.

Sam Porcini, it must be said, is no longer looking his best. With each hour in captivity the boy's vitality diminishes. His slack muscles begin to waste. His pink skin grows dull as an earth-stuck grub. And his unwitting ingestion of a cobra's venom has slowed his powerful heart to a most reluctant pump.

But the ancient woman hauling herself about the corpse-board notices nothing of this. Her cloudy eyes are focused on the hairs that shiver on the boy's shins as he shifts to kick a dream penalty towards a point twenty metres behind a goal net. Her blackened thumb hovers above these sandy sproutings, eager as a carcass fly. She rolls the bedsheet back to admire the knobbles of the boy's knees.

The air in the tomb chills.

'Snake wife, hold it there!'

A deep voice shakes the tomb. 'Just because you have thrown me away in a bag in the grass do not think I do not see these acts of perversion!'

'Pah!' Poonana dismisses the air with a slice. She has no time for marital bantering. Not tonight. She pushes the sheet further back, exposing the boy's creamy thighs and a pair of dirty green shorts. She pinches a burrowing beetle out of the pale flesh.

'Beware, snake wife!' The voice scrapes her skin like sharpened glass on bone. 'Nosiness does not end in wisdom. It ends in an ugly nose.'

The paraffin lamp that is wedging open the hatch crashes in the grass. The hatch bangs Mrs Duong on the spine, throwing the tomb into darkness.

'Pah! You are a jealous fool, Mr Dead and Dusty Bones! This pathetic lamp-luggery is the best you can do?'

'Jealous, me?' The grass rustles with laughter. 'This boy can keep this stinking snakeskin piece of so-called wife. I never wanted her myself. No desire here, I'm simply adding to the list. Not one of my so-called wife's crimes will go unpunished in the eternity. I am waiting for you, Mrs Snaky.' Inside the tomb the top fold of the sheet flops back down over Sam Porcini's knees. 'Ha,' the air taunts, 'ha ha ha.'

'Still filled with the bile of a bear about one little viper bite, husband? Didn't I warn you for years to stop with the rum jars and show your wife some care?'

The sheet flops over and over and comes to rest at Sam Porcini's ankles. 'Haaaaaaaaa.'

But Poonana has no more time for her bitter-gourd husband – the footballer is beginning to stir. She retrieves the lamp. The black box must be switched to humming.

'Try not to use it.' That's what her son had said of the box when daybreak came and he had left her. And she had tried. She really had.

She had squeezed and pinched her emperor prawn and waved him away in his jeep and returned to the longhouse to feed the chickens under the stilts and the toads and snakes in the baskets. She had scoured a cauldron and brewed up valerian root with half a honeycomb until the potion bubbled thick as corpse blood. And as the sleeping draught cooled, an unfed cobra began to growl.

She opened the lid of the basket. A black cobra's head rose from the twisting mass, its hooded neck vibrating, its tongue casting after her breath.

'You are willing, cobra? You are offering?'

The snake's peppercorn eyes gleamed. Its jaws stretched wide.

'So be it.' The old chieftain's wife clamped the snake's head with a pair of pliers and dragged the thrashing body at arm's length to the cauldron.

She paused to clear clouds from her mind. 'Try not to use it,' her son had said. He had said it of something boxy. She was sure of that much. There had been no words spoken on cobras, had there? No 'trying not to use' of Mummy's snakes. Particularly those that offered so nicely. She considered the pulsing throat. In a second it would spit. Its potent juices would be wasted. 'Pah,' she said, for Mrs Duong did not like waste. She turned the head to the cauldron and as the cobra spat she crushed the skull between her pliers. Six drops of venom glistened on the valerian brew like pearls of dew.

Mrs Duong scraped the paste into a small leather pouch that hung from her neck. She scissored open the snake's twitching body and skewered it on a nail to cure. Then she paddled her canoe back to the Island of the Dead.

The sun was high when she pulled open the hatch of the tomb. She removed the sheet from the boy's sweating body. In the midday light his flesh gleamed pale as an adder's underbelly. She measured the span of this giant's hands, his long webbed feet. No child of hers had ever grown so vast. She plucked a hair from a toe and licked it. She blew in his ears. She slid a finger around the wall of his white teeth. Then she tested the black box's hum. 'Hummm,' she said. Such a pretty sound. 'Try not to use it,' her son had said. So be it. She climbed onto the corpse-board and crouched in the corner to watch over the footballer in his sleep.

As the day's sun slipped into the forest behind the tomb, the boy began to moan. 'Daddy?' he said, his eyelids flickering faster than moth wings. 'Daddy, where are you?'

'But you need to rest,' Mrs Duong cooed. She crawled to Sam's face, which was creasing with confusion as he found himself in a deserted spectators' stand with rain coming down and a puddle of tea spreading from an abandoned polystyrene cup under the studs of his boots. Digging in her neck pouch, Poonana covered her thumb with paste and pushed it between the boy's teeth. 'Suckle, child.'

Within a few seconds his jaw slackened, his whimpering died away. She removed her thumb, marvelling at the tip's numbness. She smoothed the boy's hair. She looked at the black box. 'Try not to use it,' her son's voice repeated. 'All right,' she sighed, 'I hear you.' She shut the hatch and settled her old bones in the long grass beneath the tomb, beside the plastic bag containing her husband's remains.

Sometime before dawn the footballer woke her with his mewling. She wiped his face and nudged her envenomed thumb between his lips once more. This time she settled by him on the corpseboard to stroke the hairs on his forearm and swat those mosquitoes that dared to approach. She held her gaze from the black box with its enchanting powers. The throb of the boy's hot body drew her into sleep.

So a second day passed over the island. As the sun crept away on the Saturday evening Mrs Duong left the tomb to squat by the shore and watch for the car lights on the far side of the lake that would announce the return of her son.

But plans changed in the tip of the top of a faraway tower, and a son did not come when he should. He did not return to rescue his mother from her loneliness, nor from the gift of electricity he had lent her. The electricity that powered a strange desire beginning to pump in her old veins.

That grew quicker and stronger during the dark hours as she sat by the shore.

That now draws her back to the tomb as a moon retreats from the sky and a second night ebbs away.

Just one pulse. What could be the harm?

'Nothing but a short dance,' she informs her dead husband. 'You like to dance, I think,' she tells the sleeping footballer, peeling away the sheet and dropping it in the grass outside.

She clips the wires to the boy's manacles and plugs the end into the black box. She presses a button. The box hums. A dial rises.

And then she flicks the switch, blasting electricity down the wires: a long pulse followed by a short one.

The footballer's limbs stiffen.

Mrs Duong is entranced. She ignores her husband's huffs of ghostly rage, his wimpy heavings at the hatch. She has her very own puppeting show to watch. Two long blasts she tries, then three.

Teeth chatter.

Mrs Duong giggles.

Creamy hair stands up on the footballer's head.

Mrs Duong applauds. Mrs Duong forgets about her son's instructions. She runs the battery down.

But who could blame her? For an eighty-one-year-old woman living in a remote Highland village does not expect the gift of new pleasures. She expects only her husband to trip her up one day, to push her off the steps of the hut, or stop up her throat in her sleep. She expects no gifts of black boxes, nor visits from yellow-haired dancing giants. And certainly she never anticipated this reawakening of long-forgotten, heart-flipping delight.

Poonana wafts the scent of singeing from the air. She will tell her son that she will keep these gifts. At least a few days longer.

The boy moans.

'Hush, my child, dreams are coming.' Poonana opens the pouch and hoists herself onto the corpseboard. She crawls past a tremor in the boy's thighs and encounters a curious swelling at the crotch of his shorts. She pauses to scratch her head. The electricity has clearly attracted a rat which has scurried under the fabric and become trapped. Her husband – had he not once kept some sort of mouse in his pants?

Sam Porcini's nose retreats from the smell as a honeyed plug fills his mouth and venom sinks his veins. He drifts along the A13 to his mother's flat in evening rain. He opens the door, but he is not swamped in his mother's embrace but back on the pitch in front of the Leyton goal. A man who looks just like the father he'd had until two years ago is in the east stand, drinking tea from a polystyrene cup and crying. For some reason Sam doesn't understand, this man is crying. And then a penalty is missed. Sam runs. A puddle of tea spreads under his boots. And so it goes round, this carousel, the colour slowly fading and the noise slurring into a shushing wind.

Above Sam a sullen stalemate has descended in the tomb. Having had quite enough of his wife's perversions, the old chieftain has withdrawn to his plastic bag in the grass. He is marshalling his ghostly atoms for a final push. That cured piece of snakeskin that against the odds and despite his many attempts is still pushing out breath will soon pay for her crime. He is sure of it. Revenge is nigh.

Poonana, however, is engrossed in a most intriguing matter, namely an appendage that droops in a curly yellow nest beneath her gaze. Now that she has pulled down Sam Porcini's shorts she can see it is not a rat at all but an organ flopped and useless as an aborted piglet. But each time she pulses the electricity something remarkable happens: the piglet returns to life; it swells and stands upright in the moonlight. The old woman is mesmerised. Somewhere in her brain she knows there must be an explanation for this salute. Somewhere in her bowels she feels a tightening that seeks no further explanation. She leans close and wonders what might happen if she were to touch it.

But here it is necessary to retreat from the tomb and draw a delicate veil over the next few hours on the Island of the Dead.

Because big things are about to happen.

Adventures of a Post-Colonialist in a Pre-Civilised Land

Yes, big things are happening today: there will be partings and reunions; financial deals and rescue packages; diligent husbands will finally get their dues; and some lucky people may find themselves reborn. But as dawn does the decent thing and tips up rosy, the day begins with good news: love is in the air. Yes, just a week and a day since his eyes fell on her, Jules Chretien Bone is marrying the woman of his dreams.

Here he stands in the great white hall of a great white house, wearing an orchid-embroidered loincloth, two brass rings around his neck, a weighed hoop dangling from an ear, and his leonine curls captured in a chignon by a tiger toebone. He waves a blue glazed gourd in the air, striding over zebra skins to proclaim, 'Today the day has come at last when I, Jules Chretien Bone, renounce my British ways and embrace the life of the mountain people. Today I break the taboos of East and West. In a timeless ritual I take a mountain girl for my bride. Fortune shall favour the brave, and love will conquer all – and cut there.'

JC takes a swig from the gourd. 'Show me,' he demands of his assistant, Charlie Thoc, a bright young Anglophile he has rescued from lowly photocopying labours at Go-Go

Dalat tour company and raised to the heights of Bone Films' Director of Photography, full use of handycam included, remuneration TBC.

Astride a black rhinoceros at the end of the hall, minister of ceremonies, Uncle Mei, is checking fifty-dollar bills with a laser pen.

JC tightens his loincloth. 'We'll go again. Try a tracking shot this time. Come off the head of that stuffed mongoose and pull back onto me. End on a ten-second close-up. Got it?'

Charlie Thoc holds a square of white paper in front of the camera.

Adventures of a Post-colonialist in a Pre-civilised Land.
Scene one: Wedding day!

'Action!' JC shouts, raising his gourd.

The handycam retreats from the mongoose and wobbles up to JC as he removes the gourd from his mouth and smacks his spittled lips. 'Cheers! It's time to celebrate, because the day is come at last when I, Jules Chretien Bone—'

'All correct, Mr Bone,' Uncle Mei calls from the rhino. 'Not a dollar is missing or falsified. The girl will be brought from the holding pen for you.'

'Cut there,' JC says.

'I already have,' Charlie Thoc replies.

Standing at the top of the marble staircase the bride of the day, formerly known as Lila Duong, winces as a tenth brass ring is snapped into place around her neck. It is stretching her throat and biting into her jaw.

'One key undoes them all. But best to remove one at a time – slow slow is romantic, no?' Aunty Choccie pings a nail on the metal with approval. 'Not many take ten. Not many are swans like you.' Hot Chocolatie wrestles the key on its string down the crack of her zippered bosom. 'A swan swimming off to a new life.'

The bride makes no response.

'Aie, you look just like a doll,' Aunty caresses Orchidee's hair with a show of cheeriness she knows is necessary on such occasions. It has been cropped into a Parisian bob, as requested on the order form. 'I am certain you have an okey-dokey sort here, no obvious extremes of fetishism. Dentist's chair and these dentist's outfits he supplies – no problem. Bracework? Let's wait and see – don't worry before you don't have to is your Aunty's motto. This Mother-loving business is easy-peasy stuff!' Hot Chocolatie dribbles the requested French perfume behind Orchidee's ears. 'One girl, when her request list comes back, we all turn mute-mouth reading it, yes we do. This girl, when she left in marriage she was in chains. Branding also happened with her. But even she is happy now. Carolina, US of A she was delivered to. I have postcards.' Chocolatie gives Orchidee's nipples an enlivening tweak beneath the golden silk of her dress. 'You will find means or method to be happy. It is our great gift as women. I have to agree with Uncle Mei's wise karaoke – no woman no cry.'

There is no reaction from the bride. Her kohl-rimmed eyes shed not one tear. It is a response of such peculiarity it has led Aunty Choccie to contemplate the possibility of an ocular duct defect – probably caused by the girl's tragic accident – although a state of cold psychopathy could not be ruled out. During the past days of limberings and lecturings, of orificial openings and corset clenchings, of elastics and gymnastics, this girl had remained resolutely dry-eyed. Which was simply not normal. Every girl experienced at least three months' misery before adjustment occurred – *every* girl Choccie has helped pass through. Even the Cambodian spy Choccie employed to report on nocturnal conversations in the bunk beds disclosed no damp patches on sister Orchidee's pillow, no midnight mania, no desperate lurching for the iron-grilled window.

Unlike that poor Han girl from the lake café when the news of her father's crime got out: how near the sisterhood had come to tragedy then! For Mai Han had nearly lost the baby that night and had to be restrained from her ravings. Screamed and bucked all night, she had, shouting that her father was no murderer. He committed suicide – and that was her fault, wasn't it? – but he was no murderer. Mai would tell anyone who wanted to know it who the killer was: a Westerner with sour breath, a big nose and greasy hair.

The Cambodian had recounted the full facts to Hot Chocolatie in the morning. That day's front pages were filled with the police report that old man Han had shot Commissar Nao. He had been seen wielding a rifle and racing towards an unidentified Western man who was standing by Commissar Nao's bride when the eclipse began. The Cambodian had shrugged while explaining this: in her view, if this Westerner was turning his attentions elsewhere it was quite possible the pregnant girl's father would be enraged, and in his rage and in the solar darkness get the wrong man. Vengeful fathers were as common as coffee leaves.

And sister Orchidee? Hottie C enquired. What had been her reaction that unhappy night?

The Cambodian sighed. Sister Orchidee was magnificent. She had gone to Mai and hugged her and said she didn't think Mai's father had killed her husband and she didn't suppose it mattered now anyway. Following this she had soothed Mai by applying calming pressure to those of the girl's meridians not in restraints. She had stayed with Mai until dawn. And then after breakfast she had performed the *marathon of the twenty-three splitting positions* as requested on the *Export Quality Assurance Checklist*, without a single complaint. If Hottie Chocolatie had not discarded all her spiritual convictions on the morning of her own initiation to the sisterhood seventeen years earlier, she might just think this blind girl was not two steps removed from the village saints for all her loving kindness. Either that or she was insane.

Aunty Choccie sighs and wipes a tear from her eye. She consults the delivery document one last time. A tribal drumming starts up in the hall. 'Listen well, my dear sister,' she whispers suddenly in a low voice Lila has never heard her use before; it is as dry as desert sand. 'I give you one final piece of advice. A man's might cannot be resisted, but his desire for you will make of him a fool. Never forget this – it will be of use sometime. And now, blind beauty,' the voice brightens, 'take a hold on your Aunty's arm. We will descend you to your loving husband. Feel here with your toe, the first step is coming up.'

'Action!' JC bellows.

In the grip of her Aunty, Orchidee is led up the hall. JC reaches to take her delicate hand in his. A bolt of excitement shoots through him as he touches her soft fingers. He sniffs the fragrance of her ringed neck. 'Hello gorgeous.'

Orchidee Mei, as the delivery papers name her, smells the breath of this man beside her and finds herself assailed by memories. The sour scent transports her to a birdless silence, a nose crushed against hers, and a bruising kiss that swallowed up the seconds before a bullet broke through her husband's skull.

So this is him. Big-nosed and back for more. Her mother and Choccie were right; what a persistent beast is male desire. It is here in the clamping of his clammy fingers on hers, in the heat of his panting breath. She cannot turn her head from him, although she tries. Beneath her gold sarong she clenches her thighs. She will make her mother proud. She will resist or die in the trying.

It does not take long, the morning's business in the great hall at Paradise Plantation, not long at all. Mr Bone signs a receipt and receives the delivery papers, visa documents and the key to his wife's neck.

'Action!' he shouts.

The handycam rolls. JC signs the marriage certificate. Orchidee's thumb is inked red and pressed to the paper. Uncle Mei descends from the rhino. He feeds a long chain through a hoop protruding from the lowest ring on Orchidee's neck and hands the end to JC. 'I now pronounce you man and wife.'

Drums rumble. Uncle Mei and Hot Chocolatie applaud. A ceremonial gourd is wheeled in and the men take turns imbibing the rice spirit through a silver-plated reed.

The photographer arrives. He recognises the blind bride from the eclipse in the park only last Saturday. A double tragedy her ending up here, of course, but business is business and Mr Mei has always been very good for business. The photographer plucks at a scab on his skull and considers the options. 'Over here on the zebra skin, please. Lovely. And let's see you cuddle up with Mr Panda over there. Big smiles – perfect.' Click click click. 'Just one more. Let's have the groom feed his gorgeous bride a little rice wine. Sucky sucky on the gourd, sweetness. Beautiful. Hold it. Smile. Super.'

Lila's jaw aches from the shunting rings. It is useful sometimes, she thinks, to see grey clouds in the place of human forms. If she cannot see around her she does not have to be a part of what is happening around her. She will go elsewhere. She will go to her grandmother now, she thinks. She will recall her father's bedtime tales of this woman's resistance. Twenty American cowboys with their grenades and bayonets held at bay with a python and a chicken cleaver. 'It was ten long days before backup arrived,' her father would whisper through the mosquito net at night. 'But your grandmother never gave in. Defeat is not a word our family understands.' Lila smiles to herself and her jaw lifts a hair's breadth higher.

Beside her, her husband drains the gourd.

Uncle Mei makes a toast. 'To the happy couple! But most of all to the bride! Yes, Mr Bone, it is with sadness that I lose a daughter, but my loss is your gain. Today you acquire a woman of great flexibility, with a fertile womb and considerable oral potential.' He consults his watch. The next ceremony commences in thirty minutes. 'Hot Chocolatie, prepare for departure.'

Lila is handed a bitter-smelling tea glass. 'Drink up now for your Aunty.'

'Charlie, shoot this, will you.' JC turns to Mei. 'A traditional wedding drink, is it?'

'Certainly, Mrs Bone's drink is a great new tradition.' Mei grins golden into the camera lens. 'You purchase a songbird, you don't want it to fly the cage before it starts to sing. It is necessary to calm the feathers prior to exiting the shop.'

'Cut there.' JC chops at his neck.

'I already have,' says Charlie Thoc.

Lila refuses all Hottie C's attempts to cajole or press the glass to her lips. She listens to the rumble of a vehicle pulling up outside to take her to a place unknown. She tries to summon up pythons and a grandmother's courage.

Mei positions himself in front of the camera. 'Go-Go Dalat backroom boy, you film this now. From Uncle Mei to Mr and Mrs JC Bone, a small sign of goodwill and blessing. Whitney Houston – the world's greatest singer. I give you the world's greatest hit.'

A trapeze descends from the stuffed eagles, a boy hands Mei a microphone and he slips onto the bar and is winched into the air above the happy couple to serenade them with 'I Will Always Love You'.

Husband and wife are escorted from the building by two dark-skinned boys. 'Happy holidays!' Mei calls after them. 'Send us a postcard from the Mnongs, and do watch out for the cannibals' cauldrons!'

A thousand hyenas – or so it seems to Lila – begin to laugh. And the honeymooners' minibus ambles down the drive.

All the Money in the World Will Never Make a Man

The roads are busy in Dalat this Sunday morning. As a white minibus takes a turning off a shady road towards the town centre it passes a black police jeep heading south towards Saigon. Some indeterminate distance behind the jeep, but definitely beyond the range of its rear-view mirror, a motorcyclist on a Suzuki Spritely Mover tags along. This Sunday is going to be no kind of day for rest.

The two people travelling south in the jeep are bearded and sporting mirrored sunglasses. The passenger has accessorised with a navy beret. He is in possession of a fine moustache and is trying not to rub its strings too hard in excitement. After twenty years as a desk sergeant he now finds himself at the very heart of a Top Secret Policing Mission.

The man in the driving seat of the jeep is about to select a radio station when something in the passing white minibus makes him start. He stares in the rear-view mirror as the vehicle disappears from sight. He could swear he just saw his beautiful daughter – with a bowl of hair and a neck like a waterpipe. Chief Duong shakes his head; his eyes must be playing tricks on him. He cannot wait for the day to be done, to have his dear Lila safe behind peppermint walls and a father's foolishness forgotten. Soon to be in possession of more money than a man could probably even eat in his lifetime, Hung Duong will be doing things differently from now on. Better. Yes, he will be doing things better. Of that he is almost certain.

Chief Duong slows the jeep. Ahead of him several dozen Ma tribespeople are trudging down the road, all their belongings with them. Babies sleep swaddled on stooped backs, pots jostle against spur-wrapped cockerels in laden handcarts, pigs roll along in bamboo barrels, and yellow dogs trot behind on knotted string.

Chief Duong fingers his beard and considers the liberties a person might take incognito. He winds down the window to address the old man at the head of the procession. 'Good day to you, Father. Have the civil authorities evicted you?'

The Elder spits a betel shell into the dust, eyeing the black jeep's blue number plates. 'Who's asking?'

'A friend of the Montagnards who is sorry for your pain.'

'They came with dogs at dawn. People move out for bulldozers to move in. That's how it goes in these new times.'

'Where are you heading?'

'Tonight we sleep under the pines. Tomorrow we continue to the hills beyond Elephant Mountain. Five hectares we have been allocated.'

'Well, the soil is not so bad there. Perhaps one day you will be grateful for this move, yes?' Duong smiles encouragingly. 'Who knows, one day you may be a rich man with a coffee villa on the spot.'

The old man is slow to return a betel-stained smile. 'Mr so-called-friend of the Ma, that day will be far beyond the whistle of my last breath.'

A thin boy clutching a puppy runs to the jeep's mirror,

waggling the dog's paw at their reflections. The Elder strokes the boy's hair. 'I hope life will be easier for this one. Perhaps he will have his coffee villa some day.'

'Most certainly he will.' Duong investigates his pockets for peppermints for the child, and as he does so he discovers himself struck by a very interesting idea. It isn't out and out genius as such but it is heading that way. 'Listen, Father, imagine if tomorrow very great wealth was to land in your hands! Imagine that – then you could live wherever you choose! Would that not be a wonderful thing?' The chief slaps the steering wheel in excitement, seeing philanthropic possibilities expanding exponentially. Seeing a happy settlement of happy young boys and puppies and a smiling benevolent statue, perhaps carved by a grateful mother. 'You might even have a whole town of coffee villas – think of that!'

'So-called-friend of the Ma,' the old man's eyes soften with amusement, 'even if the clouds rained golden beans for a month, do not forget how it goes with us Vietnamese. Men may make money but all the money in the world will never make a man.'

'A noble sentiment, Father,' Duong removes his sunglasses and cannot help but beam – he feels an urgent need to stop and make a list. 'Money might not make a man but it can at least soften the bed on which he passes his life's nights. That, my friend, you cannot deny.'

The Elder looks steadily into Duong's eyes. 'A clean water well. That would be a start.' He turns to the boy. 'Come, we have still many steps to take.'

'Good luck to you,' Duong calls out, waving as he drives away. 'Do remember what I said – life has a way of delivering up surprises.'

Only he is surprised to discover he can't make himself heard over the blasts of a car horn. Flinging sheets of dust in its wake, a red taxi is hurtling up the road from the south. The car speeds past the chief's jeep. A Spritely Mover motorbike, which has been idling further back on the road, lurches evasively into a ditch.

In the driver's seat of the red taxi a Cao Dai disciple and part-time chauffeur clenches the wheel with trembling hands. He has no idea what crime he must have committed in any one of his previous existences to deserve the yellow-haired witch he is transporting north.

The driver avoids the mirror. Specifically he avoids the sight of the small silver device that the woman in the back is worshipping in her hands. The device that is forcing them towards the treacherous Highland route twenty-seven. He cannot argue for the tarmac of route fourteen against the glower of this woman's eyes – a purple he could not believe possible in any human eye. Not in any of the temple's paintings, where the whole of Creation is depicted, has he seen irises such a colour. Fear twists the driver's bowels as he pulls over at a roadside lean-to. 'Regret to inform madam of need for gasoline in engine.' He shields his eyes from her phosphorescent glare. 'Here I will purchase fuel from shop.'

In the back seat a combat-clad woman applies a ruby rim to her lips and dials a number on her cellphone.

It goes to voicemail.

Perfect.

'Good morning, boss, I hope you're doing good today. I'll keep it short and sweet for ya, Bradley. I just wanted to let you know I'm quitting. Other irons, other fires. No hard feelings and good luck with the soccer kid and all.

So long.' Sherry-Sioux blows a kiss into the phone and flips it closed.

She sits back and summons up a happy image of the shock on Burdock's gormless face when she delivers the boy safe and sound to a hand-picked selection of the world's media in a few hours' time. The fizz will pop right out of the family business when the news about Gola-Cola's covert chipping scheme hits the networks. She imagines the court scene – Goldie Hawn's daughter would be the one to play her – handkerchief at hand, witness for the prosecution: 'I understand, your honour. Microchips are illegal, and if I could take back my actions, I would. But I was simply obeying orders, as I did when Mr Burdock the Third insisted on the unpardonable delay in negotiating for the safe return of Sam Porcini. There was a corporate gun to my head, your honour, and a girl raised in a trailer park has her own reasons for not wanting to lose her job.

'But ultimately, your honour, I had to throw aside the fear that only those who have truly experienced destitution will understand, and I had to ask myself what really matters here. "Sherry-Sioux," I asked, "what really matters here?" And there was only one answer – Sammy Porcini. Getting Sammy back alive.'

She slides a finger around the waist of her combats. Ten years out of the Marines and she still fits nice and lean. The world better be ready for Sherry-Sioux Ballou. 'Yo! Driver!' she winds down the window. 'Grab us a Gola-Cola. Skylite if they have it, and take one for yourself.'

The driver nods miserably. He does not like this rot anymore now than when his American friends gave it him during the war. It ruined the teeth, fouled the stomach and emptied the wallet. There was not much that could be said for it.

If it could be conveyed to him, it might give the chauffeur some comfort to know he is not the only driver on the road today experiencing discontent in his choice of profession. One hundred kilometres north of the taxi transporting Staff Sergeant Ballou, Marine Corps Rtd, a loaded sedan is leaving a hospital in Buon Ma Thuot and turning from the city onto route twenty-seven – the recently de-mined track along the dragon's backbone to Dalat. The taxi is grunting in second gear towards the first hill. Its driver sucks on a cigarette and casts curses at the man – the oily so-called doctor – in the back seat.

This oily so-called doctor seems to have only the vaguest of notions where they are going. Not only is this the same route they drove – pointlessly – last night, but the silly man is refusing to say which of the twenty or so lakes in the region he requires. 'It will be about an hour's drive away,' he said when they set off. 'When we reach the lake of her memory she'll give me a sign and we'll stop there. That will be our destination, driver. That's all you need to know.'

The driver spits a curse against oily doctors and their many sillinesses. To add to this, the unrestrained breasts of the tomb-toothed nurse sitting beside him are proving a hazard on the muddy tracks, joggling about so wantonly in his vision. He spits a second curse out the window. They are a temptation too far for any man – let alone a tantric practitioner who has now clocked up two weeks without.

And in addition to all these woes, as if any were needed, there is the matter of the shorn-skulled and blindfolded fatty the doctor has wheeled out and wedged in the back seat, and from whom they are all waiting on a sign. Beyond a rudimentary sign of life, presumably. That's if she doesn't shatter the car's suspension at the first pothole. He spits twice more. He has only had the damned car a week.

The driver snorts and flicks his burning cigarette out the window. He reflects that perhaps he should have denied the gambling allegations at the monastery and stuck it out with the monks. Souls such as Chaura's are not reborn for labour.

The Nice New Brotherhood and Sisterhood of Ape-ish Folk

But it's not all rage on the road this Sunday morning. There is one group of travellers, heading west, who look rather chipper, despite the hardships of their journey and the distance they have already covered.

Liberation has proved a dizzying tonic for a ragtag band of individuals, formerly gathered under the titular umbrella of the Monkey Liberation Army, who are now making their way to Laos. They have survived four nights in the forest, and after a few teething troubles they are getting on surprisingly well.

'The secret to any successful operating system is order,' the silverbacked gorilla had announced, halting the weary troops at noon the day after they fled in fear of their lives from Dalat. 'Organisation and order.'

'Also, an equal weighting given to the rights of the individual and the needs of society,' the female chimpanzee murmured, rummaging in a clump of leaves for avocados.

The exhausted snub-nosed monkeys slumped in a pile and said nothing. The black baboon curled up in Grace's lap and sucked its thumb. Fang tried to keep his eyes open and pay attention.

'In addition, the humans may need to take a back seat

for a while,' the gorilla continued. 'Nothing personal, my man, just a hunch I have. After centuries of human oppression there may be some residual resentment in the ranks. It could erupt any time. I'd keep your head down if I were you.'

Fang stifled a yawn with his hand. 'If you think so.'

'Absolutely. Glad that's cleared up.' The gorilla turned to disband the already disbanded army. 'Apes fall out. Bald chimp bury cancerous smoking materials. Scour sleeping areas for signs of snake or scorpion infestation. Forage for foodstuffs et cetera. We'll rest here till mid-afternoon.'

Grace watched Fang watching the gorilla. 'He does like to thump his chest a lot,' she whispered. 'I'd love to know what he thinks he's saying that's so important.'

Fang smiled and plucked a seedball from her fringe.

Grace felt herself shiver all over at this touch of his fingers on her hair, and she planted a super-quick kiss on his cheek.

The following morning, when they had covered some fifteen kilometres by foot and tree, the gorilla halted the march in order to convene a meeting. Things were on his mind, he said. After the snub-nosed monkeys had handed out green cashews and papaya, he hammered on his magnificent chest and waited for silence. 'I have a very important announcement. It is this. I propose an immediate ditching of the moniker Monkey Liberation Army.'

'And there's me thinking you were stopping us for a reason,' Dicky said.

The gorilla ignored Dicky and went on to point out that the generic term 'monkey' was demeaning to sub-genuses, snub-nosed or otherwise. In addition, and without contradiction, he explained, the word 'monkey' was a label of exclusivity – applied in ignorance – that raised a discriminatory bar against tailless primates, preventing them from getting involved in what was otherwise a top-notch organisation.

The black baboon, who had fallen asleep, was woken by a silverbacked nudge in the belly to second this, after which a motion was put forward by the gorilla for the renaming of the organisation to GALA – the Great Ape Liberation Army.

The cashews were very tasty and this motion was all but carried in munching acquiescence when Jackie O flicked out of an upward cobra via a downward dog and said, 'Hold it there, team.' She'd been pondering a few things herself during the night and had grown rather uncomfortable with the whole idea of liberation. To her mind such a state was eternally elusive because there were always things you had to do which made a mockery of the notion of freedom. 'No matter how cageless you think you are, you will be a slave to your body to the day you die,' she said. 'Therefore, any talk of liberation is inherently misleading.' In fact, she didn't know why there was even a word for it, because as soon as an animal grew into consciousness it acquired a raft of obligations – emotional, social, physical and psychological – that were as thick as its skin. 'Which is not only warty – as Dicky will tell you – but also impossible to peel off without causing haemorrhaging and certain death.' Consequently, Jackie concluded, after so many years a captive she wouldn't be altogether happy putting her name to an organisation that gave false hope of a false freedom.

Following a brief pause to allow this philosophical dampener to sink in, the smallest of the snub-nosed monkeys, a blushing golden-headed creature who hadn't spoken a word for days, surprised herself by plucking up the courage to say, 'If I could just add, it isn't so much the Liberation as the Army part of the title that bothers me.' She said she found the notion of being in an army rather distasteful. And that no army she'd heard of had ever been one hundred per cent effective. After all, wasn't there a fifty per cent probability of defeat in any combat situation? And didn't all primates simply get tired of fighting, when they ran out of sticks or things to beat the other side with?

Hearing this, the gorilla – who'd had to smother a yawn during Jackie's discourse – could hardly contain himself. He leaped up to batter his magnificent chest most magnificently and second this fine point. 'Ape Guerrillas! That is what we'll call ourselves,' he said. Because everyone knew guerrillas had an excellent track record of winning wars. Being a distant cousin of the guerrilla subspecies he added that he was happy to put himself forward as the outfit's frontman, if they could find a weapon that didn't look too puny against his magnificent chest. Possibly, he thought, a bazooka might do it.

Whereupon the shy golden-headed monkey surprised herself and the others still further – and it was a good job her coat was such a fine burnished colour because she was blushing to the tip of her tail – by saying, 'Excuse me again, but does it have to be about weapons? Couldn't we just say we'll all try to be nice to each other?'

Which had everyone stumped and busy stacking cashew shells for a minute or two, because although the snub-nosed monkeys and Jackie had no objections to the title 'Nice Ape-ish Folk', it didn't appear to resonate with the chest-thumper in the troop.

Finally, apologising for the intrusion, Fang forwarded the notion of brotherhood, explaining there had been a Brotherhood of Man before, devoted to singing and generally being nice to everyone. The strong defended the weak when necessary, he explained quickly to the gorilla, but the foremost concept was a sense of equality.

'And?' the gorilla raised an eyebrow, while Jackie O expressed her instinctive feeling that equality was at worst a delusion and at best a pipe dream.

'And?' the gorilla insisted.

Fang looked at his feet. 'It hasn't worked out too well.'

Following a long silence, Tricky Dicky, for whom politics was not a forte, and who had therefore held his tongue for far longer than any artiste could reasonably be expected, tried to lighten the mood. 'What's green and lives in a cage? An unripe canary.'

The snub-noseds applauded politely, then the little golden-headed monkey raised her hand. 'Excuse me, please? There's no reason our organisation has to be like that human brotherhood. One failure doesn't mean we can't try again. Brotherhood is a nice-sounding name, and those ideals of singing and equality and whatnot are nice too.'

The gorilla snorted. 'Something like a *New* Brotherhood of Apes, you mean?'

'Well,' she said, flame-faced and going for broke, 'we shouldn't forget the sisters and the being nice bit. How about the Nice New Brotherhood and Sisterhood of Ape-ish Folk?'

'NNBSAF? Wet as water, if you ask me.' But with

magnificent self-sacrifice the gorilla put it to the democratic vote. There were no more cashews left, and as most members were itching to find more, it was agreed.

During a break on the afternoon of the second day's hike the gorilla approached Fang, who was reading Grace's long-overdue Reigate Public Library's Anglo-Vietnamese dictionary. He was turning the pages with a studious air, trying to conceal the fact that his stomach felt as if it were home to thousands of fluttering moths. A sensation he put down to an absence of tofu from his diet, but to an impartial observer may have had more to do with an English girl's fingers stroking his hair, checking his scalp, she said, for nits.

And Grace? Despite the tropical terrain and a lack of chocolate from her own diet, she was also thriving. Although she was finding it hard to concentrate on nits. As Fang digressed from the dictionary's Hs, abandoning hams, hamsters and harmonicas to explain to Grace how his father had lived for four years in this area with not much more than a hammock and a handgun, Grace was trying to decide whether offering a head massage would be inappropriately forward.

'Have a word?'

Grace jumped. The gorilla seemed to have materialised from thin air.

Fang looked up.

'Touchy subject. Wondered what you thought. In private, my man, best spoken about in private.'

Fang looked at Grace looking at him and he blushed. 'Excuse me a minute.' He laid down the dictionary and followed the ape into the undergrowth.

Grace shook her head and leaned back into the sunshine and giggled, wondering once again why she felt so perfectly happy.

The gorilla plucked a soldier ant from his eyebrow and threw it into the long grass, where he and Fang were crouching to confer.

'How can I help?'

'I want to talk to you about systems.'

'Systems?'

'Quite.' The gorilla glanced back at the camp, where Tricky Dicky was juggling six mangoes and the snub-noseds were politely applauding, Jackie O was meditating, and the baboon was sloping back to Grace for a cuddle. 'I mean, it's all well and good going on about niceness and wishy-washy nonsense like that. It's easy to be democratic with words. But what if things were to go awry in the real world? I'm not suggesting they would, but seriously, if they did we'd be stupider than sloths if we weren't fully prepared.'

'Are sloths stupid?'

'This has nothing to do with sloths!'

'What is it to do with?'

'Being prepared, for heaven's sake, do keep up! I'm only suggesting that you and I should have an operational system worked out in the event of an incident in which there is no time for democratic chit-chat before action is required. I only bring it up because the baboon's clearly past it, and that bald chimpanzee – well, jokers can't be leaders, can they?'

'I get it now,' Fang smiled. 'This is all about you wanting to be the Alpha male.'

The gorilla lowered his brows and looked wounded. 'My dear boy, I wouldn't dream of putting it so crudely.'

'I'm sorry.'

'But seeing as you propose – I accept!' The gorilla bared his teeth brightly and offered his hand. 'That's official then. You'll make a fantastic Beta. You won't regret it.'

'I don't suppose I will.'

'By the way, I suggest we don't bother the females with any of this,' the gorilla muttered in Fang's ear as they rejoined the camp. 'They don't seem to grasp the importance of the Alpha position in quite the way we males do. One overall boss for both sexes should suffice.'

'Good, you're back,' Grace said, seeing Fang come towards her. 'How's the chest-thumping coming on?'

'Fine.' He couldn't help smiling – a little shyly, wondering if one day he could tell her the truth. One day, maybe in some sort of animal rescue centre they would run together, with their children playing about them. He was sure she wouldn't laugh when he did.

It was such a ridiculous thought – but a wonderful one – this vision of a future that Fang realised would make him happy in all the important ways, that his face broke into a full-beamed smile.

'Golly gosh,' Grace said. One minute she'd been reading through the Gs, the next she'd been struck by a laser. And powerless to stop herself, she leaned forward and planted a kiss smack on Fang's lips.

For three days that was pretty much how things went with the Nice New Brotherhood of Ape-ish Folk (Sisterhood having been dropped from the title in common usage, with few objections on the whole and a compromise agreement to its inclusion before the word Brotherhood in all official communiqués). They hiked the Highlands, skirting settlements, feasting from wild fruit and crops they found unguarded. They crossed bridges at night and swung through forested slopes in the day – their arms growing stronger and looser. They swapped tales of capture and incarceration, and gobbled up cassava and turnip and dictionary words. Some of them applauded politely to repeated jokes. They practised Niceness.

On the fourth evening the Brotherhood made camp by a narrow waterfall that fell from grey karst boulders to a deep blue pool. After dining on roasted yams, the gorilla climbed a sycamore to consult the stars. They were only a couple of weeks' hike from the Laos border, he declared.

Fang went to sit with Grace. She was splashing her toes in the water's white spray. 'It seems we're not that far from Laos.'

'We're not?'

'A couple of weeks, if that.'

'And there was me thinking we were just running away into the forest while things calmed down.'

'Well, we have to run somewhere, don't we?'

'I suppose we do.'

'And it would be better to head to a new country. We'll be safe in Laos.'

'Oh.' Grace pulled her toes out of the cold water, feeling suddenly and most unaccountably peculiar. 'I hadn't really thought about it.'

'What's there to think about?'

'For a start, what will we do at the border?'

'We'll find a way across.'

'What do we do after the border, then?'

'Grace.' Fang took her hand in his. They did this easily

and often now. '"Leave tomorrow's cares in the care of tomorrow." That's what my father would say whenever we were scared, or too worried about something to sleep. He would invent proverbs that were meant to be comforting. "The pig that goes to its slaughter with a song is a happy pig indeed." Or, "See how boldly the snail slips along the path – while ahead, the hungry crow is waiting." That was a favourite for a while.'

'Well, they're not comforting me.'

Fang touched her cheek softly. 'Maybe they make more sense in Vietnamese.'

Grace stuck a heel in the spray and didn't answer.

'What's wrong?'

She shook her head. After a long pause she looked at him. 'I really don't know. It's just like something's gone and punched all the happiness out of me – pow! – right in the stomach. Perhaps I thought we could run forever. Stupid really. Perhaps it's this waterfall that's doing it.'

'The waterfall?'

'When I was small my dad used to tell me that the bubbles flying off the cliffs were the world's sorrows. When they smashed on the rocks below all the pain would break into pieces. A fresh approach, I guess, for a climate geographer. But, of course, bubbles don't shatter, do they? The water keeps on flowing to the oceans, to be sucked up in the sky where it falls again like fresh tears.' Grace watched the water, remembering rivers near Reigate and family picnics and how long it had been, weeks now, since she ran away from home. She shakes her head – she mustn't think of it, of home. 'At least that's my romantic interpretation of what happens.'

'That sounds like something my mother might come

up with.' It was Fang's turn to stare into the water. 'She's the guardian of the sadness in our family. She doesn't really bother with proverbs any more, though Dad says she once loved them. Now that the Duongs have been doomed, she says there's no point.'

'Doomed?'

'Oh yes, we're all done for. "Better a quick-thinking maternal hand had drowned us all at birth" she said once.'

Grace stared at Fang. 'She said *what*?'

'She was particularly unhappy at the time.'

'I thought she was a Catholic. I thought they believed you were responsible for making your own fate – your own doom.'

'She was. But after Lila had her accident she began to wonder whether there must be more doom out there that we were destined to shoulder. Of course, my parents had already both lost family in the war. But when I had my accident she felt it confirmed her suspicions. The Duongs were always doomed to be doomed.'

'But that would mean she wouldn't be responsible for the doom – if she couldn't help it happening.'

'Pointless, isn't it?'

'Not if you still *feel* responsible. I can see how that would make you pretty miserable.'

Fang said nothing.

'Anyway, what accident did you have?'

'I fell off a moped. And then I couldn't speak for a while. Nothing much really.'

'What has that got to do with your mum?'

'Not much.'

'What about Lila, then?'

Fang didn't take his eyes off the waterfall as he shook

his head. 'Poor Lila. It was just an accident really, I do know that. Mother took us both on a dig before school one morning – this was in the days when she still believed in archaeology. She was always talking about unearthing something – something that would really matter.' Fang laughed. 'She thought pots mattered. She said we needed to look out for things that would change our under-standing of the past, because the past shapes the present and the present informs the future. We went east of Dalat into the hills. We loved going because Mother got so excited. She'd be laughing and singing, but above all, talking. Warriors and empires and rites and rituals, arrow-heads, armoury, politics – if it was about archaeology you couldn't shut her up. She was a real academic, Mother. Is. She is.' Fang smiled. 'My father hated us going – the hills weren't all mine-cleared back then – but he never stopped her. He never could stop her doing anything, and I don't think he ever really wanted to. For one thing, she was always so happy when she came back. Happy in a way that fitted her properly for a while, you know, the sort of happiness that settles under the skin.

'On that morning my mother got carried away. She'd discovered shards of terracotta strewn through the soil and one or two tiny beads she thought might be agate. She hoped it was some sort of regal burial site. Anyway, she became so engrossed that she forgot about getting us to school on time.

'So we had to run, because we didn't want to be punished. It was as simple as that. Well, not quite. I asked Lila to race. We always used to race downhill when we were little, but Lila was less keen now she was growing up. But I begged her. She was ahead of me and just as we hurtled down the path onto the road, she caught the hem of her ao dai in her sandals and slipped on the tarmac. A surfacing lorry skidded to avoid her and then lost its load. Gravel in the corneas. Inoperable, the doctors said. So we were all to blame really.'

'But your dad?'

'He'd allowed the lorries to travel with excess loads. The company was owned by a friend of his. It wouldn't have lost its load if it was under the legal weight restriction.'

Fang stared into the water.

'It sounds like it wasn't anybody's fault really, Fang. It just sounds like a terrible accident. You said that yourself.'

'That was the first time my mother took to bed. She didn't get up for three months. Most of the pot shards went in the bin – "useless clay from worthless soil" she called them. That was the end of the kings and the start of the doom. Did I ever tell you how my father said he fell in love with her?'

Grace took Fang's hand. They sat watching the water crash onto the rocks as Fang talked of wars and proverbs and growing family doom. And as she listened, Grace felt her heart stiffen with sadness. She thought of her own family. She thought of Fang. She thought of Laos. She began to realise what she had to do. There really was no other way. If only she could find strength enough to do it.

Miss Marsden's Needs

Fang is already up and turning bananas in the campfire's embers when Grace wakes on Sunday morning, certain of what must be done. She goes to wash in the waterfall. Despite the chill she takes her time.

'I was thinking,' she says, heading to the fire where Fang is coaxing a snail away from the hot stones, 'if we do go to Laos there'll be no turning back.'

'You're right, there won't be.'

'I could fly out any time I want to, but you—'

'Me?'

'Well, I'm not entirely sure how these things work but you might not be able to get back into Vietnam if they have you marked as a criminal.'

'Who's saying I want to come back?'

She squats down and rubs her wet nose against his shoulder and tries to decide how to say what she needs to say next. The truth is she feels herself inexperienced in matters of the heart. She is, she reminds herself, a good eighteen months from official adulthood and it's probably all right to feel this way. Whether it's all right to do what she now needs to do, she isn't sure.

But it must be done.

She draws a deep breath and then she begins it: the end of everything.

This is what she doesn't say: 'Really, Fang? You want to leave Vietnam and never come back? So all your talk these past four days about how your father taught you to hack teak for firewood and bamboo for shelter, all the stories of how he stripped pine spears to catch fish midstream, and fermented cane rum in coconut husks, how he could start a fire with a single cotton bud – all this counts for nothing?'

Nor does she say, 'All the times you told me how your sister's hands can cure a headache or toothache with one tweak of a toe, and morning sickness with a scrape of a knuckle on a knee – this also counts for nothing?'

And she certainly doesn't say, 'And all your mother's stories of dragons and sorcerers and ancient kings, and this terrible burden of doom she feels for you all – this too is nothing to you?'

No, Grace bites her lip and rubs her wet eyes on the back of Fang's T-shirt and says none of these things. Instead she says, 'I don't want you to throw away everything for a few days of adventure. I started all this. It's my responsibility. Perhaps you should go back now. To your family. It's not too late, you know.'

Fang turns to face her, confused. 'But I'm happy, Grace. I thought we were both happy.'

Grace swipes her eyes and shrugs.

Fang frowns at the fire. 'Even if the monkeys don't need me, I thought maybe you did. If I went home now I'd be sent to jail. I couldn't do that to my family. My father, the police chief? The shame of it would destroy him.'

And not seeing you again? What do you think that would do to him? This Grace thinks, but also doesn't say. She doesn't want to think of families. She bites her lip until blood seeps into her mouth.

'OK,' she says eventually. 'I just wanted to check. I won't say another word. We'll keep on moving, then. To Laos.'

Relief bursts from Fang's smile. 'To Laos.'

Grace turns away, pretending to scan the scenery, preparing to force out the words from which there will be no return. 'In that case, if we're going all the way to Laos, I could really do with a chocolate milkshake, I'm absolutely craving one.'

Fang laughs out loud. He laughs for the relief of it. 'If you like, after breakfast we'll head to the nearest village and stock up.'

'Yes,' Grace sniffs, 'let's do that.'

Like this the die is cast.

'What's the stupidest animal in the jungle? A polar bear. Two elephants walk off a cliff – BOOM BOOM!'

The bananas have been eaten, the snub-nosed monkeys are applauding Dicky's morning stand-up routine, and the gorilla is harrumphing at the Brotherhood to hurry up the theatricals and fall in for departure when Fang brings up the issue of Grace's milkshake and the need to make a brief diversion to a village.

'In daylight?' The gorilla raises an eyebrow. 'I'd like to enquire of the human whether a detour for luxuries is a wise idea, given the imperative for constant vigilance and evasive reaction to all contact with his kind.' He lowers his brow and begins to pace back and forth, pounding his knuckles into the soft earth. 'The more I think about it the more I'm convinced it's an idiotic idea to risk the dangers associated with humanity for a quart of sweetened cow's milk. Blatant lunacy, in fact. And, if I might add, entirely lacking in esprit de corps. May I suggest the human in question makes do with chewing sugar cane? Who will second me?'

The members of the Brotherhood stare at their toes.

'Come on, come on, we don't have all day.'

Suddenly there is a nervous squeak. 'Not me!' It is the tiny golden-headed monkey. 'I mean, excuse me, Mr Kong, but I don't mind if we do detour and whatnot.'

'You don't?'

'No.'

'I see.' The gorilla glowers at the ground. In the spreading silence he is heard to mutter something. It could be anything but it sounds remarkably like, 'Damn female. She may be a fluffy midget but she's got Alpha written all over her.'

The monkey blushes. 'What I meant was, we are a *Nice* Brotherhood and Sisterhood, aren't we? So I hope we could try to accommodate Miss Marsden's needs. Perhaps members will agree with me that she's looking a little peaky.'

'The human species seems to require a vast nutritional range,' Jackie O adds, twisting herself into wise eagle. 'On health grounds, I would say the benefits to Miss Marsden outweigh the risks to the Brotherhood.'

Dicky jumps up and whoops. 'Put me down for a case of Gola-Cola and two hundred Craven A. What do you call a deer with no eyes?'

'No idea,' the gorilla growls.

And the milkshake motion is passed.

After two hours' trekking, the snub-nosed scouts climb a pine and sight a village of dusty thatched longhouses at the end of a muddy track. A long black lake spreads like a slick of oil at the far end of the settlement.

Grace, who hasn't let go of Fang's hand all morning, pulls him aside. 'I'll go in alone.'

'Don't be silly, you need me to translate.'

'We don't know what's been broadcast on the tannoys. The police will certainly be looking for you,' she says, 'whereas I can probably pass for a tourist. I'll whistle if I need you, I promise. I'm a great whistler.'

'I don't know, Grace. Your ears are on wanted posters everywhere. Even with the balaclava, they're quite – um – distinctive, you know.'

'Oh pish.' Grace affects breeziness. 'Honestly, I could do with a bit of space.'

'Space?' Fang looks up at the sky.

Grace bites her lip and forces a laugh. 'Time on my own. It's what my mum sometimes says.'

'Time without me?'

'No, Fang, I never ever want time without you. Always remember that.'

Fang blushes and looks away.

To distract them both, Grace asks what else they might need. Fang suggests cigarettes and cola for the chimpanzee. Grace asks him to write that down in Vietnamese. While he writes she turns aside and slips two hundred thousand dong, plus eighty dollars and her passport, from her rucksack into her money belt.

She takes the note from Fang, closes her eyes to breathe him in for a second and kisses him quickly on the nose.

'OK, I'm off then. Ta-rah, toodle-pip.'

'Grace?' Fang calls out as she scarpers down the hillside. 'Wait a minute.'

But she doesn't. And she doesn't look back.

The Kind of Moment the Brotherhood Has Been Waiting For

It is a sweltering almost shadowless noon. The village is deserted. Through the haze the wooden buildings shiver as if uncertain of their existence. Hens and pigs are flattened to smudges in patches of shade around the stilts. A lone dog pants in the grass beneath a tree full of laughing cicadas – the only sound of life. Even if Grace had intended to buy a chocolate milkshake she would have been out of luck. It is coffee day in Buon Ma Thuot and the villagers have gone to spread their beans at the feet of the city's middlemen.

'Good afternoon?' she calls out in her politest Vietnamese, walking down the scorched track, silent longhouses on either side.

'Anyone home?' she says in English.

Grace walks the length of the village. She passes the last longhouse – a dilapidated structure at some remove from the others. This too is deserted. But there are canoes tethered in the lilies at the lake's edge. Perhaps someone is out fishing. She can appeal to them.

'Hello, hello, hello,' she calls out.

At first she thinks it is only her voice echoing this sound that comes back across the water: 'Ho ho ho.'

She shouts again, this time as hard as she can, 'Hello hello hello.'

But now it isn't a 'ho ho ho' but a 'hop' she hears. 'Hop, hop, hopppp' – the moan hanging in the gluey air.

Grace shivers. The whole place is dead but for this voice. She reminds herself that there are no such things as ghosts. There are absolutely, definitely no such things as ghosts. And certainly not in daytime. Get a grip, Grace Marsden, she tells herself.

'Hop hop hop.' The voice is coming from across the lake. Grace peers into the water. It looks even blacker close up. And deep. Hadn't Fang's father told him fresh-water crocodiles prowled these mountain lakes?

'Hop hop hop.'

'I hear you,' Grace mutters. She pulls on the bow of a canoe. There are no obvious reptilian grins lurking below.

Grace shields the sun from her eyes. Across the water she can make out a blob of something grey. Land perhaps.

'Hoppppppppppppppppppppp.'

'Blimey, I said I heard you.' Grace clambers into the boat and takes up the paddle.

The unilateral surrender of the Monkey Liberation Army to the Vietnamese authorities will just have to wait.

Grace doesn't know what she might be expecting from the island, but it is not this: row after row of tiny stilt houses, rather like a parking lot for sedan chairs, she thinks, or kennels for high-ranking dogs. All the huts have thatched roofs and some are bound with buffalo horns. One has more horns than the others. It is from this hut that the 'hop hopping' is coming. 'Hello?' Grace goes over and lifts the hatch. 'Anyone home?'

It takes a few seconds for her eyes to adjust to the gloom. It takes several more for her brain to absorb the tableau set before her and apply an anaesthetising dollop of shock.

'That looks like Sam Porcini,' she laughs. 'But you don't look anything like you do on Emma's poster. This is ridiculous – *Sam Porcini?*'

'Hopppp,' a mouth replies which does indeed belong to the Scunthorpe striker and international icon. He is lying naked on his back on a board. And he is being straddled by what appears to be the sitting corpse of a very old woman. 'Hop hop,' he moans weakly.

'But that's ridiculous,' Grace reports, swiftly shutting the hatch and standing back to think things through. 'He isn't wearing any clothes.'

The second time of looking Grace sucks in her cheeks and bites them – a hitherto infallible method of keeping a grip on knowing who she is and where she is and that she is seeing what she is – but the scene remains unchanged. A naked shackled footballer is stretched out on a board, to all intents and purposes being ridden by an elderly female pygmy jockey whose skirts are tucked into her waistband and whose thighbones are gripping in a vice of rigor mortis.

'Goodness,' Grace blushes with sudden realisation, 'I'm so sorry to disturb you, Mr Porcini, I won't breathe a word of this to the papers.' And she shuts the hatch and turns and marches away down the shore.

Behind her the 'hopping' heightens in pitch.

'Jesus, Mary and Joseph, no need to howl about it.' Grace increases her speed, her hands clamped to her ears. 'The whole world doesn't need to hear you.'

But now she stops in her departing tracks. For Grace, while innocent in many matters of the flesh and brought up to respect a person's privacy however celebrated they may be, is beginning to wonder whether two and two do in fact add up correctly in this particular situation.

She peers past the dead old woman. It's definitely Sam Porcini. His pupils crawl towards her. 'Hop.'

'Help? Is that what you're trying to say, Mr Porcini? Certainly. One moment please.'

It is the kind of moment the Brotherhood has been waiting for; one of the members at least. Grace's emergency whistle carries far, and fifteen minutes later she is waving ashore a long canoe with Fang at the helm, two chimpanzees and a gorilla at the paddles, and several queasy monkeys and a baboon clinging to the sides.

Looking into the tomb Fang's eyes turn white as peeled lychees.

'I know,' Grace whispers, 'it's the weirdest thing. He's alive, he just isn't moving. What do you think?'

'I think,' Fang says slowly, 'that looks like my grand-mother.'

Only three times in his life has Fang come to the village by the lake. Visits made in the company of his father at an age when Fang still enjoyed playing Top Secret Policing Missions. So there is a chance he might not have recognised this ancient woman whose shrivelled head is thrown back in ecstasy. Who, in her gaping grin, looks like she is having a great laugh, possibly the last laugh. But around the corpse's neck dangles a familiar pouch from which break-fever medicine was once dispensed to a malarial grandson. And this could not be anything other than the family tomb on the island where the living did not venture for fear they would never leave. Where his grandfather had been laid out after his unexpected death four years before Fang was born. Come to think of it – Fang's head is spinning – if the footballer is stretched out here, then where on earth is Grandfather?

'Excuse me,' Fang mumbles and he turns around to vomit.

It proves no easy task, removing the old woman's corpse. Poonana has screwed her toes beneath the footballer's thighs and must be wrangled down to his knees before she can be unhooked and levered off.

Grace is quick to set about Sam's bonds with her penknife. She saws through everything but the locked handcuffs. But once liberated the footballer shows no signs of movement, nothing beyond a slow rolling of his eyeballs. Now that he is being attended to, even his hop-hopping has ceased.

Fang taps her shoulder. 'Will you come down to the shore a moment, Grace?'

'We'll be right back, Mr Porcini, don't you worry about a thing.'

'Listen,' Fang whispers as they walk away. 'I have a horrible feeling the footballer may have been poisoned.'

'*What?*'

Fang says nothing.

Grace's eyes widen with another thought. 'You meant it, didn't you? It really is your grandmother in there.'

'She was wearing this.' Fang shows Grace the pouch he took from the old woman's neck. 'My grandmother lives out this way. She keeps snakes to make venom potions and she always has a pouch like this – *exactly* like this – around her neck.'

Grace pulls the drawstring and sniffs the black paste. 'Now this really is crazy. I mean, there's Sam Porcini in there with your grandmother and they've been, well, they've been—' she begins to blush with thoughts of things as yet unsaid and certainly undone between them. 'Is he going to die?' She hangs the pouch around her own neck for safekeeping. 'Is that what you're telling me?'

'I don't honestly know. My guess is that if his body's held out this long then he might not. But he might not recover any further either.'

'Jesus, Mary and Joseph.'

'I know.'

'But how on earth would your grandmother lug him here? And where on earth did she get him from? In fact what on earth has any of this got to do with your blinking grandmother? Sorry but blimey, Fang. Blimey.'

Fang looks down. 'Did you see the black box?'

'With the wires leading to the handcuffs?'

'It's old-fashioned police re-education equipment. Grace, my father has a box just like that one.'

Grace clamps a hand to her mouth.

'All right,' she says eventually. 'Let's consider the black box. Logically it suggests this business has something to do with the police, and yes, possibly the application of force, I suppose we must concede that. But what other clues are there? Sam was given a pillow. This suggests the provision of comfort. Whoever took Sam Porcini didn't want him to die. That's my guess.'

Fang looks unconvinced. 'You think so?'

'Absolutely. He was probably kidnapped by someone

who wanted to scupper England's chances. Are there any big matches coming up?'

Fang shrugs. As far as he knows his father isn't a football man.

'Yes, that makes sense, and your grandmother must have stumbled on him by accident and done what many a lonely-hearted person might do,' Grace breezes. 'That's the good news, OK?'

Fang nods, very willing to go along with this blame-skirting hypothesis.

'Unfortunately, the less than good news is that if whoever put him here didn't want him to die, it means they'll be back for him soon.' Grace surveys their location – the dense palms, the long grass, the thickening jungle vegetation inland. 'We need to hide Sam – and quickly. When the kidnapper returns we'll have to surprise him at the tomb, overpower him and secure him with Sam's rope. With me so far?'

Fang looks uncertain. 'Couldn't we just ship the footballer back now?'

'And get ourselves into more trouble than we're already in? I don't think so, Fang.' Grace takes his hand and tries to give him a look of confidence. 'Once the kidnapper is secured, we'll ship him to the village and back into Dalat for justice to be served. We'll probably be heroes at the end of it.' What's more, she thinks, the police will have to let us off the hook for stealing monkeys, so I won't need to turn myself in after all. Which is such a totally wonderful thought that Grace plonks a kiss on Fang's cheek. Then she returns to the practicalities. 'Do you think you could get the monkeys to hide in the jungle? They do seem to follow you, and it would help with the surprise element and the overpowering if they all charged out at the kidnapper at once.'

Fang looks at her.

'Does it sound too crazy?'

'You're marvellous.'

'So are you.' Grace looks at Fang until she is sizzled to nothing. 'We should probably hunt out a suitable base camp,' she says eventually.

Working together most magnificently the Brotherhood clears the ground between three date palms in the jungle a short way back from the tomb. The snub-nosed monkeys gather pineapple and dragonfruit for lunch. The chimpanzees fetch firewood, and the black baboon, who has spent many peaceable afternoons at the restaurant with Binh Linh's hobby-loving wife, weaves reeds into a mattress for Sam to lie on. They conceal him in a bamboo thicket. Fang places his grandmother on the corpseboard. In the grass beneath the tomb he finds a plastic bag full of old bones. He puts it inside the tomb beside his grandmother's body. He bows and shuts the hatch.

The male primates draw lots. Unlucky Dicky climbs the tallest palm to begin the first lookout. In the thicket the snub-noseds take turns massaging Sam to encourage his sluggish blood.

'Excellent work by all Brotherhood members,' the gorilla says, pacing up and down in a supervisory fashion. 'Keep it up, team.'

And nestled in the footballer's shoulder, a tiny chip emits a summoning signal.

Engorged By Desire, a Boar Can Be Driven Crazy

On the back seat of a white honeymooning minibus heading out of Dalat, a bride formerly known as Lila Duong turns towards her husband and taps on the brass rings trapping her neck. 'Please, hubby,' she says in the English for Export she has recently acquired, 'you take all off now.'

JC looks up from the groundbreaking travelogue he has started – *Adventures of a Post-colonialist in a Pre-civilised Land. Chapter One – Marriage! To a divine and pure village girl in a ceremony replete with ancient traditions!!* He takes a moment to consider his wife. His *wife*! He cannot get over the way her unseeing eyes seem to stare into the heart of him. He waves his fingers in her face. Nothing. Not even a consolation blink, the poor darling. He imagines her imagining him. A mysterious stranger. A tall dark handsome mysterious stranger. That's probably what she's thinking. And a darn sight more muscular than the men she'd be used to.

Lila re-tings the metal. 'You take off, yes please.'

JC pats her slender wrist, feeling pity surge in his stomach. She'll never see how straight his teeth are. How sunlight transforms his ringlets into twists of molten amber. How his jaw can portray sensitive and strong at the same time. JC sighs and tosses his hair. He should not deny himself the chivalry this blindness entails. She will depend on him absolutely.

Thinking this is his first mistake.

His second is unlocking the brass bands.

'Thank you.' Lila rubs her throat. 'Please excuse me.' She clambers over her husband and makes her way to the front of the minibus as the vehicle takes the turning onto route twenty-seven.

'Charlie Dan Thoc,' she whispers, leaning towards the boy on the front passenger seat who is filming out the window.

The camera wobbles, the boy gasps.

'Yes, Charlie, you should be ashamed of yourself getting mixed up in all this. And don't even bother with "how did you know it was me?" I could recognise the stink of your foot fungus from the other side of the moon.'

Charlie Thoc turns away, blushing from the heat of Lila's disgust. She could always do that to him, lovely Lila Duong. 'Hello, Lila.'

'Yes, Charlie, I can feel the heat of your shame. You should enjoy the warmth now because the prison barge will be colder than a Halong winter.' Like her mother, Lila has never been one to mince words. 'Although I suspect your rotten-corpse toes will feel right at home. Because that's what you'll be doing for the rest of your life – rotting. If they don't shoot you for this. And don't think it won't happen, because I'm getting out of this mess and starting my reflexology course tomorrow, whereas you, Fungus-foot Charlie, will be transported to a watery hellhole as an accessory to the kidnapping and illegal sale of the police chief's daughter.'

Charlie Dan Thoc starts to whimper.

'Everything all right up there?' JC calls from the back seat. 'My wife's not nagging you, is she, Charlie? Say the word and I'll call her off.'

Lila nudges Charlie.

'Ha ha ha,' Charlie shouts back. 'Ha ha ha, Mr Bone. We are old schoolfriends, we chat about these days.' To Lila he whispers, 'You have to believe me, I knew nothing about this. About you. I came because he promised me a ticket to London for the editing. I want to make movies, Lila. It's my dream.'

'You want to travel? You'll make a pretty boy pet for the Westerner. I believe this one is fond of anal penetration, and I think you too might enjoy the buggery business.' In the past five days Lila's vocabulary has bloomed beyond all recognition. 'I think you'll take fist-fucky good. No need for pre-buttering with you.'

The dark-skinned driver turns, sniggering stale whisky and garlic in Lila's face. 'You're a feisty one, the boss was right about that. But he didn't mention this dirty tongue. A shame to see such filth polluting an angel's mouth. Might have to stop in a minute and do something about this tongue. Might have to put it to work, eh, Charlie? See if we can clean it up.'

After delivering a long and meaningful stare at what Lila hopes are Charlie's eyes, which is intended to convey utter disgust and this solemn message: 'Look what company you're keeping, Charlie Dan Thoc, you worm. The spirit of your poor mother must be weeping to see how you've turned out. She will never forgive you if you don't help me out of this mess. Are you a man or a worm, Charlie Thoc?' After all this, Lila turns her attention to the sniggering driver.

Leaning forward she crawls her index finger over the boy's chest, down his stomach and slips it past the bone handle of a knife sheathed in his belt. She slides her hand into the heat of his shorts. 'Any time you want to get dirty, big boy, this tongue's ready and waiting for you.'

For pragmatic Lila remembers Aunty Choccie's words: engorged by desire, a boar can be driven crazy, and thence – Lila extends the metaphor – over a cliff to his ruin.

'All right up there?' JC calls, looking up from his laptop, where he finds himself stuck on the third sentence. 'You've all gone very quiet.'

Charlie looks across to where Lila Duong, the brightest politest girl in his form class, is nibbling the Mnong boy's ear, her hands plunged into the front of his shorts. 'Ha ha ha, just fine, Mr Bone. We discuss route. Your wife want show you the best scenery. Her special gift for you.'

Charlie looks to Lila. There, he's done it. A first wriggle away from worminess. 'Also, Mr Bone, we look for good place to stop for lunch.'

'How sweet she is.' Instantly inspired, JC returns to his travelogue.

My wife – Orchidee is the name of this incarnation of innocent femininity – lives always with her first thought being her husband's needs.

And the white minibus lurches into second gear.

A few moments later the vehicle jolts off the tarmac road and onto a muddy track, passing a stationary red taxi with Saigon number plates. A yellow-haired woman is standing on the track by the car waving a handgun in the air, while a weeping man on his knees is yanking at a punctured tyre.

But with a hot tongue tormenting an ear and a slight hand unbuckling a straining belt, the white minibus doesn't stop to offer assistance. No, it continues its ascent into the Highlands on the grinding journey towards a honeymoon.

Standing at the Frontier of Medical Science

One other vehicle has made it onto route twenty-seven this morning. A sedan taxi bumping down the same track but in the opposite direction. Its starting point – Buon Ma Thuot – fifty kilometres to the north.

The driver in this vehicle is experiencing less luck in his erotic endeavours. Twice now his hand has been slapped away from jostling breasts. A third attempt was deflected by a bruising elbow to the nose. It seems increasingly likely – though quite unbelievable – that the toothy tart of a nurse only has eyes for the slug of a so-called hypnotist in the back.

For some time the driver has been observing the man's amateur mumbo-jumboing via the mirror – his pawing at the fatty's slack hand, his oily croonings in her ear. The driver strikes a match on the dashboard, lights a bitter cigarette and curses. For this man – formerly known as the Venerable Chaura – knows a second-rate charlatan when he sees one.

Obviously, the occupation had its true professionals: natural-born practitioners of talent and ingenuity, able to live off fresh air and their wits alone. But such genuine talent, Chaura thinks, has always been rare, and usually ended up suffering at the hands of jealous nobodies. Like jealous nobody monks who went snooping around other monks' cells for charms, spells and betting slips that were none of their business – and certainly none of their business to go bothering the head monk with. Even a monastery, this particular professional had learned to his cost, was not immune from such envy.

Chaura blows a smouldering cloud at the mirror. In contrast, there will always be types like this Bing Bung, with his obsessive trouser rubbing and excessive phlegm. A doctor? A quick-quacking, dib-dabbling chancer more like. It won't be long before his number is up, and Chaura, for one, won't be tossing any pennies in the begging bowl when that happens. As to whether the snoring, blindfolded fatty is truly under his spell – he really doesn't care, so long as the suspension holds up.

On the back seat Mr Bung is feeling the therapeutic strain of monitoring his patient's hand. It is due to 'rise like a fluttering songbird the moment your soul longs for rebirth'. For the past hour of intense hypnotic observation, however, it has been flapping on the seat loose as a broken-winged pigeon.

Mr Bung considers the patient's drooping head and wonders. It is gone midday. They have passed five lakes, any one of which would have done the job. Perhaps the tug of the patient's subconscious to the geography of her trauma is not as strong as he thought. Perhaps it is time to remember his position of authority and make an executive decision.

'Stop!' Mr Bung cries out on the back seat. 'Stop the car!'

He has made an executive decision.

They are passing through a village – quite deserted from

the look of things – and there is a perfectly sized lake at the end. Quite perfect.

'Continue to the shore of the lake, driver. Park as close as you can to the water. Neither I nor the patient should be disturbed during the procedure.'

'Going to attempt a walk on water, are you?' Chaura snorts, cranking up the handbrake. 'If you want my opinion, that lump'd drown itself in a puddle of piss.'

'If you don't mind, driver, you'll concern yourself with the transport arrangements and leave the healing to the professionals.' Pulling himself up to his full therapeutic height, Mr Bung exits the vehicle. 'Come along, nurse, you can help me find a good spot.'

Propped against the trunk of a banyan tree by the lake's edge, Delia Duong snoozes. The afternoon sun is soaking into her skin. Words are drifting about her and floating away, their import lost beneath the raucous cicadas and the calls of diving cormorants. Above her, Mr Bung is wiping damp hands. He begins to strut.

'Today we find ourselves standing at the frontier of medical science. It is a momentous frontier.'

Having been tasked with the 'pre-therapy' photograph, the pretty nurse is now perched in a slender bough taking notes.

'Do stop me if I go too quickly, nurse, it is vital you record this momentous moment correctly. It is a brand-new frontier. In a landmark procedure the highly experi-enced – and you can add "most remarkable" if you wish, nurse – the highly experienced and most remarkable Doctor Bung will replant a patient's memory using the power of hypnosis alone. From psychological seeds sown today, who knows what splendid trees may grow? New paragraph, new title, Case Notes. New line.

'The fifty-six-year-old female was admitted to the care of Mr Bung (Dip. Hyp. Lyons, France) suffering from violent domestic psychosis and acute identity amnesia. She proved a gifted candidate for hypnotic therapy. New line. New title, The Experimental Procedure – Rewriting History. New paragraph, my dear. Excellent. What a pretty style you have.

'In stage one of today's procedure, Mrs Po Duong will be returned to the physical site of a key psychological junction in her life. The specific junction I have selected for therapy is the morning the patient encountered her future husband. The psychological transition is that of girlhood identity – already burdened by personal sadness – encountering her future womanhood and all the responsibilities of domestic life, i.e. marriage and motherhood. Footnote, please: something this old maid had already given up all hope of happening to her. A woman should never give up hope, nurse!

'It is my belief the patient has never shed the load of misery she was carrying on that long-ago lakeside morning. She never sloughed off the past and embraced her marital future, as every woman ought. It is perhaps remarkable that she survived *intactus psychologicus* for as long as she did before her trauma manifested on a conscious level. Specifically, nurse, please register the manifestation as homicidal rage resulting in bodily harm – via a hatchet – to her civically esteemed husband. After achieving stage one – a physical return to the geographical point of transition: this beautiful Highland lake – we now proceed to stage two. The patient will be returned *psychologically* to 1972.

Employing my revolutionary "Flicker" technique – a copyright symbol here if you would, nurse – a state of profound psychological disorientation will be engendered and all distinction between conscious and subconscious states will vanish. The patient will comprehend the date and nothing more. From the moment she is engaged in flickering – copyright again, please – her reality will be exactly what I make it. Underline that sentence, nurse. She will be remodelled, remodified and reassigned new and improved memories. In a nutshell, I am about to rewrite an individual's history. Three exclamation marks there, if you would. Done? Excellent. New paragraph.

'In the third stage of the procedure the patient will be submerged in the lake under controlled conditions. This serves no specific therapeutic benefit but the emotional comfort of this placebic ritual cannot be underestimated. This marks a significant baptismal moment – a new junction, if you like – in accordance with the patient's new life. New paragraph. Nearly there, nurse, I hope those pretty fingers aren't tired.

'The stage two procedure will be repeated in stage four to reinforce learning. Finally stage five concludes the procedure with a thorough examination of key performance indicators to verify that the newly installed memories are fully operational. It will be noted that one of the key performance indicators of the procedure's success will be renaming.

'Please record that I am now addressing the patient. "Phoenix, clap your hands three times."

'Nurse, please record no response.'

'"Delia Duong, clap your hands three times. Thank you, Delia." Nurse, please note the patient's unequivocal response. At the end of today's procedure there will be empirical evidence of a complete reversal – the patient will only respond to the name Phoenix – a fitting moniker, I find. End of notes. Any questions, nurse?'

The pretty nurse blows on her fingers. 'Golly, doctor, it does sound fantastically clever.'

'Naturally, my dear.'

'Are you sure it will work?'

'I have no doubt of that, my dear.'

'Golly, well, I suppose in that case my only question is what kind of new memory you're planning to install.'

'An excellent question, nurse. Note this under the heading: Content of Patient's New and Improved History. The patient will be packed with thirty years of domestic harmony. She will no longer demonstrate academic frustration, Southern snobbery, religious delusions or an absence of spousal affection. We will not have time to fill in the details today, but broadly speaking she will discover most recollections centre on happiness at the stove. A fitting history for a woman who loves her food.'

'Golly, doctor, you are awfully clever.'

'That's fine praise from a delightful young nurse; however, the greatest compliment for me would be to return this woman to full mental health. Jot that down, would you, in the margin in parenthesis. Excellent. Now, if you would be kind enough to pass me a tissue and remove the patient's blindfold we shall commence our humble endeavours.'

It would be wonderful to jump in at this point, to take the form of a shallows-wading cormorant and come pecking at Delia's toes, to wake her from her drowsing and prevent the fun and games from starting. But such intervention is beyond any observer's control. After all, it's Delia's choice, isn't it? Perhaps she might not submit. Perhaps she will open her eyes and say, 'With all respect, that's quite a load of rubbish I've had to tolerate from you, Mr Bung, for long enough. Do shut up and drive me home at once.'

But the truth is, she doesn't.

Which leads the observer to a single conclusion: Delia is happy to let someone into the intimate spaces of her mind.

Is her current reality so disappointing, so devoid of hope and meaning, so doom-laden, in fact, that she is ready and willing to hand it over to another person? The observer may choose to agree with Chaura – to hand it to a charlatan, no less? Perhaps. But perhaps she feels she needs it, this charlatan's hand to yank her forward, just as she seized another hand over thirty years ago in the mire of an uncivil war. Perhaps.

'Delia, it is 1972, open your eyes!' Mr Bung commands. And obediently she opens her eyes and seems to accept that it is indeed 1972. As commanded, she kneels and begins to scoop out the muddy earth, searching for traces of buried kings. Willingly she seems to follow the doctor's finger, flicking her in and out of a time-travelling trance, flipping the fabric of her memories like sheets in the breeze. Mrs Duong reels up and down from her digging until she appears no more sentient than a light switch being snapped on and off as the hypnotist seeks that point where the filament hisses and the bulb blows.

'Hold it right there,' Mr Bung says after half an hour, fixing Delia at a forty-five-degree tilt to the ground. 'Excellent work all round. Ten-minute tea break. Did you bring the flask, nurse?'

Delia's thighs quiver with the strain of the position. Her thoughts are as muddy as the water that drips from her hands. But she finds, as the doctor suggests, that this sogginess of mind is not altogether unpleasant. The doctor may be right: even if she does not recall exactly who she is or where she is, she anchors herself around *when* she is. Somewhere in 1972, she hangs over the shore in what the doctor informs the nurse to note for the record as 'take-up time'.

For fifteen minutes Delia droops in her virtual 1972. Like an actor paused in a period film she awaits further direction, ignoring anachronisms like the modern white minibus that is screeching to a stop on the track outside a dilapidated longhouse she could easily recognise if she put her mind to it. Her brain does not bother to absorb the scene her eyes are following, that of her very own daughter exiting the white minibus, holding a blade to a driver's throat. Which is a shame, because there's no question Mrs Duong of old would be delighted to witness Lila's boar-subduing actions. It is possible she would not have continued any further with Mr Bung's fun and games if she had made this one simple neurological link.

But it must not be forgotten that she has made her choice, and it is really too late to back out now. Meekly she pulls her gaze from the drama on the road to devote her full attention to the next stage of her therapeutic procedure: the acquisition of a new name.

'Phoenix,' the doctor says, feeling sufficiently restored by his artichoke leaves to exert such pressure to the patient's shoulders that his toes dangle off the ground. 'I name you Phoenix. What is your name?'

'Phoenix,' the patient replies, sinking into the mud.

'Excellent, Phoenix is what I name you.'

Mr Bung daubs this catechism onto various levels of the patient's consciousness until he begins to feel quite bored. He consumes the dregs of the tea flask and decides to move on.

'Delia, wake up,' he says.

There is no response from the patient.

'Excellent. Note for the record, nurse – we have her now.'

After a pause for the expectoration of unexpected mucus and a wipe of his hands, the hypnotist is ready to install Phoenix's new memories. But before invoking delight in meeting the husband and thirty happy years at the stove, the thoughtful doctor is inspired to a commemorative touch. 'Just before we leave 1972 you will open your eyes and discover the king you've been seeking for so long. You'll probably find him standing before you, Phoenix. It will make you very happy.'

With tears of joy pouring from her eyes, Phoenix drops to the ground.

'Excellent.' Mr Bung removes his shoe from her eager kiss. 'Remember the king's face, Phoenix. Whenever we meet a small curtsey will suffice. Please note, nurse, this worship acts as a fail-safe mechanism – if at any point she does not behave reverentially in my presence she will be recalled for reprogramming.'

The baptism goes well. There is only one mildly alarming moment mid-lake: the patient seems to confuse air with water. The taxi driver must be prevailed upon to abandon his cigarette and sprint to assist the nurse in ripping Mrs Duong's fingers from hyacinth roots on the lake bed. Despite her superior buoyancy she has filled her lungs deep.

'Excellent work,' the hypnotist says when the patient's lungs have been dredged and she is propped against the banyan tree to drip-dry in the weakening sun. He crouches before the woman, who is now to all intents and purposes fully conscious. 'We'll drive you home in a moment. But you just nearly drowned, dear lady. So please set our anxious minds at rest and confirm your name and the date.'

The woman raises her sodden gaze with a shy smile. 'Your Highness does the great honour of conversing with a humble housewife from Dalat. Mrs Phoenix Duong is the name. As for the date, I am not entirely certain but I believe it to be springtime in the twenty-first century.'

'Excellent work,' the hypnotist says.

And even Chaura is impressed.

A One-Winged Butterfly That Never Learned to Fly

It has been noted in brief, the arrival of Lila Duong at a dilapidated longhouse, holding a blade to the throat of a dark-skinned driver. A detail might now be added: the boy's neck has been nicked twice. 'An unfortunate consequence of a blind hand on bumpy roads,' as Lila put it. The boy who descends from the driver's door of the minibus does so docile as a lamb. His wounds are congealing nicely.

Lila and the driver are accompanied from the minibus by Charlie Dan Thoc. In an inversion of management position, Charlie is accompanied by a camera-carrying damp-skirted Westerner. This craven creature is attached to Charlie via a chain from a hoop locked around his wrists. Such are the reversals of fortune.

Once Lila had whipped her hand out of the boy's shorts and whipped the bone-handled knife from its sheath, everything had unravelled rapidly. As she raised the blade to the driver's throat and power lurched from one side of the bus to the other, Lila felt moved to recall Aunty's first seminar. 'The charms of the female tongue often come in handy,' she whispered to Charlie, who blushed and did not disagree.

'Everything all right up there?' the Englishman called. 'Did I hear someone scream?'

'Request you place your wrists in here, hubby,' Lila said, entrusting the driver's throat to Charlie and coming down the bus holding open a brass hoop for JC.

'Oh, I don't know about that, my honeypot.'

'Yes, please, hubby.'

'Yes, please, Mr Bone,' Charlie turned and nodded. 'Necessary tribal wedding custom. Show of total trust in wife before intimacy begins. Very nice idea.'

Lila secured her husband via the chain to the headrest of the seat in front.

JC strained after her, his lips puckered for a kiss. 'When does the intimacy begin, my flower, only I think I may need a comfort break before we get cracking?'

Lila returned to the front of the bus.

Charlie handed Lila the blade and the driver's throat. 'What happens now?' He looked out the window at the hills of white-blossomed coffee and shook his head. 'We've kidnapped a Westerner and we're heading for the middle of nowhere.'

Lila shrugged. 'Keep going a while, I guess. I'll figure something out.'

'We're here,' the driver announced miserably. 'This was where I was supposed to drop you.' He had stopped the bus by a crop of half-built longhouses. According to a billboard they boasted indoor toilets, mosquito nets, genuine minority tribe outdoor pursuits and organic ethnic articles for sale. One hundred per cent government-approved accommodation for foreign bodies. Completion was due in two years' time.

'Orchidee, my sugar blossom, you can see how much I trust you, and I must say it's been a very amusing joke, but pop back here and unlock me,' the Englishman called from the back seat. 'I'm dying for a pee. You understand? Piddle. Pisspot. Wee-wee needed now.'

'We're where?' Lila leaned past the driver to smell the air out the window. 'You know, Charlie, there's something very familiar about this place.'

'Yoo hoo, hello up there, folks. Sorry to interrupt lunch arrangements, but I really am bursting. Small-bladdered inheritance, I'm afraid.'

'I don't see how,' Charlie said. 'We've stopped at one of those awful tourist home-stay compounds. When would you have ever visited? When would you have wanted to?'

Lila shook her head. What was it? The heady scent of coffee blossom, the creaking cicadas and the cormorants – all these were common enough out this way. 'Wait a minute, Charlie, we're at least a hundred kilometres from Dalat, right? I can hear cormorants, so there must be a lake?'

'Look here, darling, far be it from me to insist on instant obedience, I'm a man of the enlightenment after all, but I did take on rather a lot of rice wine at our wedding. More than most men could handle, actually.'

'Drive on, boy,' Lila said suddenly, 'all the way into the village.'

The bus lurched on, and in the back the Englishman began to sob.

'Is this by any chance the village of the snake woman?' Charlie had been sent to enquire of an old man sitting in a red plastic chair in the shade outside the first of the longhouses.

The old man shifted his thighs and chuckled softly. He said Chieftain Duong's wife, if that was who the boy meant, was not to be found at home much nowadays: she was said to prefer the Island of the Dead. Where no still-breathing body wanted to go, and particularly none pursued by the ghost of their husband, as she was said to be – and with good cause too. Which was proof of her snaky craziness, he said, if anyone needed it. Which they didn't, not after what had happened to the chieftain. He'd leave her hut well alone, and the woman too. Although – the old man looked Charlie up and down and pinched his nose – she did have an effective recipe for corpse-breath foot fungus he could recommend.

Charlie relayed most of this information to Lila, and Lila lifted her jaw high and said, 'I thought so. We'll go to my grandmother's. We could do with a base while we figure out what to do next.'

Privately Charlie thought that turning around and returning to Dalat immediately might be the finest plan of all. But wishing to stamp out any lingering intimations of worminess, and feeling more than a little intrigued about the possibility of jars of medicinal miracles for a lifelong blight, he agreed.

'Driver, proceed to the furthest house from the village,' Lila said. While in the back an Englishman started to weep over his soggy skirt.

Once the dark-skinned boy and the Westerner are installed inside the longhouse, shackled by brass rings to a teak post opposite the snake baskets, Lila and Charlie sit on the steps outside to enjoy the last of the sun before it slides into the lake. 'Thank you,' Lila holds her breath and gives Charlie a quick peck on the cheek, 'I couldn't have done it without you. Will you forgive me those nasty things I said before?'

'Oh Lila,' Charlie says leaning in close, 'oh Lila, I'd forgive you anything.'

'Oh Charlie,' Lila says, 'please back off. You're a nice boy, but your feet are too stinky for me. I'm really sorry but that's just how it is.'

After an awkward chat, in which they discuss the possibility that the provenance of the odour is Charlie's footwear ('It isn't,' Lila says) and the chances of a future together in the event of the fungus clearing up ('Unlikely,' Lila says) or a miracle cure being discovered ('Who knows,' Charlie says), they return to the longhouse.

Charlie unstacks a tower of fermenting medicine jars with disappointment, then turns his attention to the Englishman's pink documents. 'The problem as I see it, Lila, is that you appear to be legally married to him. It's all above board. Signed, sealed, official.'

'In which case, do you have your lighter on you? I think we might need an official cremation.'

'Stop!' the Englishman howls. 'That's four thousand dollars you're burning, Charlie! That's my student loan! My mother will kill me! Orchidee's mine, I tell you. I bought her, Charlie. I own her. You've no right to meddle with another man's goods. I'll have you for this.'

Charlie holds the lighter's blue flame to the corner of a pink sheet.

'All right, Charlie, you win. How much? How much do you want? I'll give you fifty quid to release me. Make it sixty. Do you take Visa?'

'I'll find you a pot, Mr Bone. You keep the ash.'

'You won't get away with this.' JC rattles his chain as the paper curls and blackens. 'The man I bought her from keeps copies in triplicate. I have a receipt!'

'And I have video evidence of a forced wedding.'

In their baskets the snakes hiss. The Englishman watches his marriage turn to ash. 'There aren't even any cannibals here to write about,' he sobs. He plugs his mouth with his thumb. 'I want my mum.'

Which Charlie interprets for Lila, who shakes her head while she smells her second day-long marriage shrivel to nothing. 'Two marriages in eight days, Charlie. What do you think of that?'

'I think there were two men who didn't know how lucky they were,' Charlie says, spotting with fresh hope a glistening orange jar tucked behind the snake baskets.

'Do you know, Charlie, I don't think I'll bother again. It's a lot more effort than it's worth.'

Charlie unscrews the jar. It is labelled 'rats' feet ointment'. He sniffs. 'Never say never,' he replies.

As the Englishman sucks his thumb and Charlie dabs orange jelly between his toes, the driver begins to sing, softly tapping out a rhythm with a brass ring on the planked floor. He sings of the day the forest birds left their nests to follow the sun, and of the hummingbird that hovered in the clearing, unable to make his mind up whether to stay or go. The boy's voice is sweet, Lila thinks, and so very young.

'I've had enough of all this,' she says suddenly. 'Charlie, will you unlock the boy, please.'

'Are you sure?'

'Quite sure.' She is remembering a brother who once sang sweeter than sugar dust. She is thinking of a father, of how unhappy he must be feeling without her, and of a once-brilliant now doom-defeated mother, shouting for stone masons to seal her away. For the first time in a long and terrible week, Lila allows her jaw to fall. 'And then, Charlie, you can take me home.'

'What about the Westerner?'

'Tell him my grandmother should be back to feed him tonight. We'll send a car for him tomorrow. Mei's boy, I'm very sorry about your neck, but if you would be so kind, could you wait for my grandmother and explain the situation to her, and then make sure the Englishman gets in the car we'll send. Tell my grandmother I'm sorry I missed her but my reflexology course starts tomorrow and I must prepare my meridians. You may as well do whatever you like after that, though can I suggest school? Come on, Charlie, escort me home.'

Charlie pockets the rats' feet jar and takes Lila's hand.

'Don't leave me here with the cannibals,' the Englishman wails behind them. 'I don't want to be eaten by cannibals. I don't want to die.'

They are halfway to the minibus and Lila is about to speculate that the odour of Charlie's feet may have marginally improved when he stops dead.

'Wow.'

'What is it, Charlie?'

'Wow, Lila, has your mother become some sort of nun by any chance?'

'Of course not.'

'But does she have a shaved head?'

'No, of course she doesn't, Charlie.'

'Only there's a figure of her approximate size and appearance approaching.'

Sure enough, with a baritone blast of 'There's my dearest daughter!' the titanic form of Mrs Phoenix Duong is bearing down full steam ahead.

'But that's impossible,' Lila says.

'Brace yourself,' Charlie says.

'My darling daughter!' Phoenix says, crashing into Lila and throwing a crushing hug around her. 'Have you come to see the king?'

Lila staggers back from this perplexing embrace. 'I came to see Grandmother.' She feels for her mother's hair and finds only a prickled skull. 'Why are you so damp, and what's happened to your hair?'

Phoenix's hand feels about her head and for a moment she is confused. 'Pah! Never mind that, you say Granny Duong's home? But this is wonderful, we must call in!'

And now most pragmatic Lila finds herself wishing for something she has lost long ago. Yes, just for a second she wishes for sight. Just this once. Just to be sure. 'Maman?' she says, running her fingers over the dimensions of the face before her. 'You didn't brick yourself up and dismantle the pulley? It really is you, ma chère Maman?'

'Pah! Let's have none of this foreign gobbledegook. Have you eaten? It must be nearly supper time.' Mrs Duong slices her daughter's arm from Charlie. 'Stand aside, boy, I'll take my daughter from here. What do you fancy, Lila? Chicken hotpot?'

'You're *cooking*?' Lila whispers as she is swivelled round in a maternal clamp and frogmarched back towards the longhouse. 'But do you know how to?'

'Or a goat hotpot. If Granny has any goats.'

A greasy voice assails Lila's ear. 'I presume you're the

daughter. If you'll give me a moment, miss, I can explain everything.'

And so Lila and Mrs Duong and Charlie and Mr Bung and a toothy nurse and a bony ex-monk troop into the longhouse as the sun drops to the horizon and a red taxi brakes by the lake and disgorges a blonde woman. This woman runs to the canoes, wielding a small silver handset. The taxi squeals into reverse and, despite a screamed foreign order to wait, it rockets away.

Inside the longhouse things are more than a little awkward to begin with. The problem is that Mrs Duong has so much to do. As a priority, provision must be made for the king, requiring the removal of rags from beneath lowlier bottoms and the shaking out of a comfortable strip of bedding roll near the fattest snakes. Supper must be made ready, of course, but before this, fresh coffee needs brewing, and before even this, the fire should be lit, but – how inconvenient! – there is a shortage of suitable kindling. This is not, Mrs Duong makes clear, how she would run her own home!

Charlie Thoc is despatched to gather firewood. Brief introductions are made in the meantime, but Mrs Duong cannot rest until she has the kettle on. The toads bounce in their buckets and the planks splinter under her hurried hostessing steps. The fire is lit, the water boils, but Phoenix can find no rest, for it is turning dark and Granny Duong is not home. 'My husband's mother is frail,' she cries, thundering to the door, 'and shouldn't be allowed to wander alone. Gracious me! Is that the sound of gunfire out there? I couldn't bear it if Granny were in trouble. We should send a search party at once.'

It is at this point that Mr Bung attempts to induce a

soothing state upon his patient for the benefit of all. But Mrs Duong is so jumpy about whether she has quite enough chicken for his regal appetite, never mind her dearest daughter, that big-nosed foreigner snivelling into his skirt, Charlie, the two drivers and that giggly piece of nurse, that she doesn't stand still long enough for the hypnotist to get an adequate grip on her brain.

'Post-hypnotic mania,' Mr Bung whispers to the nurse. 'Fascinating. Witness how she's experimenting with her new personality.'

Lila heads towards the smell of grease, whereupon she raises her chin high. 'My mother has never cooked a day in her life. She has always loathed my paternal grand-mother and never hugs people. Vietnam is a Socialist Republic, lacking even a residual emperor let alone a king to curtsey to. Would you mind informing me what the hell is going on.'

The information she receives as Charlie fetches more logs, her mother peels a cobra she has found skewered to a nail, and the young nurse hauls out a rum jar, rather disables Lila's manners. 'So let me get this straight. You're sitting in my grandmother's home telling me you've been meddling with my mother's mind for the past week, is that it, greasebag?'

'My dear, please remember,' Mr Bung calmly contains his mucus, 'hypnosis is merely a suggestive therapeutic medium. All this was merely suggested to your mother. She was the one with the desire and imagination to apply it.'

'Well, may I suggest, shitpiece,' Lila steps the conversa-tion up a gear, heedless of a gasp of maternal disapproval, 'you remake some suggestions pretty quick.'

'I understand it may be hard for a lay person to grasp,

but your mother is a pioneer, my dear. Today she stands at the frontier of medical science.'

'Oh yes!' the nurse pipes up. 'She nearly drowned and she didn't seem to feel a thing!'

'I don't want a pioneer,' Lila says with such splintering menace that even Mrs Duong stops scouring pots for a second, 'I want my mother back.'

Phoenix thunders over to blast her daughter with kisses. 'Pah! My soppy little mouse, your mummy's right here and she's not going anywhere – just back to the stove to cook up some dinner. Please excuse me, Your Majesty, and my daughter's filthy language, we always tried to bring her up to be a good girl.'

The silence that follows is colder than a Halong winter. It is broken by a screech. Then a merry whistling tune.

'What's she doing now?' Lila hisses.

'Well,' Charlie says, 'she's just slit open a toad for the pot and now she's whistling.'

'What would you rather, my dear, a depressed hatchet-wielding maniac or this happy housewife we see here?'

Lila is temporarily flummoxed for an answer and Mr Bung seizes the moment. 'There's just one other thing. During the therapeutic process your mother changed her name. She'd now like to be known as Phoenix.'

'Yes, Your Majesty?' Mrs Duong calls out. 'What can I get you?'

Lila knows how to answer this one. A left hook swings with sightless precision and the hypnotist crashes back against the snakes.

'You could get me a towel,' he sniffs, 'I think my nose may be broken.'

After the nurse has reset the hypnotic snout, the group

settles to a supper of chicken hotpot with toad and snake fritters and fried rice. Even Lila must concede it is extremely tasty.

'You see, my dear,' the hypnotist says through two nasal plugs, staying well out of range, 'the fruits of hypnosis can be harvested by all.'

Outside the longhouse the evening star appears, hunting owls wake and whoop and dogs bark at the dusk. There is no longer any hope of returning along the mountain route in time for reflexology courses in the morning. In any case, Lila does not want to let her mother out of earshot and the vile mindbender man will not leave for the tourist compound accommodation as she has asked him to do. As if he hadn't done enough already, the man is insisting on monitoring 'his patient' over a twenty-four-hour period.

Mr Bung surveys the hut with postprandial content. He is regaining air flow to his left nostril, and the blind daughter – quite a looker, incidentally – seems to be calming. In a while he will subtly offer his services; undoubtedly she could take some anger management advice. If she has inherited her mother's aptitude, there is no doubt she will experience significant mental enhancement. Harmony, he thinks, would be a pretty new name for her.

'More rum, doctor?' the young nurse asks, after a hiccup and an announcement to the gathering that her name is Kimmy and she is Mr Bung's number one fan. She has opened a second jar and is dispensing it around the hut. In fact, as beakers clink and toasts are made, Mr Bung notices with some therapeutic satisfaction that the tentacles of camaraderie are beginning to grope the dark room.

Chaura assists the now unlocked Englishman in the

smoking of his American cigarettes and quietly investigates his pockets. Charlie Thoc rubs comfrey paste into Lila's bruised knuckles, and speculatively between his toes. The nurse takes Mrs Duong's pulse and the dark-skinned boy beats out a rhythm on a pan, confessing that he is two mountains away from his family's settlement and he is feeling homesick. He is only fourteen, he says, and he never wanted to go with the uncle on his seventh birthday. But business is business, his father said at the time, and the family needed a cow more than a child. He begins to sing of a one-winged butterfly that never learned to fly. The atmosphere in the room is turning soft as duckling down.

'I'm curious, doctor,' Chaura says, lighting up a cigarette and puffing smoke rings in the direction of pot-scraping Mrs Duong. 'What you did today. Can anyone hypnotise just anyone?'

Mr Bung wipes his hands and clears his throat; after all, such a topic was only to be expected eventually. 'One does not like to generalise, but in general a great practitioner is born, not made. Although top-drawer overseas training is also essential.' He glances at the daughter and her clenched fist. He is comfortably out of range. 'But it is interesting that you ask, driver. Would anyone care for a demonstration?'

Chaura exhales slowly. 'That would be most generous.'

'Oh what fun,' the nurse giggles, 'can we get out the candles again?'

With the predictable exception of the daughter and the boy with the rotten feet (sadly, nothing hypnosis could ever do for those) the great hypnotist's offer is received enthusiastically. 'Phoenix, my dear,' Mr Bung says, 'do stop with the pots and come and join us, listening only to my voice.'

'Please, Maman, no,' Lila says.

But before her daughter can get to her, Mrs Duong has thudded across to the hypnotist, received a flick on the brow, and tumbled down.

'She's quite insensible,' the great man says.

'So it appears,' Chaura says, blowing smoke into Mrs Duong's face.

Bung turns benevolently to the driver. 'It looks like you need to stub that cigarette out. Perhaps on a heel. She won't mind, she won't be able to feel her left heel at all, it's quite dead to her. Isn't it, my dear?'

'Yes, Your Majesty,' Mrs Duong says dreamily. 'Quite dead.'

Chaura smiles. 'It would be my pleasure.'

Mrs Duong sizzles. The audience gasps.

'Please stop!' Lila cries.

'Commendable.' Chaura throws away the blackened stub. 'Tell me, doctor, could you make someone do anything you wanted once they're under? Something that would apply afterwards, when they're not zonked?'

'A post-hypnotic suggestion is the technical term for what you're talking about. A sophisticated procedure, suitable only for advanced practitioners. Essentially, the trick is to frame the suggestion so they accept it and embed it in their subconscious.'

'Like, could you have them unwittingly lose at cards?'

'That would be quite simple, my friend. Shall I demonstrate?'

'Oh no, doctor, that's too boring!' The nurse really has had plenty of rum now. 'Do another trick – you know, like—' and she feels she has grown close enough to the great man during the last twenty-four hours to whisper in his ear.

So it happens that Chaura and the Englishman are standing on the belly and thighs of Mrs Duong, who is suspended stiff as an iron girder between two timber logs, when her husband walks through the door.

Dalat's sometime Chief of Police and Miscreant Management sees his wife cataleptically converted into a human bridge. 'Po?' he says, staggering backwards. 'Po? Po? Po?' he says, rubbing his disbelieving eyes.

And there, in the shadows of the snake corner, he spots a girl who looks just like his beautiful daughter, and without another word he buckles insensible to the floor.

The Greater Vehicle

It had been a difficult day for Chief Duong long before he discovers his insane wife and the image of his daughter partying with strangers in his mother's home. For this Sunday was D-day: (re)designated Drop day; a day of deals, dollars and above all, daughters. Like all the chief's most successful days to date he had seized the initiative and begun it well before dawn in the lean-to, the place where he always achieved his most creative thinking. Settling himself on the toilet, he'd opened a can of lager, his trusted copy of *Creative Truths* and his notepad. He scored a margin, wrote the title ESCAPE PLAN and, as his manual advised in chapter nine, 'Inspired Planning', he simply waited.

It did not take long. During the second half of the second can of lager he underlined the title and shortly afterwards inspiration began to trickle from his pen.

Idea 1: <u>Take the money and run</u>. Through crowds, in and out of restaurants and over Saigon rooftops. Technical difficulties: lack of acceleration (age-associated). Innate fear of heights disabling high-rise endeavours. Risk of injury to ankle or other limb on shoddy tiling.
Success potential: 3/10

Idea 2: <u>Hire helicopter to enable accelerated escape</u>.
Technical difficulties: paper trail from booking form.
Deposit required for helicopter hire — beyond
immediate financial means. Pilot required. Innate
fear of flying.
Success potential: 1/10

Idea 3: <u>Incognito</u>. Masquerade as coconut juice
vendor. Snatch money and conceal stash in portable
ice box.
Technical difficulties: acquisition of coconuts, ice box,
cart.
Success potential: 6/10 (promising?)

Idea 4: <u>Arrange drop near Ben Dinh tunnel network</u>.
Collect money under cover of night via subterra-
nean entry hole.
Technical difficulties: potential of too-fat-to-fit in hole
(age-associated) leading to asphyxiation and death.
****NIGHT = TOO LATE FOR LILA!!
Success potential: not worth bothering with.

Along with one or two lager blots the chief's ideas crawled over two pages of the notepad and into the first light of dawn. Eight further schemes were set down, weighed up and discarded. Then, just as Duong drained the last cold can in the fridge, it happened: the perfect plan oozed from his pen.

Idea 13: Get someone else to do it.

Flawless, Duong thought. Genius, Duong thought, always

struck eventually. He belched with satisfaction and picked up the phone to call Sergeant Yung.

It had been the happiest moment of Sergeant Yung's forty-two-year administrative policing career, receiving his dawn summons. There was no question about that.

'Can you show bravery above and beyond the call of duty?' – that's what the chief had asked, beckoning Yung past the cleaner and into his office thirty minutes later.

Yung saluted beneath the portrait of Uncle Ho. He could.

From a middle drawer of the filing cabinet Duong pulled out two dusty beards. 'Uncle Ho, the Mother Country, and Mr Sam Porcini need you. Will you stand up and be counted?'

Yung swallowed a sob. He would.

'Do you promise to obey your superior officer at all times without question or demur, and do you swear on your sergeant's stripe to maintain the top secrecy of this most important policing mission?'

Yung did.

'Shut the door.'

Yung shut it. Whereupon Duong threw him a beard. 'You'll have to wear this the moment we leave the office, along with your sunglasses.' Duong opened the door, peered out at the cleaner and shut it again. 'We cannot be too careful. Now, Sergeant Yung, the time has come.'

Glaucoma wobbled in Yung's eyes. 'You don't mean—'

'I'm afraid I do – the footballer.'

Yung gasped.

'It has been brought to my attention in a Top Secret Memo that there have been several hoaxes concerning this boy. Today we have been asked to participate in a double-crossing mission.'

Yung blinked back tears of unblemished joy.

'Wearing disguise, we have been tasked with collecting a box of money from a specified drop point outside a temple in the Cho Lon district of Saigon. The drop will take place at noon, six hours and sixteen minutes from now. Following this, we make our getaway, yes?'

'Oh, yes, Chief!' Yung applied his beard, hooking the elastic behind his ears. 'Only one question, if I may, Chief. Which part of this collecting-money plan is double-crossing?'

Duong looked closely for a minute at his sergeant. 'That really is classified information. But I suppose I can trust you.'

'To the death, Chief. I shall not fail you or the unfortunate Sam Porcini.'

Duong considered his sergeant. For all his sixty years, Yung was affecting the slippery side fringe that had excited the nation in the last two days. Referred to as the Football Flop, it was sported as an act of solidarity with the missing boy.

'The hair will have to be flattened, Sergeant.'

'Yes, Chief.'

'The contact from whom you will be collecting the box is a member of the Cambodian Fun Chi cartel. Notorious, I'm afraid. They do not have the footballer – the International Investigating Team Leader who is overseeing the operation assured me of that – nevertheless they are making threats and demanding the ransom money.'

'The pigs!'

'Indeed. Therefore, the box you will be collecting from a Fun Chi gang member outside the temple will be swapped with an identical one soon after. You will deliver the swapped box to the Mekong ferry terminal. The gang are expecting this second box to be filled with ten million dollars. Naturally, that won't happen. I will return the first Fun Chi box to the Investigating Team Leader for fingerprint analysis. You will deliver a box of blank pieces of paper to the dockside, yes?'

Yung flipped back his flop and blinked. He blinked again.

'What's on your mind, Sergeant?'

'One further question, Chief. If the Fun Chis definitely don't have Sam Porcini and we're not actually giving them any real money either, then why are we bothering with the double-crossing mission in the first place?'

The chief stared at his sergeant. It seemed, to Yung, to go on for quite some time. 'That,' Duong said eventually, 'really is classified. Please fill the jeep with petrol, I have a private phone call to make.'

'Sergeant Yung, I'd like you to imagine something for me,' the chief said to his passenger as they drove down into the heat of the Southern Plains some three hours later. They had made good time, and spurred by philanthropic thoughts of Ma coffee communities (didn't philanthropists also get statues in town centres?) Chief Duong was returning to a familiar question. 'Hypothetically speaking, of course.'

Yung wasn't overly sure what hypothetically meant, nevertheless he had sworn not to let his boss down at any point on the mission. He twisted his moustache strings sagely. 'Without fail, Chief.'

'Imagine you had ten million dollars. If they landed in your lap today – hypothetically speaking, of course, what would you spend them on?'

'Do I have to have all ten million?' Yung asked.

'All.'

How much was an American dollar worth in real money, Yung wanted to know. The chief told him.

'But that's impossible, Chief.'

'Nothing, Sergeant, is impossible.'

Yung itched beneath his fake beard. He rubbed sweat from the roots of his moustache.

'Come along, this isn't an Academy-approved test, it's a short hypothetical exercise.'

After a period of intense tip-twisting Yung announced his comprehensive spending list as follows: a new television set for the grandchildren, two tickets to the Asian Football League Final in Hong Kong. A car for Mrs Yung. 'And yours, Chief?'

Duong revealed his list might include eye specialists, speech therapists, exterior wall peppermint-painting, a dumbwaiter for his wife, a carer-companion for his mother, a new seat cover for the Hero and possibly, he said, he was thinking of investing in a shrimp farm.

'That's a fair amount,' Yung said admiringly.

Duong conceded the list was lengthening. He had decided he would also be throwing a large amount of money the way of the Ma tribe.

'Oh yes, Chief,' Yung acknowledged the wisdom of this. 'Charity is a fine pursuit. It will help with the Greater Vehicle.'

'You think I should get them a jeep?'

'Certainly, Chief, if you think it best,' Yung replied solemnly. 'But as it was explained to me by the Venerable Chaura at the temple, the Greater Vehicle signifies man's tortuous transit through the cycles of suffering and rebirth. Charity eases this journey. For example, as the Venerable said only last week, those who give generously to monks will not reincarnate as anything less than a cockroach.'

'There's less than a cockroach?'

'Of course, Chief. Also, when one is a cockroach it is most difficult to ascend beyond insecthood. One must take every opportunity while in human form to advance through the cycle. Perhaps I too will give most of my ten million to the Ma. The grandchildren do not need a new television set.'

'Chaura, you said the Venerable was called?' Very belatedly Duong recalled a missed appointment at the temple on Lila's wedding day. He watched a fruit fly wander over the dashboard, stuck in its insecthood. 'Charity, yes. Perhaps a fourth peppermint wall will be forgone.'

'The Chief is most wise,' Yung replied, and they drove on through the Plains. And a few hundred metres behind them, just out of sight of the rear-view mirror, a motorcyclist on a black Spritely Mover tagged along.

At the shrimp farm that Duong had visited three days earlier he stopped to switch the jeep's blue number plates to white ones. They took breakfast. Polite small talk was exchanged with the proprietor concerning the case of the missing footballer. The television in the corner played images of the storming of a Chinese brothel, divers searching Halong Bay's underwater caves, and a Gola-Cola sponsored candlelit concert at Hanoi's Water Theatre.

Over coffee, enquiries were made by Duong about start-up and staffing costs of a shellfish outfit on a scale similar to the farmer's. 'Hypothetically speaking, of course.'

'It's a real money-spinner,' the farmer confirmed. 'Nothing hypothetical about that. Feed them, sift them, harvest them. Shrimp rarely sicken.' He confided that profits were so good he was thinking of expanding his stock to lobsters. Duong and the farmer swapped details in case hypothetical investment funds ever became available. The farmer's wife handed Duong a recipe for caramelised clams, and a bag of steamed grey shrimp for the journey.

'Interesting that. Growing export market. Guaranteed four hundred per cent return on investment,' Duong remarked when they were back on the road. He had removed his beard so Yung, who was shelling the shrimp, could pop the flesh into his mouth with ease. 'Hypothetically speaking, of course.' The flesh was delightfully succulent. 'Tell me, Yung, do shrimp also travel in this Greater Vehicle?'

'Oh absolutely, Chief. Would you like me to peel you another?'

Just before eleven, Chief Duong parked the jeep at Tan Son Nhat airport and reapplied his fake beard and glasses. He unloaded the decoy cardboard box (specifications: ninety centimetres by ninety by ninety, wrapped in black plastic) and stuck a sticker on the top: **Mr Fun Chi. Phnom Penh. By River Express. Valuable.**

Then he, Yung and the box took a taxi east through the city to Cho Lon district. Behind them, a somewhat dusty motorcyclist on a Suzuki Spritely Mover decided to head that way too.

Duong gazed out of the taxi window. 'Look at them,' he said.

'Excuse me, Chief?'

'These city women, Yung.' Duong, who often found himself prone to philosophy when gearing up for imminent action, pointed to the shoals of motorbikes streaming down the city's boulevards. The stiff-backed ladies sporting elbow-length gloves and low conical hats were wearing face scarves that covered all but their eyes. 'We people that showed such courage as a nation have become frightened of a little sun.'

'Yes, Chief,' Yung replied, attempting to re-knot the loose elastic that was causing his beard to dangle some centimetres below his chin, and wondering whether it might be possible to run through his part of the plan one more time. 'Forgive me, Chief. About the disguise. I am just wondering, while you know I am more than willing to show bravery above and beyond the call of duty—'

'I'm glad to hear that, Yung,' Duong said, transfixed by the shimmering flow of traffic.

'Only, what if the beard falls off, Chief? Or the glasses or the beret? My face would be nearly naked and clearly identifiable. I don't want you to think I'm scared or not one hundred and fifty per cent committed, because I am. It's just, well, isn't there a chance the Fun Chis will come after me, Chief? I know we live in Dalat, but Cambodians are reported to be rather ruthless, and my moustache is rumoured to be quite distinctive locally and—'

Yung stopped.

He stopped because his boss had seized him in an embrace and was shouting at him.

'Absolute genius,' his boss was shouting, and most definitely at him. 'I do believe after all this time that my genius has rubbed off on you. You're absolutely right, Yung, in every way.'

'I am?'

'Stop the taxi at once, driver.'

Yung watched as Duong leaped from the car and ran to a glove and face-scarf vendor on the street corner. He then approached a woman selling a spread of conical hats on a dusty sheet along the kerbside. He returned laden and beaming. 'Genius, Sergeant. It was lurking in you all along.'

Yung felt it might ruin the moment to enquire why.

The taxi dropped them at Cho Lon district bus station. Duong left Yung casually loitering outside with the box while he headed for the indoor market. There he purchased a large laundry bag, two sheets, string and two sets of extra-large dark-blue women's working pyjamas.

He summoned Yung to the toilets behind the electronics stall. 'A brilliant plan of yours, Yung. I almost wish I'd thought of it myself.' He shared out his purchases. 'Like this, we shall be utterly unrecognisable. Now, Yung, let us tie back these beards as ponytails and think ourselves into the minds of women.'

Yung tried. He recalled Mrs Yung's varicose veins and penchant for coconut candy. Bunions, he thought.

Duong sniffed the pyjamas in search of inspiration. 'Feel a woman's musk float through your veins, Yung. Feel your wrists flutter up and your eyes turn down. Swing your hips and flick back the silken sheet of your hair.'

'Now, Chief? Here?'

'Of course not now, Sergeant. Once you are attired in the disguise. Tie back your moustache, Sergeant. Better still, tuck it behind your ears or something. And best leave the speaking to me.'

They entered the men's toilets and exited as ladies. Duong employed his best falsetto and hired two Super

Dream mopeds from a Cantonese trader two streets back from the bus station. 'Come on, little sister,' he squeaked, averting his eye from the garage mechanic who was staring a touch inappropriately for his liking, 'pass me the candies, we mustn't be late for Papa's birthday.'

So it was that at twenty past twelve a skinny sun-fearing lady rode her moped past the bus station and along to the Goddess of Mercy temple on Lao Tu Street. Her shorter plumper sister took a side street parallel to the temple, and then hung up a couple of sheets in a narrow alleyway.

The skinny lady idled her bike by the sparrow seller at the temple gates. The street was busy with tradesmen and, unbeknown to the lady, several dozen undercover agents dressed as tourists. Fifty metres along, standing alone by the incense stalls, a trembling Consulate work-experience boy held out a black-plastic-wrapped box measuring ninety by ninety by ninety centimetres.

The lady revved her moped and accelerated up to the boy. She braked suddenly and snatched the box. It was heavier than she had anticipated and caused the moped to list alarmingly before she managed to wedge the box between her knees. She accelerated down the street at a fair wobble. Behind the temple's tortoise stall a camera was pulled from a Spritely Mover pannier and snapped a shot.

After making two dummy turns as instructed, the skinny lady ducked into a narrow alley and drove head on into a flapping sheet. She braked. The plumper lady on the other side of the sheet received the loaded box and handed the skinny lady the empty box. The skinny lady received a sisterly pat and sallied forth through the second sheet and out of the alley with her decoy box between her knees, whereupon she joined the flow of city traffic. Behind her a box was tipped into a laundry bag, two oily sheets were pulled down on top and a laundry woman waddled out onto the main road.

Getting lost only three times, the decoy box eventually made it to the docks to be hurled onto a cargo ferry for Phnom Penh.

'Good riddance to extortion gangs!' Yung could not help squealing as he wheeled away. 'That one's for you, Sam!'

He left the motorbike in an alley, his woman's clothing in a dustbin and hailed a taxi for the airport.

While awaiting Yung's return in the departure canteen at Tan Son Nhat, Chief Duong enjoyed a celebratory beer and tried not to think about money. In particular, he tried not to think about the mountain of shrink-wrapped dollar blocks in a laundry bag he had lugged into a ladies' toilet and lugged out again, re-dressed as a bearded businessman. The bag that was sitting in the locked boot of his jeep. 'After Lila is home,' the police chief told himself, 'we will see about this wealth business. Daughters before dollars.'

Outside the airport the sky clotted over with clouds, and the steamy city blurred with monsoon rain. Inside the canteen, ten tables down, a weary motorcyclist unzipped a sodden jacket, snapped a photo and also took a beer.

It was approaching two o'clock. Duong sat back, watching the moped taxi men shake out their dripping helmets and take cover under the awning. He ordered two ham sandwiches and a second beer. For one quick moment he indulged himself with a delicious thought: he had done it – Lila would be home safe tonight. He belched, gassy with relief.

In truth, Duong had to reflect that the day had been most civically useful. It had provided a valuable insight into miscreant behaviour patterns. It was interesting to note how stepping outside the law could make you a new man within it. If that's what he chose to do. Because with a heavy bag in the car boot, any future was now possible, any one at all. Duong beamed at a passing waitress. She had a look of Lila about her. Dazzled, the girl went to dim the restaurant lights.

Thirty minutes later Yung appeared, retransformed into a desk sergeant: beard and beretless, excitable and on the right side of the law. 'Did it go off all right, Chief?'

'Perfectly.' The chief seized his sergeant in an embrace. 'The International Investigating Team Leader was delighted. The fake notes have been destroyed. We have foiled a hoax plot that could have jeopardised the footballer's life.'

Yung's eyes misted with tears.

'Thanks to you, Yung, this Porcini boy will probably survive.'

'And you, Chief. You were instrumental.'

'I suppose I was.' Duong beamed. 'I have purchased sandwiches for the journey, so let us return to Dalat forthwith. There remains much to be done today.'

A Fool's Dream of Statues

Night had long claimed the Highlands by the time a government jeep pulled in at the gates of Paradise Plantation. The jeep's driver dismounted and applied himself insistently to the buzzer on the gatepost. 'I have come to retrieve my daughter. It is Chief Duong. I have the money, let me in at once.'

A slow chuckle seemed to ooze from the intercom. One gate slid aside sufficient to squeeze a soft body through. The chief cursed and took a torch to unlock the boot. On the road a motorcyclist whizzed by in a flash of light.

Duong removed two green blocks from a laundry bag, tucked them into his trousers and squeezed inside the plantation. The gate clicked closed. He followed the puddle of his torch beam towards the house.

'I have learned my lesson well.' That is what he would say to his Lila when he saw her. 'No child, do not disagree with me. Just as there is always a bruise under the most perfect of peach skin, so every father sometimes makes mistakes. Never again will I be so careless with the most valuable thing in the world. Next time, my precious daughter, you may choose whom to marry. And if no one takes you because of this blindness – which, to tell you the truth, Lila, was my worry in the first place – if this is how it is to be, then I will care for my silkworm until the day I die.' That is what he would say.

Thinking of this speech was making the little chief quite drippy-eyed during his trudge through the undergrowth. He reconsidered the last sentiment. Death was perhaps too depressing a notion to introduce into the reunion. Perhaps the wording required minor adjustment. He recalled the opening chapter to *Creative Truths*, 'Maintaining Purity in Mind and Motivation'. Perhaps a better motive behind his borrowing money from Mei was to raise funds for overseas eye surgery. He tried it out, addressing the moths somersaulting through his torchlight: 'It was for your sight, my silkworm. Everything I did was for that.'

This would be undoubtedly easier to say, and a purer motive, if marginally less honest. Which had the chief stopping for a second and wiping his brows, perplexed. Lila's vision was clearly the noblest of causes. If he hadn't borrowed money for that, why on earth had he got himself mixed up with Mei? He could not think. Still, he consoled himself: it no longer mattered, Lila was coming home.

'Lila, your father's come for you,' he shouted, crashing out of the undergrowth, imagining his daughter on the verandah ready and waiting for him; her mother in her jaw and hair and general grace, and his own small part in shaping her brows. 'Lila, Daddy's here.'

'And in such haste.'

There was no Lila. There was only a tiny shadowy figure rasping its bottom on a stuffed water buffalo.

'Welcome, welcome, always a friendly welcome in Paradise, even out of office hours, Mr Duong. A pleasant surprise to see you. I am just enjoying a nightcap in tranquillity. It has been a busy day for business.' A green coconut was raised. 'I assume you have brought me something important, to arrive so late in the evening?'

A block of dollars thudded onto the moonlit marble. 'There's your money. Now fetch me my daughter.'

'You surprise me, Mr Duong.' Mei abandoned the coconut and dismounted slowly via a stepladder. 'It is not often I am surprised.' He picked up the gleaming block and ripped the plastic. He flicked the corner of the wad, sniffing the notes as they whirred under his thumb. 'What a fresh scent this American money has. Permit me to congratulate you, you have done well. Better than expected.'

'There's ten thousand for you, Mei. More than three times your asking price. Now bring me my daughter.'

'Come now, friend,' Mei said as he tucked the block down the front of his loincloth, 'no need for belligerence. Never in business. A drink perhaps?'

'You have my money. Give me my daughter.'

'Oh my dear friend.' Mei began to snigger. 'My dear little ex-chief, let me begin by reminding you that all was fair and squarely agreed, was it not?'

'Why are you laughing? I don't understand. Where is Lila?'

'Let me explain.'

'It's the fifth day. I had five days to raise the money. And I did.'

'Indeed it was, Mr Duong. It *was* the fifth day. Before business hours ended.'

'Business hours?'

'I wish you could have seen her off yourself, she looked beautiful. Watch yourself there, Mr Duong, take a pillar and hold on tight. Yes, your daughter was very beautiful, and now very married. This morning, early to beat the heat. We did not set an appointment time for the fifth day, did we? That was remiss of me. But do not worry, Uncle Mei made a good match. On her way to Europe no less.'

Swaying against the pillar, it was all Duong could do to pull out the second block of dollars and throw it at the buffalo. 'Another ten thousand. Take it. Unmarry her.'

Mei tucked the block away and laughed on. 'Oh my dear Mr Duong, whilst I compliment you on your sudden good fortune and thank you for the generosity you show to an old friend, I fear you do not understand me. I shall speak plain. Your daughter is honeymooning as you and I chat here. Most regrettably, she no longer belongs to me to sell back to you, it's that simple. In addition to this, I no longer know where she is.'

'You no longer know what?' It was proving difficult for Duong to follow the man's words. They were coming at him in a common enough string but they made no sense. No sense at all.

'I no longer know where your daughter is. Puff. Gone. Vanished to a happy overseas life.' Mei ignored the slow groan emitting from somewhere deep inside the little police chief. 'Now perhaps you'd be kind enough to release my pillar and trot off home. Unless of course, you're interested in purchasing a substitute daughter? I can offer many pretty specimens at a fair price for all budgets.'

Duong swayed against the pillar, groaning. His eyes took in the tiny laughing figure plucking at his loincloth and sauntering through the door of the great white house, the door that was slamming closed.

Duong's mouth moved to beg the man to wait. His vision was filled with Lilas. Lilas bundled and brought home from hospital, Lilas on the first day of school, Lilas on the final day of pepperminting, Lilas on Tet days, birthdays, wedding days.

'By Ho, Hung Duong you have been a fool,' he whispered. 'Lila, your father has been no more use to you than the lowest of insects. I am less worthy than Yung's cockroach.' The chief slid down the pillar onto the cold marble and all his Lilas were crushed to black.

'Chief Duong?' Dark hands were taking a hold under his shoulders and lifting him to his feet. 'Steady there.' The door to the white house was shut. No lights were showing. 'You must leave now, Chief, you have exceeded your allotted time on the premises. We will escort you to your vehicle.'

For many minutes a police jeep parked on a shady road did not move. The lights of a passing lorry illuminated a round face howling at the wheel. The lament took this tuneless and wretched form: the driver was richer than many men under the sun and yet he had nothing of worth. His daughter had been lost for a fool's dream of statues.

And as happens when sorrow starts spinning, several threads became tangled on the loom. For now this man was thinking of other failings: of the sensitive son he had driven away; of a wife whose dreams he had suffocated in marriage; of a widowed mother living alone.

He would throw all this money down the Ma's well, he sobbed, if his daughter could be found. On the life of them all he swore it. He would abandon his job and travel the earth to find her. And if she had truly vanished then he would step back into his pothole on route twenty. He swore this too.

A fruit fly stepped over a shrimp shell on the dashboard. The hours passed.

Eventually the engine of the jeep was engaged, headlights splashed the tarmac and wheels began to roll upwards in the direction of town. From here the vehicle turned onto route twenty-seven. For whatever the misery crushing the driver's shoulders, a hostage awaited liberation and he would keep his word; another thread tangled by him must be cut loose.

And in his miserable state the driver was unaware of a car that crept along a kilometre behind, steady as a wolf hunting in the dead of night. All the way to the lakeside village this car tailed the jeep. It parked at a distance and watched as this weariest of chiefs got out of his vehicle, climbed the steps of a longhouse, cried 'Po? Po? Po?' and fell toppling down.

Mistakes Happen Even in the Best-Run Families

Inside the longhouse damp towels are applied to Chief Duong's forehead by the nurse. Two men jump off his wife's belly and thighs. Lyons-trained Mr Bung effects a speedy return to consciousness for Mrs Duong, who rushes to involve herself in the revival of her husband with a wail of wifely delight.

'This will be most fascinating,' the hypnotist informs the assembled guests. 'We will observe.'

Mrs Duong is observed shoving the nurse aside and wrapping herself around her dazed husband, tight as a python. Her husband is observed retracting like a snail in an attempt to protect his vital organs from whatever implement his wife must be concealing. He shoots a look of alarm at the oily face that is hovering above.

'Don't be alarmed,' Mr Bung smiles benignly, 'you'll find your wife has nothing but love for you.'

The little husband's look of alarm dissolves into one of chalky terror. With good reason, as it happens. Having swept him into her arms, his gleeful wife now lumbers off to the bedding corner, where she sits rocking her spouse like a cloth doll, a lullaby drone on her lips.

'A touch of mania remains in the system,' Mr Bung

informs the bystanders. He crouches down and pats the limp man's shoulder. 'Nothing to worry about, Chief. Therapy is in progress. You will observe.'

The hypnotist knocks a knuckle on Phoenix's forehead and whispers in her ear. The cradle ceases to swing. Mrs Duong places her husband with all propriety on the bedding roll, where the nurse takes his pulse and presses restorative drops of rum between his lips. Warily the man eyes the woman who claims to be his wife but who is rustling up supper and blowing kisses his way. Wearily he closes his eyes. 'Doctor, my wife is much changed.'

'Improved, no?'

'Like hell she is.' Lila is elbowing past the nurse to run her fingers over the cherished contours of her father's face. 'Oh Daddy, I'm so glad you've come. Wait till I tell you what this man has done to Mother.'

'Lila?' A fresh bout of dizziness blasts through the policeman's veins and then ebbs away. 'Oh, girl, your voice sounds just like my dear Lila's.'

'But it *is* me, Daddy.'

Duong shakes his head sorrowfully. 'Your voice is the perfect echo of my little lost silkworm's.'

'Daddy, it *is* your silkworm.' The voice is firm. Exceedingly.

'There is no one quite as firm as my silkworm,' Duong says sadly.

'Open your eyes, Daddy.'

He opens his eyes. 'But,' he cries with wonder, 'but it is my silkworm! But this is a miracle! But how can this be?'

Lila laughs softly. A laugh as forgiving as a spring tide. 'I thought you always said there are no such things as miracles, Daddy.'

'But I thought you were—'

'I was married, Daddy, but there's no need to worry, it's all cleared up now. I shall start my reflexology course the day after tomorrow. A day late, but I'm sure I'll catch up.'

The chief scrutinises every inch of his wise silkworm's face. He takes her hands and turns them to check for signs of injury. He bursts into tears. 'But you don't look a day older than you did five days ago. You are just as perfect, just as *unsullied*.'

'Well, I did pick up a few tips.'

'Oh Lila, your father is a fool,' he sobs. 'Lila, I am glad you are blind, yes, and you cannot look on your unworthy fool of a father. I am useless as a peach to you. I am worthless as a cockroach. I will give the dollars away. All of them. I do not need a shrimp farm. I never needed a shrimp farm. The Ma shall have the millions – every dollar of them.'

'Hush now, Daddy, mistakes happen even in the best-run families.'

'If I may, sir,' Mr Bung says, stepping up promptly to offer therapeutic assistance. For this is a family of some torrid emotion and – so it seems – tremendous wealth, and he has been thinking of starting a private practice at weekends.

Lila knots her fist and raises it with a growl towards the smell of grease. 'Stand back, spunkbreath, you've done quite enough damage for one day.'

Spunkbreath? His daughter's language has possibly sullied slightly these past days. Duong lets that thought go and clutches his daughter to his chest. 'But this is a miracle, yes? My lost silkworm is here, alive and not carried away to Europe.'

'Of course I'm here, Daddy, I wasn't going anywhere.'

A slim finger presses his babbling lips, another smoothes the wriggle in his brows. 'Hush. Blow your nose. Charlie Thoc, you remember him from my school – Fungus-foot Charlie – he's helped me. Your silkworm's fine, Daddy, she really is.'

Held by his wise silkworm, Duong blows his nose and weeps a while longer. In truth, he thinks he could sit and weep away the Mekong. Except that a knuckle is knocking on top of his head.

'Husband? Sorry to disturb. His Majesty said only if it was important and it is.'

'Don't even ask about the so-called Majesty,' Lila whispers.

'How can I help?' Duong looks at the woman who resembles his wife but who is kneeling respectfully before him.

'It's your mother, husband. We've been waiting up for dear old Granny and she hasn't come home. It's black outside and I don't mind telling you, I'm worried.'

'That is very strange,' Duong says slowly. 'Not home, you say?'

'All afternoon.'

'Oh dear.' With a sudden stab of anxiety Duong recalls the reason for his night drive to the village. He blots his eyes and gets up. 'Lila, my precious, there's something I've got to do.'

'What now? It's the middle of the night. Don't be silly, Daddy, you're not feeling yourself. Do it tomorrow.'

'I have to be getting along now, Lila.' Duong gets up, avoiding her frown of concern. 'Charlie, watch out for Lila. Don't let her out of your sight for a second, you hear me, boy? There's fifty dollars in it if you take her straight home tomorrow morning.' Duong is hurrying for the door.

'Daddy, stop! I'm sorry but this really is as stinky as Charlie's feet. Sorry, Charlie, but really it is. You clearly had no idea Mother and I were out here, so why on earth are *you* here? It was hardly to visit Grandmother at this time of night. And come to mention it, what are we going to do about finding her?'

Duong pauses at the door. He pauses because Lila is blocking the way. He takes her hand. 'Lila, I know I have been a fool, but please trust me this one time – just one more time. I really can't say any more. It's Top Secret.'

Lila takes her hand back and folds her arms. 'Sorry, no. No way.'

'It's a policing mission.'

'Sorry, Daddy, I don't believe in those any more.'

'Don't laugh at your father!' Mrs Duong shouts from the pots. 'Policing mission or not, he has to go.'

'Yes, that's right,' Duong says, taken aback – pleasantly – by this spousal support.

'And where your father goes, I go too.'

'Well, actually on this occasion perhaps not—' Duong begins.

'And where my patient leads, I follow,' Mr Bung shouts.

'I'm not letting you alone with my mother,' Lila spits.

'And your safety is my concern,' Charlie says.

'I'll bring the rum,' the nurse giggles.

And this is how, despite Duong's pleas and protestations, the chief and his wife, and her doctor and nurse, and Lila and Charlie, and an Englishman and a homesick boy, along with an ex-taxi-driving monk turned hypnotic trainee, set off for the Island of the Dead. In a very long canoe.

The Law of the Jungle

It is necessary to return to the island in advance of this giddy expeditionary party, to rewind a few hours and revisit a small camp guarding a famous footballer, waiting with the sun still warming the day for persons with purpose unknown.

Much is to happen in the hours after Tricky Dicky takes up first watch in the date palm. Incidents that will inspire a myth whispered years into the future. A myth of a heroic Nice New Brotherhood (and Sisterhood) of Ape-ish Folk, a cross-species organisation which not only tried hard to be nice to each other but also turned out to be very courageous when the time called for it.

Dicky's watch passes without incident. He rehearses a few puns and descends to a peaceful camp. Fang is practising knots on a binding rope, remembering childhood games of cockerel twists and hangman's loops, and trying to keep his mind off a black box in a family tomb. The gorilla is on its back, basking in the attention of four snub-nosed masseuses. Jackie O is feeding him almonds. 'All crucial preparations for combat, old boy,' he winks at the bald chimp glowering above him. 'Second watch, assume sentry position at the double.'

The black baboon looks up from his weaving and limps arthritically to the date palm. He begins to shunt his old bones up the trunk without enthusiasm.

Under Grace's watchful eye Sam Porcini sleeps peacefully in the bamboo thicket a little way up from the camp. She has tested his nerve endings, alternating the application of a splinter and a blade of grass at various points on his body. Mr Porcini responded 'hah' (hard) or 'hob' (soft) accordingly. It was difficult to be sure which answer was which, but the fact that he was responding to stimuli was a good sign. She takes his pulse and it seems to be slightly stronger. She tries not to think about Fang's father and black boxes, and the burn marks on Sam's wrists. 'Let's be positive,' she whispers.

Tricky Dicky accepts a handful of nuts from Jackie O and is sufficiently mollified to divulge his sentry observations to the camp. 'I witnessed some curious human prancing about on the other side of the lake, and one attempt at drowning,' he is saying as a whoop of alarm from the date palm has everyone turning round.

Fang's hands tighten on the knots of his rope.

The gorilla springs up from his massage. 'What is it, Baboon? Report findings immediately.'

'There appears to be a vessel approaching,' the baboon calls down with some surprise. He is clinging to a gnarly fissure halfway up the trunk. 'At least I think it's a vessel. It's definitely longer than a crocodile – unless there's two of them swimming nose to tail and splashing about. No, ignore that, it's not a crocodile, it's almost certainly a boat.'

The gorilla rolls his eyes at Fang. 'Look to the boat, Baboon. How many assailants do you see? What arms do they carry?'

The baboon squints and leans out as far as he dares. Even in his salad days his eyesight had never been the sharpest. 'One. White-skinned. White-haired. Possibly albino. She might be female. She looks human-ish.'

The gorilla pulls a doubtful face at Fang. 'Climb to the very top, Baboon, and confirm report.'

The baboon mutters to himself. Fifteen years in a pen on the ground could instil vertigo in any animal. He inches himself higher and squints and confirms his report.

'Any on-board armaments you can see? Cannons or suchlike?'

'I'm not sure. No, I don't think so.'

'Any other weaponry?'

'Excuse me?' the baboon's hearing is not what it was.

'Confirm status of weaponry, Baboon!' The gorilla begins to pace. 'Rifles, machine guns, grenades? Rocket launchers, machetes, firecrackers? Do you have a positive or negative sighting of any of these?'

'Negative.'

'Are you absolutely sure? This is a very important question, Baboon.'

'Negative. Yes, negative.' It is true – most unfortunate but true – the black baboon can see no weapons in the boat.

'What good news!' the golden-headed snub-nosed exclaims.

'Indeed.' The gorilla slumps, succumbing to a moment's dismay, 'An armless female.' It is Tricky Dicky who offers the great ape solace. 'In my experience females can be most ferocious even when not carrying a weapon. Once had the misfortune to get on the wrong side of an orangutan called Pimple. You know the type, a dainty piece but possessive as all hell. Came at me tooth and claw when I was halfway through my set in a packed zoo. Didn't like how I'd looked at some lemur in the crowd. Never made that mistake again, I can tell you.'

'Now's not the time to speak of matters of the heart.' The gorilla raises himself onto his hindlegs. 'Brotherhood, convene the council of war.'

As there is only one (female, unarmed) assailant, the suggestion is made that Fang, Dicky and the gorilla overcome her at the tomb. The females and the baboon will wait in the concealed camp with the paralysed footballer. 'No need for anyone to take unnecessary risks,' the gorilla says. 'Clear? Splendid. Let's roll.'

'Just a second please,' the little golden-headed snub-nosed says, blushing. 'Sorry to interrupt, but I just wanted to ask – we are rather assuming malevolent intent, aren't we?'

'Naturally. Shoot first ask questions later, my dear lady. The law of the jungle where humans are concerned.'

'But should we?' Jackie O weighs in, rolling herself up into a shoulder stand. 'Should one always assume the worst – even of a human?'

'Oh absolutely,' the gorilla says, 'in my experience, most definitely.'

'But it's not very nice, is it?' the snub-nosed says quietly. 'If we did something terrible – something irreversible even – and the albino hadn't come with any kind of ill intent, that wouldn't be, well, *nice*, would it?'

'*Nice?*' the gorilla splutters, quite unable to believe his ears. '*NICE!* The enemy is at the gate and we're sitting here debating manners!'

The golden-headed monkey blushes to the tip of her tail. 'It's important. Nice is what we agreed on.'

'The building blocks of civilisation – manners.' Jackie

O descends her legs over her head into a plough. 'Manners mean respect.'

'Very well,' the gorilla grits his teeth. 'We shall endeavour not to harm the aggressor prior to establishing her ill intent. Satisfied, ladies? Come along, men.'

'There's just one more thing,' the snub-nosed says. 'What about backup? I've got a good pair of teeth on me. I mean, only after establishing ill intent, and only if it was totally necessary. But in those circumstances, we snub-noseds would probably be happy to contribute to the team effort.'

'Equality in endeavour,' Jackie mumbles in agreement.

'Obviously, we'd have to vote on it first,' the snub-nosed says.

'Obviously,' the gorilla replies wearily. 'The call for snub-nosed backup will be two chimp cackles. Combat troops, fall in.'

'I've got something to add,' Jackie O says, ignoring the gorilla's impatient hopscotch on the edge of the clearing. 'I'm as strong as Dicky. Stronger, actually. If there is going to be any fighting subsequent to the establishment of ill intent, the battle would probably fall under the category of a Just War. In morally defensible circumstances, the snub-nosed is right, each ape should contribute as it is able. I will swap places with Dicky.'

'Fine, fine, fine,' the gorilla says. 'Whatever you want.'

'I'm not too good with the sight of blood,' the camp's number-one performance artiste mutters, looking more than a little green around the gums. 'It plays havoc with my comic timing.'

'Enemy vessel approaching the shore!' the baboon shouts from the palm.

'Combat troops!' the gorilla screams, bouncing up and down, 'You will adopt combat positions or face court martial!' He drops onto his knuckles and races for the shore. 'Good luck, everyone.'

What now ensues on the Island of the Dead can be described as nothing less than a tragedy, for which, one day, a shrine will be erected on the shore in remembrance. It will be tended by a reclusive mesmerising millionaire called Chaura and sponsored by Scunthorpe RSPCA. It will be hoped that sacrifice will not be forgotten, at least not in the minds of a few.

But that is a future day and a future memorial, and such things hold little meaning for these troops locked into the present moment and steeling themselves for what- ever dangers are drifting with the canoe into shore. The troops assume positions. Fang climbs into the tomb with his grandparents and coils rope about his fists. He lets the hatch door down and waits in the dark to grab the hand that will open it. The gorilla lurks in the long grass beneath. And some twenty metres from the shore, Jackie O hangs in a fig tree cracking her toes and preparing to launch a sprinting tackle on the aggressor, should ill intent be clearly revealed and assault be morally justified: the Brotherhood is ready.

The first indication of a problem comes from the baboon in the lookout palm. 'That's peculiar,' he mutters, squinting and shaking his head and squinting again. 'Surprising, really. Excuse me,' he calls down to the camp, 'I don't know how to tell you this but there's something glinting in the albino's hand. Black and shiny with a little snout. She's out of the boat and pointing it about the shore.

Anyone know why she might be pointing something snouty all over the place?'

The second alarming development is noticed by Jackie O through the fig leaves. 'This isn't right at all,' she whispers to herself. Because the gun-toting woman isn't heading for the tomb. Glancing at a silver handset strapped to her belt, on which a green light pulses, she is making a slow-stepping beeline for the jungle. 'Gorilla!' Jackie calls out. 'She's got a gun and she's heading straight for the camp.'

In the long grass under the tomb the gorilla follows the woman's movements. The heart in his ebony chest is pounding.

'Gorilla!' Jackie hisses. 'Did you hear me?'

A rushing wind fills the gorilla's ears. He is watching the woman and her gun, but he is seeing a prone black shape with a heaving chest and bleeding eyes that roam and roam and fix on him. He is remembering his mother. He is recalling what happens to apes when human guns are fired.

'Gorilla!' Jackie is urgent. 'She's going for camp. We've got to act.'

His mother's eyes were still bleeding when the net fell over his face and he was pulled from her. He tried to fight of course, to stay tucked in the wet fur on her chest. But he wasn't an Alpha then, not an Alpha at all.

'Gorilla! We're running out of time!'

There is no doubting it now, the woman's shadow passes by the tomb. With unswerving steps she is moving steadily towards the jungle and the camp.

'Gorilla, what's going on out there?' Fang taps on the tomb floor.

The gorilla tries to force back memories of the net that swung him from his mother. He tries to shut out the image of her blood-filled eyes that did not look up to see him being dragged away. He must concentrate on the issue at hand. Is he or is he not an Alpha male? That is the question.

'Where are you, Gorilla?' Jackie's call is sudden and high and screaming.

He doesn't know the answer. All he knows is that the Brotherhood depends on him. Who is he to fail it? And roaring with a rage to scare the dead, the silverbacked mountain gorilla leaps out of the long grass and charges.

She sees him coming, of course she does. Nothing gets past Staff Sergeant Sherry-Sioux Ballou. She spins a neat ninety anticlockwise, she checks her aim and she fires twice. The silver and black body freezes mid-air, its momentum trapped in an invisible net. And then it falls, catapulting backwards and thudding down in the grass. Sherry-Sioux consults her handset and keeps her course. She hadn't been known in the platoon as Sure-Shot Susy for nothing.

In the clearing the monkeys hear gunshots and they tremble.

'My sisters,' the golden-headed monkey whispers, 'it grieves me to say it but I think we may be at war.'

'But we haven't had the backup signal,' Tricky Dicky protests. 'We'd hear the backup signal, surely—' he looks up and falters: the baboon is sliding down the palm trunk. Every hair on his head is drooping.

'The human's shot the gorilla,' he says.

'But is he—'

'But surely—'

'He's not moving. And now she's heading this way.'

Tricky Dicky whimpers and runs away into the bamboo thicket, where Grace, having heard shots, is dragging Sam Porcini deep under cover.

The snub-nosed monkeys form a huddle and pull in the slumped baboon. For a moment there is dejected silence, then the little golden-headed monkey looks up. 'Ladies, Baboon, listen up. We are a Brotherhood and Sisterhood, aren't we?'

The monkeys nod.

'And we have an ape down.'

The monkeys agree silently.

'So, ladies and gent,' the little snub-nosed shakes out her fluff firmly even though her tiny voice is wavering, 'what are we waiting for? I'm going in. There is no obligation on any of you to follow. But whoever's with me, fall in behind!' With her tail held high she dashes out of the clearing.

And every one of the five snub-noseds and an arthritic old baboon follow her onto the shore.

'Freakin' Indiana Jones, that's what this is!' Sherry-Sioux whoops, spinning and shooting *bang!bang!bang!* The rush of adrenaline has Ms Ballou pink-faced and quite beside herself with glee. White flashes burst from the gun's snout as she swings and aims and shoots the monkeys down. 'Freakin' rabid sons of bitches! Bring it on, baboon boy!' she whoops, mixing it up – head shots, heart shots, one in the belly just for fun.

Fang smashes his heel through the rotten corner of the hatch.

'Freakin' crazy shit!' Ms Ballou cries, caught by surprise by a golden-headed monkey leaping for her face. She steps back and blasts it one between the eyes. 'Bring 'em on for Sure-Shot Susy!'

Sherry-Sioux clears the shore in a few easy seconds. In silence she reloads her cartridge. And in the fig tree behind her, a female chimpanzee with a philosophical penchant for fairness flexes her toes and drops quietly to the ground.

'ARGGGGGHHHHHHHHHHHH!'

Sherry-Sioux falls. She has been dealt a blow to the back of her neck. She reaches behind and touches teeth and fur. 'Help me!' she shrieks. 'I'm being attacked. Please God, someone help me. Sweet baby Jesus, save me, I'm being savaged by a rabid animal!'

Fang crashes out of the tomb and races, rope in hand, to the ball of snarling spinning black and blonde hair on the shore. He pulls at Jackie. 'Get off her.'

The chimpanzee glances at him, her eyes boiling with a fury so wild it may as well be rabid, her teeth locked into the woman's white neck.

Fang pulls at her shoulders. 'Not this way. I promise you she'll pay, Jackie, I promise you. But not like this. Not like this.'

Slowly the chimpanzee's snarls quieten.

'Let me handle this, Jackie.' Fang pulls at her arms.

Slowly Jackie unlocks her jaw. She spits out the screaming woman.

Sherry-Sioux slumps forward, prone on the shore.

Fang kicks the gun away and unravels the rope.

'Thank you, friend. Sweet lord Jesus bless you,' Sherry-Sioux babbles, squirming and trying to sit up. 'You're a true Samaritan.'

But Fang's knee is in her back. 'Lie still. You're bleeding badly.'

Jackie O picks a flap of skin from her teeth and turns away.

Fang sets to work with his rope.

And purple-eyed Sherry-Sioux babbles on. 'Please, friend, would you keep that thing off of me? Wouldya do that for ol' Sherry-Sioux? I think it's diseased or rabid or something. Sweet Jesus, don't let it be rabies. Listen, friend, I hope you can understand me, but if you could just fetch me some clean water – agua – shit, I don't know what you call it round here, but I need bottled water to wash out the wound. I'll pay you whatever you want. However much you want, comprendez? Hey! Watch my neck!' Bonds are bending back Sherry-Sioux's limbs and tugging her thoughts from gratitude. 'Ouch!' she yelps and tries to kick. The bonds tighten and burn. 'Hey, boy scout, whatcha playing at, we don't need no rope here. Why don't you do us both a favour and go tie up that rabid chimp? You speakee English – Inglese, boy? No rope. I said *NO ROPE!*'

Fang is taking no chances. He trusses the woman into a bent-backed bow, exactly as his father once taught him. He gets up, his hands shaking. 'Don't say another word,' he warns her in English, and he walks away.

Sherry-Sioux cranks up her head and spits out a centipede. 'Yo! Did you hear me, boy? I have money. Dollars. You like dollars, sweetheart? Hey, come back. Don't walk away. Nobody walks away from Sherry-Sioux. Visa? Amex? Diners? Come on back, baby. We haven't finished talking. You like dollars? Everyone likes dollars, baby.'

Fang hurries to the gorilla. He is lying on his back at the foot of the tomb, a crimson ribbon streaming from a hole in his chest.

'My man, is that you?' The gorilla feels his head, heavy as a boulder, being gently raised. 'How'd we do? Did you see that snub-nosed go at its *face*? Damn fine piece of fluff when it came to it. Female, of course, but Alpha all over. Listen, my man,' the gorilla's eyes are wandering, searching the sky as if looking for something up there. 'Between the two of us, I don't mind saying I'd have liked to have been of more assistance. I rather hope I didn't let the side down.'

Fang pulls off his shirt to stem the gorilla's wound. 'Hush,' he wants to say, 'you were an Alpha today. You were *the* Alpha.' But all of a sudden he can't find the words.

'Told you females were tricky ones, didn't I tell you that?' the gorilla whispers, pink bubbles popping on his lips.

Fang nods. He has no words for this. He holds the gorilla as best he can.

'Wait till Laos, my boy, wait till we tell this story in—'

The gorilla's eyes stop searching.

Fang's howl brings Grace running from the clearing.

She stops by the first of the bodies – that of an arthritic old baboon. The air is sharp with the tang of blood. Grace sees Jackie O shuffling about the shore, lifting snub-nosed monkeys to the setting sun, searching for signs of life.

'Yoo hoo! Hiya there!' a woman calls out, flopping in the grass. Her arms and legs have been roped back behind her. 'Boy am I glad to see your sweet face round here. Must have stumbled into one of those rabies colonies you read about. You're a tourist, right?' The woman begins to shunt herself towards Grace. Her face is bearded in blood and she seems to have one purple and one brown eye. 'Western? Sure you are. Well, sugar, you arrived at just the right time. Now, the first thing to remember is don't panic. You just loosen me up here and I'll take damn good care of you. Don't get too close to that chimp, honey, that's the critter that took a chunk from me. Don't look it in the eye. Move slow. Nice and easy. Say, if you just reach me my gun I can get a good pop at it.'

Grace stares at the woman.

'You do speak English, don't you, sugar?'

Grace nods.

'Sure you do. You're just a little scared and that's natural, sugar. You pass me the gun and we'll keep that last one at bay. Say, what's your name? My name's Sherry-Sioux. Sugar, why don't you come on over?'

Grace begins to move towards the woman.

'That's my girl. You come up real close. Listen, I don't know if you're with that kid over there, but let me tell you he's bad news. He's kidnapped some soccer ace and he's gone and done this damn rope trick on me. You ain't so bad-looking, get them ears pinned back and you could do much better than a native, sweetie.' A dark slug of blood slides from her neck as Sherry-Sioux tries to rock herself up on her knees. 'Here's an idea, you loosen me up and pass me that gun and we'll finish that chimp off. Kindest thing for it. Then we'll sit ourselves down nice and quiet and figure a way to get you outta this mess and home. Everyone wants to go home.'

'But your wounds are bleeding,' Grace says slowly. 'I've got something for that.'

Sherry-Sioux winks her brown eye. 'Look at that, I

think I found me an all-original Brit girl scout. Am I right?'

Grace pulls on the leather string around her neck.

'Say, you don't have a penknife, do you? Gee youww! Goddamn, that medicine of yours has sure got some goddamn—' and Sherry-Sioux's words cut out as the envenomed paste soaks in.

Grace goes to the water's edge and washes her hands. She walks to the body of a snub-nosed monkey, a bullet ripped through its brow. The lowering sun is burnishing the monkey's fur to copper.

Grace strokes the tiny curled fingers, opening and closing them into the soft palm. 'I'm sorry, monkey,' she says. 'I didn't manage to save you after all.' Cradling the body she falls to her knees, and she sobs and sobs and sobs.

A Path of Diamond Dust

Fang looks over at Grace and nothing is said.

The sun slips ruby into the lake.

Tricky Dicky emerges from the clearing and helps Jackie O gather the bodies of the snub-nosed monkeys and the black baboon and lay them in a row under the tomb. Jackie closes their eyes.

Grace and Fang haul comatose Sherry-Sioux into the camp. They carry Sam Porcini out of the bamboo thicket and lay him on the bed the baboon had been weaving.

Night falls on them quick and black as leeches. The air chills. Fang builds a fire. Darting bats snap up mosquitoes and flying beetles. The last four members of the Brotherhood shuffle close to the flames. They avoid each other's eyes and nothing is said.

On his grassy bed Sam Porcini is stirring. Dreams are softening their hold on his mind. His toes are twitching. He opens his eyes to the night. The Milky Way swirls a path of diamond dust high above the island. A tear slides out of Sam's eye to see such beauty. 'Good morning, Vietnam,' he murmurs.

Snails Making Love in the Rain

As the moon descends the sky exhaustion sinks Grace. Twisting into herself by the fire her eyelids drop and she falls into a dream of golden-headed monkeys marching up Surrey streets. Fang pulls a T-shirt from her rucksack and covers her shoulders. He breathes a kiss on her cheek and curls himself around her.

The fire burns down to its embers. The humans sleep. Tricky Dicky turns to Jackie O. He lays a long arm over the hunch of her back and squeezes her shoulder. 'Shall we?' he says at last. He stands and holds out his hand. 'It's for the best.'

Together the chimpanzees creep into the dense jungle and swing up into the trees and vanish from sight.

A sudden scream wakes Fang. He sits up, his blood racing.

Silence. For a moment he thinks it nothing more than an owl about its killing work.

But then something somewhere begins to groan with a despair such as only humans are said to feel. The sound is so deep Fang thinks he can feel the earth vibrating. It is a very familiar sound.

'Mother?' He jumps up, casting around. 'Mother, is that *you*?'

A short distance away a woman currently known as

Phoenix Duong is indeed groaning. She is on her knees before the hooked corpse of her mother-in-law in a stilted tomb hut. 'Aieaieaieaieaie,' she is crying, 'abandoned and alone. We did not seek you in time, and in what peculiar agonies you have departed from us.'

To which not a lot can be said, given the evidence. And indeed not a lot is said. The assembled local and international guests of the expeditionary party stand awkwardly as Mrs Duong sways and clutches for vanished hairstrings. The party atmosphere that had looked so promising – boat rides, rum, a nurse's uniform – has quite evaporated.

At least the Duongs are putting on a show of sorts. Mrs Duong has progressed to a hysterical beating of the ground, while her husband – who had insisted on rushing ahead of the group to the tomb – has not budged from where he has fainted for the third time that night, falling like a bowled skittle onto a big furry cushion. His shirt is being unbuttoned by nursing fingers. 'Only you, Mummy Prawn?' the little chief is mumbling. 'But where is my VIP present to you, Mummy? Where has my present gone?'

'Preliminary post-traumatic shock,' is the trainee nurse's giggled opinion. 'I will administer medication. I wonder whether a strong-armed gentleman would be kind enough to raise his head for me?'

'Is that really wise?' Lila says, sniffing rummy vapours and hearing her father sucking on a nursing finger.

The nurse scowls at the exquisite blind girl. 'Please leave the professionals to their work, miss.' She turns and flutters her eyes at the big-nosed sour-breath Westerner, who has come to assist in the leverage of the police chief. However attractive a girl is told she is, when that girl also happens to be pushing twenty-five, and has a tooth or two wider than the average, it doesn't do to be choosy.

Nothing that a good brace wouldn't fix, JC thinks, scooping up the policeman and swinging a lantern around the black mound the chief had fallen on. 'Christ!' he shouts, nearly dropping his charge in surprise. 'It's an ape! It's bloody King Kong – bloody hell! Will you look at the pecs on him! Jesus – and there's more. There's a whole row of them! Charlie, take the canoe, go get the camera from the van!'

Charlie does not move. However, JC's new friend, Chaura, takes speedy steps to join him. He crouches by the snub-nosed monkeys. 'Tribal,' he says sniffing. 'Fresh offering. You hungry, my friend? Want to make barbie breakfast?'

'But this is awesome. This is too good to be true. This is a whole new twist to the blog. Charlie, are you going back for that camera or what?'

Charlie ignores JC. He is trying to describe to Lila as delicately as he can the peculiar hooked shape of her grandmother's corpse, but is interrupted as Mrs Duong's bellows abruptly hiccup into silence.

'Charlie?' Lila is anxious. 'What's happening now?'

'Well, actually right now, your mother's started eating soil.'

Lila sniffs the air for grease.

A hypnotist ducks a blind punch.

'You made her behave like this,' Lila rages. 'She's eating soil! Do something!'

With an eye to the girl's range, Mr Bung draws himself tall. He senses a declamation coming on. 'Even if we could manage to roll her over, my child, it would be to no avail. She must walk the paths of her grief alone.'

'That's bullshit, spunkbreath, and you know it. Mother's

going out of her mind over someone she's only met twice in her life.'

Charlie shines the torch on Mrs Duong. 'She's eating worms, Lila.'

'She's eating worms!'

'Grief takes a person to strange places,' the hypnotist exalts. 'Grief cannot stay locked within a body – as it has in this one – for a lifetime. It must out. We will observe the intensity she is experiencing. We will wait and watch and see if this grief will wash her clean.'

Lila isn't waiting for anyone, especially not someone under the instruction of a man she personally would like to wash clean under the lake for a very long time. She crawls to her chomping mother and digs her knuckles into the digestive chakras on her soles.

'She's spitting out worms!' Charlie marvels.

Lila presses deep.

The expeditionary group loiters on the shore for some time as the sky begins to lighten, prodding monkeys, practising reflexology and passing round rum. Under her daughter's touch, Mrs Duong quietens and begins to snore. Propped against one of the tomb's stilts, her dazed husband hugs a jar of rum and mumbles over and over, 'Where is your VIP present, Mummy? Where did you put him?'

Chaura removes a snub-nosed monkey and takes it to the shore to skin. It can be sold to the Englishman for breakfast.

JC builds a fire and is sent to gather young reeds for tasting the brain.

The Mnong boy takes this moment to slip away to the shore. He steps into an abandoned canoe, singing of a brown-feathered parrot and its family. He picks up the paddles and begins his journey back to a village home.

And beneath the tomb things are at last starting to happen. Chief Duong is shaking his bleary head. After two unsuccessful attempts to stand, he takes hold of a stilt and pulls himself upright. The rum jar clinks invitingly. Though in truth he would like to consume a little more, he pulls up his socks, tightens his sandals and lurches past his wife and barbecuing guests to the lake's edge.

'What's he doing?' Lila asks Charlie.

'It looks like he may be trying to wash himself.'

'Or drown,' the nurse giggles. 'Perhaps it runs in the family.'

'Daddy!' Lila starts for the shore.

'Leave him to me, ma chérie.'

'Maman?' Lila says.

'Who else?' Mrs Duong is on her knees and rising. She stands for a moment over her daughter, stroking her hair. 'You know you make me very proud. I have not told you this often enough, Lila, but it is true.'

'But Maman you sound—'

'Like my old self? Why, I was never anything else, chérie, not really. I spent a few days having a rest and trying to play things a little differently. You should try everything once in life, Lila. I do not regret it. During this time I came to a few conclusions.'

'What, Maman? What conclusions?'

'Later, chérie. I have a feeling your papa needs me.' And leaving her daughter open-mouthed, Mrs Duong follows her husband down to the lake.

Wading out, his sandals slurping in the mud, Chief Duong takes a deep breath and dunks his head into the cold water. He counts to five and reminds himself that he is not a man of lily-livery, that worriers waste time and that while the swift eagle snatches the hesitant mouse, the patient toad also manages to catch a fly or two by sitting quietly. Fortified, he pops up for a quick breath of air and then reimmerses his face. This time he reminds himself that logic – a provincial policeman's best friend – means the footballer has to be somewhere on the island. And reason – logic's cousin – doesn't want him to forget that he has Lila back safe, which is the most important thing of all. If the boy does not reappear he will simply give the money back. That is what he will do. Duong emerges beaming with the wisdom of Uncle Ho: 'To every man a shadow; to every problem, a solution.'

There is a squelching behind him. He turns. He stares in some amazement.

It is his wife.

His wife is walking along the shore, scrawling in the mud with a piece of driftwood. Scrawling muddy words as she once did by a Highland lake thirty years before.

'Po?' he says softly, going over to her.

He reads the words she is writing. His eyes suddenly fill. 'Oh my dear Po.'

Two halves of oyster shells – she writes
– they may not always seem to fit the best –

He waits for her to finish, wiping his eyes, remembering the words, speaking them aloud to bring them into being as she sets them down.

– but even so, they grow pearls inside.

He takes the stick from her.

My perfect oyster shell – he writes,
– would you consider re-gluing your end to mine?

He writes more, hurrying along the shore.

For marital unity is as vital as the moon to the earth and the clouds to the sea.

His wife trails behind him, reading as the words fill with water and soak away. He turns and sees that she is starting to smile, just like she used to.

We may not fit as snug as snails making love in the rain, not every marriage can be that. But we do all right, don't we?

'How your proverbs are coming on,' she says.

'Oh Po, things are going to get better, I promise you.' He takes her hand, as he first did nearly thirty years before. 'Your husband has been as foolish as an ass in fresh grass, but he's learned a few things lately. It might take a week or two, but things will improve, you'll see.'

Mrs Duong considers her husband for a long pulseless moment. This little man who could always light up a corner inside her, if only for a second. And then she reaches a finger to smooth his brows. 'No more doom,' she says. 'Doom is all done for the Duongs.'

Chief and Mrs Duong stand in the mud holding hands as the sun comes up. Tears are plopping onto the man's sandals, and for the moment he is quite unbothered with how he will deliver the promised reversal in family fortunes. He has quite forgotten about empty tombs and missing footballers. He is planting as many kisses as he can on his wife's soft cheek.

So it comes as some surprise to hear a voice call out behind him, 'Dad, is that you?'

Duong stops mid-kiss. 'Po, did you hear that voice?'

'It sounded like our son to me.'

'Our son,' Duong exhales slowly. 'Our son.'

Duong turns round with great care. By the jungle's edge stands a slim figure. 'Hello, Dad. I think we've got what you're looking for.' With that the apparition vanishes.

And at once the little chief is running. On legs grown strong as young bamboo, he is running to haul in those soft words before they disappear in dawn mists, running to catch a voice put away for three years, running to hold on to his son.

Every Dog at the Carcass Must Get a Bite of a Bone

The Duong family reunion at the edge of a clearing on a small island in a Highland lake occurs as follows: Chief Duong stands on his toes and grabs his son in a paternal headlock; Lila kisses her brother's cheeks and takes his hands; and Mrs Duong pulls her children to her and smiles without having to think about it. She smiles remembering the little light inside her that only one man in the world can switch on. 'No more doom,' she says firmly. 'Doom is all done for the Duongs.'

'*Doom?*' Mr Bung mutters. He has been observing events ever since Mrs Duong stepped into the mud with her husband. Now he clears his throat and approaches. 'Phoenix, a word if you please.'

But changes are happening in the clearing as fast as the day's sun is rising, and Mrs Duong is turning to Mr Bung with a face set cooler than night frost on strawberries. 'Please listen carefully, Mr Mesmer,' she says. 'Apart from the wandering hands, I won't deny the past few days haven't been a bit of a jape in their own way. Rather a holiday in fact. But life is what it is, and you must make the best of it. Yes, Mr Mesmer, you did help me realise that. There can be no substitutes, no new and improved alternatives, and no blaming of problems elsewhere. So now, if you don't mind, please remove your nose from this family's affairs and leave us in peace.'

'Listen closely, Phoenix,' the hypnotist wipes his hands hurriedly on his trousers, 'you're feeling very sleepy.'

'Actually, I'm feeling rather perky. And if it's all the same with everyone, I think I'll go back to plain old Delia.'

'If I say you're feeling tired, Phoenix, then without question you are.'

'I've said my piece, please don't interfere further. This is family time.'

'I see.' The hypnotist flexes a thumb for a flick on a forehead. 'In that case, you just stand still, Phoenix, dear.'

Except his thumb is knocked off course by a blind fist. 'Back off, greasebag. You heard her – my mother's name is not Phoenix.'

'*Phoenix?*' Fang says.

'It's not important, mon fils, just a little role playing.'

'But you look happy, Maman.'

'I am happy, son!' Mrs Delia Duong hoots. 'Curious sensation but it's growing on me. You can't be miserable forever.'

'And you can't stay silent forever,' Fang says, blushing.

'Family,' the chief says, feeling giddy as a dragonfly and beaming brighter than the splendid dawn, 'that's the thing.'

'I think I'm going to be sick,' the Englishman groans, staggering up behind Lila. 'That monkey brain's turned my stomach.'

'Who's he?' Fang says, watching JC run retching into the undergrowth. 'And what monkey brain?'

'Only my husband. Ex. Utterly unconsummated,' Lila

replies. And sensing a dangerous tremor in Fang's voice she applies soothing pressure to the pulse in his wrist. 'It was just something he ate in Dalat.'

So the happy family and attending guests proceed to the campfire to be greeted, in varying degrees of inertia, by an English girl, an American woman and a famous footballer.

'Is this what you were looking for?' Fang asks his father, pointing at a sleeping Sam Porcini.

Duong hurries to Sam, who is smiling in his dreams, finding himself no longer on a football pitch facing penalties and runaway fathers, but whisking up zabaglione before school, with the help of a few monkeys. 'The footballer. You found him.'

'He was in Grandfather's tomb,' Fang pauses, 'with Grandmother.'

'Of course he was.' Duong smiles brightly at his son. Could it be that fortune really is returning to the family? 'Well done everyone.' And in a spirit of openness Duong adds, 'Children, you're probably wondering about all this, yes?'

'Yes,' Lila says, 'what footballer?'

'Your father got himself into a spot of bother. A rather large one, actually. He was silly. Very silly.'

'It's OK, Daddy,' Fang says, 'you don't need to explain.'

'I think I probably should.'

'I think so too,' Mrs Duong says.

'No more Secret Missions,' Lila reminds him.

'Agreed.' Duong smiles at the clever women in his family and stoops to check on Sam's breathing. Quickly he unlocks the handcuffs and pockets them. Then he redirects every inch of his beam towards his children. And it is worth noting, just one more time, the stunning intensity of the smile that might, on a warmer day, have started jungle fires – the smile that comes with a realisation that against sizeable odds and despite logical expectations, all might yet be well. With a polite nod to a cabbage-eared Western girl hunched over the fire's ashes, Duong starts his full and forthright confession. He starts with the dream of statues. For without the terrible spark of desire, he explains, no action ever ignites.

But as he talks Duong notices Fang go over to the Western girl. Duong needs no psychological policing manual to spot the sorrow in the boy's eyes. 'But what is this?' Duong says, rising from the flames of his desire on a gust of poetic wind. 'Every son's action his father sees, and when he feels pain, he also grieves.'

Fang looks down at Grace. Eventually he says, 'There's been a bit of an accident.'

'An accident!' Duong exclaims joyfully. 'Is that all? Well, not to worry, son. Your father's here now, and clearing up accidents is what he does best.'

Fang leads his father to where Sherry-Sioux lies, her bonds loosened but not undone, her eyes open and blinking occasionally but showing no further signs of life.

'That's a nasty bite on her neck.' Duong bats off the circling flies.

'She attacked the monkeys.'

'Ah.' Duong does not enquire further. 'But what's this?' He crouches down to Sherry-Sioux's hands to investigate. 'Am I looking at a double-twisted reversible running knot?' For a moment the chief finds himself lost for words. 'It's perfect,' he says, blotting his eyes. 'A perfect choice in the circumstances. See how it has optimised the angle of curvature. An excellent tension in the binding. Yes, it's been quite expertly done. You see the beauty of a reversible running knot is that it is—'

'Always reversible?'

'Quite an achievement. A natural talent, knotting a double-twisted running knot like that.' Duong is overcome with the need to find a stick and scratch out some words in the ground. But instead he simply fixes his sleek-browed son in his gaze. 'You know I always knew you were my boy. In my heart I never doubted it for a minute. Closer than finger and nail, you and I.'

Fang blushes and looks at Sherry-Sioux. 'I don't think she's very well.'

'Nurse!' Duong calls. 'I have a patient for you.'

And what of Sam in all this? What of the boy who became a hostage to a man's need for fortune? For Sam's adventure in the East is coming to a close and finally things are on the up. The dreams of his runaway father have faded, so too the Leyton pitch and any ambition Sam may have once had for penalty shoot-outs. And in their place? Visions of ziti and zabaglione, panettone and Parma ham, and standing at the helm of a busy kitchen serving nutritionally balanced food at affordable prices. Delicious feasible dreams, Sam thinks (if he excludes the monkeys swarming through the kitchens). More than dreams, if he so chooses; it could be a new future.

It has crossed his mind these past few hours, finding himself handcuffed in the jungle, that something untoward has happened recently. Something possibly involving monkeys. Which is alarming, if he thinks about it. But he doesn't, because he is feeling so relaxed and incapable of movement that any anxieties are dissolving like dawn mist.

In fact, his day is getting better and better. Because wrapped in golden light and floating through the mist towards him is a heavenly creature. Such an angel that Sam finds himself wondering whether he has died and gone to heaven. Which could explain a lot.

Unfortunately, Sam's bliss is broken almost immediately by a yelp.

'Bloody hell!'

Brushing past the angel and sprinting at him head on is an Englishman – and not exactly the type Sam might choose to consort with if he were in paradise. But Sam finds he has little opportunity for further metaphysical speculation because the lumbering man is increasing his pace and bearing down until he is almost on top of him. 'Bloody hell! It's Sam Porcini! I mean, *bloody hell* it's *Sam Porcini* everybody! Get this for bloody luck!'

JC crashes down at Sam's toes. 'I worship you, man. You're a legend. That free kick in last year's final. That was legendary. You're a god, man. Jesus – Sam, is it really you?'

'Yes,' Sam says after a short pause. 'Yes,' he says more definitely. 'I think so.' Perhaps things are returning to normal. This man reeks of vomit and is wearing a very short skirt, but at least he seems to be responding in a fairly predictable way.

'But what on earth are you doing here, Sam? The whole bloody world's looking for you.'

'We found him,' Fang interrupts. He doesn't trust Lila's big-nosed ex-husband for one second. 'We found him here and we're going to return him safely home.'

'Awesome. That's so cool.' JC crawls alongside the footballer's legs. 'Sam, would you mind if I touched you?

Just a toe. I mean, not just a toe – *the* toes. Jesus – the world's finest toes!' And webbed, he notices. That's got to be worth some cash with a tabloid somewhere: EXCLUSIVE: 'THE DAY I RESCUED THE WORLD'S FINEST WEBBED TOES.' If only Charlie had brought the bloody camera.

'Touch as many as you like,' Sam says.

While JC hovers in selective ecstasy the footballer's gaze returns to the angel who is bending over the hunched Western girl by the fire. 'You don't happen to know who that is over there?'

JC turns and shrugs. 'Yeah, just my wife.' JC is warming to his potential role as football god confidant (EXCLUSIVE: 'THE DAY I RESCUED MY MATE SAM PORCINI'S FINEST WEBBED TOES'). 'Actually, I bought her,' he says with a grin.

Sam says nothing.

'That's my sister you're talking about,' Fang growls. 'And by the way, Mr Porcini, the marriage has been annulled.'

'Really?' Sam watches Lila's fingers find a route down the English girl's spine and feels himself longing for those hands to touch his own sluggish limbs. 'Really?' he says again, floored by such a weight of desire he can say nothing more.

'Mr Footballer?' Chief Duong is bending over Sam. 'How do you do?'

Sam smiles nervously at the beaming face. He is not sure why but somehow this face makes him nervous.

'He's going to be fine, Dad,' Fang says. 'Grace took care of him.'

'Well, son, you've obviously found yourself a top-notch girl. Something about Grace reminds me of your mother.' Duong beams again at the footballer. 'Fang, please convey to Mr Porcini my gratitude for everything he's done for us.'

Duong offers his hand to the footballer to shake. But Sam's fingers flop and slide away.

'I'm afraid he's been paralysed, Dad.'

'Paralysed?'

'I think it was Grandmother's paste.'

'Ah. Now I come to think about it, I believe your poor grandmother's mind might have been going.'

'Yes,' Fang says, sparing his father the details of how far her mind had taken her in the end. 'But he's improving all the time.'

Duong pats Sam's knee. 'We'll have you back home and kicking your ball in no time. Please translate that for me, son, and tell him not to worry – the paralysis will almost certainly fade, leaving little in the way of permanent residue. No harm done.'

While Fang relays the good news to Sam, Duong smiles encouragingly. Once more he begins to dream of dumbwaiters and eye specialists and peppermint walls. And a shrimp farm breeding succulent emperor prawns, possibly co-owned by a Ma co-operative, possibly with a plywood figure, if not a statue, out the front. He can almost feel the revving of his Greater Vehicle.

But when Duong stands up his Vehicle stalls.

For wandering by, sucking on a cigarette and watching proceedings with professional interest, is an ex-monastic taxi-driving hypno-studying charlatan called Chaura. 'Good morning, Chief of Police,' he says. 'Good morning, missing footballer.'

On entering the clearing Chaura had clocked the British

footballer, first with surprise, then with potential. Now he winks deliberately at Chief Duong and goes to whisper in the hypnotic ear of Mr Bung. For Chaura is willing to concede he may have been overhasty in his assessment of the man yesterday. He might have the makings of a colleague after all.

'Tea's ready,' Mrs Duong shouts from the fire. 'Gather round everybody, before it goes cold.'

'Seems to me, Chief,' says Chaura, a smile forming like a crust on his lips, 'you're in a lot of trouble.'

Duong beams. 'Why would you say that?'

'You expect us to believe you found the footballer here by chance? And then you expect us to hold our tongues about it.'

'I'm afraid I have to agree.' Mr Bung blows on his tea. 'Your little secret's out.'

'Seems to me every dog at the carcass must get a bite of a bone, Chief.'

'I'm afraid I have to agree.' Mr Bung sips his tea. 'Every dog, Chief.'

'Seems to me you need a plan.'

Mr Bung expels a clot of mucus into the fire. 'Now, what we thought was this . . .'

The proposal is simple enough. It involves a spell of hypnotic oblivion for Sam, during which time he will take a ride in a sedan taxi to a hospital in Buon Ma Thuot. There he will be wheeled in by a pretty young nurse, having been discovered on the roadside suffering from amnesia.

'All this will be made possible,' Chaura says, 'for a three-way split in the takings.'

'Agreed!' Duong beams.

'Dad!' Fang looks at his father in horror. 'Surely you're not going to allow yourself to be blackmailed by these parasites?'

'Well, son, it's not strictly my money we're talking about, and there is rather a lot of it for one family. Besides,' Duong takes out his notebook and jots down the details on a list of to-dos, 'the plan doesn't appear to be a bad one. Quite watertight, I'd say.'

'But Dad—'

'Fang, listen to your father, please,' Mrs Duong intervenes sternly. 'He's very experienced in these matters, and whatever else he may have been, he's not a greedy man. Now tell me, is that your girlfriend at the fire? She looks unhappy.'

Fang goes to Grace, who is staring as a slug creeps towards the embers. He hugs her, but she doesn't respond. 'I think she might be in shock.'

'Pah!' Mrs Delia Duong is rising. 'Look at the poor dear, all she needs is love.' Fang is elbowed aside and without a word of protest Grace is scooped up in maternal arms.

'Such munificence!' Mr Bung sighs with admiration. 'Observe the generosity of the larger lady. Chief Duong, you are a lucky man.'

A second round of tea is taken. Lila asks Charlie to lead her to Sam Porcini. She kneels and runs her hands, light as courting butterflies, over the footballer's sluggish limbs. 'This heart is weak,' she says in English, placing her palm on his chest. 'I will make it strong.'

'You can make it anything you want,' Sam whispers.

Lila smiles. Charlie turns and walks away.

Lifting Sam's left heel onto her knee, Lila begins to knead. 'Please relax.'

Sam feels tingles beginning to travel the long tunnels of his nerves. His body is waking.

Fang comes over. 'We're nearly ready to leave.'

'Don't stop,' Sam whispers as her hands lower his heel to the ground. 'Please carry on, miss. Please don't go.'

'You're going home,' Fang says to him, 'isn't that what you want?'

'But, but – but—'

Fang laughs kindly. 'It's OK, she has this effect on all the boys.'

'But I – I would like to invite her to England.'

By the fire Mr Bung drains his last glass of tea and wipes his hands.

'Please – please will you ask her if she'll come?'

Fang looks at his sister, who is leaning over Sam and gently rotating his kneecaps. 'Another one's fallen in love with you. This one wants you to go away with him.'

'I felt as much.' Lila smiles and moves up to kneel beside Sam's shoulder. Her hands flutter over the contours of his face. Her fingers grow warm and her smile grows strong, too strong for her to put away out of sight. Softly she shakes her head. 'But please tell him no. I have my reflexology course to think about. Tell him true love takes time to grow its roots. Tell him I am not going anywhere. Not for any man. At least,' she smiles at Sam, 'not for a long, long time.'

'But this course – how much time will it take?'

'Three years,' Fang says.

'I'll wait. Please tell her that's what I'm going to do. I'm not going to give her up.'

'Excellent,' Mr Bung says, coming to sit on the other side of the footballer. 'The patient is in a mild trance already. Fang, if you wouldn't mind telling him to keep his eyes on your sister, we shall seize the moment and get things under way.'

Fifteen minutes later four men carry a deeply entranced Scunthorpe striker to a long canoe. These men return for Sherry-Sioux. The nurse jumps in next to her patient. Charlie, Lila and Mrs Duong, who is clasping Grace tightly to her, get into the second canoe. They wait for Chief Duong, who plucks a dragonfruit and fills two glasses with tea to leave as offerings with his parents in their tomb. And they wait for Fang, who crouches below the tomb, lowering his head and touching his hand to a row of furred bodies.

The canoes push off from the shore.

And the Island of the Dead is left with its dead.

Internal Affairs

Chief Duong, as has been previously established, is not a man of lily-livered constitution. Unfortunate intestines and buttery kneebones certainly, but cowardice, no. Consequently, when he spots the chopstick-thin figure of his co-chief waiting on the shore with Sergeant Yung drooping beside him, and sees three squad cars flashing their lights on the road, Duong is resolved on a response of great fortitude.

'Ahoy there, officers!' he shouts. 'Do help pull us in.'

Sergeant Yung rushes, sploshing into the water lilies. 'It's bad, Chief, very bad,' he blurts. 'Please say it isn't true.'

'Of course it isn't true,' Duong says bravely, trying to ignore the shadow of the second vessel coming up behind. He turns and waves. 'Terrible tide! Hold off and maintain your position.'

'Good morning, Co-Chief Duong,' Jimn shouts. 'Out early on the lake, I see.' Jimn tiptoes his shining loafers back from the mud. He is carrying a leather briefcase. 'Both vessels will moor up immediately, by order of the Central Highlands Provincial Police Department.'

'A commendably eager policing strategy, Jimn.' Wobbling in the prow of the canoe, Duong attempts a bright smile. 'But I hardly think it's necessary to net these particular fishermen.'

'And what you think, Co-Chief, is no longer relevant. Yung, moor them up. All bodies will disembark all vessels immediately.'

Yung sploshes up weeping. 'So sorry, Chief,' he blubs, dragging the tips of the two canoes to the shore.

'Make it easy on us all,' Jimn says, 'form an orderly line without histrionics.'

Nine bodies wobble out, splash through the lilies and stumble ashore. They stand in front of Co-Chief Jimn, silent and wary as refugees. Even Duong's brightest smile is sagging, and despite his resolution, his disobedient knees begin to quiver.

Jimn stands his briefcase on dry ground and paces along the line. He allows a minute or two to pass, so anxiety can soak deep into the criminals' hearts, then permits himself a dry laugh. 'A shabby band indeed.' He strides to where Grace is staring miserably at the sand. 'But wouldn't you know it, Yung, while we've been fishing for big fry, it would appear we've gone and caught ourselves some monkey thieves.' He pinches her chin, lifting her face to left and right. 'Got the ears for it. Yung, get the posters from the car. Let's match her up. No case is a closed case in my book.'

'Wait!'

Fang steps forward. 'You're wrong, and your posters are wrong. It was me, I took the monkeys. Leave the girl alone.'

'Well, isn't that quite remarkable?' Jimn's lips peel back in a sneer. 'Isn't it remarkable how the dumb speak? Curious how every criminal finds his voice when faced by the unimpeachable image of the law.'

Grace turns to look at Fang, who is offering his wrists

to Jimn. Her face grows animated, first with curiosity and then realisation. 'Oh no,' she says. She fights to clear monkeys and murder from her mind. 'No, Fang, don't you dare,' she says, and now she is frowning. 'This is wrong. They'll lock you up for years for this.' Her cheeks are growing pink. Suddenly she is advancing on Jimn. She is prodding the lapel of his blazer, her face flushed with intent. 'It was me. I did all the taking of the monkeys. I planned it alone, I carried it out alone. Fang had nothing to do with it. In fact, I forced him to come. Yes, I forced him at gunpoint.'

'What on earth is she wittering on about?' Jimn enquires of Fang, holding her off with a white palm. 'That is an extremely grubby finger she has, and this suit is clean on.'

'Get off him, Grace,' Fang whispers.

She turns, her eyes burning hot as her cheeks. 'I won't let them take you, Fang. I'll keep on saying it and I'll kick up such a fuss they'll have to let you go. If it wasn't for me none of this would have happened. In fact, I'll starve myself. That's what I'll do, I'll go on hunger strike till they let you go. I let the monkeys die, Fang, and I tried to kill someone too.'

'Did I just hear that right?' Down in the lilies at the end of the line, JC's ears prick up. 'Attempted murder? There's monkey theft, celebrity kidnapping *and* attempted murder. Does anyone have a pen?'

'Shut up!' Fang and Grace shout in unison.

'Seems we have a rift in the gang.' Jimn shakes his slim head. 'It is always the way in the end. But I should have suspected foreign involvement. And female. Statistically, their sentimentality gets them into all sorts of bother.' He unclips his pistol and points to the banyan tree. 'Miscreant

Duong Junior, take that grubby girl and sit down over there, and make sure you tell her you are both ordered to shut up. We'll officially arrest the two of you in a minute. And that big-nosed foreigner, he can join you until we figure out how he's involved. And for all your sakes, keep his mouth shut too.'

Jimn turns his attention to the canoe that is lying lower in the water than any of the other boats. He tiptoes into the mud as far as his loafers will allow and peers at the slack bodies laid along the hull – one a Western woman with a thick bandage around her neck and staring purple and brown eyes, the other a sleeping, smiling footballer in a filthy green soccer strip. 'But gentlemen, and ladies, of course, you appear to have left something behind. A couple of things actually. Would you like Yung to give you a hand in getting them out? Sergeant, come over here.'

'Sergeant, stay where you are.' Duong steps forward. 'With all respect, Co-Chief, I must insist that my investigation is not jeopardised. I am on a Top Secret Policing Mission. I don't like to pull rank, but I shall.'

'And I like to pull out evidence, Co-Chief, and I shall.' Jimn smiles the smile of a man who knows he is about to enjoy a moment so perfect it must be savoured with precision. He steps his loafers back onto dry land. 'I have in my possession a tape recorded in an office where a ransom demand was made. Yes, your suspicions were correct, Co-Chief – the new armchair. You didn't look beneath the seat. Thirteen per cent of people never look under the seat of furnishings for as long as they own them. I suspected you might be one of these types.'

Duong's knees begin to loosen. 'The new armchair, you say?'

'*Underneath* the new armchair, Co-Chief. And I have you to thank, or rather you have you to thank for all this.' Jimn's lips have disappeared inside his smile of precise satisfaction. He opens his jacket and flashes a shiny badge. 'Internal Affairs. You yourself notified Hanoi of the cancerous corruption in the district force with the superintendent's shocking attempt at bribing Commissar Nao. I must commend you on your whistle-blowing ways. With my reputation being what it is, Hanoi sent the matter my way, with a small budget attached. I've just had the superintendent arrested. It appears he was behind the murder of Commissar Nao after all. A sniper in the pedaloes confessed. Who will police the police? Isn't that how they put it, Co-Chief?'

Duong's hand rubs at his trembling brow. 'But—'

'Fortunately there are a few officers, such as myself, who are incorruptible. Incorruptible and willing to embrace cutting-edge surveillance technology. It's a simple fact that bugging devices pay dividends far beyond the instalment cost. Indeed, the spring issue of *Policing Today* reports a seventy-one per cent yield in some form of indictable information. Very cost-effective. I am in the process of drafting a report to the Interior recommending the adoption of concealed electronic listening devices as a primary resource in all criminal investigations. Take this case as an example. Why would I ever suspect you of involvement in kidnapping a footballer? The sheer thought is ludicrous.'

'It is,' Duong says bravely.

'Without the bug I would have had to agree with you. But as I say, it yielded incontrovertible evidence, and this released funds for a police tail. All the way to Saigon and back. Don't look surprised, Co-Chief, eighteen per cent of people never make full use of their rear-view mirror. A most fuel-consumptive investigation, by the way, not to mention the cost of the photographic development. Following the tail's return to the office, I made a call at twenty-three forty-five to a local businessman. Not a nice piece of work, given, shall we say, his track record with the ladies. Nevertheless, to keep to the matter in hand, he called himself a friend of yours. In fact, I believe you'd just left him. Mr Mei was most co-operative, not to mention intrigued. Where on earth, he wondered, would a local government employee find twenty thousand American dollars? Every note can be traced – even unmarked ones, Co-Chief – one way or another.'

Jimn removes a handkerchief from his top pocket and inhales. 'So, really, it didn't need Yung here blabbing about a top-secret mission with cardboard boxes and fancy dress – the net about you was already tightly knotted.'

'I didn't say anything, Chief,' Yung blurts out. 'Please believe me.'

Jimn's glance falls fast as a pick on an ice block. 'Sergeant, it is a sadness of modern policing that one is sometimes required to question an officer's sense of loyalty. I hope yours will not have to be so questioned. I believe the recommended sentence for acting as an accessory in a case such as this is twenty years.'

Sergeant Yung squeaks and seems to shrink.

'While for the perpetrator,' Jimn casts his glacial smile at Duong, 'it is the firing squad.'

And despite recently formed resolutions and all his best endeavours, Jimn's co-chief wobbles on traitorous knees. His vision blurs and gunfire crackles in his ears. Then a marital hand reaches out and takes his arm.

And he stands firm.

A Peppermint-Painted House

This is where it could have ended. With one chief driving another off in handcuffs. One destined for a golden future in the capital and even, perhaps, a statue commemorating 'The Incorruptible' on the roundabout outside the police station in Dalat; the other despatched at dawn against a stained prison wall. It is possible there might have been clemency appeals from Sam – if he remained stricken with love for Lila – but it is more probable that by then spin doctors would have spun him away from dreams of angelic fingers. The post-trauma doctors would have diagnosed and treated his trauma and he would have returned to rejoin Scunthorpe in time for the new season.

This is how things could have ended. But it is necessary to heed Mrs Duong's earlier expression of hope and say further doom will not do. This is not where it ends, and thanks for this must go in part to a small brown beetle.

To be genus-specific, the heroine that now appears in the unlikely role of bacon-saving deus ex machina is a *Blattella asahinai*. Yes, unnoticed by the assembled humans blind to all but their human-sized concerns, a tiny caramel-coloured Asian cockroach comes crawling out of Co-Chief Jimn's open briefcase, little scraps of paper falling off her legs onto the shore. She twitches her antennae, dazzled by the sunlight after five days in darkness. For this cockroach has been inhabiting the seam of the co-chief's brief-case, along with her two surviving children, after a fire killed thirty-eight of her young and robbed her of her home.

The cockroach rubs the paper scraps from her legs and, as displaced beings do, scans the shore for a friendly face. Squatting in the shade under a tree she sees the boy from her cousin's restaurant. The one – if the rumours were true – who could interpret the rattle and rub of an insect's legs. Who might provide the means to a mother's vengeance.

While co-chiefs contemplate glory and despair, the beetle crawls up the boy's arm over his shoulder and into the drum of his ear. Here she recounts the story of her infants' callous murder, starting with the brutal relocation of their home – a blue plastic bag in the black soil of a seedling bed – and ending with her desperate leap from an office inferno into a briefcase. Where she had discovered, she tells Fang with a disgusted click of her foreleg, a block of green notes, all unburned – unlike her babies. Twenty-four notes, she counted, had been removed over the next few days for the acquisition of titanium watches and snakeskin loafers. All gone, but for the one she had minced into a nest for her two surviving babies along the seam of the briefcase. Yes – she sticks a leg out of Fang's ear to indicate – that briefcase right there.

Suddenly Fang laughs out loud.

His parents turn to look at their son, trying their best to conceal their disappointment as he removes a cockroach from his ear and lowers it to the ground.

'Such a lot of sickness in the family,' Jimn sighs, taking in stubble-headed Delia holding her troublesome little husband straight, admiring for a moment proud blind Lila, then turning his attention to the lunatic son, Fang. Laughing Fang. Who is pointing at a shabby longhouse and waving at nothing at all on the ground. Nothing but a cockroach skirting past the wheel of a great vehicle on the road and making for the longhouse.

Fang waves and laughs and points. A suitable home, she had asked him for, with vacant possession. Fang stops waving and laughing and goes to pick up the tiny crumpled scraps the cockroach has left scattered on the shore.

'Any idea what these are, Dad? Only they look like bits of American dollar money to me.'

Dazed, Duong turns to his son.

'They look like scraps of twenty-dollar bills,' Fang says.

Duong shakes his head slowly.

'Twenty-dollar-bill scraps that fell out of Jimn's briefcase. Although before that they may have been in a blue plastic bag.'

'A blue plastic bag?' Duong says slowly.

'Any idea how Jimn would have all this Western money?'

Jimn snatches up the briefcase. 'An inheritance.'

Fang laughs. 'Really? What do you think, Dad?'

'Could be. Or could it be—' Duong says slowly, his eyes moving from Jimn's fine snakeskin loafers to the shiny watch that is glinting on the bone of his wrist. 'A dowry?' He begins to smile. 'A five-hundred-dollar dowry stolen from a dead man's house.'

The assembly on the shore gasps.

'Careful,' Jimn snarls. When he speaks each word is iced in threat. 'You will be careful what accusations you throw. And at whom you throw them. I walk a righteous line and the law is my friend. I am Internal Affairs.'

'In which case this could ruin you,' Fang says.

'That is nonsense. Pure supposition. Desperate, distracting talk.'

'It isn't, actually.' Fang holds out the handful of scraps in his palm. 'Every note can be traced. You said so yourself. Now, perhaps you'll be so good as to hand over the briefcase to Sergeant Yung. I'm sure there'll be all sorts of forensic analysis to be carried out on it, won't there, Dad?'

'Oh absolutely,' Duong beams.

'No,' Jimn hisses, clutching on tight. 'No briefcase.' Maybe, just maybe, civic statues are crumbling before his eyes.

'So, just to be clear, in front of all these witnesses, you are refusing to hand over evidence?'

Jimn's eyes boggle and bulge. His mouth opens and closes.

Fang turns to Grace and hugs her hard. Surely neither of them will be locked up now. 'Of course,' he smiles, 'there is probably another way. What do you think, Dad?'

Which is when Duong lets out a sudden laugh.

He clamps his hand over his mouth.

He needs to rein in his beam, which is threatening to burst out with blinding effect all over the shore. For he is beginning to feel the stirrings of genius. Yes, he realises, the genius with which he finds himself assailed at this most pivotal of moments is quite incontrovertible. And growing stronger by the second. 'If I may be of assistance, I believe what my son means is now that we know about your unfortunate oversight concerning the dowry, and now that everyone here has seen the accompanying evidence first hand, well, perhaps – how can I put it?'

Duong takes his time to select a proverb. 'Perhaps one hand can wash another clean.'

Jimn's mouth twists in a sneer.

'Clean and dry and beautifully fragrant, Co-Chief,' Duong adds.

On Jimn's face the battle between revulsion and desire rages hard. So hard it is beginning to seem to the people gathered on the shore that there may be a legion of tiny living things crawling over the bones beneath the surface of his skin. 'The dowry was, I admit, a slip on a bad day. But Duong, really, if you think someone like myself, with a practically perfectly unblemished record of integrity, would ever – *ever* – accept a bribe of dirty money, would ever stoop to your level—'

'Not my thought at all, Co-Chief,' Duong interrupts. For a second he pauses to let Jimn deflate. 'Not at all, Jimn.' Then he lets his genius fly. 'I am merely thinking that thanks to your fine work in arresting the superintendent, there is now rather a large vacancy in the force. I am thinking, Co-Chief, that like nature, a District Police Superintendent position dislikes a vacuum.'

Slimn Jimn is obliged to whip out his handkerchief and inhale sharply.

'And I for one am happy to give way to youth and vigour, and never say a word about the disgraceful theft of my dowry – a theft that was the cause of a chain of illegal and most unfortunate events. I believe, by the way, the youngest superintendent we have ever had in the Highland province was fifty-six.'

Jimn exhales. Inhales. Exhales. He allows himself the thinnest of smiles. 'I cannot say that your plan isn't without its charms. But the fact remains that the evidence—'

'Points directly to a great white house,' Lila says, stepping forward. 'A great rotten prison of a house.' For Lila has discovered she also has some thoughts about the ideal solution to this mess. She might not call them genius, although her father possibly would. 'The evidence points to a great white house where an odious little man is sitting on twenty thousand dollars of traceable ransom money.'

The audacity of Lila's suggestion causes a tremor down the shore.

'It is his word against that of the town's police chief.'

'And I know who I believe!' Yung exclaims.

'Let's imagine,' Lila continues, 'the glory of arresting such a sex-trading worm of a creature. Let's imagine crushing his evil ways for good. We can easily imagine the gratitude of Britain and football fans across the world for Sam's safe return – the glory for that is already yours, Jimn. But what about those of us left in Dalat? What about properly policing the community? I'd ask you to try and imagine the appreciation of the women Mei has imprisoned as they are returned to their fathers and husbands and children – the photo opportunities, the reporters and TV cameras capturing these happy moments. Imagine the feeling when the wrecking ball strikes the walls of New Universe. Think of all those happy households, the safe futures restored to so many girls – not to mention the temptation removed from our town's menfolk. Imagine, Jimn, the huge amount of good that you, and you alone, can do. It would lead to high places in government, surely, for any superintendent who could achieve so much. Imagine that. But you know, Jimn,' Lila pauses for dramatic effect, 'it doesn't just have to be imagined.'

Slimn Jimn, whose spine has been steadily stiffening during Lila's speech, suddenly scowls. 'But you are forgetting something.'

'I am?'

'The footballer's testimony.'

'Don't you worry, Chief,' Mr Bung jumps in. 'As a man of science trained in the arts of the unconscious, I can assure you he is one hundred and fifty per cent on side with whatever you want him to say.'

'On side,' Lila says softly, 'without any hocus-pocus necessary.'

'Well,' Jimn says. 'Well well well.' And if a smile can be said to spread it does so now, from his thin lips to his dry eyes, and then it jumps lightly from him to Lila. Soon this smile is hovering on the faces of each of the humans on the shore. It is the happiest of contagions.

'That's my daughter.' Mrs Duong steps forward to slap Lila on the back, and as she does she stubs her toe on something hard and smooth just beneath the soil. 'Well I never,' she says, crouching to investigate. 'Who'd have thought it. Surely it can't be? Surely not?' And instantly oblivious to everyone around her, she drops to her knees and begins to dig.

'So, Jimn,' Fang says, 'what about it? You have to admit it is a logical solution.'

Jimn applies eucalyptus drops from a bottle to his handkerchief and sniffs. Then he folds the handkerchief into quarters and tucks it back in his pocket. He squints into the sun; it is turning out to be a beautiful dawn. 'I suppose criminal justice does abhor a vacuum.'

'Absolutely, Chief Superintendent,' Duong replies.

*   *   *

So Slimn Jimn stays schtum. He returns to the station, where he gathers his squad and, in full view of the international media, arrests Mr Mei that afternoon. As Lila foresaw, it is a touching scene: thousands of dollars of incontrovertible evidence are bagged and removed; a gust of wind whooshes up the moneylender's loincloth as he is hauled into the squad car (laying to rest all rumours about additional rear appendages), and forty girls are released into the arms of their waiting fathers and husbands. Pink paper scraps fly through the air like confetti. In time the great white house will be razed to the ground to make way for a taxidermy museum of local wildlife. This popular venue will be run by a plastic-toothed lady, who remains long into her retirement a vision in lilac PVC.

'Stainless' Slimn Jimn is swiftly promoted for his efforts. An exclusive serialisation of 'Inside the Porcini Investigation', featuring eyewitness accounts of 'a hell called Paradise Plantation', is commissioned by a British broadsheet and optioned by a Hollywood studio – its author a modest young English writer called JC Bone.

A white minibus is driven back to the Go-Go Dalat travel agency by Fungus-foot Charlie, where, with a jar of rats' feet in his pocket and a fungicidal odour solution on his mind, he promptly resigns.

Mr Bung and his pretty nurse supervise the transportation of a speechless woman and a footballing star with a fuzzy memory and a girl's name on his lips to Saigon's international hospital. They are driven by an ex-monastic mesmerising trainee called Chaura. The boot is stuffed with dollars.

Sam Porcini returns to England with a piece of his heart left in the Highlands. The chip in his shoulder is never discovered. Nor are the plans of a Communications Executive called Sherry-Sioux Ballou, who resides in silence in a home for the militarily traumatised in Montgomery, Alabama. Thousands of lumps of valuable human flesh continue to transmit green lights around the world.

As for the Dŭongs, they return with their house-guest, Grace Marsden, to Dalat. In time, there may be reflexology clinics, sex-worker safe houses, ape sanctuaries, charitable coffee plantations, shrimp farm co-operatives and international archaeological digs. For now though, there is a peppermint-painted house awaiting them, and later, Mrs Duong says, there might be a hot meal on the stove.

And this, they agree, is enough.

Acknowledgements

I'm very grateful to everyone who read drafts of the manuscript: Helen O'Toole, Anna Sadowy, Kathy Hale, Emma Conder, Tassy Lichtarowicz and Thuy and Scott Thomas. A special thank you to Gabrielle Murphy for cheerleading for ten years without once dropping a pom-pom. I owe a great deal to the 'Easy Riders' of Dalat for sharing their knowledge and love of this wonderful region of Vietnam. Thanks to Tom for the first adventure, to my nephews, Mieszko and Wojciech, for keeping me on my story-telling toes, and to my family for the support over the past year.

Thank you, Clare Alexander, for the steady hand on the tiller, Rose Waddilove and Jason Smith at Random House for all the hard work, and thanks to the inimitable Jocasta Hamilton for motivational fancy dress and everything else.

PAULA LICHTAROWICZ

The First Book of Calamity Leek

Lying in her hospital bed, broken, burned and scared, Calamity still believes that Aunty loved her. For as long as she can remember, Calamity, along with her sixteen sisters, lived in a Garden behind the Wall of Safekeeping. Like it said in Aunty's Appendix on the first page of the Ps: 'Everything has a purpose', and they were being trained for a very special one. In the Ns the Appendix said, 'Nosiness leads to nonsense.' As Calamity sees it, this is what led to their Garden's downfall, because when the sisters started questioning what was outside the Wall, they started questioning what was happening inside it too.

But doubt is contagious. Watching your world crumble is frightening. And people who are frightened can be dangerous.

'Wonderfully strange'
MARK HADDON

'This hypnotic debut novel — one of the hottest reads of the year — is no ordinary book. It combines pitch-perfect teen angst with a fantastical setting and premise; as much a hymn to reading as a gripping story'
ELLE

'Like a mash-up of Margaret Atwood and Roald Dahl ... once picked up it's hard to put down'
THE LADY